Grabbing
Mane

Natalie Keller Reinert

This story is for all the re-riders, amateurs, and dreamers.

Also by Natalie Keller Reinert

The Hidden Horses of New York: A Novel

The Eventing Series
Ambition
Pride
Courage
Luck
Forward

The Show Barn Blues Series
Show Barn Blues
Horses in Wonderland

The Alex & Alexander Series
Runaway Alex
The Head and Not The Heart (A Novella)
Other People's Horses
Claiming Christmas (A Novella)
Turning for Home

Historical Romance
Miss Spencer Rides Astride
The Genuine Lady
The Honorable Nobody

Short Stories
Horse-Famous: Stories
Deck the Stalls: Horse Stories for the Holidays (Editor)

Introduction

Whenever Casey Halbach, age thirty-two, thought about horses, she smiled.

She'd done this for as long as anyone could remember. It wasn't just any smile, either. It was a delighted curve of the lips which reached right up to her green eyes and made them sparkle.

Her parents had found Casey's happy horse smile so endearing that they'd taken their little daughter for her first riding lesson when she was only five years old. She was barely able to hang onto the saddle as the chubby lesson pony wandered around the riding arena at a bored walk. She cried when the riding instructor plucked her down at the end of the half-hour. Then she turned and beheld the pony snuffling at her shoulders, and Casey smiled again.

Thus Casey's destiny of becoming a horse girl was made clear at a very young age. She rode horses non-stop for the next decade, with brief pauses to sleep and go to school and scribble out her homework.

After that decade, though, real life won out. Colleges were jostling for her attention, but all their correspondence really meant was that they wanted *her* to impress *them*. Stuck at a crossroads which felt more like a cliff, Casey was forced to choose between spending her last junior year horse-showing and hoping for the best once high school ended, or going all-in on school. Her parents made it very clear which side they were on. *If* she made it as a professional horse trainer, and that was a very big if, she'd almost certainly struggle her entire life. If she simply worked hard at school and got a good job, she could afford to be as horsey as she wanted without the broke lifestyle. This was the way her parents, teachers, and guidance counselors all broke it down for her, anyway. Her mileage, they stressed, would not vary.

And so, beginning at age seventeen, Casey commenced doing everything she was *supposed* to do in life: she sold her horse, she concentrated on her schoolwork, she got into a good college, she began a sensible career in marketing, she dated and dumped several unreliable boyfriends before settling on one very good one, and by all measures, she wound up fairly happy.

After four years in Gainesville, Casey settled back down in Cocoa, the coastal Florida town where she had grown up. She live in a rented townhouse with a nice guy who held a good job, and she had her very own desk in her very own cubicle, a square of beige carpet she could roll her chair across in two seconds, located within a frostily air-conditioned office which featured blue-tinted windows to keep the Florida sun at bay.

Casey then proceeded to live her life to the fullest. She never hit reply-all on emails, and she said things like: "let's circle back on that" in meetings. She spent too much money on cheese. She went on cruises to the Bahamas, and had long weekend brunches with friends. She talked about, but ultimately wasn't willing to take the responsibility of, adopting a dog.

Casey's modern life was in nearly every way living up to the ideals her parents had hoped for. Maybe they wondered if she and Brandon were *ever* going to get engaged, and maybe she wondered if she was ever going to get a promotion, but, all in all, things were good. Things were proceeding at an acceptable pace.

And if a secret smile sometimes played at her lips and creased the skin beside her beguiling green eyes, neither her coworkers, nor her friends, nor even her boyfriend, knew it was because she'd suddenly seen something which made her think of horses.

Chapter One

At about five years into employment at Bluewater Marketing Partners, Casey realized she was bored.

She countered this by escaping the office whenever she could. She didn't look for another job, like some other, more rash person might have done. She had *five years* of employment there, remember? Things were bound to look up. Sure, all of her moves had been lateral so far, but that would change. Her work spoke for itself. In the meantime, she'd just look for ways to jazz up her days on her own.

Luckily Mary, her accounts manager, liked to extend a little "white-glove service," as she called it, whenever she thought it might close a deal. This often meant dispatching someone junior to hand-deliver a proposal or a contract, during which time they were expected to show every courtesy possible to illustrate what an exceptional marketing agency Bluewater was. Not just a marketing agency, Mary was wont to lyricize, but a true business partner, *every step of the way*. You could almost hear the TM at the end of her little slogans.

Casey usually called ahead to the office she was visiting and offered to pick up coffees for the receptionist and the object of her sales-closing desires, and that tended to get the point across.

She'd first put up her hand for a courier job about six months before, on a sparkling-blue November day when she'd suddenly realized that if she wrote one more Thanksgiving-themed marketing email before the holiday weekend, she would simply not be able to tolerate the sight of a turkey and stuffing on Thursday. This would offend her mother, and that would not do. So when Mary stepped out of her glass-walled office holding up an interoffice envelope, Casey stood up and put her hand in the air. It was a job usually given to much more junior employees, but Mary didn't seem to have the least bit of hesitation in handing it off to Casey.

Which was something Casey had tried not to think about as she triumphantly took the envelope from her boss's hand.

She picked up the lattes, she closed the deal, she made it to the end of the day without writing another Pilgrim pun, and after that, Casey volunteered for every single errand which could take her out of the office.

It was becoming kind of a joke around the office. She didn't let that stop her, though. The courier runs became her special thing, and the more she was away from her cubicle, the more she didn't miss it.

The moment she overheard an opportunity to ditch her desk, Casey put her hand up in the air like an overeager student. She didn't stop with courier runs, either. Casey answered emails with requests for client site visits or media event reps so quickly, she often eschewed proper punctuation and the confines of professional sentence structure in favor of getting the first response to their inbox.

Which was really something, considering one of Casey's job requirements as an email marketing strategist was to be a total Grammar Nazi.

Casey couldn't help it; once she'd found something she liked, she became obsessed with it. What's more, she got competitive about it. She'd always been like this, ever since grade school—the first one to jump when the school bell rang, the first one standing in her row when the bus pulled up to her stop, the first one lining up when the airport's gate crew started prepping the queue for aircraft boarding. It had certainly served her well when she'd been an equestrian, too—her desire to be first in all things had made her an incredibly strong rider and a determined competitor at horse shows all over Florida.

Her high school friend Heather, who had dabbled a little in riding lessons herself and would occasionally join Casey for a trail ride on a borrowed horse, used to joke that Casey was like one of those horses who stood for hours with her nose pressed to the pasture gate, testing it every so often in hopes that the chain would give way and set her free.

Her boyfriend, Brandon, who had come on the scene well after her horse phase had passed, just thought she was fidgety and a bit of perfectionist.

Casey would have heartily agreed that she had a perfectionist's personality and a competitive heart, but there was something else dogging her these days. She felt like there was something better waiting for her, if she could just catch up with it. And so while she wasn't crazy enough to give up her place in line at her job, she still wanted to get out whenever she could, just to see what else was out there.

As the months went by, the changeable Florida autumn turning seamlessly into two chilly jacket-weather weeks of Florida winter before giving way to the blue skies and warm days of Florida spring, Casey found herself looking harder and harder for something better than what she had.

She didn't tell any of her friends or coworkers about this feeling, naturally. It sounded kind of striving, or maybe it sounded kind of pathetic, or she was afraid it would sound that way, anyway. She had quite a lot in her life, actually, and if she told her coworkers she didn't think her life was good enough, wasn't she also implying *their* lives weren't good enough? They spent all day inside at desks, rushing out at the stroke of five to make it to waterside happy hours or to get back home to deal with dinners and homework, depending on the family situation. They lived for the weekend and its rounds of pancake breakfasts and Little League games and gymnastics tournaments and lawn-care, for the family types, or for brunch and beach time for the singletons and the young couples.

Everyone else seemed fine with this lifestyle, Casey reasoned, so who was she to call it unfulfilling? Anyway, she *liked* brunch, and hanging out at the beach, and invitations to go jet-skiing on the Indian River. Hell, she even liked writing marketing emails (although she could use some more interesting clients). She wasn't necessarily unhappy.

She just wanted something more, and she didn't know what more might be, and so she just kept looking. In other office buildings with blue-tinted windows, in the dreamcatcher-hung living rooms of beachside rentals, in the antique-heavy home offices of Mediterranean Revival country club homes, she looked at how other people were living their lives and wondered what she could learn from them. She wondered if they had enough, or if they were just as confused as she was.

And at work, standing around the Keurig as it hissed and steamed, she brushed off her colleagues' teasing. Casey joked that her office escapes were actually her coping mechanism to help her deal with her crippling perfectionism. After all, everyone knew her tendency to sit at her desk for hours without getting up for a walk or a coffee, squinting at copy until the last possible moment she could send it out and still make deadline. She was known to frequently work through lunch; hell, she'd even sit through mid-morning snack and afternoon gossip sesh at the coffeemaker.

These were the unofficial mileposts of an office workers' day, intended to break up the monotony of spreadsheets and emails with gentle infusions of caffeine and carbohydrates. Missing them was kind of crazy, in everyone else's view, but Casey generally missed her team's snack and gossip time at least three days per week, utterly absorbed in her work.

But when she left the office midday and went blinking into the intense Florida sunlight, all of her mind's tightly wound cogs and sprockets loosened at once. She felt an intense freedom, a lifting of her heart. She would turn her face to the hot, blazing sun and close her eyes and smile. She would stand there for a moment and just bake, letting the sunshine seep into her pores. She would remember the old joy of spending her days outdoors: the fresh sea breeze playing in her hair, the blue dome of the sky, horses grazing green grass, everything gleaming and sharp in the white, tropical light. She would smile.

"So you can see why I needed to drive that contract down to Melbourne," she'd laughingly explain. "The change in scenery helps me reset my brain."

"I heard you were here an extra hour the other night," a colleague might reply, shaking her head. "Casey, nothing we do is that important!"

Casey didn't find this comforting.

"Plus, it's so hot," someone would always add. "I hate going out there this time of year."

"It's gorgeous out this time of year!" Casey would exclaim. But being the lone Floridian in the room generally resulted in Casey's protests being shouted down. *No one* liked being outside in Florida, especially in summer, unless there was a pool and a drink involved. Those were the hard facts, according to her colleagues.

"Well, I grew up outside," she had defensively told Marty Barker, who sat two cubicles down from her. He was a brown-haired and pale-skinned Michiganer who had questioned her ability to withstand Floridian UV rays for whole minutes at a time, suggesting that perhaps she was just a crazy person. "I used to ride horses and do chores in all that sun and heat. It just feels right to me."

"I can't live without the air conditioning running at all times," Marty had replied, dead serious. "Sometimes I don't even think *that's* enough. Walking from the office to the car is like torture. I would like an air-conditioned tunnel to my car, actually. Someone invent that, pronto."

"Hey Casey, do you still ride horses?" This was from Amy Hickstead, three cubicles down, with blonde curls and creamy skin which burned if she opened her living room curtains. She was originally from Pennsylvania. "My sister rode horses when we were kids. I didn't, though. They're so *big.*"

"Agreed," Marty exclaimed. "Nothing should have that many muscles!"

"I don't ride anymore," Casey said with a little shrug. "That was all strictly pre-college. Pre-Real Life, you know?"

Although she'd wondered, after saying it, what exactly was so real about her current life of air conditioning, tinted windows, and long drives to peek at other people's lives.

"I make things designed to be deleted," Casey had told a new face at Sunday brunch a few weeks ago, and all of her friends had laughed as if it was the first time they'd heard the joke. In truth, the nature of her work was a little tough on her perfectionist side. Casey was all too aware that as an email marketer, she spent her days writing words so ephemeral, she might as well be outside trying to blow the best bubbles, or count the most falling leaves. She liked writing emails, but the truth of where all of her hard work eventually went—into the trash, either immediately or after a few days—was too painful to think about very often.

Her work title was email marketing strategist. This was a fancy way of saying that she wrote emails designed to get past a spam filter. Of course, her considerable writing skills were not limited solely to crafting emails convincing consumers to *Click to Learn More*. She was also known for such hits as the pop-up boxes on websites which encourage users to *Sign Up Today For Our Newsletter* and *Save 10 Percent on Your First Order*.

Her profession had come up over the past weekend.

"Really? But I love those emails," the new guy at brunch, a round-faced IT guy named Lee from Brandon's coding group, had assured her. "I never unsubscribe from emails because I would feel guilty about all the work that goes into them. And here you are, in the flesh."

"Well, I don't write *all* emails."

"No, but I'm… I mean, I get a lot of emails. Too many, if I'm being honest. *But,* I don't unsubscribe. I'm a supporter of your work." He smiled broadly.

"But you don't read them all, either," Casey pointed out.

"Well, no."

"So eventually your inbox realizes you're not opening them and classifies them as spam."

"Well… yes."

"You unsubscribe by inaction." Casey took an elaborate sip of her mimosa and smiled at Lee, who was beginning to look a little unnerved.

Casey's friend Heather, who didn't like tension to mar the sanctity of weekend brunch, leaned in to change the subject. "Lee, did you know Casey used to ride *horses?* We were just talking about that last weekend, weren't we, Casey? *Horses."*

"Oh, no way?" Lee replied, looking relieved at the change of subject. "My sister used to ride horses. I didn't, though. They're so *big."*

Casey had drained her glass in lieu of answering. Brandon, sensing trouble, had nudged her gently, but she ignored him. She didn't want to talk about how horses were big and scary. She didn't want to talk about horses at all. She didn't mind thinking about them—Casey smiled, thinking of horses, and everyone at the table had assumed she was over her little pique and the conversation turned naturally to jet-skiing—but she didn't want to talk about them. Casey found that she missed horses too much to talk about them to anyone... even her friends, even her boyfriend. They were a subject best left buried. She'd jumped into the jet-skiing conversation, inadvertently promising that she and Brandon would come try out Lee's new Sea-Doos.

Now, she looked at the words on her screen and sighed at them. "Patio furniture, why don't you just sell yourself?"

"Still working on patio furniture?" Ah, hello to Brian in the next cubicle, eavesdropping yet again. Not that she could blame him; the office was whisper-quiet, the doldrums of mid-afternoon settling over the squares of cubicles like a winter fog. A neighbor's problems were a welcome distraction from the way letters seemed to gel into one another on the screen as the day wore on.

"It's a patio furniture liquidation store," she explained, pushing back her long brown bangs and tucking them behind her ears. Sometimes, on particularly windy days, she thought long bangs had been a mistake, but she always came back to the gesture of pushing them aside. They were a built-in nervous tic, so convenient! "This company is *always* in liquidation, that's why they constantly need new subscribers."

"Hello, thank you for calling Going Out of Business Everything Must Go!" Brian chanted in a chirpy customer service voice. "One of those?"

"You got it." Her top client, after five years in the game, was barely removed from a scam. "They have a great deal on glass-topped patio tables this week, if you're in the market."

"I'm all set, thanks."

"You and all of my subscribers." The conversion rate on these emails had been abysmal for the past few weeks. The patio furniture store was brick-and-mortar, and Florida in May was not like the rest of the country, who were just starting to prep for summer fun. Here, folks were generally pretty set for deck chairs and pool loungers all year round. Casey had been revising, and *revising,* and revising *again,* trying to please the perfection quadrant of her brain, and trying to figure out a way to get a middle-class mother of three or a retired couple in a deeded manufactured-home community to decide today was the day to redo the pool deck furniture.

She put the email's obligatory call-to-action, a SHOP NOW button, above a photo of plush lounge chairs on a spotless white pool deck, and considered the effect. She moved the button below the image, and then back again, and frowned for a moment. No, it needed something more drastic than that.

She changed the lounge chairs out for an elegant dining set, framed before a green-and-blue summer's day shining on a cerulean swimming pool. She thought about being outside, soaking up the sun of late spring. She hadn't been outside between the hours of eight a.m. and seven p.m. since Sunday. Today was Friday. Today was Friday! A little jolt of excitement fractured her sleepy calm. She wiggled in her seat, and experienced a range of discomforting physical responses as a result.

Her right foot had gone to sleep. There was a crick in her neck. Her left side ached, gently, without definition. Her tongue was poking anxiously at a slightly sore spot behind her molars. Casey began to suspect there was something wrong with her, something that had gone soft after too many hours motionless in this chair, hunched over this keyboard, glaring at furniture emails.

Her dark bangs fell back over her eyes and she pushed them back impatiently, less amused this time. Her friend Alison had said long bangs would accentuate her small, neat features and her pointed chin, but all they'd really done was block her view of the computer monitor, and get caught in the arms of her blue-light reduction glasses. She should trim them immediately, she thought, eyes flitting to the scissors in her pencil jar.

"Casey?"

She looked up so quickly that her neck cracked. Audibly. The snapping was actually a relief. The tingling of revitalized nerves prickled with a delicious sort of pain that drowned out all the indistinct aches she'd been suffering from a moment before.

Mary was looking down at her, a faint mask of disgust creeping over her usually flat expression. "Was that your *spine?*"

"I guess I've been hunched over too much."

"You're going to need a chiropractor." Mary lived and died by the chiropractor on the first floor of their building. She went three evenings a week; Casey sometimes saw her through the blinds as she walked down the sidewalk towards her car, Mary greeting the receptionist with a warm smile she never extended to her staff, Mary retreating through a door into a treatment room, already looking more relaxed as she anticipated the bone-cracking session ahead of her. "You should see Dr. Blanding."

"I should," Casey agreed, as she always did. Her eyes shifted to the manila folder in Mary's hands. "Is that… do you need a delivery?"

"If you have time."

"I'm just going to send this revision to the client…" *Save. Attach. Send.* It was done. They'd better like it.

Sending the email instead of playing with it for another frustrating minute sent an instant feeling of relief over her, as if she'd ducked beneath an incoming ocean wave and let cool saltwater rush over her hot skin.

Newly energized and email-free, Casey shoved her chair back from her desk so quickly the wheels struck the back wall of her cubicle and made the entire cubicle village shudder violently. There were a few gasps from her neighbors, and the sound of calendars and papers slipping free of their push-pins and sliding to the desks and floors below. This was followed by a few gusty sighs of exasperation. But no one actually complained. Everyone knew Casey. This was her *thing*. The girl liked playing mailman. Better her than them. So her coworkers probably thought as they put their wall decor back up and went on with their afternoons.

Mary was looking at her now with a slightly raised eyebrow. She had always found exuberance distasteful. "You're sure you have time?" she asked, holding the envelope just out of reach.

Casey, who had already switched off her second monitor, closed her laptop, and was slipping her purse over one shoulder, did her best to smile winningly at her boss. This was an uphill battle. Something about Mary tended to make her expressions freeze up. "I have time," she assured her. "I forgot to take a lunch. I'll grab something on the way back and make up for it that way."

Casey had spent five years at this office, and she'd spent the first two years trying to win over Mary. She'd survived the last three years by trying not to get her feelings hurt. The older woman's frosty demeanor had made her tough to read and tougher to connect with, and Casey had only been able to assure herself of her own good standing in Mary's graces by her own continued employment. There was certainly no daily indicator that she was doing a nice job. Her annual reviews were terse affairs which usually revolved around whatever spelling errors Casey might have made in drafts that year, before the minimum salary adjustment was approved.

She had hoped for and been passed over for promotions twice in the past two years, but she hadn't made any spelling errors recently, either, so she wasn't sure what else she could do but wait it out.

"It's perfect timing," Casey now assured Mary. "I'm all caught up on the patio furniture campaign. I'm good until the new brief arrives Monday."

"You did a total rewrite? They wanted an all-new email. They didn't like your last send at all."

"I did. It looks great. They're going to love it."

Mary nodded, but she still didn't look happy as she handed over the envelope. Her expression made it plan that she didn't think the clients would like the new rewrite, and that Mary would not be surprised when they sent yet another revision request.

Casey dropped the envelope into her big leather purse with a savage satisfaction, ignoring Mary's unspoken implication that she wasn't doing well enough. At this exact moment, she didn't care if Mary didn't like her, or if Mary found her work lacking something. She simply wanted to get *outside*.

These moments were cropping up more and more often. After years of trying and failing to make Mamma Mary proud, Casey found she'd stopped caring so much whether her stone-faced boss liked her. Or even whether anyone in the office liked her. Or even whether *clients* liked her. Casey still did her job with a vicious level of dedication, but that was just the way she worked—the way she was wired.

Her actual satisfaction in the work? If she was honest with herself, she'd have to admit it was dissipating, quickly, like a brief morning rain shower sliding over the beach and onto the dry mainland.

Casey told herself she was just having a little bit of a slump. She needed an interesting new client, or a really good creative brief, or maybe she just needed that promotion to account manager to come up at last and give her a new challenge, and then things would be fine.

In the meantime, though, she was all for getting out of this stagnant office whenever she possibly could, escaping the work and her constant drive for quality which no one ever noticed, a perfection which was either deleted or marked as spam.

Mary had already lost interest in her and was turning away. "The address is on the envelope. If you pass a Starbucks on the way back, I'll take a grande latte with an extra shot and two shots of vanilla."

"Is someone going to Starbucks?" a voice called. A gentle buzz of interest floated from the cubicles and encircled them with hopeful coffee orders.

"No one is going to Starbucks," Mary announced. "It's just wishful thinking on my part." But she looked over her shoulder and winked at Casey.

Casey was startled into winking back, or she thought she did—she'd never been very good at winking, and Brandon still laughed at her whenever she tried it—but with her fingers gripping that magical envelope and her car keys clenched fast in her other hand, she had everything she needed to make her escape. She'd gladly pay for her boss's six-dollar latte if it bought her an hour away from her desk, and cheap patio furniture which was never, ever going to sell the way clients thought it should.

Chapter Two

"Well, this can't be right."

Casey always talked to herself when she drove. She gave herself pep talks: *you can make this light!* She gave other people driving lessons she felt they sorely needed: *you don't have a stop sign you MORON OH MY GOD okay thank you, good job.* And she narrated the weird feelings which sometimes cropped up when she found herself on a street she remembered from her childhood.

Anyone who has stayed in their hometown past childhood knows these disorienting moments, but they're super-charged when you live somewhere that has been growing at a lightning pace for years, like coastal Florida, and old memories suddenly burst at you from unfamiliar new surroundings. You're driving down a road surrounded by the endless plate-glass gleam of strip malls and suddenly a wooded lot where you remember playing with friends appears, somehow untouched by development, like a ghost who got lost in the sprawl.

In this case, the weirdness struck as she made a turn off an everyday residential street, the curb lined with bland beige houses, and found herself driving on hard-packed crushed shell. This road was blindingly white and straight as an arrow, disappearing into the distance in either direction. Both sides were lined with appallingly deep drainage canals. Tall Australian pines dipped their feathery needles into the still black water. Every few hundred feet, the canals were bridged by earthen embankments, where a driveway to some hidden homestead crossed the canals.

Looking around at all of this, Casey had the distinctly unnerving feeling that she knew exactly where she was. She just couldn't quite pinpoint why.

Then, she saw the leaning mailbox, with its peeling, faded number stickers, and she realized where she was.

"But this road used to be in the middle of nowhere," she muttered to herself. "I remember thinking this drive took forever. My parents used to complain about how far in the middle of nowhere it was."

Casey pulled up to the driveway next to the mailbox, put her car in park, picked up the inter-office envelope from her passenger seat. She looked at the address on the envelope again. In Mary's old-fashioned hand, the note read *12201 Old River Road.*

She studied the battered mailbox, clinging by rusting screws to its dangerously leaning post. The impressive fire-ant hill mounded around its base appeared to be the only thing keeping the post upright. Its peeling decals were almost, but not quite, too faded to read. The numbers were correct. *12201.* A small wooden sign graced the gate ahead: *St. Johns Equestrian Center.*

She had to admit that this particular address had seemed familiar from the start. When Casey had first tapped them into her phone and looked at the map, she'd had an inkling, a stirring memory, something buried deep, telling her she'd been to this address before.

"But this *can't* be the same place," she said aloud, looking ahead to the rusting farm gate, the twelve-foot earthen bridge leading across the drainage canal, the tall barrier of Australian pines which masked whatever lay at the end of the driveway from the peering eyes of passing drivers. "It can't be. But I think... it *is.*"

With that suspension of disbelief, the sense of homecoming

rushing over her was so strong that all Casey could do for a few moments was sit very still and take deep breaths.

She was remembering it all now, the memories lifting up hazily from her childhood. She knew what had once waited at the end of this driveway: a long, low horse barn with square windows running down each side; the pricked ears of curious horses as they leaned over their windowsills to see arriving cars; an ancient tractor parked out back which children were warned away from via dire threats of expulsion from the farm; an arena of red clay footing scattered with brown jumps arranged in a simple show-hunter course, *outside-inside inside-outside;* a sagging single-wide trailer with broken blinds in the windows and a pot of geraniums on the porch; a jungle-green ribbon of lawn out front and and fenced paddocks behind, abruptly cut off at the back fence by the fawn-colored savannah which stretched out to the marshy St. Johns River.

Casey could see it all as if she was out there again, still standing under four feet tall, clad in rubber riding boots and cheap polyester breeches, her life feeling like it had just begun that day. In a way, it had.

Because her first riding lesson had happened at the end of this driveway, on a spring morning with blue skies and a sea-breeze ruffling through the long grass. This was where it had all begun for Casey: riding a shuffling school pony in endless circles while learning to post, learning to jump, and, eventually, learning to clamber aboard bareback and how to hang on with her knees when the barn-sour school pony took off for home.

Oh yes, this was the place. But whatever was at the end of this driveway wouldn't be what she remembered. She had to remind herself of that before she got herself too worked up.

Because that barn had closed a long, long time ago. The ponies she'd ridden and the kids she'd ridden alongside had scattered to new trainers, new barns.

That barn had been long gone before she'd even left elementary school, before she'd even gone to her first horse show. It was like a dream, a place which had vanished from her life before she'd had her own horse, or her own dreams of equestrian stardom… a memory immeasurably distant from her current life, which was so horseless, it sometimes felt like her entire childhood was someone else's memory.

Casey realized she had been sitting in her car staring at someone else's farm gate for some time, and that wasn't considered social behavior in the countryside. In fact, in rural Florida, this could be considered an act of aggression. Without knowing who was on the other side of that gate, she thought, she'd better not piss anyone off with too much lollygagging.

So she climbed out of her car and opened the old gate with a few practiced gestures. Her fingers knew just where the latch was, how to lift it and slide it back without looking or fumbling or pushing the bar the wrong way. Buried under her neat black office suit, somewhere under her soft sun-starved office skin and her tidy office pedicure, there were still the freckled brown hands and dirty fingernails of a barn brat.

She pulled the car through, put it back into park, and closed the gate behind her. *Always* leave a gate the way you found it: another lesson of her youth she'd never forget.

The driveway was made of crushed shell and long, with a few impressive ruts to shake things up. The tire lanes were dotted with puddles of black water from a recent storm, and palmettos on either side reached out to tap the mirrors of her car and slip long green fingers along the doors. All of this matched the pictures in her head. Her father used to complain so much about driving his car back here that her mother stopped asking him to take Casey to lessons.

Then her car emerged from the tree-lined alley and there it all was, like a doorway into the past—the past, with upgrades. Casey took in the familiar sights with pleasure: the long, low barn with horses looking curiously out of their windows; the red clay arena with its course of jumps, although they were now featuring rainbow colors; the patchwork squares of green paddocks, now surrounded by new black-board fences; a serviceable-looking doublewide trailer where the sagging single-wide used to be. The rusty old tractor was gone.

Behind the barn, the summer-green grass still ran up to the fawn-colored edge of the savannah and stopped abruptly at a wire mesh fence, dotted with wildlife refuge signs. On the other side, the watery grasslands surrounding the St. Johns River spread out for miles under the bright blue sky. A low line of cypress far in the west was the only sign that the swamp had another shore.

The potted geraniums were gone, but there were new signs of life: the barn's front overhang now featured a soda machine and some patio furniture, none of which appeared to have come from Casey's liquidation client. Across the barn's center aisle there was still a set of cross-ties, and there was horse standing there now, looking bored or maybe just napping. Even the horse, bay with a white star, could have been transported to this place from twenty-five years ago. Admittedly, from a distance most bay horses looked alike.

"This is not happening," Casey whispered to herself, putting her car into park alongside a railroad tie which seemed to mark a parking area. "This doesn't even feel possible."

A pair of oddly spotted dogs came running out of the barn, followed by a young woman with a long blonde pony-tail. She was wearing riding clothes: dark breeches and a long-sleeved top, with argyle knee socks and dusty brown paddock boots. The woman whistled as the hounds reached Casey's car and began to bellow a welcome—or was it a warning? She couldn't tell.

Casey decided to sit tight and wait it out.

Luckily, the dogs bounded back to the woman and hopped around her, blissfully reaching up to lick at her fingers, her elbows, even her ears—they were practically kangaroos, Casey thought with astonishment, although they'd be very odd-colored ones, with their red-and-gray roan coats liberally splattered with black dots.

The blonde woman snapped her fingers and pointed at the ground, and eventually the dogs, with a lot of pawing and regretful glances at Casey's car, threw themselves down on the ground and put their noses on their front paws. Casey was impressed.

The blonde woman gestured at Casey, grinning: it was safe to get out.

"Sorry," she called, as Casey climbed out, the big yellow envelope in one hand. "They're idiots. I usually keep them inside when there are people around."

"What kind of dogs are those?" Casey's interest in animals got the better of her professional manners.

"Catahoula hounds," the woman said., and laughed at Casey's immediate confusion. "Never heard of them? Don't feel bad. Most people haven't. They're a really southern hunting dog. I don't hunt… I just like their energy. And their spots. And they bark so much at night it scares off intruders, which is kind of the point."

"I love their spots," Casey ventured. She was a little surprised by the woman's complete lack of any accent; she'd think someone with a penchant for southern hunting dogs would have an accompanying twang in her voice, even if she *didn't* hunt. "Very handsome," she added, looking the dogs over. Noticing her scrutiny, one of them lifted his head hopefully. The young woman snapped her fingers again, and he put it back down, his tail thumping the grass.

"You just have to train them," she explained. "They've got too much crazy to let them run wild. *But* I never trained them enough to have them out around people, unfortunately, so they're only out when I'm alone. Hi, by the way. I'm Sky. Skyler Thomas, I mean, in case you're who I think you are."

Casey looked at the envelope in her hand, the name written in bold black ink. *S. Thomas.* "Yes, I am," she laughed. "I'm Casey. I was just running this out for the team. I gotta tell ya—this is going to sound weird—but, I think I rode here when I was a little kid."

"Did you?" Sky looked utterly delighted. She had a smile which took over her entire face and made her green eyes dance. "That's amazing! I moved here three years ago... my mother bought it from the bank and then we fixed it up. It was in really rough shape. The last people went bankrupt and then this place just sat to rot. When I first saw it, I thought the property was all jungle. My mom was looking at it as a land investment, nothing more. The barn was a total surprise."

Casey let her eyes run over the tidy stable behind Sky. It was hard to imagine this place had ever been buried in weeds and vines, but that was definitely how Florida operated. "I guess it was at least twenty-five years ago," she said, nearly wincing over the size of that number, "but the barn looks just the same as I remember it."

"Well, you have to come in and see it! I'll bet it's nicer now, not gonna lie... we put a lot of work into the stalls and tack rooms. My mom and I saw a big opportunity up here. I'm from Wellington— yeah, I know," Sky laughed, seeing Casey's eyes widen. "Richie-rich horse country, it's true. But I wanted to get away from that whole Wellington horse show scene, relax a little bit. I grew up with all that, you know? We have fun here, way more fun than I could have down there. When we need to show, we load up and go, but it's nice to have a quiet place to come home to."

Every bit of Casey was yearning to see the barn, but a sizable portion of her mind knew she would be due back at the office— *with* a latte, since that had been a direct order disguised as a casual request—and Mary would be counting the minutes until she returned. But Sky's enthusiasm was so infectious… and the barn was so alluring…

"I know what you're thinking," Sky teased. "Work beckons. But come on… this is your old barn! It was meant to be!"

The horse in the cross-ties, who had been napping, suddenly woke up and turned to face them, his sleepy eyes slowly widening. Their gazes met, human and equine, and Casey felt a sudden rush of need to get closer to him, to put her hands onto a horse's warm hide, to sniff the stable smells of hay and shavings and leather, to see the wooden rafters and brass nameplates and brightly-colored halters hanging neatly from their hooks on the stalls. She needed to be in a barn again, more than anything else in the world. Fifteen years of missing all of this was swelling up in her chest, and she had no choice but to give in to her heart's urging.

"You're right," she agreed, tossing her boss's approval to the warm wind blowing across the St. Johns. "This was meant to be!"

Chapter Three

"I should be going," Casey said again.

She'd said it, by her own count, four times already.

Once, after Sky walked her down the center aisle of the barn, prettily redone but still recognizable as the barn where she'd ridden as a little girl. The new touches were decidedly luxurious. There were brass nameplates mounted on every stall door, rows of wide tack lockers along the walls in the boarders' tack room, and best of all, an air-conditioned lounge, complete with a big picture window overlooking the arena.

Casey lingered inside the lounge, the cool air on her sweaty skin giving her the shivers, and imagined parents clustering here to watch their little darlings riding in their Saturday lessons. Her parents would have loved this! How many hours had they spent sweating it out while she bounced around that very arena? *Too many,* her father would groan.

The bones of the place were unchanged, and felt comfortably like nearly every Floridian horse barn she'd ever been inside: high, open rafters, with a steel roof pinging gently from the clumsy assaults of midday insects swooping in on the breeze; wooden stall fronts with black steel bars, pocked with the teeth-marks of gnawing horses; an overhang at either end sheltering cross-ties, where you could groom your horse while the sea breeze teased your skin.

The second time she'd declared that she really must get going, they'd been exclaiming over the cuteness of Sky's latest project-horse acquisition, a dark bay Thoroughbred gelding with a small white star and an expression of extraordinary serenity. He looked as if his soul had been bound for a Buddhist monastery but had accidentally been becalmed within the sleek shell of a hot-blooded racehorse.

The horse blinked with quiet interest at the women as they cooed over him through the stall bars, then poked his nose through, allowing Casey to run her fingers over the silky-soft skin between his nostrils. He blew gently on her palms, and she felt like swooning with instant, heart-melting love.

"What a doll," she sighed.

"He's only been here two weeks, and I haven't even ridden him yet," Sky explained as Casey cuddled with the horse, "but he was such a gentleman in the video his trainer down at the track sent me, I just sent her the money online and said to put him on the next trailer up here. The girls are calling him James, like James Bond, because he's a total lady-killer. I mean, *look* at him. Look at that nose!" James was wiggling his upper lip on Casey's fingers, as if he knew his adorableness had no bounds. "That's his favorite trick. He gets the girls doing it for half the afternoon sometimes. I have to drag them away."

The girls! Casey had to bite back a sigh. She'd been one of those barn girls once—that feral pack of adolescent and teenage girls every boarding stable had. Girls who spent every free moment at the barn, constantly fighting small civil wars when they weren't working relentlessly towards their next horse show.

Casey felt a pang of nostalgia and loss just thinking about her life in those days. They'd been so wild, alternating between fierce friendship and equally fierce enmity, changing teams with artless abandon whenever the mood struck.

The third time that Casey said she should be going, Sky had just finished showing her the framed photos from the lesson program's very successful winter eventing season. So many bright-faced teenagers, so many determined chins jutting as they jumped their horses over piles of logs and attractive flower boxes!

"No one evented when I was a kid," Casey said regretfully. "It was all hunters and jumpers back then."

"A lot of them are still hunter-jumper kids, but I like to give them options. We do both, when we can." Sky tapped her finger on a framed photo of a grim-faced small girl, who was sending her horse over an alarmingly high jump. "Some of them have what it takes to be professionals. I can't wait to see where this one goes."

"She looks insanely talented."

"She is. Good old Gwen." Sky nodded with satisfaction. "Future Olympian, I have no doubt."

Casey remembered when *she* had planned on being a future Olympian. Hell, they all had. There hadn't been a girl in her group who hadn't believed they were going all the way to the top.

The fourth time she'd said she just *had* to be going, it was because her phone was ringing and the caller was Mary, wondering if everything was okay. "Did you get lost?" her boss asked caustically. "Flat tire?"

"I *just* found the place," Casey lied into her phone, winking her unconscious half-wink at Sky, who was grinning back at her, enjoying the show. "I'm so sorry to have taken so long. It's in the middle of nowhere and the driveway was hidden. Then there was a gate I had to get open. Took forever. But I got it now. I think I see the owner coming now—I better get off the phone!"

Sky was holding up a can of Diet Coke, waggling it enticingly as Casey put away her phone. By now, they were in the barn office, which in Casey's childhood had been a dark place where her riding instructor had accepted weekly personal checks from Casey's mother and placed them into a metal lockbox atop the old wood-laminate desk. Now it was brightly-lit and refreshingly chilly, with a much more twenty-first-century desk of Swedish flat-pack origin.

On top of the desk, a laptop was peeking from a smudged leather case, half-buried by tack catalogs. Cool air slipped through the mouth of a vent in the ceiling. "This room is always freezing," Sky laughed, slipping on a jacket to cover her bare arms. "We added the air conditioning to the central rooms when we remodeled the barn. My dad runs a construction company, so he always manages to find equipment when he wants it. Try *stopping* him from adding AC to something. I think he'd do the whole barn if I let him."

Casey accepted the Diet Coke gratefully, telling herself she'd get going in a few minutes. This was just something cold and wet for the road. It was insanely hot under the May sun, and they'd been walking around for... she checked her phone... more than half an hour! "I *really* should be going," Casey said, the fifth time. "Seriously this time. My boss is going to flip, and now she knows I'm here."

Sky sighed, clearly disappointed her visit was over. "Well, damn, I hope I didn't get you in trouble! It was just fun to meet someone who was here when they were a kid. I mean, what are the chances?" She stood up and opened the office door. The humid afternoon air rushed to meet them, along with the scent of hay and shavings. A horse whinnied hopefully. "And it was nice to talk to an adult. All of my clients are children. Boarders, students, leasers: everyone is under eighteen."

"It's funny. I was *really* little when I was here, but—" Casey swiveled her head around as they stepped back into the aisle, "—this just brings back so many memories. Stuff I'd totally forgotten about. There was this pony I rode, he was in that stall over *there,* and he had this big white star, and even though he was super-grumpy and pinned his ears every time anyone came near him, I loved him because, I don't know, he felt like *my pony* in my head. I hadn't thought about him in years, but now I can picture him perfectly."

They both looked at the stall she'd pointed out. It was the one where the new Thoroughbred was living now. James gazed back at them with his dark, thoughtful gaze, his silky black forelock nearly obscuring his little white star before falling rakishly over one eye.

Casey again felt that rush of adoration. That horse really was *too* cute. Her palms tickled and she put them behind her back to stop herself from rushing over and rubbing his smooth muzzle again.

Sky was nodding thoughtfully. "I totally get the whole possession thing, every little girl is like that with her school pony! But if you don't mind me asking, why on *earth* would you stop riding?" She sounded utterly befuddled, as if Casey had given up horses so that she could take up a new life of dog-napping or uprooting flowerbeds.

Casey wasn't sure how to answer at first.

They started walking up the barn aisle, Casey leading the way, feeling painfully resigned to go back to her job and her real life. After this little trip down memory lane, she wanted nothing more than to stay. The horses watched them through the stall bars. The bright blaze of the horse she'd seen in the cross-ties flashed from within the end stall as he looked up from his hay. The pull of the place filled her with a hopeless longing.

"I quit riding when I was in high school," she finally admitted. Her voice was low, as if she was sharing a weakness. "Before senior year. It's been... fifteen years." Fifteen years, as if none of her hard work had even mattered. Of course, everyone had told her it *didn't* matter—everyone being her guidance counselor, her teachers, even her parents. Riding had been her hobby, but it couldn't possibly be good enough to be her career. She couldn't throw herself away to be a two-bit trainer when she had so much potential!

Potential for *what?* Casey took a deep gulp from her soda and clenched the can tightly. She was not going to have one of those little anxiety attacks about her job and her life right now. They'd been growing in strength and frequency lately, sure, but now was not the time. She was going to say goodbye to this nice woman and get into her car and drive back to her good-paying job and she was going to *remain calm* and she was *not* going to think about how pointless it all was.

After all, the last time she'd let herself think too much about the general void of meaning in her life, she'd wasted a lot of time and emotion for no return. It had happened like this: she'd had a particularly rough drive home after an uninspiring day of writing emails about patio furniture—yes, much like today!

She'd slammed into the house, already in tears, drank several beers before switching to whiskey, and applied to thirty-seven jobs with customized cover letters and resumés before going to bed at midnight. Several weeks later, sixteen different hiring managers wrote back to her requesting interviews. Naturally, this was well after she'd calmed down and realized she couldn't possibly rearrange her life in such a way that she could become an apprentice at a French bakery or join the National Park Service as a forest ranger in Gatlinburg, Tennessee. So one could argue their delayed timing had been good, and that her entire fit had been a waste of time.

"You should start riding again," Sky was saying eagerly, interrupting Casey's rapid-onset depression. "It's never too late to get back in the saddle! It's like riding a bike! I have some time on the weekends—I could fit you in with a private lesson, get you back in the habit, and then later you could join a group lesson if you want."

Casey felt a rush of excitement, which she promptly tamped

down as hard as possible. How could she fit horses into her life? Her parents had always groaned about having to drive her to barn, that extra commute, plus the endless hours she spent there. Horses were a massive time-suck, and it was a solitary hobby, if you were the only one in your household who did the riding. Even if she just rode on a Saturday morning, Brandon would be left alone half a day, a quarter of their weekend time together. That would be totally unfair.

She shook her head regretfully. "I never have much spare time on the weekends. My boyfriend keeps us hopping—he's always got something he wants to do. Plus we have brunch with friends, and someone's always asking us to come ride jet-skis or something. I don't know how I'd find the time."

Sky pushed on. "Any weeknights free? You could come after work. I'd find some time for you."

"I don't know. It's almost summer, it's going to start raining every evening…" The excuses bubbled up without any effort at all. Casey knew picking up riding wasn't in the cards. If she was meant to start riding again, wouldn't she have done it sooner than this? It was too late now. She had a real life to contend with: a job and a boyfriend and regular weekend brunch with friends. She was in a middle place right now. Horses were for kids and rich older women, before and after the middle place, assuming she ever got rich. Maybe in ten or twenty years she could be a wealthy amateur. Of course, that would mean her job situation would need to improve twentyfold. "I mean, I'd love to but—"

Casey could tell Sky knew excuses when she heard them, but the other woman pressed on anyway. "Just take some time and think about it. I'm telling you, it's doable. You can come early on a weekend morning and I'll have you in and out before your boyfriend notices you're gone. Start on Saturday morning with a private lesson. I have an opening at nine but it will fill fast, trust me. And just watch how great you'll do—you'll pick it all up again in no time! We have great school horses and all of our boarders and students are super-nice—" Sky's sales pitch went on and on, all cotton candy and buttered popcorn and ice-cold lemonade, and Casey found it easy to believe that nothing bad ever happened here and that if she rode a horse here, clover would spring up in their wake and rainbows would arch over her helmeted head.

Then her phone rang again. *Mary*. Casey held the screen up to show Sky. "I really have to go."

Sky dug in the back pocket of her riding breeches and drew out a business card, curved and slightly damp with sweat. "Call me."

Casey took the card in one hand, and answered Mary's call with the other. "Yes, I'm on my way back, the papers are delivered—"

She looked in the rearview mirror before her car entered the green tunnel of the barn driveway, and she saw the spotted dogs sitting alongside Sky, watching her go.

Chapter Four

Back in the office, Casey tapped her toes under her desk through the remaining two hours of the day, her thoughts so full of horses that she accidentally typed *canter* instead of *counter* in an email for an appliance store. Luckily, she caught the error in a revision before it went out for approvals.

I'm a mess, she thought, but she had to bite back a private smile as she deleted the mistake. Who knew horses would still have this kind of effect on her? She felt like a twelve-year-old girl. She felt light and fresh and free, and—Casey looked at the time and smiled more broadly—in just a few minutes, she would be.

"Happy Friday," a departing coworker said as she passed Casey's cubicle, purse over shoulder.

"Almost that time," a cubicle neighbor agreed.

"Big plans this weekend?" the first woman asked, pausing for chit-chat.

Casey mouthed along with the next line, her head down so she wouldn't be caught. "The usual. Projects around the house. Kids have soccer."

"Well, have a good one." The woman moved on.

The same conversation, the same time, every Friday, Casey thought with a dismissive chuckle. She busied herself on her laptop, clicking windows closed. Then she let the mouse hover over SHUT DOWN while she watched the clock on her monitor. In three…

two… *bye!* Casey dropped her laptop into her bag, slung it over her shoulder, and marched out of her cubicle without looking back. Free for another weekend!

Brandon was waiting for her when she got to their usual Friday-night hang, looking admirably relaxed already. Of course, Casey reasoned, since he got to set his own hours, he had probably started his weekend earlier than she had.

He had secured their favorite table by the dockside, with dark water lapping on the opposite side of a fence made of old fishing nets and rope, and a pelican sitting on the closest fishing boat, watching the restaurant diners with beady black eyes.

"Hey, you!" Casey called, smiling as she doled out a light kiss, and sliding into the chair across from Brandon. "Thanks for ordering the fritters!" She dug into the bowl of corn fritters in the center of the table before she'd even settled into her seat properly. "Mmm. Mango's makes the greatest fritters."

"Dixie Crossroads makes the greatest fritters," Brandon corrected her. He grinned, his dark brown eyes twinkling at her. This was a weekly tradition.

Casey chewed elaborately to make her point, then swallowed with as much emphasis as possible. "Mmm. Delicious. I'm so glad you agree that it's important that we have this conversation every Friday, to keep the moon from crashing into the sea."

"Oh, I totally agree. But now can we talk about how nicely I trimmed my beard? I did it all by myself." Brandon ran his fingers under his chin with the feathery touch of a QVC presenter.

She admired the neat edging work he'd given his close-cropped brown beard. "I like how the hair on top of your head is twice as long as the hair on your chin. It really gives you a finished look."

Brandon ran an appraising hand over his hair. "This extra-hold mousse I found on your side of the bathroom cabinet is doing wonders for me."

"Well, you look fantastic, that's all I can say."

"You should try it sometime." He smirked at her.

Casey gave him a light kick under the table. "Keep it up and I'll hide my haircare products, thief!"

Casey might have found her coworkers' repetitive weekends depressing, but if she was really honest with herself, her weekends were filled with rituals, too. Starting with these three: Casey and Brandon always ate dinner on the dockside patio of Mango's Island Grille on Friday nights, and Brandon always ate more than his share of the fritters, and Casey always had one more margarita than she had planned.

These were some of the constants of their three-year relationship, along with Brandon's perplexing out-of-state devotion to the Baltimore Orioles and Casey's steadfast refusal to agree to a cat and their mutual admiration for kitschy old Florida memorabilia. Their political views meshed. Their favorite t-shirts were the same shade of blue. Their jokes were *all* insider jokes.

After her last anxiety attack, the one in which she'd applied to dozens of jobs, she'd had a striking thought: that a relationship like this was a reassuring place to find yourself after you'd felt like you were drowning and finally came up for air. One half of a perfectly cohesive unit: what a safe and enviable way to go through life! Although she had to admit that when her thoughts did run wild, it was frustrating to realize she couldn't actually run away to be a forest ranger or a baguette apprentice. Not without ruining this perfect balance she had with Brandon.

A cruise ship was sliding past the patio of Mango's just now, its soaring metal curves just a few hundred feet away from their table. Loud dance music pumped from the upper decks, and seagoing passengers clowned around and waved to all the unlucky souls remaining on shore. Most of them were drunk already. Some of them would be drunk for the next three days. There was no hangover like a three-night Bahamas cruise hangover, a fact which Casey could attest to.

"Man, I'd love to go on a cruise," Brandon sighed, watching the ship sail serenely past them. "If I hadn't just signed on to this crazy new project, I'd be booking us a weekender so fast. Maybe this fall we can go."

Casey watched the ship's prow push through the deep-blue channel water, turning up white foam which cascaded into rippling breakers. "I used to want to work on a cruise ship." She paused, thinking about far places and tropical islands. "I thought it would be a cool way to see the world. Although, maybe being a flight attendant would have been more fun, I don't know. Neither of them really fit into my career."

"More living space for flight attendants," Brandon remarked, nodding. "Cruise ship quarters are *tight*. They're packed in those rooms like sardines, from what I hear."

"Well, too late now," Casey said, and turned to accept a margarita from their server, who knew her order without asking. "Thank you, Jaycee. This is perfect."

The ship was halfway past them now, moving at a decent clip. Some of the more tame passengers were watching the shore slip past from their stateroom balconies, enjoying their own private parties while the kegger raged up top. A couple raised their champagne flutes in a toast, and Casey held up her margarita glass in return.

"Yeah, all of that running away to see the world, those are like, college things," Brandon agreed, nodding to the server as he accepted a beer. "Gotta get them done young, before life takes over. Now we just have to save up for vacations a couple times per year."

They were old and wise, Casey thought. They were passengers now. They got on, they stayed a few days, they got off again. No commitment, no hard times, no shared rooms.

The ship's stern was passing them now, the water churning behind it, while seagulls and pelicans dipped and bickered over the fish caught up in the slipstream. Casey took a long sip from her margarita, wishing the tequila would hurry up and quiet her discontented brain.

"So what's your new project?" she asked finally. "You were being pretty secretive about it all week. Afraid you'd jinx it?" Brandon worked from home, tapping away at something mysterious involving coding and firewalls and security, and all week she'd been coming home to find him holed up in the guest bedroom upstairs, door closed, deeply engaged on conference calls while he tried to work out the scope of work his latest lead would actually need.

"I really was, yeah." Brandon laughed and ran his hands through his hair. "Things got intense. They weren't sure I could do it alone... for a while *I* wasn't sure I could do it alone, honestly. But we worked it out. A huge new site. All the bells and whistles. Integrations out the wazoo. But here's the best part."

He took a swig from his beer, mischievously letting a little anticipation build. Casey waited, smiling. Brandon had a theatrical streak.

"It's for a new charitable arm of a marine company. The founder is ready to give back to society. So I'll be saving the ocean! Finally!"

Casey gasped. Then she leaned across the table and took his hands in hers. His dream job, at last! "Brandon, that's *amazing*. This is what you've always wanted!"

"It is!" Brandon's face was alight with happiness. "After writing websites for endless crap for years, I finally get to do something that *matters.*"

"I'm so, so happy for you," Casey assured him, and she was,

but something in his words made her insides twist into a little jealous ball. She put his hands to her lips and kissed them, closing her eyes so he wouldn't see any hint of of envy. "You deserve this."

She meant it. She just wanted it for herself, too.

"Thank you." Brandon took a deep breath and looked out over the choppy waters. A few pelicans were flapping lazily in the wake of the departed cruise ship, looking for disoriented fish they could scoop up without too much effort. "It's going to take a lot of time, though. I'll probably have to do some work on weekends to keep up, definitely at first."

Her eyes fluttered open and she looked up at him. "Weekends?"

"Not *all* weekend, but I'll have to do some stuff. Saturday mornings, maybe? That way it doesn't interfere with the rest of the weekend."

Casey bit her lip to avoid smiling too much. That would be suspicious, right? To grin like an idiot as her boyfriend announced he'd be keeping office hours on Saturdays?

She hadn't planned on going back to the horse farm. She *really* hadn't. But this was surely a sign!

Casey thought of the business card in her bag, of Sky saying *you can start on Saturday mornings*. Of the dark, liquid gaze of that sweet Thoroughbred watching her through the stall bars. What had his name been again? James, that was it. The celebrated ladykiller James. She'd bring him some baby carrots, or maybe some cookies. Which one did he like best? Her old horse, Wilson, had *loved* Thin Mints. Casey used to make her mom buy them by the carton every time Girl Scout Cookie season rolled around. Then she put them in the deep freezer in the garage, taped shut so that her father couldn't break into them. She wished she had a box of them now, but Thin Mints didn't last more than an hour in the same house as Brandon.

While her mind wandered, Brandon had plucked the last fritter between his sugary fingers, then paused with his prize halfway to his mouth. "Uh, is this one yours? I wasn't counting."

"You *never* count!" Casey protested, laughing. "Lucky for you, I wasn't counting either. Eat the fritter."

"Are you sure?"

Casey considered the effect of several years' of Friday night fritters eaten at this very table. "I'm good. Let's order some dinner. It feels like a salad night."

Brandon looked at her. "You usually get a burger."

"Well, it's hot out. And summer is here. Beach body and all."

Brandon didn't look convinced, but he ate the fritter anyway.

Casey picked up her menu and flipped the page to look over the salads. "Yum," she murmured. "Mmm, looks good." She'd shout the praises of arugula and sprouts and lean grilled chicken all night long to stave off questions about the salad if she had to, but what she wasn't going to share was that she was thinking of taking up a sport which required skin-tight pants.

Not yet, anyway.

Chapter Five

Tight pants were just one of the requirements for Casey's first riding lesson in over a decade. She felt a mild thrill late that Friday night as she typed *tack shop* into her phone and started skimming websites, recognizing lots of familiar names from her past. Dover Saddlery, State Line Tack: they were still around! There were some newbies on the block too… newbies, she thought, until she noticed at least one of them was celebrating their ten-year anniversary.

God, she'd been gone *so long*. And looking at the listings for things like riding tights, sun-shirts (that explained Sky's long-sleeve shirt, which had seemed really unusual for a hot May day in Florida) and silicone-grip breeches, riding clothes had changed. Sure, she hadn't *really* expected full chaps with fringe to stick around… or maybe, in the back of her mind, she had.

Casey decided she needed to get personal with the new generation of riding clothes. Mail-order wasn't going to cut it. So on Monday's lunch break, she tried out an old standby, Jack's Tack and Feed. She remembered the place as a good source for cheap riding clothes, but times had changed for Jack's. It was now little more than a garage in an industrial strip mall, filled to the rafters with pallets of livestock feed. The tack section of the store was a small corner with a few plastic storage shelves loaded with cardboard boxes. Everything was still wrapped in the plastic it had been shipped in. Casey lifted a bag containing a pair of polyester breeches, beige and sorrowful, and dropped it back into the box immediately.

"Spider," she whispered, trying to avoid screaming—Jack was watching her with unprofessional interest. "Spider, spider, spider." She smiled at Jack and walked by and didn't allow herself to collapse into a trembling wreck until she'd closed and locked her car doors.

"I forgot spiders came that big," she said out loud.

That was all the fun she had time for on Monday's lunch break, but on Tuesday she tried going a little further afield, to a new and excitingly named tack shop called Horseland. There was not a tiny castle filled with happy cartoon horses painted on the sign above the doors, which was disappointing, but at least Horseland occupied an actual suite of a strip mall designed for stores, rather than for autobody repair shops. There was no feed or hay in sight, and she suspected their budget included regular pest control. Casey duly went inside with a much more confident feeling than she had left Jack's with the day before.

Inside the small store, racks of jewel-tone breeches and exuberantly printed riding shirts jostled for space alongside boxes of boots and displays of gloves. There was a jewelry case by the cash register filled with twinkling stock tie pins and horsey earrings, which apparently were still the standard horseshoes and snaffle bits. The back wall was lined with new saddles and bridles, filling the atmosphere with that timeless scent of leather Casey remembered from tack shop trips as a kid. The entire place felt magical.

A teenage girl who probably should have been in school lurked behind the jewelry case-slash-cashwrap, looking at her phone. "Hi," she seemed to hint rather than actually speak as Casey walked in, and she didn't look up.

That was fine; Casey didn't want some sales person hovering over her. She walked over to the breeches and began to poke around the racks. Fashion had changed over the years. Half-chaps were what you wore now, over paddock boots, and smart breeches with silicone grips on the seat and inner thighs. Tech fabrics had taken over, and the price tag for all that tech was steep, especially without an online-store discount. Flipping price tags, Casey realized that the cheapest items here were at the top of the budget she'd been planning on. The tip-top.

The teenager wandered out from behind the counter. "Can I help you find anything?" she asked in a monotone.

"I could use a little help," Casey admitted, feeling defeated by the sheer volume of choices. "I haven't bought breeches in a long time."

"Oh, do you wear tights? They're just small, medium, large, you know? Easier than breeches." The girl flicked through the rack, eyeballed Casey's hips, and flicked some more. Casey felt compelled to explain herself.

"I just haven't ridden in a while. And when I did, I never wore breeches and boots unless I absolutely had to, like for a show."

The girl lifted an eyebrow as she pulled out some potential breeches. "What did you ride in?"

"We wore chaps," Casey said. "Full chaps. So we could wear shorts to the barn and just zip the chaps over to ride."

"Weird." The teen blinked at her, startled into making eye contact. She was wearing too much mascara. Tiny flakes were sloughing from her lashes and dotted the skin under her eyes. "It sounds like that would be really hot."

"It was actually cooler, though because we wore shorts all day," Casey said lamely, but the conversation had floundered. It had never really existed.

Trying on six different fabrics and sizes of breeches, Casey was forced to admire herself in a full-length mirror while four-way stretch fabric allowed for no illusions. It was a shame, she thought, turning and adjusting herself as she tried to find a palatable reflection, that nineteenth-century riding fashion was relegated to eccentrics only. At least give a girl some whalebone and steel to cover up how soft she'd gotten while sitting at a desk. The breeches the sales girl had found for her hid nothing, accentuated nothing, and gave no confidence. At least they were under a hundred bucks.

When Casey emerged from the curtained dressing room, the teenage girl had gone back behind the counter. She came out again, with a sigh, to help Casey size the half-chaps, which had to fit through the calf, the ankle, *and* from foot to knee. It was a very precise request for an off-the-shelf product, but this time, Casey kept her thoughts about them to herself. As she got zipped into the third pair, though, the silence began to wear on her.

"Do you ride near here?" she asked.

The girl glanced up at her. "I ride at Karen's place."

"Karen…?"

"Karen Devos?" She tugged at the zipper; it was too snug for Casey's calf. "At Holly Hill Farm. Down by Melbourne."

"Oh, I don't know it." Casey sighed, wondering how much the farm scene had changed. "I don't get down to that end of the county much."

"She's the best," the girl said simply. "Here, these won't work."

The fourth try yielded half-chaps which felt miraculously custom, wrapping themselves like a tight glove around Casey's lower leg. She took a few steps and found the half-chaps so comfortable she thought she'd like to wear them all day, but her lunch hour was almost up and she wasn't prepared for those kind of stares, anyway. She quickly picked out a pair of zip-up paddock boots in the same brand she'd worn as a teen, Ariat, and gathered everything up, taking it to the register with a feeling of real accomplishment.

Wrapping the purchases up in a bag, the sales girl was still thinking about the implications of full chaps.

"I just don't get it. How was all that leather cooler than wearing breeches and half-chaps?"

"I meant when you weren't riding... when you were just clowning around the barn, or doing barn chores or whatever. You had shorts on then. Instead of wearing pants all day."

The girl shook her head, unconvinced. She swiped Casey's credit card, charging her an alarming sum of money, and then looked thoughtfully at her as she handed the card back. "Did you want a helmet?"

Casey shook her head. Helmets had changed so dramatically that the choice seemed to be between a glorified bicycle helmet and a six-hundred dollar, Formula 1-grade crash helmet, and Casey wasn't prepared to make that decision yet. "There are helmets at the barn."

"*Lesson* helmets?" The girl's teenage disgust was expert-level.

Casey took her purchases and fled.

She left the big Horseland bag in the car, and marched back into he office with just a take-out salad. (Salads were still in order, thanks to the riding breeches.) She had just settled down to eat around her keyboard when coworker Amy went wandering by and noticed the desk lunch.

"Errands at lunch?" she asked, leaning on the cubicle and settling in for a chat.

"That's right," Casey said agreeably, stabbing lettuce with her fork. "Busy day." She wished Amy would go away. There were several emails with aggravating subject lines glaring at her from her inbox, and she didn't feel like sharing her client issues with anyone. Amy, a bit of a teacher's pet, had the sort of interesting accounts Casey would kill for: a surfboard company, a regional chain of bakeries, the South Florida Association of Tropical Horticulture.

"What did you do?" Amy asked chummily.

"Oh, had to return some clothes. And the line was long, and then my receipt wouldn't scan, it took forever." Casey talked around a mouthful of tomato, hoping to indicate how very pressed for time she was. "And *then* of course there was an issue with their credit card reader. It was a whole thing." She waved her fork for emphasis and a few drops of salad oil hit her desk.

"Oh." Amy had clearly been hoping for a better story. "Well, at least it's over with. Enjoy your salad!" She sauntered off.

Casey crunched her way through some purple cabbage and moodily began to open the offending emails. Yeah, she'd lied to Amy. What about it? She wasn't about to share with the office that she was going to spend Saturday morning re-learning how to ride a horse. For one thing, it wasn't anyone's business. For another… Casey sighed and leaned back in her chair, disappointed in herself for just thinking it. But it was true.

She didn't want to be the office horse girl.

There was just a little bit of a stigma associated with being a horse girl, that was all. You saw it all over social media, and social media was what passed for social mores these days. The lines had been drawn and the decisions had been made: society had decided normal people didn't ride horses. Horse girls were measured on a scale of slightly to moderately to very weird, but no matter what, there would definitely be a weirdness to contend with in any horse girl situation. This was understood.

Casey already had enough of a status issue in this office. Look at the clients she was stuck with! There was no way she was going to make things worse by being a horse girl.

And anyway, she reminded herself, this was just one lesson. It might be terrible. She might hate it. She might never go back again.

It might have been a secret at work, but she still had to tell

Brandon. There was a chance she could have hidden it from him if he worked out of an office, but with Brandon home all of the time, he tended to notice what she was up to. With him working from home all Saturday morning, she'd have no way to get to the door in her riding clothes unseen, or creep back in a few hours later, sweaty and disheveled, without being discovered.

So that night, as they sat on their back patio trying to sneak a few minutes of outdoor Florida living before the mosquitos started whining in their ears, she decided to come clean.

"Hey Brandon? You know how you're working on Saturday morning?" She bit her lip, realizing she'd opened the conversation like a kid who was trying to get something without really asking for it.

"I do know, yeah." Brandon grinned at her. "I heard something about it."

"Right, of course. I don't... I don't know why I said it like that. *Obviously* you know. I mean, it's... yeah." She took a breath.

"Are you okay?"

"Yes! Yeah, I just... Saturday morning, I'm going to take a riding lesson." She said the words all at once: *imgoingtotakeuhridelesson.*

Brandon looked at her with astonishment. Then his surprised mouth broadened into a smile. "Well, Casey, that sounds like fun! My little cowgirl!"

She swallowed before she could tell him how wrong he had it. *Actually, I used to ride hunter-jumper* was not a lecture Brandon needed or, frankly, deserved. "Yeah," she agreed instead. "Just like the old days."

"What brought this on?" Brandon swiped at something near his ear.

"The craziest thing," Casey began, and she gave him an abbreviated version of her meeting with Sky. "It's just going to be

46

so wild to ride in the same ring where I learned to ride all those years ago," she concluded, artistically allowing a little wistfulness to creep into her tone.

Brandon was inspecting his arm. Then he slapped it, and scraped his palm on the armrest of his chair. "Mosquitos are out."

She blinked at him, disappointed. "Brandon, did you hear my story?"

"Of course I did," Brandon told her, standing up. "It's like a fairy tale. Come on, let's go inside. I'll start dinner and you can tell me more horse stories." He grinned and at her and held out his hand. "Did you get a cute cowgirl costume?"

Casey rolled her eyes and took his hand. Better nip this in the bud. "Brandon, my boy, you have a lot to learn about horse girls."

Chapter Six

Saturday morning at the stable: grass shining with dew, a cool breeze breathing through a shadowy barn aisle, dust motes dancing in the golden sunbeams, horses nosing through hay and chewing quietly. Casey climbed out of her car, half-chaps in hand, feeling her heart rise up like a hot-air balloon.

Sky was waiting for her, arms folded, head tipped back against the barn wall. She was dressed in the same uniform as the week before: wine-colored breeches, a gray and blue sun-shirt, and wore a blue hat over her blonde braid. Casey felt like a dark-haired, more wobbly version of the younger woman, and their twinning good looks made her smile as she ran her hands over her navy-blue breeches and matching sun-shirt. She might be keeping things casual for now, but she felt like a horse girl again already.

Sky pushed off from the wall. "Is this the perfect morning, or what?"

"It's insane," Casey agreed, smiling so broadly her cheeks hurt.

"I'm really glad you're here. Come on, let me introduce you to the horse you'll be riding."

The white-faced horse in the first stall was watching them through the bars. Casey waggled her fingers at him as she passed. They passed a few more stalls, housing eating horses who couldn't be bothered to notice them, and then she saw James, his soft eyes glimmering in the shadows as he looked up from his hay and saw her. His ears pricked, and he stopped chewing.

"Hi, buddy," Casey whispered, feeling shy and foolish.

She saw his nostrils flutter in a silent greeting, and her heart began to pound with excitement. He remembered her! He'd practically neighed at her—in that silent, inscrutable way most horses actually spoke.

Casey wanted to stop and give his nose a tickle through the stall bars, but Sky was already stopping at another stall two doors down and was looking back at her expectantly. She hustled to keep up, feeling regretful at leaving James behind.

Sky had stopped outside a stall housing heavyset bay gelding. He was not interested in Sky, or Casey. The horse kept his nose buried deep his pile of hay while Sky picked up his halter and lead from the hook outside the door and undid the door-latch, signaling her intentions to take him out. He just went on chewing, as if he thought ignoring the women would make them go away.

"This is Mikey," Sky announced. "Mikey, say hello!"

Mikey flicked his tail and snorted loudly into his hay. Casey became aware that she was in the presence of a supremely indifferent animal. Mikey's attitude was the opposite of James's welcoming nature. She couldn't help but frown a little. This wasn't the rapturous return to riding she'd been picturing.

Sky grinned at Casey's disappointed expression. "Yeah, he's a little tough to impress. Mike's my adult babysitter. Maybe you're too advanced for him, but he'll be perfect for your first ride in a while. Nothing bothers Mikey."

Casey glanced around the quiet barn aisle, hoping there was no one lurking in a nearby tack room to overhear that line about an *adult babysitter*. She found the thought of being mistaken for a beginner unspeakably depressing. She'd put *years* into this sport! The best years of her life, if one was strictly measuring life satisfaction by general flexibility, joint health, and a reason to get out of bed in the morning. There was no way she was going to look like a beginner out there this morning. Sure, she'd be a little stiff, but honestly, wasn't getting back on a horse just like getting back on a bicycle? Sky had said so herself!

Casey looked at Mikey through the stall bars, and he turned his head to gaze impassively back at her, jaws still working as he chewed through his hay. This was a very tall horse, Casey noted. Taller than sixteen hands? Maybe. She wouldn't be able to see over his back when she stood next to him. He had high, sharp withers at the base of his long neck, which would make the saddle ride even higher on his back. When was the last time she'd hitched her leg high enough to mount a horse?

She'd been, what… seventeen?

She was thirty-two now. Her mind whispered the words to her in an ominous undertone.

Casey's hips began to ache in nervous anticipation as she realized she had been wrong.

This was not going to be easy.

A horse was *not* a bicycle, and she was *not* going to hop right back into the saddle like a general returning to battle. Yes, she had spent her childhood building up her riding muscles. But she had spent her adulthood forgetting they'd ever existed.

One of these tricks had been easier than the other.

Casey heard a whisper—a malicious little giggle—and she turned around just in time to see a pair of young girls disappear into a tack room, white-blonde pony-tails whipping over their thin, tan shoulders. Great! Barn rats! Just what she needed, a bunch of judgmental kids watching her every move.

"Ignore them." Sky grinned. "This place is overrun with boarder kids. You know the drill. Their parents drop them off every morning and they're my problem until dinner."

Of course, she knew the drill. Casey had been a barn rat once, too. She knew their habits and their schemes, and she knew there was nothing they liked better than watching an adult flounder at something they all excelled at with virtually no effort. She'd knew she'd have an eager audience watching her lesson, all of them waiting to see her fail at her first ride in fifteen years.

Casey's cheeks flushed preemptively, already prepared for her public embarrassment.

"Well, it's the best way to grow up," she managed to reply. "And here I thought the place was pretty empty for a Saturday morning."

Casey had forgotten that cars in a parking lot meant nothing at a boarding stable. When the average customer age was fourteen, *everyone* was a drop-off.

A gaggle of girls suddenly spilled out of the boarders' tack room and into the barn aisle, all of them talking at once, their arms filled with tack: bridles, martingales, girths, stirrup leathers, saddles. They were universally lanky, coltish, although there was a definite variety between the ages—anywhere between twelve and seventeen. They were alternately wearing breeches and paddock boots, or shorts and old sneakers, all topped off with tank tops or sun-shirts and long braids or pony-tails, like they'd been issued uniforms for the rapidly approaching Florida summer.

Oh good lord, Casey remembered, summer! Memorial Day was almost upon them, and then, right after the holiday, the kids would be out of school. They'd be here all day, every day. Casey suddenly remembered the stretching days of hot barn summers, all the sweat and the hunger and the friendships, and she felt a longing which ached like homesickness.

"Girls? What on earth are you doing?" Sky's voice had deepened in pitch to a firm, no-nonsense Mom tone. Casey had previously guessed Sky was only about twenty-five or twenty-six, which made her less than ten years older than the tallest of these girls. She probably had to really work to make them listen to her.

"Callie read something about stripping tack with ammonia and then dipping it in neatsfoot oil," one of the older teens explained. "So we were going to—"

"Well, you don't have any ammonia," Sky cut her off.

"I was going to *say,*" the teenager continued, with an air of great forbearance, "that we were just going to oil our tack really, really good to make up for not having ammonia. It's already dried out from this yucky dry weather. We shouldn't need ammonia. Unless you have some we can use, to try it out?"

"I don't, and I don't want any of you looking for it at home. It's dangerous. No ammonia in my barn. Got it?"

"Got it."

"Sorry, Sky."

"Yeah, sorry we interrupted your lesson, Sky."

Casey watched the girls parade down the aisle to one of the cross-tie bays at the far end of the barn. She'd hoped to tack up Mikey down there, where the breeze would be playing off the river and might offer some relief from the still air hanging in the barn aisle.

Now, though, she just wanted to keep her distance from that pack. She remembered the old routine when a new rider came to the barn. To barn kids, a new student was the equivalent of a blockbuster film release. Everyone gathered and found a place in the aisle to watch the show. Judgements were made. New kids had to be evaluated: did they know how to ride already? How would they fit into the pecking order? Who would be displaced? Was their horse any good?

Beginner kids without their own horses were not yet real concerns. They wouldn't be part of the pack until they improved enough to warrant their own horse. The barn kids would watch the beginners ride out of pity, and with a general disbelief that any of *them* had ever ridden so clumsily.

But no one ever pitied the horseless adults.

Casey remembered how ridiculous they'd always seemed, those middle-aged exiles walking so uncertainly into their barn in their new boots (or museum-quality riding habits, depending on their hoarding habits and the amount of weight they'd put on since their teenage years). Knowing that as teenagers they were untouchable, the rulers of the barn, the future champions of the equestrian world, she and her friends had watched the adult riders strictly for the laughs. At least they sort of knew how to groom, tack, and mount a horse.

In contrast, adult beginners were rare, and adult beginners who stuck around for more than a few lessons were even more scarce. It was the re-riders, the experienced adults who had given up riding for college and jobs, and had come back after years exiled in the Real World, who might be mildly interesting to the barn teens—but only as museum specimens, or examples of What Not To Do.

After all, what kind of sicko gave up riding? What kind of crazy person sat at a desk when there were horses to ride and stalls to clean?

All valid questions, then and now, Casey thought with a shrug. She looked back at Mikey. The horse had returned to his hay. She could stand there all day and he still wasn't going to make the first move.

"You okay to get him out?" Sky was beginning to sound a little nervous. Maybe she was wondering if she'd misjudged Casey's competency.

"Yeah, I'm good," Casey assured her, coming back to life. She slid open Mikey's stall door and paused, waiting for the horse to walk over and greet her. He turned his head and considered her for a long, searching moment, and, just when Casey was deciding he hadn't found her up to snuff, the horse sighed and made a creaking turn in her direction.

"Hey buddy," she crooned softly, holding out her hands. Mikey snuffled at her fingers, rubbing his upper lip against her skin in search of hidden favors. His whiskers were long and prickled at her palms. "I don't have any treats for you right now," she told him softly. "I didn't even have breakfast myself."

Usually by this time of day, she'd be finishing a mug of coffee, sitting alongside Brandon on the couch, and they'd be thinking about making toast or maybe cooking some bacon, or even getting dressed and going to the diner.

Right now, Casey thought, as she stood here in this barn, sweating in the thick humidity of the morning, trying to shake off the stares from a pack of feral horse girls, she could be sitting in air-conditioned comfort, biting into a crunchy strip of bacon.

Suddenly, that reality sounded vastly preferable to trying to remember how to ride a horse while a lot of teenagers giggled about her poor position.

Be realistic, she chided herself. Brandon was working all morning, so their usual Saturday breakfast wouldn't have happened, anyway. She might as well be here, blushing furiously, blaming her pink cheeks on the heat.

Also, she was going to learn something about herself. This could change her life, opening the door on Equestrian Casey Part Two.

Or, this riding lesson might be a first-time, last-time kind of thing. She'd get a fresh feel for riding, realize she'd been right to give up horses in favor of a Real Life, and move on, forever comfortable and confident in her life decisions. She'd fry up the bacon herself next weekend, and make Brandon take a breakfast break.

Mikey pushed his head against her, forcing her back into her current reality.

"Go on, you can take him," Sky was saying, holding out a

cotton lead-rope. "See what you remember."

And so, for the first time in fifteen years, Casey took charge of a horse.

Chapter Seven

Miraculously, it turned out that Casey remembered *everything*.

Maybe there are some things that are simply engrained upon a person's memory forever; or maybe it was the obsessive attention to order which had come with learning to ride at English show barns which had etched the process permanently into Casey's brain.

Grooming and tacking up a horse were carefully performed rituals, with many small, important steps to be followed in a precise order. That sort of thing, repeated daily throughout one's most formative years, obviously became part of a person.

It certainly helped that amongst all the new inventions which had invaded the equestrian world, Casey's old standbys were still present. From the brush box, she was easily able to pluck out her favorite type of curry comb: one of those fat, round, rubber ones with cone-shaped teeth, which she remembered a variety of horses leaning into, grunting with pleasure when she found their itchy places. These had been new inventions when Casey had been a child, a fresh-faced rival to the black oval curry combs with hard, ridged teeth which had been around for decades. Now, she didn't see the old oval curry comb at all.

She also plucked out a wooden-backed, medium-bristled brush and a finishing brush of soft black horsehair. With these familiar pieces in hand, she whisked the sand and shavings and loose hair from Mikey's mahogany-colored coat. She bent over and picked out his hooves with the same sort of plastic hoof pick, one side a metal pick and the other side studded with stiff plastic bristles, that she'd been using since she was seven years old.

Tack hadn't changed much, either. When she chose a saddle pad from the tack room's towering stack, the one she selected could have been a quilted cotton pad from her own childhood collection, an inventory which had been dispersed to friends long ago. The saddle which went onto Mikey's back was a close-contact Collegiate model which was probably already old back when she'd quit riding, the leather weathered with age but still recognizably of good quality.

"Nice job," Sky said cheerfully, watching Casey work from the sidelines. "Next time, show up early and you can do all of that outside your lesson time. You definitely don't need supervision to get tacked up."

Casey checked her watch, noting with resignation that it had taken her twenty minutes to tack up, all of which was part of her hour-long riding lesson. "For sure," she agreed, thus admitting she'd be back for a second round, after all. So much for one and done. She'd been crazy to think this one ride would be enough, anyway.

She put on a helmet borrowed from Sky's lesson tack, then slipped on Mikey's bridle, the horse opening his mouth for the bit without fuss. The straps went into their places almost of their own accord, her fingers forgetting nothing, and Casey remembered with a wry smile the struggle of being a little girl trying to figure out how to bridle a pony. That had been a hard lesson that she never had to learn again, she thought, and the realization gave her a little hope for all the other things her body might remember. Maybe today's ride wouldn't be too terrible, after all.

Together, the three of them walked out to the red-clay arena. A sprawling oval big enough to comfortably host a horse show class with a dozen or more horses at once, the arena was lined with a low wooden fence, and dotted inside with a course of jumps cheerfully painted in white, red, yellow, green, and blue.

"Right over here's the mounting block," Sky pointed to a narrow wooden staircase: three shallow steps and a small platform. "I'll hold him while you mount."

"I didn't used to need a mounting block," Casey said ruefully.

"Oh, you do now. Even if you could mount from the ground, I ask everyone to use the block most of the time. It's just easier on the horses' backs. The kids mount from the ground every now and then to make sure they can in case of an emergency."

Another change. In the old days, using a mounting block would have been an admission of weakness. She and the other girls would have absolutely shredded anyone who succumbed to its promise of an easy way up into the saddle.

Casey led Mikey up to the mounting block, appreciating this particular change. The horse seemed even taller out here than he'd appeared to be back in his stall, and he had a broad, full body which required a wide-tree saddle. She thought of how little she'd asked of her hips over the past fifteen years of school and office life. She thought of how much she'd be demanding of them this morning.

Things were going to get painful.

Casey placed the shiny toe of one new boot into the left stirrup, placed her open palms atop the pommel and the cantle of the saddle, and prepared for her jump. The saddle seat was level with her chest. It didn't seem like an insurmountable height; she just wasn't sure how she was going to convince her body to get up there. How had she mounted before? It had been instinct. Where were her instincts now?

Nothing came to mind.

Positive thinking, Casey! She could do this. Piece of cake. Like falling off a bike.

"Uh… you okay, Casey?"

"Fine… why?"

"You've been standing there a couple of minutes, I think."

Mikey stepped forward, bored with waiting, and her foot twisted in the stirrup. "Ow," she muttered, starting to pull free so that she could start over.

"Nope!" Sky insisted, her stern trainer's voice making its presence known for the first time. "Time to get on. Right now. Face his tail and use the momentum of your turn to swing you over the saddle. One—two—three!"

Casey did as she was told—and *almost* made it into the saddle.

Everything went right, the jump and the turn, until she got to the part where her right leg was supposed to swing all the way over the saddle's cantle… which didn't *quite* happen. She managed to hook her right knee over the cantle and then just hung there, in limbo, for a moment. She hadn't had enough jump, she guessed, but she wasn't sure how to fix it.

Casey felt a hot rush of adrenaline flash through her… which ignited a slow-burning shame. She was stuck—there was no going up from here. Only down. Back down to the mounting block, failed in her first attempt, while all of those eyes were upon her. The idea of dismounting in front of the barn kids was horrifying, even worse than falling off for a semi-legitimate reason, like a hard buck or an unexpected duck and spin.

Luckily, Sky came to her rescue.

"I got you," Sky announced, ducking around the mounting block. She didn't ask for permission to grab Casey's ass, she just planted her hands on each cheek and gave a mighty push. The shove was enough to get Casey's body up in the air, freeing her right leg to swing the rest of the way over the saddle. "There we go. Nice work! You got halfway there on your own… not bad."

It *felt* bad, Casey thought. It felt embarrassing and babyish. But here she was, in the saddle. That counted for something.

Casey sat down more firmly, feeling the familiar pressure points in her seat bones and her thighs, and a calmness spread through her limbs. Whatever happened next, this was a place where her body knew what to do.

She kicked her feet into the stirrups, doing that at least without looking down, or needing assistance, and pressed her heels down. Everything flexed as it was supposed to, ligaments and tendons and muscles eased into place and held position, ready for whatever command came next. The sensation was intoxicating.

Casey had the sudden, irrational feeling that, for the first time in years, she was alive and in tune with her body.

Of course, she'd better feel the same way about the horse she was sitting atop. Casey looked down at Mikey's neck, his neat black mane rising up in front of her. His ears were tipped back, listening to her breathing, weighing the feel of her in the saddle and deciding if she was a balanced, capable rider who was just having an off day, or a loose-limbed beginner he could cart around the arena his way, without worrying about too much interference.

Evidently, Mikey decided on the latter, because he suddenly picked up his hooves and began to walk over to the arena gate, knowing exactly what trajectory this ride was on, and perfectly willing to handle all of the details.

Casey knew she should have stopped him, reined back and made him wait until she asked for a walk. But she let him go, savoring his motion. Her body knew just what to do with every swing and sway of the horse's body. Her hips rolled with the reach of his hind legs, her hands moved forward with his nodding head, bobbing with each step of his forelegs. Her core muscles, which she would have sworn in front of a judge did not actually exist, rose to the occasion to keep her back straight.

She turned an excited face towards Sky, regardless of the grinning peanut gallery in the background. "This feels so *right!*" she exclaimed.

Sky laughed and held out her arms like they were sharing a long-distance hug. "I know it does! You're back where you belong!"

Twenty minutes of walking punctuated with a few minutes of very painful attempts at posting to the trot: that was the sum total of Casey's first riding lesson. There was no mention of cantering, no suggestion of two-point position, the pretty pose of rising out of the saddle to balance above the horse's motion.

All three of them, Mikey included, knew she couldn't have handled it. Cubicle life had jellied Casey's leg muscles to the point of non-existence. She wasn't even sure if her heels were *truly* down or just felt that way, and that had once been the most simple of reflexes. She couldn't keep her knee close to the saddle, she couldn't keep her toes turned in, and she couldn't keep her eyes open against the sweat rolling into them. The initial feeling of rightness had slipped away as she struggled to maintain a position she just wasn't strong enough to hold, and she'd started to feel instead that she was doing something extremely difficult she hadn't been trained for, like mountain-climbing or a swim race.

Along with all of this, the weather was conspiring against her. The humid morning sea breeze was blowing in stiff gusts across the arena, a sultry blend of salty ocean air and dense urban heat picked up over the beaches and island sprawl. It licked at her wet shirt and made her feel like she was melting.

So as the first riding lesson wrapped up, Casey felt a strange combination of emotions: a delirious happiness with her life; heartbreaking disappointment in her lapsed riding abilities; the very intense desire to be inside an air-conditioned space.

When she dismounted, Mikey's impressive height was not

helpful. She staggered backwards, her legs wobbly. Sky, holding Mikey's reins, smiled sympathetically before saying: "You're going to hurt tomorrow."

It was a phrase Casey was going to become intimately familiar with.

Chapter Eight

"Casey! Are you coming down? If we don't leave now we'll be late for brunch."

Casey sat on the edge of the bed and considered saying something insane in reply, something truly mad, something like: *I'm not going to brunch, go without me!*

Brandon would come upstairs looking for her. He would check her temperature. There would be questions.

The thing was, Casey had been pretty vocal about weekend brunch and how much she loved it for years now. Once a week, usually at brunch, she announced that brunch was the highlight of her week. So there were plenty of witnesses. She couldn't get out of it easily now.

Brandon and Casey's weekend brunches were an institution they'd been keeping intact since they'd gotten together. Every weekend, they met up with old friends to day-drink and eat with general abandon. Their group grew a little smaller each year, as people moved up north for higher salaries, or had babies and switched their weekend routine to pancakes at home with the kids. Sometimes, Casey wondered how much longer weekend brunch would last, but she'd always figured she'd be the last woman standing.

Alison and Heather were all that was left of Casey's old gang from high school. Brandon's friends, from farther down the coast, made occasional cameos. Once, there'd been a standing reservation for eight, with occasional expansions to ten or even twelve. Last year, they'd downsized to a regular six-seater at Waves, their favorite brunch spot. Now another, younger group dominated the big table against the windows overlooking the water, shouting with laughter as they worked their way through bottomless mimosas.

Big or small, brunch was Casey's chance to catch up with her friends and be reminded of the person she used to be, or maybe the person she was trying to be—she was never sure which one of those was more accurate. At brunch, she was fun, sometimes even funny. At brunch, she was one of those lucky people with smart, stylish friends who could talk about politics and late-night TV and whatever arthouse movie had made it to the local theaters and, very occasionally, a book they'd all read—or at least all heard of, and could pretend they were going to read as soon as they had time.

At brunch, her job could sound interesting, because she could word her anecdotes just so: a soul-sucking project became a hilarious failure, an obnoxious cubicle neighbor became a table-slapping joke. She could pretend for a couple of hours that everything about adulthood was going the way she'd expected— even hoped—and when she faltered, the bottomless mimosas helped that illusion along.

If she wasn't really that person Monday through Friday, at least she had a few golden hours on the weekend to pretend. She needed that.

Unfortunately, on this fine Sunday morning, with a brunch table waiting, Casey was pretty sure she was never rising from this bed again. Not with the way her hips and thighs and whatever *that* was... her groin, maybe? Was this her groin? Did women have groins? Whatever it was, brunch was no match for the way all of— *that*—hurt.

"This is my punishment for giving up riding for fifteen years,"

Casey whispered to herself. "Or maybe it's my punishment for thinking I could do it again. Either way, I am definitely being punished."

"Casey?" Brandon's voice was edging closer. Now he was at the foot of the stairs. She imagined him climbing the stairs, coming into the bedroom, surveying her as she sprawled along the edge of the bed, her uncombed hair tousled on the pillow. What an unprecedented predicament! *He* was usually the one to make them late. "Hey, babe? You need me for anything?"

Yes, Casey thought. She needed him to carry her down the stairs and gently place her in the backseat of their car, stretched out lengthwise so she didn't have to bend her legs. But that probably wasn't what he meant. She clenched her fists, resolved herself. She could do this.

She stood up slowly, groaning all the way. "I'm coming, I'm coming. Be down in a second."

She tugged a sundress from its hanger and pulled it over her head, then coaxed her sore shoulders into letting her put her hair up in a knot. She looked at herself in the mirror. At least her face looked normal—no indication of the agonies below the neck.

There was no graceful way to get down the stairs with her uncooperative thigh muscles or the searing sensation in her hips, and so by the time she'd stumbled into the little hallway of their townhouse, Brandon was watching her with undisguised shock.

"Casey, do you need to go to the hospital?" he asked, carefully keeping his voice neutral.

"No, I'm just a little sore from that ride yesterday." She plucked her purse from its hook by the door. "Let's go."

He watched her walk unsteadily to the car before he spoke up again. "But you were fine yesterday."

"We sat around all afternoon. I must have stiffened up after the ride."

"I didn't know riding was that hard."

She laughed despite herself. "It's not that it was *too* hard. I'm just not in shape. It'll take a few more rides to put this body in order."

As usual, Brandon opened the car door for her. She liked the chivalrous side he always showed her. It was especially welcome today. She didn't love the way he watched her slowly fold herself over to get into the car without too much agony in her legs.

"So… you're going to go back and do this again next weekend?" His voice was skeptical.

Despite her soreness now, Casey remembered the way her body had rolled with Mikey's strides. She'd felt like a sailor going back to sea after too many years on dry land.

"Oh, I'm definitely going back. Every Saturday. I have a standing lesson now." She had set it up with Sky: Saturday morning private lessons for the foreseeable future. As long as Brandon was working on his save-the-oceans project, she'd work on her horse project. After that? Well, she would have to see.

Brandon settled into the driver's seat. "How serious is this? Are we talking full horse-girl status? Mid-life crisis kind of thing?"

She glared at him. "First of all, I am not old enough to have a mid-life crisis. This would be a *quarter*-life crisis. And second, I don't know, can I just be allowed to have fun, please?"

"Sorry. No, you're right," Brandon shook his head. "I guess I just thought all of that horse stuff was part of your childhood or whatever. It's like if I just announced I was going to take up baseball again, because I played in Little League when I was a kid and it was fun." He started the car and busied himself checking mirrors, pulling into the road.

Casey saw nothing but holes in his argument, and her cramped leg position made her peevish. "Why would playing baseball be weird? There are a million adult leagues. You could play anything you wanted and people would say it was a great hobby. You could say the same thing about riding. You don't have to put it down immediately as something just kids do."

Now that Casey had committed herself to taking up riding, she was feeling militant in her defense of the sport. Riding wasn't just for teenage girls! Anyone could do it. *She* could do it. And if anyone questioned her motivation, they were just being rude. This was to be her stand.

"No, you're definitely right." Brandon offered her a sheepish smile. "I was just surprised, that's all. I'm happy you found a new hobby. Or an old one."

"That's fine," she said, forgiving him with a quick pat on the wrist. "It's good exercise and I can do it on Saturday morning while you're working, so it's all for the best."

Although, she thought, shifting uncomfortably in her seat, it would be better when her body caught up with her mind.

"You went *riding!*" Alison exclaimed, leaning back in her chair. She'd been the first to arrive at Waves, and as usual she'd slipped into the chair which was thrust most deeply into the dining area's covered patio, using the shade to supplement her huge hat and long-sleeved shirt. Alison's skin was the ethereal white of a Victorian ghost who had returned to haunt the residents of the boarding-house room she'd died in. She had long, straight, strawberry-red hair and was sensationally, frustratingly, beautiful. Her boyfriend, Grayson, was a noted hermit who had never come to brunch. "I can't believe it! Casey is back in the saddle!"

"I knew this day was coming eventually," Heather proclaimed. She pushed her long black bangs out of her eyes with an unconscious gesture. Heather was married to her career, which was some involved some sort of mysterious aerospace security clearance, and she was legendary for putting off haircuts for a year at a time. Luckily, she had perfectly straight, raven-dark hair which looked ravishing no matter how much time had elapsed between salon visits.

Casey was always envious of Heather's easy beauty: all her friend had to do was tie her hair into a knot and smudge a little shadow around those dark brown eyes, and she was the picture of sophistication, whereas Casey couldn't even go out in the humidity of the day without a handful of product to keep her coffee-colored hair from standing on end. Plus, as a sort of bonus, her face turned beet-red in the heat. Someone at school had once called her a chocolate-covered strawberry after they'd all had to run the president's mile, and she'd never really gotten over it.

"When we were in school, Casey lived for her horse," Heather was confiding to Brandon. "We were barely friends, honestly. You never saw her after school, she wasn't on any teams, nothing. Then, her senior year comes along and all of a sudden she was in everything: debate, community service, yearbook. We were like, *oh, look who showed up!*"

"I had to do all that. It was all for college admissions," Casey said defensively. "Everyone was really adamant that I wouldn't get into school anywhere without extracurricular crap. As it was I *scraped* into UF."

"But when you didn't start riding again, we were all shocked," Heather pointed out. "All those horses up in Gainesville and everything. They had a college riding team. We thought it would be your dream come true."

Casey remembered the flyer for the scholastic riding team. More than one person had slipped it under her dorm-room door, thinking it was a kind gesture. They didn't understand that without her old horse, Wilson, she couldn't see herself riding again. "I didn't want to ride other horses," she said now, toying with her glass. "I missed my old horse."

Brandon looked sympathetic. "The one you sold in high school?"

"Yeah." Casey wished they'd talk about anything else. She'd never felt right about selling Wilson. The day he'd left, she'd cried for hours. Losing him had been a gaping hole in her life that she'd tried to fill with constant homework and extracurricular activities. *That* was the real reason she'd shown up for everything from debate to yearbook. She took on so much, she barely kept up with her schoolwork. The irony was not lost on her.

"It's too bad," Alison sighed. "He was a nice horse. I used to give him carrots and he never bit me even one time."

"I should have leased him out and then taken him back after I graduated," Casey muttered.

She had realized she still angry with herself, deep down. She'd thought about this mistake a thousand times back in college, but in the past few years it had stopped bothering her. Wilson had died five years ago; the family who had bought him kept him in their backyard paddock after he retired from showing. They used to send her a photo of him every Christmas. She took to putting them into an envelope, and stuck the envelope in a box in the hall closet, someplace where she wouldn't accidentally see them and get stuck on a trip down memory lane. But taking up riding again was dredging up all of these memories without needing the visual cues.

If she'd kept Wilson, would she have a different horse right now? Would her life look completely different?

Her legs would certainly feel better.

"I just never thought anyone over sixteen actually rode horses, unless they're like, cowboys," Alison declared. "Seems like everyone quits to focus on school and then, you know, real life. Just like you did."

"Real life is over-rated," Casey declared thoughtlessly, tossing back the second half of her mimosa.

"I would agree with that," ventured Tyler, sitting across the table. He was one of Brandon's friends from high school. They'd grown up in a beach town about thirty miles south, far enough away from Casey and her friends to have never co-existed, to have never hung out in the same malls or visited the same Taco Bell at two in the morning; yet close enough to consider themselves all from the same place. Tyler was a quiet programmer type, and at the sound of his voice everyone turned and looked at him in surprise, until he blushed and went back to his menu.

"Real life is *exciting*," Heather announced with a militant look on her face. "Especially with a top security clearance. Casey, if you're looking for something exciting in your life, you should come work with me. You wouldn't need a single distraction, trust me."

Alison snorted, to hide the fact that no one knew what Heather did, and set about defending Casey's work. "Come on, Casey has a great job. She's a whiz at email marketing. Right, Case? You did an awesome job on that wedding mailer for my hotel. They loved you. They're coming back next year, but don't tell anyone I told you that."

"I won't," Casey promised, wishing they would talk about literally anything but work. All of their jobs were so boring, except for maybe Heather's, and Heather couldn't actually tell them anything about her work, hence the obscure boasting.

"Casey, you okay?" Brandon touched her arm. "You look down."

Everyone at the table peered at Casey with interest, ready to make their own judgements about her emotional state.

"I'm fine." She smiled brightly to get them to stop staring at her. "Just sore from riding!"

"Oh, *tell* me about it," Heather cut in dramatically. "You wouldn't believe how sore I am from kayaking yesterday. My arms are like spaghetti!" She held up her arms over the table to illustrate.

Everyone looked appreciatively at Heather's arms, which were slim and muscled, tanned to the smooth brown of ocean sand.

"I would die of sun poisoning if I went kayaking," Alison declared.

"They make *clothes,* you know," Heather pointed out. "You are allowed to go outside once in a while."

"Casey and I have talked about kayaking," Brandon said brightly. "But I can't quite get her to commit."

"There are gators in that water." Casey shook her head. "Absolutely not. I am committed to no. And I've told you that."

"Gators won't bother you," Heather said, shrugging. "Alligators are mostly harmless. They're more scared of you than you are of them."

"There are videos of gators climbing right onto kayaks!"

"Where, on *Facebook?* You need to delete that mess. I deleted Facebook last month and I have never felt better."

Everyone at the table now had something to say about Facebook and the well-documented reasons for deleting it. Casey refrained from her usual argument that she couldn't exactly quit social media networks when she worked in digital marketing, because she was so relieved that both riding and kayaking were forgotten.

Still, *she* couldn't seem to let the topic of hobbies go, and when the server finally arrived, she'd been so busy wondering why kayaking was considered an adult-appropriate hobby and riding horses was not that she panicked when he got to her, inquisitive eyebrow lifted and pencil hovering over his pad, and she ordered pancakes instead of waffles, and then had to chase down the server to change her order.

She'd been thinking about waffles *all week,* right up until the exact moment when it mattered. How typical, she thought, returning to her seat sheepishly under the amused gazes of her friends. She thought she knew what she wanted, and then right when it mattered, she forgot everything she knew and did something else instead.

The Sunday night blues set in hard that afternoon. Even with the ocean waves crashing onto the sand and the shouts of happy children mingling with the cries of hungry seagulls, Casey could feel the heavy weight of tomorrow morning's slog to work, the nine o'clock meeting with Mary and the other members of her team, the overflowing email inbox as vendors and clients and partners from other departments started sending in their demands for her time and energy, and, above all else, the hum of that one noisy fluorescent light bulb near her desk, not quite above her cubicle but close enough, that was going to be the death of her yet.

"Well, I'm really glad you had fun riding this weekend," Brandon said, his words seeming to come out of nowhere. He was stretched out beside her on a blue-and-white striped towel, sunglasses crammed against his eyes, the sun reflecting a hard white glare off his lightly tanned, skinny frame. Brandon had been trying to get a decent tan since he'd moved to Florida with his family at the age of fourteen.

Twenty years in, he had not yet fully succeeded but his zeal was undiminished. His skin seemed to repel the sun, as if he'd been coated with some kind of Armor-All for humans. He didn't have so much as a mole to show for his efforts, although by midsummer he could achieve a light golden glow which Casey thought was pretty nice.

She herself had lost her deep childhood tan years ago, probably when she'd stopped riding, and in her adult life she had given in to the constant headlines advising her to hide from the sun, ducking beneath hats and umbrellas like an Edwardian debutante. Alison was always bequeathing to her gorgeous cover-ups and caftans from her own large collection, like today's number: a silky sky-blue shrug of some see-through material mysteriously guaranteed to block UV rays.

"Well, thanks," Casey finally replied, for lack of anything else to say. They'd been sitting mostly in silence for the past twenty minutes, just listening to the waves and the gulls. Casey had been thinking about horses, about her riding position and the many things she had done wrong. Her seat had been all wrong, for example. She needed to tighten her core, tilt her pelvis...

She realized her perfectionism was setting in and tried to still her brain. "It's good exercise, anyway" she said, to fill the quiet creeping between them.

"Yeah! Well, I've been talking to the guys down in West Palm and it seems like this project is going to get bigger for a while. So if riding is something you want to keep doing for a few months... you'll have the time, is what I'm saying. If you choose to keep it up, and it didn't hurt too much or anything," he added.

Casey glanced over at Brandon with affection. He was adorable to think that riding was a choice. She already knew, despite the aching in her thighs and the pinprick tingling in her heels and a mysterious throb somewhere deep within her shoulder blades, that she was getting back up in that saddle as soon as possible.

Somewhere, out at the farm where she'd ridden as a child, there was an answer to all the questions about life that she couldn't yet frame in words. Mounted atop that big bay school horse, she'd felt comfortable in her own skin for the first time in years.

The only question was whether she could wait until next Saturday to feel it again.

"Thanks, babe," she told Brandon lightly, as if they were talking about a trip to the craft store, or a visit to the library. "I do think I'll keep it up for a while. See where it goes."

Brandon smiled against the sunlight. "That's good. I'd hate to think you were sitting around all day waiting for me."

Casey looked out at the waves and shook her head, the thoughts of the office chased away by the thoughts of—what else? Horses, horses, horses. They thrummed in her mind with a steady pulse of obsession usually relegated to eight-year-old girls. But Casey remembered being eight. Remembered being wild and free and fearless. Being eight had been amazing. She couldn't be further from that wild little girl now, but she wanted desperately to change who she had become.

Maybe, once she was back on a horse, she'd finally be the person she'd wanted always to be.

Chapter Nine

"I heard you might be an accomplished equestrienne!"

Casey nearly jumped out of her heels. She'd thought she was alone in the office building's upstairs corridor, where she had been lingering after the brain-numbing nine o'clock meeting which started every workweek.

The session had been so frustrating (no, there really *wasn't* anything else to say about walk-in bathtubs that hadn't already been said in the previous six emails!) that she had started stealthily tapping into her phone, texting Sky about any extra riding time she might have this week—even though her leg muscles were still screaming and she was pretty sure she was walking with a little bit of an uncouth straddle in her stride.

Now, Casey dropped her eyes to focus on the short woman who had appeared next to her, a paisley-draped earth mama named Leslie who worked in accounting and was known for her impressive collection of desk succulents. Casey had always suspected Leslie was a modern-day witch, but appreciated whatever magic the older woman sprinkled into her homemade chocolate-peanut butter granola, which she casually baked up and brought to potlucks the way other people brought deli-made potato salad.

"I took a riding lesson over the weekend," Casey replied cautiously, wondering how word had gotten out. "I wouldn't call it accomplished or anything, though. I'm pretty rusty."

"My daughter says you looked just fine up there," Leslie declared. She grinned at the confusion suffusing Casey's face. "Oh! She didn't say anything? My girl rides out at Sky's place. Short, looks like a pixie, answers to Gwen when she feels like it? Which isn't very often, with me. But she spends most of her time out there. Her horse is called Juniper."

Casey remembered seeing a brass nameplate which read *Juniper,* although not the horse within the stall. She'd heard the name Gwen somewhere, too... wait, wasn't that the girl Sky had been talking up on her first visit to the farm? The one she said would go pro someday? "I had no idea you had a horse in the family!" Casey exclaimed, completely astonished. Leslie did not look the part of a horse show mom.

Leslie grinned. "Well, that's the way it is around here. You know, this part of Florida isn't all tourists like the rest, so we still got a lotta horses in backyards and little barns. Everyone knows someone who has a horse. You just have to ask the right questions." Her eyes seemed to twinkle at Casey. "My girls, of course, were not content with little barns, so I have to work my fingers to the bone to get them into fancy show barns like Sky's place."

"Sky's barn *is* really nice. But I haven't ridden in years," Casey admitted. "So your daughter is probably much better than me."

"I wouldn't take that too hard. We've always had horses in the family, but Gwen's the one who got really serious about it and she's a real pistol out there. That girl wants to be a professional eventer, with a side of show-jumping." At this, Leslie sighed theatrically, as the mother of a horse-crazy girl was expected to do, but her expression suggested she was pretty pleased with her daughter's ambitions. Which, Casey thought, seemed rather open-minded for someone with a practical, prosaic career in the accounting department of small marketing agency. It must be the witch side of her personality that did the parenting.

"If you need any help, you just ask Gwen or me," Leslie continued. "We've got plenty of old stuff laying around the house, tack, bins of riding clothes. Her big sister's older stuff might fit you, now that she's up at Florida State. There's saddle pads, bell boots, you name it. When you've had a few horses that stuff just accumulates like you wouldn't believe!"

"I wouldn't need anything like that," Casey assured her. "I'm just taking some lessons. I don't want to buy a horse or anything."

Leslie grinned at her. "That's what they all say."

Casey shook her head rapidly, feeling like she needed to banish *that* idea as quickly as possible. "No, I mean really—there's *no* way a horse could be in the cards. I'm just taking a few lessons to catch up. I mean, I couldn't possibly afford a horse, working here!" She laughed a little forcefully, hoping to turn it into a mutual joke, but of course Leslie worked here, too, and she had a horse.

So it fell a little flat.

"What kind of horse did you have before?" Leslie asked, taking a small step forward, which encouraged Casey to take one as well. Just like that, they were hall-walking together.

"I had a Thoroughbred, named Wilson. We did hunters for a while, then we moved into jumpers. He was really talented—not like, A-Circuit talented, but he had good form and he loved to jump. We went to C and B-rated shows, places like Fox Lea and Tampa, you know." Leslie nodded, speaking Casey's language perfectly. "When I got to my senior year of high school, I sold him to a really nice family, and they kept him after he retired and everything." Casey paused, her thoughts deep in the past. "He had a white star and a little snip on his nose, like he was supposed to have a stripe but someone ran out of paint."

"Sounds like he was sweet." Leslie's steps were shorter than Casey's, but quicker, as if she was used to moving twice as fast as the taller people around her. "Gwen's sister, Tory, *her* horse has a snip, too. Cutest little marking. And a white chin. The rest of him is dark, dark bay, but that wobbly little chin of his! I love to take it between my fingers and give him a kiss on the nose. His name is Barclay. She took him to Tallahassee with her and works off his board, otherwise I'd have had to lease him out. Paying for two horses *plus* college? Forget it. But I could never sell him, the big dummy."

Casey swallowed. "I never really felt like I should have sold Wilson," she confided. "I still think about it."

"Oh, honey! I'm sorry, I didn't mean it like that. We all do what we have to do. And at least when you sell a horse, you know what you're doing with yourself. When you lease one out you're just waiting around for him to come back. *You* gave yourself permission to grow up and learn something new. Nothing wrong with that."

Casey wanted to ask Leslie how a person knew if they'd made the wrong choices, but she bit her tongue. There was no sense in airing all of her insecurities to a coworker, no matter how warm and motherly and good at baking granola that coworker might be. Word might get around the office, might even get to Mary, and the last thing Casey needed was a boss watching her closely for signs that she wasn't fully invested in her job.

So instead, she put on a false smile and nodded and told Leslie to have a great day, but she needed to get back to her desk. Casey hustled back to her cubicle and opened up all the assorted programs she needed to get through her work, and looked at the creative briefs scattered across her desk. She appeared remarkably busy for the next two hours. But in fact, until she'd gotten a text response from Sky, confirming she could have her second riding lesson on Wednesday evening after work, Casey didn't get a single thing done. Even then, it took a cup of coffee and some light raiding of her snack drawer to get her brain back on track.

Late in the afternoon, as Casey put the finishing touches on a requested rewrite from the walk-in bathtub people, Mary sidled up to her cubicle. Casey placed her hands decorously into her lap and looked up with an innocent smile. "What's up?" she asked her boss, as brightly as possible.

"You remember that proposal you took out to that horse farm, a week ago or so?"

Casey's heart thundered in her ears. "Yes?"

"You didn't close for me. Did the client say anything to you about it?"

"Not a thing." As if they'd talked about anything except the horses.

"Hmm." Mary looked into the distance, her mouth turned down.

"Did something happen?"

"Oh, the client declined to sign, that's all. I was just wondering if you got any vibe about the state of her business, or if she was just kicking tires, or what."

Casey shook her head. "Nope, I didn't get any impression at all. I mean... the business looked like it was in good shape, physically speaking."

"It's a horse farm, right?"

"That's right. Newly renovated barn, riding ring, nice fencing..." Casey trailed off, wondering if she was giving away something about Sky that she shouldn't. It felt vaguely like telling tales to report back on the business.

"Well, that's fine, then. Someone must have undercut us, that's all. Probably Sunglow, they always seem to come in a few hundred below us." Mary fixed Casey with a hard stare. "Next time you deliver a proposal, read the file and work on your sales push on the way out there. I don't like losing accounts when we're offering white-glove service like personal delivery."

"Yes, ma'am."

Mary tapped the top of the cubicle with her fingernails and then strolled off, looking for someone else to harass.

Casey leaned back in her chair and let her eyes wander over the her email for a few seconds more. This was as good as it was going to get. "Come and get your walk-in tubs," she muttered.

Clicking *send,* she thought about how much more fun it would have been to write an email about riding lessons or sales horses. What a shame that Sky hadn't gone with their company for marketing! Casey would have loved to take on that account.

Imagine being *interested* in a job.

Casey couldn't relate.

Chapter Ten

Wednesday afternoon brought dark and stormy skies, a cool wind blowing behind a lingering layer of clouds. It would have ruined Casey's day if she'd been one of the tourists flocking to Cocoa Beach, but for an evening ride in a flat, shadeless riding ring? It was absolutely perfect. Her favorite sort of riding weather! Casey was absolutely giddy as she peered through the office windows.

She left work a few minutes early to beat the evening traffic on the causeways, and drove inland with her heart singing. Time for another riding lesson! Time to get her feet back in the stirrup irons and feel like *herself* again!

She was did have a little bit of a shock when she arrived. Casey had forgotten that weekday afternoons belonged to barn kids blowing off steam. In the summer they tended to wear out by afternoon—Casey remembered the constant work, the sweat and the dirt, of a horse girl summer. She remembered being dropped off by her mom at eight thirty in the morning and not picked back up for another ten hours. When school was in, though, they were just running wild after a day of being pent up at desks.

When she arrived, the barn aisle was dark with the cloudy evening, and the lights were switched off. As she parked her car, Casey wondered if Sky had forgotten her lesson. What if no one was here? Did everyone cancel their rides because of the weather?

Her heart sinking, Casey got out of the car—and hit a wall of sound. All of the laughter and screaming coming from the barn told her she wasn't alone at all.

"Okay," she murmured to herself, clutching the duffel bag with her riding clothes snug inside. "Just a lot of kids… I can handle this…"

She walked into the barn and stood in the aisle, looking around for signs of human life. Horses looked eagerly through their stall bars at her, but she didn't see any people. The source of the screaming seemed to be from one of the tack rooms halfway down the aisle. It sounded like she was interrupting a slumber party. Or a ritual sacrifice.

Suddenly, a long, lithe girl darted out of the boarders' tack room. The girl spotted Casey and stood still for a moment, regarding her. Then she sprinted across the aisle and into the barn office.

Casey heard a hushed consultation within and then Sky came out, her face barely visible in the gathering gloom. There was just enough daylight to see her big smile. Casey sighed with relief. *Not* forgotten, then. Thank goodness!

"Casey, you're here! Arden, turn on the lights so Casey can see where she's walking. It's pitch-dark in this barn aisle. Sorry," she added as Casey walked up to her. "On rainy afternoons, it gets crazy dark in here, but I leave off the lights if it's just the kids running around. I don't mind having them around at all hours, but I try not to let them run up my electric bill. Lights are for *paying students!*" She shouted this last bit towards the tack room, where the laughter did not abate.

"It's fine," Casey laughed, looking up as the fluorescent bulbs lit up the center aisle. "It's funny, I absolutely hate fluorescent light at work, but I love it in a barn."

"Me too," Sky agreed, grinning. "It's so gross in like, a Winn-

Dixie, or the DMV, but there's just something reassuring about the way it lights up your aisle and…" she shrugged, "how it shows you that *someone hasn't been sweeping after herself!*"

This was directed at a petite, dark-haired girl who was leading a horse into a stall. When she had closed the door behind the horse and turned to face them, Casey realized this must be Gwen, the girl from the photos, and Leslie's daughter. She looked abnormally serious for someone of such small stature, and yet somehow just as witchy as her sweet mother.

Gwen gave Sky a beguiling smile. "I was going to sweep after I was done with the new horse." She hung the halter on its hook rather pointedly. "And now I am."

"You might as well have left him in the cross-ties. I thought Casey might like to see him up close."

"Which new horse?" Casey enquired, not sure where the conversation was going. Why would she want to see a new horse, anymore than any other horse in the barn?

"That racehorse, James. The one with the little star and the long forelock? You met him in his stall the first day you came out."

"Oh, right. He was cute." Casey remembered his lips tugging at her fingers, the beloved old sensation of horse whiskers prickling her palm.

"He's even better out in the light."

Casey nodded and smiled, not sure what was expected of her. She wasn't going to ride the new racehorse, right? So what was this about?

"I'll get him back out," Gwen said, pivoting in her paddock boots. "He'd rather be out with us, anyway." The horse inside the stall rapped at the door with his hoof, punctuating her words. "I know," Gwen told him. "Hang on, you're so impatient."

"He's not really impatient," Sky assured Casey. "He just loves being spoiled. The girls get him out for hours every day, they're all fighting over who gets to groom him and who gets to lunge him and who gets to graze him. Apparently they adored him at Gulfstream, too. He didn't race or anything for this whole past year, they just had him in training for months. Weird, right? I don't really know why. But he's here now." She shrugged, consigning the whims of racehorse trainers to the gods. *Who could explain them?* her shrug said.

Gwen emerged from the stall with James, the horse's shoes ringing pleasantly on the concrete. Casey looked him over as any horse-person does when confronted with a new specimen. She thought he looked just the same as he'd appeared through the stall bars a week ago: a pretty, dark bay Thoroughbred of moderate height and build. He was not unique, but he was quite nice at the same time. Thoroughbreds were like that.

Gwen halted James in the aisle and he looked their way curiously, then neighed. He had a pretty, appealing voice. Unfortunately, every other horse in the barn immediately felt compelled to join in. Gwen rolled her eyes at the racket.

"Oh my god, why are all the horses being so *loud?*" someone shouted from the tack room, and then they all started laughing again.

"Come on, noisy boy," Gwen said, and led the horse off down the aisle towards the cross-ties. Sky and Casey followed a few strides behind. Casey watched the way his hindquarters rolled with each step, the way his tail swung from side to side. He had precious little white anklets on each hind fetlock, hoops of ivory beaded with tiny black drops of ermine. His tail was a rich black, falling full to his fetlocks before ending in a sharply-cut bang.

"He looks very European," Casey observed. "I feel like he would speak with a French accent."

"He might," Sky agreed. "But the girls all say he's British."

"Why's that?"

"James *Bond,*" Sky reminded her.

"Oh, right."

Gwen turned him around in the cross-ties and snapped the hooks to his halter. "I'll stand at his head," she said. "He still isn't sure about the cross-ties."

Casey tipped her head curiously. "Does he go back on the ties?"

"He sure does."

"I never knew why racehorses did that."

"Racehorses always get tied in their stalls to groom or tack up," Sky explained. "They get used to the confined space. It feels safe. So if they're cross-tied in the aisle and something startles them, they tend to go backwards. Once they feel the cross-ties yanking on their halter, they pull backwards... and there you go, they're going back on the tie until it breaks. Takes a while to fix, but it's fixable... I'm sure you know that."

"Yeah," Casey agreed. "Just... no one ever explained that to me. The *why,* I mean."

"The why is important," Gwen said gravely.

"You're right," Casey said, wondering what else she had done with horses without knowing why. Things seemed to have changed in the horse world, maybe because of the Internet. There was more questioning, and more studying, and less of "my trainer said it's that way, so that's the way it is." That could only be a good thing, but it also made Casey feel a little left behind.

And the idea of *that* made her perfectionist soul absolutely twitchy.

Together, the girl and the two women looked at the horse. The horse looked back at them. Casey wondered why they were observing the Thoroughbred. He was lovely, for sure, and she really liked his quiet nature, but she didn't see what James had to do with her in the grand scheme of things. She was just starting out. She couldn't possibly ride an ex-racehorse fresh off the track.

"Gwen, you have any cookies?" Sky asked.

Gwen dug into her back pocket and came out with a packet of Oreos, fresh from the vending machine. The horse's ears pricked at the crackle of plastic wrapper, and he danced expectantly, his dark hooves curvetting on the concrete. Gwen handed the packet to Casey.

"Do the honors?" Sky suggested.

Casey shook a dark cookie into her hand and stepped up to James. He looked at her like he wanted to devour her entire hand and arm, and for a moment she was afraid of what he might do, with all that power in his neck and jaws trembling in front of her. He was nearly overcome with excitement for one little cookie. The horse was like a toddler who had been given a giant's body and a wrestler's strength, and the combination suddenly seemed dangerous to her.

But she resolutely held out the cookie, unwilling to appear afraid in front of the other horsewomen, and James dipped his head towards it, his lips tender against her palm, slurping up the cookie without so much as grazing her skin—she never even saw his teeth—and after he crunched it he came back for the other one. Then, he licked her palm for the crumbs, lapping slowly and with great care, as if he was a mother cat and her palm a delicate little kitten, and Casey felt her heart turn over, and that's when she knew she was lost.

Sky grinned at her expression as Casey took back her hand. "Nice boy, isn't he?"

Casey nodded slowly, trying to straighten out her face. She must look like a kindergartner who just spotted a white pony: completely enchanted and utterly obsessed. "He's really nice. *Right* off the racetrack, you said?"

"Yeah. Spent two years there," Sky said. "You can tell because he wants attention all of the time, and he's spoiled to death with treats. Every horse I get from this trainers' barn is the same way, but James is the nicest of the bunch. Someone's going to get very lucky with this horse."

Casey was sure Sky was deliberately holding her gaze. "Someone sure is," she agreed finally.

Sky nodded and straightened her shoulders. Casey thought she looked a bit... *satisfied.* As if she'd gotten what she was looking for out of this interaction. "Well, let's go get you set with Mikey! Gotta ride while the sun shines. Or at least before the flood comes."

When Casey walked down the aisle with Mikey at her side, she was startled to see Leslie, her paisley bulk draped over one of the patio chairs opposite the cross-ties. "Well, Casey!" Leslie announced. "We should have car-pooled!"

"We don't live near one another," Casey pointed out. "So it would only work if we just stayed in the barn all night."

"Gwen wouldn't mind that."

"Are you here to watch her ride?"

"To pick her up. Or, I was hoping to. But she's been here since school got out and still doesn't want to leave, so I'm heading out to run a few errands before I come back for her." Leslie suddenly leaned towards Casey, and lowered her voice to a conspiratorial whisper. "I saw them pull out that new Thoroughbred to show you."

Casey had been rummaging through the brush box, looking for the curry comb she liked best, but now she straightened and sauntered across the aisle, trying to look nonchalant. She leaned in close to Leslie. "And what was *that* about, do you think?"

"Sky doesn't keep a horse in her name very long," Leslie confided. "That's not how you make money in the horse business. Not that you *do* make any money—I'm pretty sure her wealthy mother pays for this place. But you can bet she's looking for the right person to point at that horse."

"Well, it's not me. I'm not in the market for a horse." Casey shrugged. "And he's just off the racetrack... I'm not the right person for him, either way."

"You rode before, didn't you?"

"Sure, of course I did, but—"

"Thoroughbred?" Leslie had her eyes narrowed shrewdly, as if she was sizing Casey up. "Did you say Wilson was a Thoroughbred?"

"Well, yeah." Casey couldn't help but be impressed Leslie remembered her old horse's name.

"I thought so. You strike me as a Thoroughbred girl."

"That's—wait, what does that even mean?"

"And if I see it, so does Sky, that's all I'm saying."

"She's not selling me a horse," Casey said adamantly.

"No, of course not. You're just here to take lessons once a week."

"Well... twice a week."

"Twice!" Leslie laughed. "Casey, hide your checkbook. Sky is young but she's not *that* young. She knows exactly what she's doing."

Chapter Eleven

"I—don't—remember—posting—being—this *hard*," Casey panted.

Rising with the horse's motion at the otherwise bouncy trot was English Riding 101. It was the first lesson students learned after they achieved not falling off at the walk. Casey had been acing this gait since grade school. Now, though, she felt like she was trying to maintain a stately waltz in a bounce-house on a windy day.

She knew she was flopping around horribly on Mikey's back, but she couldn't seem to make her legs hold her up properly. It was one thing to rise from the saddle when his stride propelled her upwards; it was another thing entirely to hold her balance as she slowly rejoined the saddle under her own power. More often than not, she ended up just falling back down.

"You're doing fine," Sky called from the center of the arena. "It'll come to you. Keep your heels down. Really flex your ankle to loosen up."

A younger Casey could never have imagined being thirty-plus years of age and still having to hear *"keep your heels down"* like she was a schoolgirl on a pony again. She had expected riding to be good physical exercise, but she hadn't been prepared for what an exercise in humility it would be.

"Flex," Sky advised.

Casey flexed her ankles obediently, and winced.

Flexing hurt.

It *all* hurt.

At least the picnic table was empty—no peanut gallery today. The barn kids had already lost interest in her. This was half-insult, of course; if she'd been a *good* rider, they'd have been watching her hungrily. But bouncy adult re-riders were not worth their valuable time, which left Casey blissfully, if somewhat offensively, audience-free for this second ride. Unless, she reminded herself, they were hiding out in the lounge, enjoying her struggles with the added bonus of air-conditioning, and maybe a bag of microwave popcorn.

Oddly, this made her feel a little better.

Mikey had slowed his trot to a shuffle at this point. At this point, he was barely moving, so when he actually stumbled a little, a stronger rider would barely have noticed the change in his motion.

Unfortunately, the tiny stumble was enough to cause Casey to lose her rhythm mid-rise, and she plopped down in the saddle hard, her hands grabbing at the pommel for security. For a moment she thought Mikey might take the opportunity to swerve or bolt forward, but the long-suffering school horse simply slowed to a walk of his own accord.

Casey stifled a groan and slumped forward, resting her hands in his fluffy mane. It was a wild bush of stiff black hairs which clearly defied all attempts to tame it into a civilized English coif.

"I feel like I'm wrecking your nice horse," she moaned to Sky.

"Oh, he doesn't mind a little bit of banging around on his back if he knows it will stop soon. And it won't be hard as soon as you put in a few rides and get your muscles back," Sky assured her, laughing from her perch on a roll-top jump in the center of the arena. "Or at least get all the way around the arena a few times."

"I can get all the way around!"

"More than once?" Sky grinned provocatively.

Casey frowned down at Mikey. He dipped his head towards the ground, perhaps to indicate that their lives could be so much easier if she just quit for the day. But they were only a half-hour into their ride. "Twice, at least," she replied with a confidence she didn't really feel, and shortened up her reins again. "Maybe three times." There had to be at least that much in her, even after all this time out of the saddle.

She squeezed her aching legs around Mikey, and he fluttered his nostrils in a snort, resigning himself to a few more rounds. Thunder rumbled in the distance, and a cool, humid wind wandered in from the river, winding itself through the sweaty strands of hair slipping free of her helmet. At least there was a breeze, she reminded herself, and clouds. Not every ride had those comforts.

Mikey slipped into a slow trot, and she rose with every stride, striving to remember the right balance of thigh and calf and heel. Someday, she promised herself, this would feel natural again. Someday, this would all be second nature. Again.

Someday came more quickly than she expected.

Twenty minutes after her decision to try posting trot again, she was leaning over Mikey's neck with her arms wrapped around him, squeezing him with a grateful hug.

"That was awesome!" Sky called from her seat on the roll-top, sounding moderately impressed. "You really got it that time."

"Everything clicked," Casey said, straightening up. "And not in like, a clicking joints kind of way. Although that definitely happened, too. I just... I just remembered how to do it!"

"'Atta girl." Sky hopped down and walked over to the arena gate, swinging it open for them. "Now it's all going to be easy-peasy from here on out."

Casey's natural inclination was to be dubious, but it seemed like

Sky might be right. When her body had, suddenly and without warning, begun moving *exactly* the way it was supposed to, she'd nearly burst into tears at the familiarity of it all. Muscle memory was a magical thing, even when it took one and a half riding lessons to kick in. Better late than never, that was for sure. "I feel like I'm still going to need some recovery time after this ride, but all I want to do is come back tomorrow and do it again."

"Well, I'll save your hips from total destruction, because Thursday afternoons are booked solid. But you can keep your Saturday morning slot. That gives you two days of recovery."

Casey dismounted at the entrance to the barn. "Definitely. I'll be one hundred percent by Saturday for sure." She was ready to skip the next two days completely. The thought of getting that perfect posting trot back again was *so* intoxicating.

She flipped the reins over Mikey's head and walked him into the cross-ties. The lesson horse followed her with his customary absent-minded walk. She'd already noticed that Mikey was a been-there, done-that kind of horse, not really interested in her overtures of affection beyond an appreciation for any carrots she might produce. His lack of affection was a little disappointing, even though she knew indiscriminate love was too much to expect from a lesson horse.

Mikey was probably ridden by seven or eight different people in a week, few of whom would be distinguished by their riding abilities. Great lesson horses were recognizable by a few remarkable traits, like patience and steady temperaments, but one of their most important abilities was probably the capability to simply disassociate from their surroundings: to not form lasting attachments or care too much about what was happening either to, on, or around them.

So, Casey knew Mikey wasn't going to be her buddy. She would have to learn to live without his love. She gave him an affectionate rub between his ears anyway, tousling his thick forelock, which the horse endured with an air of quiet martyrdom.

A few girls were hanging out in the cross-ties across the aisle, playing with a round-bellied white pony. Gwen, her dark hair knotted back severely, was using a pulling comb to even out the pony's thick bush of mane. She took the job very seriously, judging by the expression on her thin face. The pony leaned into every tug on his mane, dark eyes blinking stoically beneath a thick tuft of white forelock. He had a small, dished face and a brilliantly alabaster coat, making him the classic show-pony archetype, despite the hay belly.

"Cute pony. Is he yours?" Casey asked Gwen, because ignoring the girls, although an attractive option, was not going to make her invisible to them. And she knew that even if they had ignored her ride, they were still watching her every move within the barn, trying to decide how this almost-middle-aged woman might affect their barn dynamic. Casey could easily imagine their suspicions, because she'd played this guessing game herself: was this lady just another adult rider who was going to ride after work now and then, or was she going to get serious and be a contender for their trainer's time and attention, things all of the girls jealously fought for?

Casey had been asking herself the same questions, with different motivation, but she could finally admit to herself now that after two lessons, she was one hundred percent hooked, totally back in the game. Her only worry now was how deep into the game she was going to end up.

"He's Sky's new pony," supplied a relatively friendly-looking girl, all long limbs and straight red hair, who was perched atop an overturned muck bucket. Casey recognized her as the one who had stared at her blankly when she'd arrived earlier. "He's a sales project. Or maybe a school pony, we don't know which yet."

"I'm training him," Gwen said, dropping a tuft of white mane to the ground. "He needs to be started over fences. He's just green-broke."

"Gwen's the official pony rider," the red-head said with a snicker. "Because she's tiny. Aren't you, little elf?"

"Ha. Ha. Go ahead and call me elf. I'm going to be *rich* because I can ride ponies," Gwen told her witheringly. "Wait and see. What do parents want? Broke ponies. What can I do? Break ponies. Have fun being super-tall and riding horses like every other trainer in the world."

The other girls laughed. This was clearly a regular conversation.

Satisfied that she'd broken the ice with the barn girls, Casey turned back to Mikey. She untacked the horse slowly, already feeling the return of Sunday's ache in her hips and pelvis. She took the saddle and bridle back to the tack room. On her return, she was surprised to see the red-haired girl on her side of the aisle, where Mikey was watching her with evident interest.

The girl held out a knobby brown horse cookie. "I know you were trying to give him carrots, but I happen to know that Mikey loves these cookies the best."

The big horse was well aware there was a cookie in the vicinity and had pricked his ears, watching them with growing excitement. He shifted his weight from side to side and stretched out his neck, lips quivering. Across the aisle, the pony was watching, too.

Casey took the cookie. "Thank you! I'll have to order a box of these, so we can make friends."

She handed Mikey the cookie while the girl hung around, watching her carefully. Waiting for what, to see if she knew how to feed a horse a treat without losing a finger or looking like a toddler at a petting zoo?

"So, I'm Casey," she finally offered, as the silence between them began to weigh on her mind. "It's nice to meet you."

"I'm Arden," the red-head said, still watching Mikey. "Arden

McKnight. I learned to ride on Mikey like, three years ago. He's really special."

"Oh, that's so nice." Casey unspooled the garden hose hung from the barn wall. She was keenly aware of the stares from across the aisle while everyone waited for Arden's recon mission to yield results. "I learned to ride here when I was little. On a pony called Smoke. Not as nice as Gwen's pony there, but he was pretty cute."

"Then what happened?" Arden asked, her voice curious.

"When? After I learned to ride?" Arden nodded. Casey started spraying off Mikey. "I quit before college. I had to save some money, buckle down, all that sh—*crap.*" She caught herself mid-cuss, then realized it was ridiculous to think a bunch of barn girls *didn't* swear like sailors. Her old trainer used to say that the expression had clearly been altered from the original "swear like horse girls."

"I'm going away to school in Virginia in a couple of years," Arden said. "At a college with horses. I'm going to work for some big-name trainers while I'm there. Then I might start a marketing company for upper-level riders. Have you ever been on their Instagrams? Some of them are just terrible. Maggie Kinsey doesn't even straighten out pictures before she posts them, and she's a four-star event rider. She could try a *little.* But they never do," Arden finished, with the air of washing her hands of the lot of them. "So that's my idea, anyway."

"Wow, that's kind of crazy. I work in digital marketing and—"

"My mom said I had to come up with a professional job and said the key to happiness at work is specializing in something you love and understand," Arden said, running her fingers along Mikey's nose. "That's why I'm sticking with the horse business, no matter what, even if I don't make it as an upper-level rider. There's no point in spending my life working with things I don't give a shit about."

Casey didn't stop hosing the sweat from Mikey's flanks, but her eyes flicked back to Arden. The girl met her gaze. Then she shrugged—*what?*—and strolled back across the aisle to join her friends. If she knew she'd given Casey a line that would run through her head that night when she was trying to fall asleep, she didn't give any indication of it.

Sky was sitting behind her desk, typing away on her phone, when Casey stuck her head into the office. The barn lights were still on and everything inside was drowned by white fluorescent light, but through Sky's window, she could see the evening sky was all golden glow streaked with pink and blue; the late storm clouds were moving off over the Atlantic and leaving behind a gorgeous sunset. Casey wished she could hang around and watch the colors change over the river, but Brandon would be fixing dinner and she didn't want to keep him waiting. Brandon could rarely be bothered to cook breakfast, but he got very passionate about his dinners.

"I'm out," she called to Sky. "See you Saturday?"

Sky looked up from her phone, blinking like a bleary-eyed teenager. "Sorry—yes! Hey, before you go… you did a really nice job today. I can see now you weren't bullshitting me—you definitely know what you're doing out there. You just need to build muscle. But you're good!"

Casey burst into surprised laughter. "Wait, did you think I was *lying* about being able to ride already?"

"Hey, you never know! I mean, you were fully capable of tacking up on your own, so that was a good sign, but you wouldn't be the first woman to show up claiming she rode at A-circuit shows as a child and then climb into the saddle looking like the sum total of her experience was walking a pony around a pasture with a bareback pad. Let's just say I have learned to set my expectations low, and then I can be pleasantly surprised."

"Well, thanks. I think." Casey grinned. "I better head out. Tonight was fun. I didn't expect to jump to two rides a week right away, but hey... no regrets, right?"

"Casey, that reminds me of something I wanted to ask you: what are your plans?" Sky stood up from her desk and walked around it, coming close to Casey. Her gaze had turned serious. "Do you want to take this somewhere? Showing? Buy a horse?"

Casey resisted the urge to take a step back. "I don't know," she said, trying to keep her tone light. The truth was that Arden, dropping her little truth-bomb and then going back to her group of carefree horse girls, had shaken Casey's resolve to keep this return to riding as casual as possible. Yes, she *had* a life already, but what was the point in trying to keep horses from disrupting it, when she didn't even really like it?

Wait... did she really dislike her life?

Was she ready to go down this road?

Casey took a deep breath, absorbing the old familiar scents of horse and hay, leather and molasses. Now was not a good time to do a massive re-evaluation, she warned herself. No sudden moves.

"I just want to keep riding," she said. "I want to see where it goes. I'm not ready to make plans yet."

Sky nodded. "That's fair." But she still didn't look satisfied. Casey wondered which part of her Sky was sizing up: her ambition or the thickness of her wallet.

The trainer stepped around Casey and into the aisle. "Wow, that's quite a sunset. Nice backdrop for turn-out. Girls!" She raised her voice. "Let's get these horses out!"

Arden led the charge, emerging from the cross-ties as a slim silhouette against the fiery sunset, and soon all the girls began opening stall doors, swinging halters from their hooks as they went down the aisle, fetching horses out with little clucks and stern warnings to back off when they got too pushy. Hooves began to ring on pavement. Casey weighed the keys in her hand and found them oppressively heavy. She dropped them back into the little pocket of her new breeches. "I can take Mikey out," she offered, and Sky smiled back at her.

"Third paddock on the left. Halter off when you get him out there."

As Casey plunged into the group of horse girls, she heard a low *whuff* of breath from the stall next to Mikey's—not quite a nicker, just a little request for attention, or maybe a statement of recognition. She turned, and saw the soft dark nose belonging to James poking through the stall bars. "Hey buddy," she called in a gentle voice, "I don't have any more Oreos, if that's what you're looking for."

He regarded her calmly, taking the news about the Oreos very well, while Mikey grew increasingly impatient in the stall next door, pacing in a circle.

Hooves passed behind her, a teenage voice saying: "Oh, come on slow-poke, you know you want to go outside," Sky calling to someone called Maria to stop and put fly spray on the horse she was leading. All of the buzz of the barn slipped past them; James was only interested in her, and she was only interested in James.

"He's cute, isn't he?" Suddenly Sky was next to her, unwittingly breaking the spell linking Casey with the Thoroughbred. James turned away from the aisle and started to make a circuit around his stall, as if he thought Mikey had the right idea all along. "Very easy horse. A little more turn-out and light work to stretch out his muscles, and he'll be ready for his new job."

Casey nodded absently. "Sure," she said. It didn't have anything to do with her, not really. She picked up Mikey's halter and lead-rope, all the while wondering which of the barn girls would be lucky enough to call James her own. She'd been a hotshot teen with an electric seat once, happy to get on any old ex-racehorse which came through the door. Too bad she wasn't that girl anymore. You didn't always look into a horse's eyes and feel an instant connection. But she wasn't anywhere near ready to get on an off-track Thoroughbred. Maybe she never would be, never again.

Mikey shoved his head through the doorway as she slid his door back, and she had to push him back into his stall before she could enter and slip on his halter. Sky hovered nearby, as if she was making sure he didn't push her around too much. Then, as Casey led the horse into the aisle, Sky rushed and showed her hand.

"James would make a great project for someone like you," she burst out.

Casey stopped and looked at her, while Mikey tugged at the lead impatiently. "How can you think that? I'm green as grass and so is he. You know the saying: *green on green makes black and blue.*"

"But you're *not* green," Sky insisted. "You're just out of practice. By the time I'm ready to sell him, you'll be looking for a horse. I'm just saying... I think you're too experienced for an old packer. You're going to want a little bit of a challenge. But you know... if not James, maybe another horse like him, down the road... when you're ready, I'll help you find one."

Casey could only stare at her, completely out of arguments against buying a horse and certain that was a terrible place to be, mentally-speaking, and Mikey took the opportunity to push forward, practically dragging her down the aisle after the departing horses in front of him. "All right, all right," she huffed, getting herself back in front of the horse, so that it at least *looked* as if she was in control. "Let's get outside."

After Casey had turned Mikey out and was strolling back to the barn, beneath a big open sky ablaze with color, the evening echoing with whinnies and the hoofbeats of joyful horses, she let herself imagine, just for a minute, that this was her life. Not hurrying home to eat dinner before her boyfriend got annoyed, not waking up at seven tomorrow to get to the office and write marketing copy about appliances all day. Just this: just horses, and people who loved horses, and that cool breeze blowing off the river.

It sounded dangerously wonderful.

Chapter Twelve

"We were getting a little worried about you," Casey's mother sighed. She settled into a padded lounge chair overlooking the turquoise-blue swimming pool and adjusted the plush headrest behind her. "You haven't come over in weeks. And the pool is perfect right now. Where have you been?"

Casey put her sweating glass down on a bamboo coaster. Her parents' pool enclosure was an extension of their house, a sort of indoor/outdoor living room complete with stereo speakers, soft lighting, and enough ceiling fans to create a breeze on the most still evenings. The furniture was of some rich chocolate-colored wood which somehow reminded Casey of sailboats. Out here, she wouldn't have dreamed of putting down a glass without a coaster. It was *that* kind of pool deck.

And that was one reason why she and Brandon used to come over on weekends very frequently. Her parents were social butterflies, fluttering in and out (mainly at the behest of her mother) on dinner dates and lunchtime bar crawls and day-trips, but Casey had a house key and had always been encouraged to use it even if her parents weren't home.

Over the past few months, though, they just hadn't come over. Their excuses were nothing special. Brandon was busy with work. Casey didn't have the energy. For some reason, all spring she'd felt a little draggy and it had felt like work just to go to brunch and see her friends on the weekend, let alone add in a trip over to her childhood home where she might run into her parents, who would have questions about her life she didn't feel like answering, questions like *so how is your job* and *anything exciting on the horizon?*

But Memorial Day was a pool-based holiday, and there was no escaping a visit home on all pool-based holidays (actually, most holidays in this part of Florida could be considered pool-based). So Casey had put on her sunblock and girded her loins for this holiday of obligation. There would be hot dogs, and deviled eggs, and cold beer, and rum with an extensive selection of tropical juices, and questions.

Brandon looked at her from across the table with sympathy written in his face. He was lucky, Casey thought darkly, that his parents were almost an hour away—and didn't have a nice pool to use as a lure.

Casey rubbed at her temples, anticipating a headache. "You know, Mom, it's just been really busy at work and I haven't felt like doing anything extra."

Her father came onto the deck with a bowl of potato chips and settled at the table between Casey and Brandon. He put the bowl into his lap with a sigh of satisfaction—evidently it was not for the group—and looked around at the guarded expressions surrounding him. "What are we talking about?" he asked cheerfully, choosing to ignore any warning signs.

"Casey's tired," her mother said, without much sympathy in her voice.

He peered at Casey, worry written across his forehead. Her father had a young face, but when he was concerned about his only daughter, a frown deepened in his high brow, drawing a horizontal line beneath his thick head of salt-and-pepper hair. "Is that so? How can we help, Case?"

She squirmed under the scrutiny. Casey hated to worry her

father. "I'm fine, really. I just haven't wanted to do anything extra lately."

Brandon lifted his eyebrows. She shook her head at him. She wasn't ready to tell them yet. That was a whole other line of questioning to deal with.

Casey's mother shook her glass. "Ugh, all ice again. Casey, would you mind grabbing the pitcher of juice from the fridge? And the spiced rum."

"No problem." She hopped up, forgetting how stiff she still felt from Saturday morning's riding lesson, which had involved a *lot* of posting trot and a little bit of two-point position at the canter. Her thighs had felt like they were tearing themselves in two yesterday, and today wasn't much better. She stumbled away from the chair and bit back a howl of pain before proceeding, stiff-hipped, into the house.

When she came back, everyone was watching her progress with interest. Casey held up the pitcher and the rum, looking around. "Are we ready for refills?"

"Casey," her mother began slowly, "are you okay?"

She bit her lip in frustration. *Here we go.* "I'm fine. Just... a lot of exercising. To try and build up my energy levels. You know."

"What kind of exercising? Marathon training? You look *really* uncomfortable."

Casey gave it up. Why had she thought she could hide this? Just tell the world. Just own it. Just plaster social media with horse pictures. The time was ripe. "I just started taking riding lessons," she admitted. "So I'm sore from that. It's been a long time since I rode."

Casey's mother stared at her for one long, heavy moment. Casey felt her throat get hot and tight. *You're always like this,* she chided herself angrily. She always wanted her mother's approval and she was never, ever going to get it—

"Well, that's fantastic," her mother said finally. "What a relief! After all that money we spent on you. It's nice to know it wasn't wasted."

Casey was at a loss for words. Something angry sparked inside of her: *You wanted me to quit! You told me to concentrate on school!* But she knew that saying these things wouldn't get her anywhere. Her version of history and her parents' would never be the same. She settled for an extra-long tipple of rum into her glass.

"Thanks," she said eventually, once the rum had loosened her throat. "Oh, and you won't believe where the farm is."

"Oh, let me guess. It's back on River Road, isn't it? I heard that place where you rode as a little kid started up again. Remember, John? Remember that driveway that felt a mile long?"

Casey's father shook his head. "Awful on my car. Just awful. Take it easy on that driveway, Casey. Your car's suspension will *not* like it. Brandon, you tell her."

"How could you possibly know that's where I'm riding?" Casey asked incredulously. "There are a million other places it could have been."

Casey's mother shrugged. "You've always been the nostalgic type, honey. The minute I heard it was open again, I thought you'd eventually end up there."

Casey drank her rum and juice in mutinous silence. She hadn't wanted to give away her little secret yet, but the least they could have done was act surprised, or pleased, or hell, even have let her spring the news about the old farm on them without shrugging it off! *She* thought it was kind of amazing that she'd started riding again at the place where it had all began! It would be nice if someone agreed with her!

Casey realized Brandon was watching her with a concerned expression. He'd seen this play out before. This was what happened every time she told her mother something. They were locked in an endless mother-daughter battle for supremacy, and Casey should really accept that she was never going to come out on top. Just like she accepted that Brandon was going to tell her all of this, for the millionth time, on the drive home.

So instead of letting the silence get to her, Casey pushed back her chair. "I'm going to change into my swimsuit and get into the pool," she announced. "Anyone coming in with me?"

"Enjoy it, Casey," her mother said absently, looking at her phone. Her mother rarely got in the pool. She liked looking at it, sitting beside it, knowing it was there.

Brandon followed her inside the house. "You know, you and your mother—"

"I *know,*" she sighed, stopping him before he could launch into his lecture. "It doesn't stop me from trying. It never will."

"At least they're happy for you."

"That's true." She pushed open her bedroom door.

Casey's old bedroom had been gussied up and turned into a bright guest-room version of its former self. She appreciated this upgrade whenever she entered the room. The familiar light streaming through the blinds, the palm fronds tapping the window, the vase of silk orchids on her old dresser and a new white duvet spread on her old bed: it all conspired to give her the best of her old room without making her feel like an overgrown child whenever she came over for a visit. Her mother really did have good instincts about some things. Maybe she'd been right about Casey's riding gap, too. She sat on the bed and looked up at Brandon.

"I guess she could have said I was wasting my money on horses and then asked when I planned on having kids, like sitcom parents."

"See? It's all good." Brandon pulled his swimsuit out of their bag. "And now we can enjoy their luxurious swimming pool, eat their potato chips, and drink their rum. You have wonderful parents, Casey. I am grateful for them on every holiday."

Casey knew he was right. She pulled out her own swimsuit and started to wriggle out of her clothes. She had lucked out in the parents lottery, even if you discounted the pool parties. There weren't enough nice things in the world to say about middle-class parents who bought their children expensive large animals and then paid fees on top of fees to have them fed and housed and cleaned up after every month for years on end. Casey might be sore now, but she was lucky to be so sore, lucky to be able to ride at all, to canter on her third riding lesson and feel the wind licking at her sweaty face, her horse powerful beneath her, and she knew that she owed it all to her parents.

That was something.

Even if they'd convinced her to quit later, that history was worth something.

When Brandon and Casey went back onto the pool deck, her father was shaking his head in disapproval. He stopped as soon as he saw them and tried to erase the frown from his forehead. Casey's mother looked as if she'd just stopped talking.

Casey gazed at their guilty faces. "What did I miss?"

"Nothing," her father said quickly, but his face tinted a delicate red.

"We were just looking at the prices of boarding a horse these days," her mother confessed. "My god, Casey, how can you afford a horse? Prices have gone up!"

Casey's good feelings went out the window. "I'm not getting a horse! I'm taking riding lessons! God, you guys!"

Her mother pursed her lips. "We're just looking out for you."

"Why does everyone think I'm going to buy a horse?" Casey knew her voice was too loud, but she couldn't stop now. She had to get this out. Everyone was making her *crazy!* This had to stop! "My coworker: *you're going to buy a horse!* My trainer: *when you want to buy a horse, just tell me!* My own parents: *you can't afford to buy a horse!* Guess what everyone, I have *absolutely no intention* of buying a horse! It has never even entered my mind!"

She picked up her glass and drained it. When the ice slid forward and smacked her upper lip, she slammed the glass back on the table without looking for a coaster. Brandon darted over and put the wet glass back on its coaster, swiping at the wet ring left behind with the side of his hand. She glared at him, then took two giant steps and leapt into the pool.

She made sure she splashed enough to get her mother good and wet.

"That was a decent blow-up today," Brandon observed.

Casey glanced over at him from her spot in the passenger seat. In the darkness, his expression was impossible to read; she didn't know if he was amused or annoyed.

In the end, all of her shouting about never buying a horse hadn't ruined the afternoon. In fact, her parents had barely registered that she'd been upset at all. They were quiet and satisfied people, not easily moved to react, and Casey suspected they had always considered her a little fractious and easily upset, since she occasionally had emotional reactions to things.

"I didn't mean to have one today. I thought this would be a nice, quiet afternoon."

"It really was. Except for about five minutes in the middle, I would say it was extremely calm." He paused, as if measuring the effect of his next words. Then he pushed onward with the air of someone who must be brave. "Something about horses makes you react very strongly. Last weekend, at brunch, you got a little upset when the girls turned your horse-talk into a conversation about hobbies. You stayed quiet, but I could tell you were mad about it."

"That's true," Casey sighed. "I can't explain it."

"I think you're afraid no one will take you seriously if they find out you're riding horses."

"Why wouldn't they?" she asked, instantly suspicious.

"No, I think that's what you *think,* not what people will actually feel."

She considered this. He was right, of course. She was afraid of getting labeled a horse girl. She was afraid of the memes and the weird cultural place horses sat in, somewhere between spoiled and privileged, and backwards and redneck; and she could still remember the gross jokes guys in high school used to make about her. She was afraid of the way she saw the media constantly, purposefully, belittle girls who loved horses.

"It's just a confusing place to be in," she said eventually. "And you know, everyone at the barn is between eleven and seventeen."

"You're like Peter Pan with the Lost Boys," Brandon suggested. "You can be in charge."

"I'm like Wendy. Old enough to know the Lost Boys are lost."

"Where is this metaphor going? I'm kind of sorry I made it."

"Me too," Casey laughed. "You're too literal for metaphors. Better leave them to the experts."

Brandon turned down their street just as a flash of lightning illuminated the world around them. For a split-second she saw her little home life in negative, electric-white and drained of color.

"Well, I think it's nice you're riding," Brandon said, once they'd recovered from the shock of the unexpected light show.

"Me too," Casey said. "Thanks."

"And I'm glad you're not planning on buying a horse," he added, pulling up in front of the house. "It might make future plans difficult."

Thunder rumbled through the neighborhood, the postage-stamp lawns and the identical little townhouses. Casey felt the sound waves deep within her chest. "What kind of future plans?"

"You never know," Brandon said, shrugging. "I have a good feeling about this job I'm on right now. I think it could turn into something big. And then who knows?"

He got out of the car. Casey watched him walk up their little sidewalk and put the key into the door, then turn back to look at her. Another flash of lightning dazzled her eyes, and she knew she couldn't sit out here all night, wondering what the hell he was talking about but not bold enough to come out and ask him. So she got out and ran up the walk to join him. And they went inside for the night, tired from rum and salt and swimming, and so another Memorial Day ended, with a late-night storm and a sudden wakening, at three o'clock in the morning, to stare into the darkness and question everything.

Chapter Thirteen

Casey was so engrossed in the email she was working on, she didn't notice Mary until her manager was standing right next to her, practically waving an inter-office envelope at her head.

"Oh god, you scared me!" Casey gasped.

"I hope everyone who reads that email is as captivated as you are writing it."

Casey resisted the self-destructive urge to pick on Mary for such an awkward sentence. She focused on the envelope instead. "Did you need something signed?"

"I need someone to run this over to Cocoa Beach and get it back here before six. Can you do it?"

Casey glanced at the clock on her computer desktop. Nearly four thirty. On a Friday, at the head of summer. And she still had half an hour's worth of work to get out before she could sign off for the week. Traffic was going to be brutal by the time she was finished; she'd noticed several coworkers had already begun slinking out of the office while she had Mary's attention occupied. *Nice,* she thought sarcastically.

"I have to finish two revisions yet," Casey said. "And pull new graphics." She was dreading that part. Sorting through the stock image library, her eyes crossing as she tried to find the perfect image, something that could hold a reader's attention for a split-second before they hit *delete,* was one of the most tiresome parts of her job. Worst of all, she'd already sent over images for this email campaign. The client had taken one look at her choices and requested changes. So many changes, for one stupid email.

Casey, well aware that her perfectionist nature meant she had already lavished far too much time and thought on these emails, was used to spending too much time on her revisions. Today, however, she was not planning on staying a moment past five. She had a treat waiting for her.

"I can't possibly manage it," she told Mary, who had not taken the hint and was still hovering. "I'm really sorry. But I have to be somewhere by five thirty."

"You can finish your revisions from home later, if you want." Mary smiled graciously as she offered the privilege of working from home, secure in the knowledge that this was a truly fantastic offer. "I just really need this signed before the end of the day."

Casey carefully placed a smile on her face and spread her hands wide in apology, feeling like a previously well-behaved teen who was now refusing to turn in her homework on time. "I'm really sorry, Mary. I can't do it. It's going to have to be someone else this time."

She added *this time* to make all of her other courier runs seem like impositions, rather than treats. It was a subtle lie, but that's just where Casey found herself now. Making little revisions of the past so that she could insert her new equestrian life into her professional, and personal, life.

Mary pursed her lips sourly and gave Casey a look which promised future trouble. Then she stalked off, her heels thunking brutally against the berber carpeting.

Casey took a deep breath, one of those really body-moving breaths that caused her shoulders to lift and release, and then she turned back to her email. From the other side of the cubicle wall, she heard Marty chuckling softly. That was fine. Whatever. She could handle all of the work conflicts this place could throw at her right now.

Because, once this workday was done, she was spending the *entire weekend* at the stable, playing barn rat!

The whole thing had come together so quickly, she still couldn't believe it was really happening. Her week had started out so normally: brunch on Sunday, work on Monday, breathless anticipation for her next riding lesson on Wednesday. But before things could progress on their regular course, Brandon went down to West Palm Beach to meet with his client. It was supposed to be two days' worth of catching-up with their staff. It turned into the entire work-week, plus a weekend invitation to stay with the founder and go boating, visiting some of the research sites the company's charitable foundation was funding. Brandon couldn't say no, and Casey didn't expect him to. She told him to expense some new shirts and underwear and have a good time.

Just like that, Casey was in charge of her own time for six whole days. Not to complain, but she hadn't been the mistress of her own destiny in years. She was part of a couple, a couple who did nearly everything together. Or rather, they had been, until she had started riding. The horses seemed to have changed things, and pretty quickly at that.

She'd seen Brandon beginning to look rather resentfully at her paddock boots, which now occupied a permanent place on the linoleum near the front door. She'd noticed Brandon's eyebrows lift up when she received packages from companies with words like *saddlery* in their names. She'd heard Brandon sigh when she rushed into the house, muddy and sweaty, later and later each Wednesday night. And that was impressive considering he was generally all the way back in the kitchen when she got home.

She knew he was watching her new hobby with silent alarm, and she knew why. It was because of the time it took—massive chunks of time that didn't include him.

Horse-time seemed to operate on its own clock. A riding lesson was an hour. Arriving early to tack up was a half-hour. Staying after the lesson to untack and hose off the school horse, to graze the horse until he was dry, to wipe off the lesson tack and carefully hang it up, to swap a little gossip so that she felt like part of the barn family... it all added up. This past Wednesday night, she hadn't gotten home until after nine—from what was billed as a one-hour riding lesson, from five thirty to six thirty. Brandon hadn't said anything, but he'd given her a *look*.

A look that said: *Where have you been?* That said: *Is this our life now? Should I just get used to you being gone? When does it go from two days to three, from three to five?*

Casey wanted to believe she would find a balance. Things were just shaking out! In the meantime, yes, the riding was snowballing, she could admit that... but the way her horse-time was taking over her life felt good, and right. When she was busy with grooming and tacking and grazing at St. Johns Equestrian Center, she wasn't anxiously ticking over everything that had gone wrong at work that day. She wasn't thinking about the next day's drama waiting for her. She was just present. She was living in the moment! Wasn't that meant to be a good thing?

And her barn hours were the only moments in her entire week when she felt centered and present.

Now that she knew an anxiety-free mental space actually existed, she was hungry for more of it. When Casey was at home on a regular evening, she found herself craving the peace of watching sunset over the river, with the long-legged egrets folding up their necks and flying for home, black silhouettes against a pink and yellow sky. She missed the burbling laughter of the barn girls as they played with ponies, threw down hay bales, dragged horses out to the paddocks, and swept up the aisle after the evening's work was done. She longed for the clarity and purpose of riding, of repeating actions and maneuvers over and over until she got a movement right, however briefly.

The bottom line was: Casey didn't want to be at home, or at work. She wanted to be at the stables. She wanted her barn-time to be full-time. That wasn't practical, and her mind fled from the idea, but still... the horses beckoned.

And how did Brandon fit into all of this?

How could she explain that she didn't want to come home after work and sit on the couch with him for hours?

How could she tell him she didn't want to go to brunch on Sunday?

How could she explain that she wanted to spend more time at a horse farm, hanging out with teenagers, working at a sport or a hobby or a lifestyle or whatever it was that had nothing to do with him, which didn't interest him at all?

She didn't know where to begin.

All she knew for certain was that riding was filling a hole in her life she hadn't even realized was there. And until she figured out a good way to explain *that* part of the equation to him, she couldn't see a way to explain that he wasn't the problem preventing her from solving it, nor that their time together wasn't somehow less fulfilling than it had been before.

It was just this: now that she knew she needed more in her life, she *really* needed more in her life.

The one person who seemed to get it was Sky. When she'd casually mentioned during her Wednesday night lesson that Brandon would be out of town all weekend, Sky had wasted no time coming up with the perfect response: "So, you're coming out here to hang out all weekend, right?"

Casey hadn't hesitated. "Obviously!"

"Good. Come out whenever you want. We'll find something

for you to do!"

"Are you sure? I don't want to get in the way."

"Please. The kids are here twenty-four seven. Maybe we'll ditch them with the barn chores and go get dinner on Saturday night. I haven't hung out with an adult in months."

Sky wanted to hang out with *her!* Casey was so thrilled, she barely acknowledged the irony in agreeing to trade barn-time for yet more time sitting around a table in some restaurant. At least this time the conversation would be about horses.

"And you can take Mikey for a hack around the arena on Friday night, if you want," Sky had added. "Now that you're getting your seat back, you'll be a good tune-up for him."

That evening, she drove home positively glowing, and proceeded to offend Brandon with her obvious glee when they chatted over FaceTime before bed. His frown had been another tip for her to tamp down her new enthusiasm around him. It was another reminder that he wasn't on this journey with her. She didn't tell him about her weekend plans.

After they'd clicked off the call, Casey let herself wonder for a few moments how she was going to include Brandon in her horsey new life. Then she shrugged.

Maybe he'd pick up on it through osmosis. Whatever. She'd figure it out.

She didn't manage to get out of the office early like some folks, but she did escape by five. Unfortunately, so did most of the other office drones on the barrier islands, with Kennedy Space Center and two Air Force bases included. After a long, creeping commute across the causeway bridge back to the mainland, she was relieved to finally put her foot down once the traffic started paring off into the various subdivisions which hugged the riverfront towns.

The arena was packed with horses by the time she arrived, but most of the riders were just walking along side-by-side, chattering away. They reminded Casey of friends getting drinks after work, except that all the gossiping and catch-up was taking place in the saddle, rather than sitting across from one another at some rickety outdoor table while a local band played covers of sixties rock.

This was *undoubtedly* the superior venue for Friday night wind-downs, Casey thought, heading into the barn. Her usual spot on the patio at Mango's, waving *bon voyage* as the cruise ships blasting their horns, could not have been farther from her mind.

Gwen was in the tack room, pulling down an ancient jumping saddle from a shadowy corner rack. When Casey poked her head in, she looked up and her lips twitched in what was almost a smile. Casey counted these half-hellos as wins, because Gwen was just not a naturally outgoing person.

"Hey Casey!" Gwen said. "I was just getting a horse ready for you."

"Oh?" She certainly hadn't expected an invitation for a comp ride to include groom services. "I didn't realize—"

"Sky needed Mikey for a last-minute lesson at four thirty, and she felt bad. So she asked me to tack up James for you."

"James? But I've never ridden him." *And he's an ex-racehorse,* she thought, a little panic fluttering in her stomach. *Who knows what he'll do out there?* The full arena suddenly seemed like a disaster waiting to happen. One horse could spook another, and another, until there was a domino effect of out-of-control horses, which would have all started with Casey. She felt queasy at the idea.

"Oh, James is dead quiet," Gwen said, interrupting Casey's doomsday thoughts. "I've been riding him all week. You practically have to beat him into a trot. There's a reason he's here and not at the racetrack anymore. Anyway, I'll ride Juniper alongside you and give you some pointers, but you've got nothing to worry about."

Casey mentally shrugged and accepted her fate without another peep. It was ride James or go home. And Casey wasn't *so* thrilled with Brandon being out of town that she was looking forward to the empty house waiting for her. The only pleasure she'd get from his absence was the time she got to spend here, playing with horses. Better not look an ex-racehorse in the mouth, in this case.

"Okay then. Thanks, Gwen." Casey decided she would swallow her fear, put on her big girl panties, and get on James. "But can I help you tack up?"

"His bridle is the one with the loose-ring snaffle, hanging by the door," Gwen said, nodding her head at a brown leather bridle.

Casey tugged the bridle off its hook and followed Gwen down the barn aisle.

James was in the cross-ties at the far end of the barn, and he watched their approach with his ears pricked and his neck cocked to give him a better view of the barn aisle. Across from him, Gwen's golden chestnut gelding, Juniper, was the exact opposite: snoozing with his head hanging from the cross-ties, the ropes taut with the weight of his big noggin. He was a big warmblood, and when you added in his coppery sheen, Juniper was the opposite of light-boned, dark James in nearly every way.

"Yeah, so I got James standing nicely in cross-ties this week," Gwen said, dropping the saddle onto a rack. "No more flying backwards and breaking everything. But he does best with another horse to keep him company. That's Juniper's job. He's a great nanny." She busied herself with the saddle pad, and Casey jumped to help, picking up the saddle and girth to hand to her. She hated feeling like the younger girl had to tack up for her.

"I can do this, if you want," she offered.

"If you can bridle him, I can get Juniper tacked and we can go out together."

"Perfect," Casey agreed.

James was agreeable about being bridled, and a few minutes later, they were walking single-file out to the mounting block. Casey could feel the stares of everyone in the arena. When she met their gazes, no one bothered to look away.

Teenagers were wild that way. They were so transparent in their curiosity and constant need to be in each other's business. Casey felt like she was a world away from the passive, whispered gossip of the office. There was surely plenty of drama here with more than a dozen girls somewhere constantly flung together, but no one went to any effort to pretend they weren't endlessly fascinated by it. There was an honesty to barn life, even with all the theft and backbiting and bad-mouthing that Casey remembered from her own teenage years, which seemed refreshing as hell.

"I'll hold him while you mount," Gwen said, pulling up Juniper in front of the mounting block. "Be quick. He won't stand still for you. Just hop on and turn a circle while you get your stirrups."

Casey bit her lip, her tenuous confidence suddenly barraged with doubts. What if she wasn't fast enough? What if she couldn't get her stirrups when she mounted, lost her balance as she leaned over to try and get her feet into them, thus spooking James, and causing him to take off running, leaving her in the dust or worse, dragging her—because now in this mental scenario she was playing out, she *had* gained her stirrup but at the last possible second, at the worst possible moment, pushing her foot too far into the iron and getting it twisted there when she tried to wrench it free.

"Just get on him," Gwen advised. "Don't make it complicated."

Casey refrained from asking how a fourteen-year-old already knew how to give deceptively simple life advice like that. She just took the girl's words to heart and went for it, letting her mind slip into autopilot the way she had begun doing in her lessons.

In a few fluid motions, she had handed off the reins, stepped up onto the block, pressed a foot into the stirrup iron, and swung aboard. It all happened so quickly, she barely registered any of the movements as separate from one another.

She was in the saddle, reins in her grasp and feet balanced in the stirrups, almost before she even realized she'd done it.

Gwen tossed her a grin as she released her hold on the bridle. "You're getting there."

Casey had never expected to feel so proud of a half-assed compliment from a girl twenty years her junior. But there was something upside-down about *everything* in her life now. This moment was the new normal.

And, she thought, it was better than the old normal.

"How was James?" Sky was standing by the tack room door as Casey finished wiping the horse's bridle off, her damp sponge leaking soapy water onto the concrete floor.

Casey tried to think of an adjective which wouldn't make Sky start seeing dollar signs. The truth was, James had been an absolute delight, his slim Thoroughbred body awakening memories of riding her sweet boy Wilson. He had been polite, interested in his surroundings, and happy to mosey around the arena while the other riders alternated between chit-chatting and doing a little light trot and canter work of their own. She had never once felt over-horsed on him.

Saying all of that out loud would invite more happy speculation that Casey might make a good buyer.

"He was really nice," Casey said carefully.

She shook the sponge into the wash-tub sink in the corner, feeling Sky's eyes on her back.

"Gwen told me he'd been really quiet all week, so I figured he'd be a good match for you. Sorry I had to use Mikey."

"Oh, I understand! Paying riders have to come first. It was so nice of you to give me a hack at all." Casey turned around, leaned back on the wash-tub, and smiled at Sky. "How can I pay you back?"

Sky gave her an assessing look. "I wasn't going to charge you. But, since you offered… it's time to feed dinner and then get everyone turned out for the night. Want to join the girls while I get my weekend calendar in order? Then we can grab some dinner."

Casey couldn't think of anything she'd like more. "On it, boss," she said, and headed out into the barn aisle, ready to get to work on evening chores.

Chapter Fourteen

By Saturday evening of the Weekend Without Brandon, Casey was sweaty and sunburned, exhausted and elated. She'd been at the barn since nine a.m., and after her game-changing lesson on Mikey (They had cantered! And hopped over a little cross-rail! It was all happening!) she had changed out of her breeches and into some old shorts so that she could help the girls dump and clean some of the big water troughs in the paddocks. Then, she'd made a lunch run, picking up sandwiches at the grocery store along with five bags of potato chips and an industrial-sized flat of chocolate-chip cookies, making herself the hero of the day. In the afternoon, she'd been appointed ring steward for a jumping lesson, and spent forty minutes dragging around poles and fixing jump heights for Sky while Callie, Roxy and a few other advanced riders jumped course after course.

Just as they'd finished their lesson, the sky had clouded over and a big thunderstorm rolled up out of the southwest, the lightning stabbing at the open savanna, and they'd all run inside screaming, having what felt like the best time of their lives.

Now she was relaxing in a patio chair across from Sky, who looked as wiped out as she did. The girls were in the lounge; they retreated to air conditioning whenever left to their own devices. No one's parents had shown up to get them yet. Sky confided that they usually left the kids at the barn until seven or eight in the summer.

"I'm a free babysitter," she said with a shrug. "Or else they think it's rolled in with the cost of board for the horse."

"Do you resent it?"

"No, of course not. It's how I grew up, too. And you, right? I thought so. Yeah, I just make them do plenty of work to make up for all the time they take up, all the free lessons and extra help I give them all summer, and I guess it evens out."

Not in your bank account, it doesn't, Casey thought, but she'd never known a riding instructor who had been savvy with money.

"Now, let's talk about dinner tonight. What about hot dogs grilled on my front porch? Would that work for you? There's beer, too."

"You had me at hot dogs," Casey laughed. "But now I am *craving* a beer."

It felt like the perfect ending to a perfect day.

The Catahoula hounds joined them on the front porch, a big roofless deck built next to the front door of the doublewide. This was evidently where Sky kept all of her spare buckets, lead-ropes and hay twine. Casey tried not to look at the mess, but Sky noticed her gaze.

"Don't judge me," she pleaded, setting up a toddler gate across the steps to keep the dogs from running loose while there were still kids in the barn. "Anything the kids leave out, the dogs pick up and drag up here. You should see these dummies running around with buckets stuck on their heads. One good thing, though: I never have to go searching for missing bell boots." She brandished a battered rubber bell boot, the Velcro fasteners frayed from whatever horse's hoof had ultimately torn it free. "When I brought in Cowboy this morning he was missing his right boot, and here it is."

"Bell boot retrieval is a very important trait for any dog," Casey agreed, sinking down to let the spotted hounds get in close for a greeting. She hadn't seen them much since her first day here. She remembered the first day she'd pulled in the lane and seen these two dogs: that had been just a month ago. What a difference a month could make in her life!

Something else occurred to her about that first day. "Hey, Sky?"

Sky was pulling the grill away from the side of the trailer. "What's up?"

"You know, about that proposal I brought out here that first day… it's a shame we couldn't make it work. I'd love to be writing emails for you instead of some of my boring clients."

Sky shrugged. When she finally replied, she sounded embarrassed. "Oh, that… I was probably shooting a little too high when I requested that quote, anyway. I was thinking of putting together some advertising, but I couldn't afford your agency. Or any others. So I let it go."

"Oh, that's a shame." One of the dogs was licking Casey's chin, which was just a little too affectionate for her taste. She stood up again, pushing the hounds back down. "What kind of business were you hoping to build up?"

"Riding lessons, mostly," Sky said. "I have good ponies and plenty of connections to get more. I did really well with ponies back home. You start a kid riding, get them hooked, sell their parents a nice pony to board with you… it's a great model, trust me!" She laughed. "But it's tough getting the word out, especially when we're back here on a dirt road with no frontage or shiny white fences for people to drive past." She turned around and saw the dogs still trying to climb Casey's legs. "Remy! Clyde! Get down or go in the house!"

The dogs plopped to the ground and rolled over, writhing apologetically, their tails thumping the porch floorboards.

"Remy and Clyde? Those are cute names."

"They were cute puppies," Sky said, shaking her head with mock sorrow. "Here I thought all that cute would stick." She reached her hands out and the dogs flowed to her before collapsing into a rapturous puddle of adoration. "Idiots," she told them. "How about you guys go inside and I'll give you dinner. I'll be right back," she added to Casey.

Alone with the rippling clouds overhead and the orange glare of the sinking sun, Casey sat down on a creaking deck chair and looked out over the farm. The girls were starting to turn the horses out for the night; she saw Gwen leading the little white pony she was training, and Arden, so coltishly tall and blazingly red-headed, walking out her huge warmblood, Phineas.

Then came one of the older girls, indistinguishable from an adult at this distance, leading a dark horse. Something about his walk caught her eye. *He's so cute,* Casey thought, sitting up for a better view. Who was it? A shifting ray of sunlight burst from behind a cloud and in the golden glow she suddenly spotted those white socks, with their little speckles of black ermine, on his hind legs.

Of course, it was James.

She'd barely sat back to analyze her feelings about the little Thoroughbred when Sky reappeared, arms filled with hot dogs and plates, buns and beers. "The dogs are eating in the kitchen," she said, sounding a little breathless. "I would never try to grill with those fools out here."

"There's something funny about feeding the dogs in the kitchen while you bring all your food out to the porch."

"That's what they thought! You should have seen them watching me walk away with all the interesting people-food." Sky placed some hot dogs on the grill. "The kids are doing turn-out?"

"Yeah. Just started."

"I'm honestly so thankful for them in summer. Almost makes

up for what poisonous little snakes they can be in the school year. Something about the show season and the stress of school makes them gang up on each other. Nonstop turf wars. I probably shouldn't tell you this, you'll never want to board here..."

"I don't have a horse," Casey pointed out. "Wouldn't worry about it."

"You'll get a horse *eventually,*" Sky said, a teasing note in her voice.

Casey opened her beer. "Maybe," she allowed. "My boyfriend would have a fit, though. I better give him some time to get used to all this."

"Boyfriends are tough," Sky agreed. "Chips?"

"Yes, *please.* Yeah, he doesn't understand why I'm spending so much time here all of a sudden."

"They never do. That's why I don't bother with one." Sky winked. "I can't have someone questioning my every move. If I want to be micro-managed, I'll just ask my mom for some money."

Casey sensed an opening for some details on Sky's personal life. "Does she live around here?"

"No, down in Wellington." Sky leaned on the porch railing, watching the girls at work. "She's a real estate broker. Big equestrian properties, million-dollar mini-ranches, that kind of thing. She bought this place years ago as an investment, then she let me open it up when I finished college. That was the deal," she explained, smiling wryly at Casey. "Get a business degree, and I get the farm. I had to write a whole plan, prove I wouldn't go under."

"So far, so good?"

"Except when I have to beg for money." She laughed, but the sound was a bit hollow to Casey's ears. "Hence: the advertising idea. I wanted to start doing more small kids and show ponies. I picked up that prospect that Gwen is riding *really* cheap, and she's game for more once he's ready to go... a few lesson ponies and lease ponies for the kids who are begging to start showing and I could stop asking my mom for a loan whenever it's time to buy a load of hay for winter. A few more serious students and I'd be turning a profit. Sounds like a heck of a goal, right?"

"Hay on your own terms. That's the dream."

They drank in silence for a moment. The hot dogs crackled and spit on the grill.

"I'm glad you're here," Sky said eventually. "It's lonely being the only adult."

"Have you thought about going after more adult riders?"

"I have. But kids stay with horses at least until college. Adults come and go. They don't stick around."

Casey considered her own case. "Boyfriends get in the way."

"And husbands, yeah. And kids. Adults have too many commitments. It takes them a long time to give in and just buy the damn horse. It takes them a long time to give in and just take the riding lesson, to begin with." She stretched and sighed, then went to the grill and started rolling the hot dogs. "But aside from business, all of that... I'm just really happy to have you here."

"Thank you," Casey said, feeling both delighted and absurd over how pleased Sky's words made her feel. "I'm really happy to be here."

She watched Sky tear open the bag of hot dog buns and start placing them on paper plates. The sounds of the farm washed over her. In the barn, kids laughed and yelled; a few horses whinnied from the paddocks. In the house, a dog scratched at the door and whined softly. In the Australian pines blocking the farm from River Road, the last of the day's sea breeze rustled the needles. A mockingbird *titched* coarsely a few times before launching into his full repertoire of melodies. Casey felt a million miles away from her poky little townhouse living room, where the musical accompaniment would be the thumps of bass from a neighbor's stereo, and the constant swishing sounds of traffic out on the main road.

This place would make Brandon crazy, she thought. Brandon wanted to live in a city, with everything close at hand. He thought the towns here were too spread out. He talked about moving somewhere more dense, but she always changed the subject.

Why move away towards density and away from this? Casey admired the luminous twilight creeping westward towards the fading gold of sunset, the long-legged herons winging home to their rookeries, the country quiet settling over the landscape.

Sky had it good out here, even if building up a business was a constant struggle. She knew what she was doing; she had good instincts, she just needed a little more capital and the chance to succeed. Casey looked over at the younger woman, bustling over the grill with a chef's authority, and wondered if Leslie had been right to warn her that Sky would try to get into her wallet. What if all these overtures of friendship were really just cold calculation?

Casey didn't think she could stand it if that were true. She *liked* Sky, really liked her. This was that amazing unicorn: adult-onset friendship. *This has to be real,* she thought desperately. *This can't be a transaction.*

"Ketchup or mustard?" Sky turned, a bottle in each hand. "I will confess right now, I always do both because I can never choose."

Her face was open, her eyes were bright, her smile was broad. Sky wasn't hiding a thing, Casey decided—and if she was, then she was a damn acting genius.

"Definitely both," Casey laughed, shoving her fears behind her.

The sea breeze finally died as the sun sank below the horizon, and they were forced to retreat into the living room to avoid the whining hordes of mosquitoes. The dogs welcomed them with ecstasy, clambering up Casey's legs until Sky restored order with the sharp voice a horsewoman could turn on and off with such efficiency. Casey herself could blast a dog into humble obedience with a voice so deep it startled her friends. "It's just from being around horses," she'd shrug, while they gasped and stared and clutched at one another with over-the-top fake shock. It was so nice to be around someone else who *got* it.

"I swear they're good guard dogs," Sky groaned, shoving a licking mouth aside. "My mom said I could only live here if I got myself some loud dogs, and you've never heard such loud dogs as these two when a possum runs by my bedroom window at three o'clock in the morning."

Casey laughed, letting her eyes run around the doublewide's living room while she tumbled onto the worn-out plaid couch. The trailer was a pretty recent model, but scarcely furnished at all. The cheap wooden coffee table and a sagging TV table against the far wall seemed to huddle in the expansive living room. A few framed horse show pictures and a whole lot of rosettes adorned the plain white walls.

"Did you get this place new when you moved here?" she asked.

"Yeah. The old place was unlivable. It had been here a good twenty or thirty years… it was probably here when you rode here as a kid!"

"I do remember a trailer here, and yikes, if that's the same one. I never went inside."

"Trust me, no one had been inside that place for a long time." Sky laughed and gave a little shudder at the same time. "My mom wanted to let the place sit, and then sell it to a developer in a few more years. She swears the subdivisions will make it out this far as long as the housing market keeps cooking and we don't have any big hurricanes to scare people off. I don't know. If she'd had her way, I'd still be in Wellington. But that didn't feel… I don't know. *Everyone* knows my mom. I wanted to do something on my own, you know?"

"Sure," Casey said, but privately she thought that line was a lot of bullshit, perhaps the first truly bullshit thing Sky had said to her. Getting the loan of a farm from your wealthy mother's real estate portfolio, plus money to run it on, plus your father's renovation work, hardly fell into the "on my own" category. Was this the first checkmark in favor of the *Sky is stringing you along* argument?

"It's a reputation thing, you know?" Sky went on. "Not to get business just because my mom makes some lady a fortune on a real estate deal and her kid wants to get into ponies, so she hands the lady my business card and poof, I have a new client. I want to get students because I'm a good trainer, and my kids win at shows. And I want to create genuinely good horsemen. Having an army of riders who show up for lessons, but expect a groom to do all of their work…" she shrugged. "I mean, it pays. But it's not what I want to be known for. That whole show-up-and-ride Wellington mindset, I just never got it. It feels different up here. That's why I decided to move."

Casey nodded eagerly. "I totally see what you mean. It's more casual up here than down in south Florida. It's still kind of southern and outdoorsy, and parents think it's totally normal for their kids to be outside all day."

"That's it. And that's why I really love it here. I'm so glad I moved up here. And it doesn't hurt that I think there's a ton of potential here to get kids into showing ponies. This is your hometown, right?"

"Yeah." Casey tugged at Remy's soft ears. He gazed up at her with adoring brown eyes. "I grew up here, then I went to school in Gainesville, then I came back. And then I stayed. It's nice here. Calm." She wasn't sure if that was the best reason to stay somewhere, but nothing more enticing had come along, either. "Beautiful," she added.

"I could stay here if my plans worked out," Sky said dreamily. Her gaze was far away. "I'd build a nice house here, give this trailer to a manager or a couple of working students, and add another riding arena so we could have really nice horse shows. There is just so much potential here. So many people and so many kids and no A-circuit barns in my way at all!" She laughed. "Or maybe that's not what people around here want from a barn, I don't know. Maybe they aren't big-time horse show people. But it's worth a try."

"I agree." Casey considered the kids she'd met. They were hungry to advance, but their tendency towards eventing wasn't going to drive arena-based horse shows. They wanted to go up to Ocala and gallop around big fields. "But you want ponies and kids, and that's not what you've got. You have teens who want to go eventing."

"Yeah, that was my marketing thing, you know? The idea that brought you out here, the quote I couldn't afford. To widen my clientele a little. Well, who knows how I'll make that happen." She shrugged and smiled. "That's okay."

"I'm glad *I* made it out here, anyway." Casey leaned over and tapped her beer bottle against Sky's.

Sky smiled back at her. "Me too. It gets lonely out here. I'm out on the edge of the world. But I just sit back and imagine all the things I can do and the empire I could build here, and that's pretty good company late at night! Still, it's better with friends."

Remy (or maybe it was Clyde?) nudged at Casey's knee, then jumped up on the couch between them. Sky laughed. "Oh, you help too," she told the dog, pulling him against her side. "I couldn't do it without my dogs."

Casey was laughing too, but she was impressed by Sky's resolve. She hadn't realized Sky was ambitious for more than a neighborhood boarding stable with local horse show ribbons hanging in the tack room. "I think you'll make it," she said. "If I can help, please let me know."

Sky gave her an intense look. "Thank you," she said. "I'm just really glad you're here."

Chapter Fifteen

Sunday night, six p.m., saw Casey at the end of her weekend without Brandon. She was giving James a bath in the cross-ties at the end of the barn. The early evening air was still as sizzling hot as it had been at noon. The usual afternoon thunderstorms had skipped the Atlantic beaches today, content to rain themselves out inland while the coast baked in the sun. For anyone but Casey, today would have been the perfect beach day.

In fact, Casey had received more than a few calls and texts early in the day from friends who wanted her to join them at the beach, at a pool party, or just for drinks down at the port. Their invitations had been tempting. Their reactions, when she turned them down, had been bewildered.

"But, it's *hot,*" Heather had gasped, bewildered, when Casey declined an afternoon by the water. "You can't possibly want to be around the horses in *this* weather."

"It's like this all of the time," Casey had replied flatly. "It's June. In Florida."

"It's not always like this. It usually rains in the afternoon. And that doesn't change my argument that it's too hot to mess around with horses when you could be at the beach. With *me.*"

"I'm really sorry," Casey had said. "I'm already at the barn."

She understood why her friends were so confused. They'd always spent steamy summer weekends looking for fun anywhere they might enjoy a good stiff sea breeze, some icy margaritas, and the possibility of getting dunked in the water. And for her friends, nothing about this summer had changed. This year would be the same as last year, and the year before that.

For Casey, though, everything had changed.

And not even the peak of June heat could keep Casey from wasting a minute of her all-horse weekend.

James was shifting restlessly in the cross-ties, beads of sweat still rolling down his cheekbones from where he'd gotten lathered under his bridle. She hadn't even ridden him that hard; James was just a sweaty kind of horse, who managed to drench himself five minutes into every ride. Casey viewed this as a plus. She remembered horses from her childhood who had abruptly stopped sweating. Vets were consulted, kitchen cures like a daily pint of Guinness were attempted, but eventually the horses were either moved to a more temperate state or retired from work until the cooler months came. Florida could be hard on horses.

"I know it's hot, buddy," she cooed, spraying him off with the hose. "I have a nice surprise for you, though. I put witch hazel in the rinse water."

"What will that do?" Arden was hanging around nearby, playing with her phone.

"It cools off the skin," Casey explained. "And it helps the horse dry faster. Hot water sitting on top of their coats keeps them from cooling off."

"Hmm, did not know that." Arden didn't look up from her phone, but Casey supposed she was filing the information away somewhere.

Her own phone buzzed noisily from the plastic grooming box where she'd set it down. "I swear, Alison won't leave me alone," Casey sighed. "This will be the tenth text today."

"Too much friend time?" Gwen was in the cross-ties across the aisle, tacking up one of the barn's lesson ponies. Sky had found the girl earlier and and asked if she could give the pony a "tune-up ride," which was code for "this pony has forgotten how to be chill in riding lessons."

"Something like that." Casey finished with the hose and grabbed a big, soft sponge to start rinsing James with the doctored wash water. "There's some celebrity wedding going down at her hotel tonight. She's the event planner and they gave her an invite at the last minute, so now she wants me to come join her."

Arden glanced up. "She doesn't have a date?"

"Her boyfriend hates parties." Because who else would a party planner fall for, but a rocket scientist who couldn't stand going to parties? "Arden, will you reach down and see if that's her?"

Arden elaborately leaned over and plucked Casey's phone from the grooming box. She squinted at the screen. "It's from someone named Brandon. *I just crossed into Brevard County, see you in an hour.* Who's Brandon?"

Casey dropped the sponge, splattering water everywhere. James jumped. "Oh, shit."

"An ex? A stalker?"

"No, he's my boyfriend."

Gwen looked over, interested. "I've never had a boyfriend, but I don't think that's the reaction you're supposed to have when one texts you."

"It's fine," Casey said anxiously, patting James to settle him. "I just didn't expect him to get home so soon. He was out of town this weekend."

Arden handed her the phone and Casey thumbed back a quick *can't wait!* while double-checking the time. It would take her twenty minutes to get home, twenty more to shower and get her barn clothes in the wash before he noticed they were damp and dirty. Would he notice? What would it matter? Why would he care? He wasn't spying on her, and she wasn't doing anything wrong by spending all of her time at the barn, instead of at the beach!

"So you have to run?" Arden asked, eyebrows lifted elaborately. "Are you not allowed to hang out here?"

"Don't be ridiculous." Casey put the phone back and resumed sponging off James. The horse leaned into the tingly witch hazel, his rapturous expression making Casey smile despite everything else on her mind. *So freaking cute!* "He doesn't allow me or not allow me to do things. It's just..." She trailed off, not sure how to explain.

"New?" Gwen suggested. "Because you've only been riding a little while but it changes so much about your life?"

Why did Gwen see so much? The kid was fourteen, dammit! "That's it," Casey agreed. "I've been here a lot. It's not what he would expect me to be doing."

"Oh, I guess you should be lying around a beach, touching up your color," Arden said sarcastically. "Like all the girls at school do on weekends. What a waste! Not one of them has arms like me, even if they have perfect tans." She flexed for them.

"Very nice," Gwen said indifferently, and went back to bridling her pony.

"I don't think he necessarily cares whether I choose to tan or ride," Casey said thoughtfully. "It's just that there's so much space between the two things. I don't want him to think... I don't know, that he doesn't know me any more? Does that make sense?"

Arden looked at her for the first time. "That makes," she said firmly, "a *ton* of sense."

Gwen was putting on her helmet. "You're afraid that he thinks riding is changing you."

"And that he won't understand you anymore," Arden added. "Totally valid. Men get scared so easily."

"You have to move slowly," Gwen suggested. "Treat him like a young horse who needs a lot of time to absorb new things."

"Better go home," Arden said. "Do you need help putting away your stuff?"

Casey realized that she was receiving relationship advice from young teenagers, possibly a dubious source, and also that she was taking said advice very seriously—possibly a sign of just how worried she really was. She tossed the rest of the wash water over James's back. "I can put my own things away," she sighed. "But thank you."

Gwen was buckling her helmet, almost ready to ride. "I hope it works out," she said.

Jesus, Casey thought. *When you put it that way, I hope it works out, too.*

She started moving faster than she should have, plucking a plastic sweat scraper from the brush box and slapping it hard along James's neck to squeeze away the excess water in his coat. He twitched and side-stepped away from her, lifting his head as the cross-ties tugged at his halter.

"Calm down," Arden said critically. "You're getting him all keyed up and he's not going to cool out that way."

"Sorry." Casey was embarrassed. "You're right." She took a moment to soothe James, rubbing the horse's withers with her fingernails. James cocked his head and eyeballed her, his ears lobbed out to either side as he tried to decide whether or not he should forgive her.

"Seriously, if you need to rush home to your boyfriend, I can finish him up for you," Gwen offered, her tone unreadable. "This little brat could use some thinking time in the cross-ties before we go out to the arena." She gestured at the pony, who was lifting one trembling foreleg, preparing to paw at the concrete if Gwen didn't get a move-on. "He apparently bucked in his last lesson, so I want him good and annoyed before I take him out. I need him to try it with me so I can wear him out. I can't fix the problem if he doesn't present it to me."

This training premise of building to a bad climax was an interesting one, and Casey wanted to talk about it more, which made her even more irritated with her present situation. "Thank you," she said, surrendering the sweat scraper. "I feel terrible about this."

Gwen shrugged and started to run the scraper over James with slick, professional strokes. "It must suck to be an adult and still not be able to run your own life," she said. "That's what it always seems like, though. Sky says no one has freedom like teenagers and even though we have to ask permission to do literally anything, I think she's right."

For a moment, Casey stood still and stared at Gwen, too stricken to move.

Then she was annoyed. Why was this kid always so able to pinpoint her exact feelings? Gwen was a little bit of a witch—even more so than her mother.

"It's not like that," she managed to say.

Gwen shrugged again. It was her signature move, a wordless gesture which said everything about what she thought of the people moving around her: they could all lie to her all day long if they wanted, and she, Gwen, would keep on traveling her own path, unaffected and unmoved. "It's whatever you say it is. Will you be here tomorrow?"

"Wednesday," Casey amended. "For my lesson."

"I'll probably ride James on Tuesday, then." Gwen put down the bucket and tweaked the Thoroughbred's nose. "Just to keep him tuned up for ya."

Casey pushed down an upwelling of jealousy as she turned and left the barn.

* * *

Casey was still in the shower when Brandon came home. She felt him come in; the bathroom door rattled as the front door opened and closed, shifting the air pressure in the entire house. Her weekend was over. Her real life was back. That was fine! She loved her real life. Of course she did!

She just wasn't quite ready for it to start up again.

She had just stepped onto the bathmat when Brandon opened the door and pushed his head inside, a smile on his face which quickly turned into a leer.

"Hey you!" she said, snatching at a towel. "I missed you!"

And she *had* missed him, despite her irritation at his early return. She felt a sudden surge of courage. She could do this. It would be easy to live two lives—look how well she was doing. She could slip from one to the other as quickly as she could shed her breeches, shower, and pull on a sundress. Everything would be fine.

She rewarded Brandon for her newfound confidence with a long kiss, during which her towel fell down, water got all over the floor, and the bed covers ended up getting extremely rumpled.

Downstairs, while Brandon ordered pizza, Casey willed up the courage to tell him about her all-horse weekend. She poured a glass of wine for herself, popped a beer for Brandon, and carried both into the living room. He was sprawled on the couch, looking extremely comfortable in blue boxers and a loose gray t-shirt. Casey tugged down the yellow shirt-dress she'd pulled over her head before coming downstairs, thinking Brandon was better at dressing comfortably than she was. Must be nice to be a man sometimes.

"Twenty minutes!" he announced, ending the call. "I will be amazed if it's that fast, but also thrilled, because I'm starving."

"How was your weekend?"

"Sunny." He accepted the beer from her and shoved himself over to make room on the couch. "The boat trips were fun. There's a lot of great work being done out there. The workweek was not so fun. A lot of typing, a lot of squinting at monitors. The same thing I do here, but I did it in West Palm instead."

"Seems like that part was a pointless drive, then."

"Well, I talked their team through some of the front-end stuff they'll have to know. You know how it is; you write the code but someone else is going to manipulate the end product."

Casey nodded; she had a superficial understanding of the issue from her own work. She wrote emails with code, which was hidden behind a pretty facade of fonts and graphics. Clients would try to alter her work by cutting, copying and pasting, subsequently breaking the entire email structure by doing it. Then they came crying back to her and she had to rescue them by redoing her hard work. "Civilians," she offered with a shrug.

Brandon grinned back at her. "Precisely. Enough about my boring job, what did *you* do with your weekend? Lots of time with the ladies while I was out of your hair? You look like you got some sun."

Casey glanced down at her forearms, which were possibly a little more brown and definitely a little more pink than they had been on Friday. Yikes, did she have a farmer's tan already? She resisted the urge to tug at the sleeves of her dress.

"And what's this?" Brandon traced her ankles, where faint pink lines gave away the elastic grips of her riding breeches.

"Well, since you were away, I actually spent the whole weekend out at Sky's place!" Casey admitted, jumping right into her equestrian confession. "I pretty much lived in my breeches. Guess they left their mark!"

Brandon met her gaze, eyebrows raised in surprise. "With the horses all weekend? Well, that's cool! And unexpected. I thought you'd at least go to the beach without me around, get a little break from all my complaining about how much sand you always bring home."

"You *do* complain about sand a lot. But that's neither here nor there. No, so, I just started riding this horse this weekend—he's an ex-racehorse, actually, and he's really sweet, and I've just been spending a lot of time with him, and the other horses of course, helping Sky out..." Casey realized she was babbling and stopped talking. She waited for him to react.

But Brandon just grinned at her. "Well, look at you! My little cowgirl!"

Casey didn't have the heart to tell him how wrong he was. Although, she thought, giving in to his cuddle, she had better make it really clear that she rode English before he did something truly awful, like buy her rhinestone-studded cowboy boots for her birthday. She could just imagine the looks on the girls' faces if she showed up wearing those.

Chapter Sixteen

Wednesday afternoon, end of June, east coast of Florida: it was a specific time, a specific place, and a specific feeling. Casey couldn't have summed it up in marketing copy, which was a shame, because it definitely would have sold houses and rented out hotel rooms.

There was just something about the atmosphere of this very moment: a moment that was midweek and mid-summer vacation, with kids on the loose and schools shuttered for the season, the work-week halfway to the weekend, which brought a half-forgotten feeling of freedom back to adult hearts as they considered their approaching long weekend. The weather was invariably the same on this day, every year: a sky bright and sunny, studded with cotton-ball clouds, a hint of distant thunder in the air. The Fourth of July decorations were up, with red, white, and blue bunting flying from the car dealerships strung along the wide, flat highways stretching inland from the beaches. The traffic was thickening, a stream of cars lobbing back and forth from the theme park interior to the beachside hotels. Staycations and vacations and backyard pool parties were on everyone's minds.

Casey loved this time of year, always had. Even in her most intense horse girl years, she hadn't been immune to that midsummer feeling, to those sunburned days by friends' pools and windblown afternoons at the beach. Late June tasted of hot dogs with mustard and ketchup, it smelled of charcoal and sunblock, it felt hot and gritty and sticky—but like, in a *good* way.

So she wasn't immune to all of the good feelings permeating the air in her office on Wednesday afternoon, at the end of June, seven life-changing weeks into her equestrian renaissance.

She was humming a little tune to herself as she moved images around on an email, planning out the next sales campaign for the appliance liquidation center just a few miles down U.S. 1, helpfully located next to a window blinds outlet and a flooring showroom. It was weird, Casey thought idly, the way retail arranged itself into little districts. Their patch of concrete was the home remodeling district. It was too bad Cocoa didn't have a horse district, with a tack shop and a feed store and maybe a horse trailer outlet—

"Casey!" A large duffel bag landed on her desk.

Casey shoved her chair back in shock. She looked up, wild-eyed, and saw Leslie smiling down at her. "Um, hi," she said weakly.

"Present for you!" Leslie announced, tugging at her paisley scarf. Today's colors were turquoise and hot pink, which were really quite the combo on Leslie's oak-tree frame. "Tory's old things. I kept forgetting to bring them for you. Go on, take a look."

Casey stood up and opened the duffel bag. Inside she found an impressive assortment of riding gear: breeches and boot socks, string gloves and spur straps, even a flexible black safety vest.

"She left it all in her closet and when I finally asked her what to do with it, she said she had all new stuff now," Leslie explained cheerfully. "I said, 'Tory, I've got a friend at work who just started riding and she could use a hand.' She said: 'sure Ma, hand it over.'"

Casey wished Leslie would lower her voice. The entire office had to be listening. She pitched her voice low when she replied: "This is very generous."

"Well, I know how expensive this sport can get. This safety vest alone is two hundred dollars new! I could have put it online to sell but I don't have the time or the inclination, and if Tory wanted the money she should have taken it up to Tallahassee with her and sold it herself."

"Thank you," Casey said, feeling equally overwhelmed and embarrassed. "I don't think I need all of this for riding once or twice a week but it's great…"

"Oh, you'll be riding more than that before long," Leslie told her knowingly. "Gwen tells me you're riding that new horse of Sky's quite a lot." She looked dangerously close to winking.

Casey rushed to shut down the conversation. "Only in lessons. He's really Sky's project. I mean, he's too green for me. There's no way I could train him myself."

Leslie had just shrugged her paisley-clad shoulders and smiled. "You know how these things have a way of working out. Well, I'll be seeing you out there. Enjoy your ride tonight!"

Casey watched Leslie disappear into the maze of cubicles, long shawl trailing around her sensible brown flats, and felt her gratitude morph into utter exasperation. Why must Leslie be so determined to convince her that Sky only wanted to sell her a horse? And *James* of all horses? Sure, Sky had brought it up, but Casey had told her she didn't think it was a good idea and that had been the end of it. Period. Sky had just read the situation wrong and she knew that now.

Plus, if Sky really wanted to sell her a horse, it wouldn't be a green-broke off-track Thoroughbred. It would be something with show miles and pro training which cost four times as much as James would command.

Unless, of course, Sky had already sized up the size of Casey's wallet and decided a green off-track Thoroughbred would be the limit of any potential horse-shopping budget.

Amy Hickstead from a few cubicles down, the one whose sister had ridden as a kid, walked past with her purse slung over her shoulder. She paused at Casey's cubicle. "So you're riding horses again? That's neat."

"Yeah." Casey zipped up the duffle bag of riding clothes. "Thanks. It's nice to get back into. Good exercise." An inane thing to say, but that was what coworker conversations were like. A group of people with nothing in common, thrown into close quarters every day, were bound to say inane things.

"I like spin class," Amy said. "My sister rode horses when I was a kid, but they were so big."

"You told me," Casey replied.

They looked at each other for a moment.

"Well, have fun." Amy started off down the aisle.

"You're leaving?"

"It's almost five," Amy said over her shoulder. "Finish up and go home! Or," she added mischievously, "go ride a horse, I guess!"

Casey sighed and looked at the bag. She'd been keeping her riding quiet around the office, mainly because Brandon had rightfully pointed out she got defensive when people immediately began poking fun at an adult playing with ponies. So, to avoid detection, she usually changed into riding clothes in the barn bathroom. Then, last week, she'd seen a really big spider in there. This had been a source of distress for her every time she thought about going straight to the barn from the office. It was one thing to see a large spider while you were fully clothed. It was another when you were stripped to your underwear.

Now, however, she was presented with an escape from the restroom spider. If everyone on the second floor had now been made aware she rode horses, there was no point in trying to keep it quiet anymore. Her breeches, sports bra, and riding shirt were all out in the car, but she could try on some of the goodies in Leslie's bag right now. She had a package of makeup-removing wipes and a tube of sunblock in her purse. "Let's do this," she muttered, gathering her things.

So Casey moseyed on into the office restroom, enjoyed the luxury of an arachnid-free private stall, and underwent a transformation, trading linen shirt and dress pants and make-up for a blue workout top, slate-colored breeches, and a slathering of sunblock.

When Casey emerged from her phone booth in full superhero garb, some of her colleagues were standing in the hall chatting, work bags and purses in hand. Sahid was the first to break off his conversation and stare at her, utterly fascinated.

"Honey," he said after a moment. "What is *this?*"

"I'm going to my riding lesson," Casey said simply.

"Well, you look fantastic."

"*Thank* you, Sahid." She smiled at the rest of the group, who were slowly shifting their expressions from astonished to encouraging. "See you later, guys!"

In the sunbaked car, air conditioning blowing full blast, Casey looked at her pink cheeks in the rearview mirror and laughed at herself. So she looked a little crazy to them the first time out. That was no reason to hide her horse habit! She'd be part of office culture in no time: Leslie was loud, Mary was scary, Jacob ate salmon every Tuesday and Thursday despite the notes written with increasing desperation requesting no fish in the microwave, and Casey paraded around the office in horse girl clothes once a week.

The bunting along the highway thinned out as she drove west, heading inland from the party atmosphere at the coast.

"The sun is shining on the beaches, but there's still a decent chance of a thunderstorm this evening along the coast," a lively woman on the car radio announced.

Well, Casey thought, *she* wouldn't complain if a storm brought a little shade. The air conditioning was still blowing on high, but she was sweating just from the glare of the sunlight through the car window.

"If you're out there, Mister Storm, now would be fine," Casey muttered, turning into the barn driveway and stopping at the closed gate. But she didn't have any real hope that the storm gods would heed her permission.

So she was surprised when a shadow fell over the countryside the moment she hopped out of the car. One second she was sweating beneath her seat-belt; the next she was standing next to her open car door as a gray cloud, high and mighty, swept over the white sun. Far in the distance, beyond the little scrap of barn she could see through the tunnel of the driveway, the western sky over the wild river lands was stained the deep cobalt blue of an impending storm.

"Okay then," Casey sighed, feeling unreasonably disappointed. "I *did* say you could come. But can you hold off long enough for me to have a riding lesson?"

The wind picked up in response, rattling the palm fronds lining the driveway. Casey had to take that for a *maybe*.

The barn was full of girls when she walked in; the normal crowd at their normal afternoon routine of gossiping, grooming, and griping. Gwen was out in the arena, a streak of speed on the white pony she was schooling over fences.

Sky was in the cross-ties grooming James, who was already saddled, and Casey had to push down a wave of disappointment, an unpleasantness which started in her stomach and rose up towards her throat. She scolded herself not to be so sensitive about things. Why should she be bothered that Sky was going to ride James, instead of her? It was just that Gwen had ridden him on Saturday, and although Casey had enjoyed her ride on Sage, a speckled red roan lesson horse who was a little more plucky than old reliable Mikey, she had still missed the Thoroughbred. She'd hoped to get back on him today.

Well, Casey told herself, she needed to get over it. James wasn't *her* horse, and he wasn't going to be. Casey knew this. She just… really liked him. Maybe more than she had realized.

She put her hand out and James reached his muzzle out to sniff at her palm. He loosened his lips and let his big pink tongue lap at her fingers. Casey burst out laughing. "Again with the licking?"

Sky looked over at her and smiled. "Hey Casey! If you want to get Sage tacked, you can go ahead and warm up without me. I have someone coming to see James in about ten minutes. I'll be ready for you as soon as I've shown him to these buyers. Is that okay? Sorry, they were kind of last-minute."

Casey opened her mouth to say it was just fine, but no words came out. She looked helplessly at James, who was still licking her hand with dog-like dedication. His dark eyes regarded her with a calm expression. Casey thought he might be the kindest horse she'd ever met. He was so gentle, so careful when he could be rowdy and shove his weight around.

"Thanks!" Sky said, not waiting for an answer, and ducked under the cross-tie rope to grab his bridle. "I gotta hustle. They're serious but they're only in town today and then they're back in a week. Just here to get on a cruise ship tomorrow and decided to go horse-shopping in their spare time." She laughed. "Some people have all the luck."

Casey backed away to let Sky get the bridle on, her mind stuck on the idea of James being sold, James leaving the barn. How was this happening already? He'd only been here about two months, just a few days longer than she had been here. He was still green as grass. Sure, he was doing solid flatwork in the arena and Sky had let her hop him over a few cross-rails just to see if he'd like the idea (he did, a lot).

But he still got fast when other horses were cantering around him. He still couldn't be cross-tied in the aisle, it had to be in one of the bays with a rail behind him in case he forgot himself and went backwards. He had terrible transitions between gaits; he had no notion of tucking in his head or rounding his back or bending around turns. He went around the arena like a battleship half the time, ponderous and hard to guide with anything like precision. He had never been to a horse show, he had no ribbons or "miles" that could add value for a prospective buyer.

To Casey, James still seemed like a baby racehorse. But maybe to Sky, maybe to everyone else who had been riding all these years while Casey had been sitting at a desk, he was just another prospect who needed a little work: a green horse who was on his way, not just ready to *start* a career, but already actively working on his career.

It had just happened so fast.

"Oh, crap. Can you hold him for me really quick?" Sky was standing in front of her, the reins held out, her phone in one hand. "I just need to run to my desk and grab their phone number quick."

Casey took the reins as Sky ran down the aisle. She looked James in the eyes. He blinked at her, and blew warmly on her hands. She felt an upwelling in her chest that was something like ecstasy and something like pain, and from deep within her she realized it was the agony of love.

"Shit," she whispered.

Chapter Seventeen

The following Friday afternoon, Brandon's Saturday morning came miraculously free. He texted Casey party details with a few happy-face emojis. *New roll-out postponed. Nothing to do tomorrow. We can to go Kim and Mike's birthday brunch after all!*

She glared at her phone mutinously.

"Problems?" Leslie was passing by her desk, a few folders tucked under her arm and a clay mug of something herbal-scented in her hand. "You look like someone gave you bad news."

"Annoying news. I was planning on riding in the morning, but my boyfriend seems to have accepted brunch plans."

"Oh, brunch." Leslie laughed. "You kids and your brunch. Is it really worth all the hype?"

"It is if you like sitting around by the beach drinking with friends in the middle of the day," Casey answered honestly. "Which, generally speaking, I have always liked. I just wanted another ride this week."

With this second ride, she had been hoping against hope, she might get to ride James. On Wednesday evening she'd obediently tacked up Sage while the horse-shoppers gave James a try-out. The pretty, lanky teen who rode him was more than competent enough to handle James's green-horse antics, and she seemed to like him, lingering to play with him in the cross-ties after her ride was finished. Her parents weren't ready to commit, though. They just said their ship would be back in port in a little over a week, and they'd have an answer for Sky by then. Sky had given them a twinkly-eyed smile and said she hoped James would still be available by then.

Casey hadn't had the guts to ask if that was an idle piece of sales banter, or a real threat. What if James was already a hot sales horse with lots of interest? What if Sky's inbox was full of email inquiries from serious buyers with plenty of cash to spend?

What *if?* Casey tried to remind herself of a few simple facts when this impossible question popped up in her brain. One: she'd known from the start that James was going to be a sales horse. Two: she'd only ridden him a few times, as a favor from Sky, and she had never planned on buying a horse anyway. Three: she had *no business* falling in love with him or any other horse.

Casey reminded herself she needed to learn how to guard her heart, and be more careful around horses, or she was just going to keep getting hurt. Like she was hurting now, before the sales horse she'd fallen for was even out of the barn.

Her self-lecture went on: James would be a valuable lesson to learn. This was part of being an adult, like when she gave up Wilson to concentrate on her future. She had made that decision for her future-self's brain, not for her aching present-self's heart.

Great job, Casey, she congratulated herself. *You are adulting like a pro. Don't think about James.*

"You okay?" Leslie was still surveying her with a concerned expression. The office came back into focus around her.

Casey realized her shifting emotions must have shown on her face, and she made an effort to compose her features. But her smile felt like it was gummed up at the corners with sticky school paste. There was nothing real about it.

Suddenly, Leslie leaned in close. Casey started to draw back in alarm, then made herself wait. Leslie was trying to be an ally. It wasn't her fault she was bad at social cues. The older woman's breath, medicinal with anise, tickled her ear. "Gwen told Sky that girl wouldn't be a good fit for James."

Then she stood up, waggled her fingers in a goodbye, and went off down the hall, leaving Casey blinking, alone in her cubicle with a new set of troubling questions to work through.

Like what the hell was *that* supposed to mean? Did Leslie think it would help her somehow if James stuck around a few more days? How was Casey supposed to get over her crush on him if he just stayed in the barn? Casey suddenly realized James *had* to leave, or she was just going to fall deeper and deeper into love. That teenager's parents needed to buy him before Casey... what?

Before she did *what,* exactly?

Rather than face the question, Casey looked back down at her phone, at the cheerful group text confirming brunch at eleven on Saturday, a date and hour when she wanted to be holding the lead-rope of a grazing horse after a satisfying ride, and then back up at her computer monitor, which was filled with the code for an email about washing machines.

She stared at the screen with a sudden hatred. *This* was what she had traded Wilson for. *This* was what she had traded for everything good and real about a horse: an email about *washing machines.* She felt a nearly overwhelming urge to just walk out of the office, away from the evidence of her life-ruining decisions.

If Mary hadn't walked by just then, giving her a beady-eyed glance as she passed, Casey thought she might actually have done it.

The birthday brunch was held at Orson Oceanside, an extremely sleek new restaurant overlooking the Atlantic. In keeping with current trends for acceptable brunch parameters, the cocktails were all decorated with fresh herbs and everything on the menu seemed to come with lobster. Kim and Mike were nuzzling each other, practically sitting on one another's laps, as usual. Casey couldn't remember whose birthday it actually was; Kim and Mike looked remarkably similar, and they were really Brandon's friends, anyway. Casey never knew what to say to the genius-level computer programmers he tended to befriend, but luckily Heather and Alison were there, plus Brandon's semi-normal college friend Monique and her boyfriend, Saul.

Everyone was dressed to the nines in honor of the birthday boy, which for Cocoa Beach meant the ladies were wearing sundresses, the men were wearing button-downs over their shorts, and everyone was wearing their nice flip flops which they reserved for special occasions—because in Florida, nice flip flops were an essential part of anyone's wardrobe.

Brandon was receiving a lot of attention for his new leather flip flops, which were from Hawaii, and everyone was taking turns admiring them when Casey came back from the restroom.

"We're looking at your boyfriend's feet!" Heather announced as she sat down again. "Very impressive."

"It's always bothered me that his second toes are longer than his big toes," Casey said. "Have you noticed that?"

"That's normal," Saul said. "Mine are, too." He lifted up his hairy legs to display his toes for all to see.

"Ewww," Monique said, wrinkling her nose. "How have I never noticed this? I feel like I've never seen your feet, and now I can never unsee them."

"Another relationship destroyed," Brandon said mock-seriously. "Casey, how could you?"

Casey wasn't particularly interested in the conversation. Gwen had texted her earlier that morning to tell her there was another interested buyer coming to see James today, and all she could do now was stare at her phone, waiting for updates. Between the cruise ship kid and now this, she was a total nervous wreck.

"Casey, your little toe looks smashed," Alison observed, peering under the table. "Did one of those horses step on you?"

"What? Oh, no," Casey said absently. "I think my riding boot is just squeezing it a little. I should probably invest in custom boots at some point. My feet are shaped kind of strange and nothing really fits them. It doesn't matter when you're always wearing sandals, so I didn't think about it much before."

"Custom boots," Kim remarked, impressed. "How fancy!"

"How pricey," Brandon murmured.

Casey shot him a look. He raised his eyebrows at her.

"Think of it like a new hard drive or something," she replied caustically, rolling her eyes.

"Whoa," Monique pronounced. "Casey is on fire today. Are those toes really getting you down, sweetie? Brandon, let's go to Macy's and get you some closed-toes after brunch. You have to stop torturing your girl with those messy metatarsals."

Casey's phone buzzed and she picked it up quickly. *They are coming late but Sky is really excited,* Gwen had typed. *Says they are very serious.*

"Shit," Casey whispered.

"Lobster egg rolls," a waiter in white linen and black bowtie announced. "For the table?"

"That's right," Mike said. "In the middle."

"Birthday lobster egg rolls!" Kim sang. "This is the dream."

The waiter set down the plate and everyone reached for a bite. Everyone except Casey, who was typing furiously back to Gwen, demanding constant updates.

"Everything okay?" Brandon asked.

"No," Casey said dismally. "I mean—yes. Nothing I can do about it."

"What's going on?" Alison asked.

"Just a horse thing," she said, waving it away.

But Alison wasn't ready to let it go. "Is someone sick? I heard horses can get sick really easily. Someone told me once if you look at a horse wrong it can just drop dead."

That someone had been Casey, she remembered, back when they were both in high school. And she'd been explaining why she could no longer afford to go on the science class snorkeling trip in Key Largo, as Wilson had just presented her parents with a traumatically high vet bill for a prolonged episode of colic.

"No one is sick. Just… a horse I like to ride is up for sale and it looks like he might sell really quickly. I'm going to miss him."

"That's terrible!" Alison looked horrified. "Right after you start riding again, too? Ugh, that sucks a lot."

"Yeah, it's too bad they didn't hang onto him for a while," Monique agreed. "Well, that will be you someday! Once you've been at it for a few years, I bet you'll be ready to buy your own horse."

Casey's gaze shot back to Brandon. He was looking at Monique with a worried expression. He was wondering, Casey suspected, *why* she would say something so provocative to his horse-crazy girlfriend. Or, perhaps he was realizing there was only one possible ending to the road Casey had embarked upon.

Casey felt like she was just realizing it too.

"I couldn't possibly buy a horse," she said, to chase the truth away. "It would be crazy to buy a horse."

"But if you like him…" Monique shrugged. "I mean, you were going to buy a horse eventually, right? My cousin has three, but she only needs one, so I know how you horse-people work." She grinned wickedly.

"I don't know about eventually…" Casey's voice trailed off as new ideas began to crowd into her brain, rudely elbowing her old certainties out of the way.

What the hell had she been thinking? Casey's brain demanded. What, she was just going to live the rest of her life taking riding lessons twice a week? Falling for horses and watching them move on to new riders? Breaking her heart over and over?

That was insane, right?

She felt like someone had flipped a switch in her brain, and black was suddenly white.

Casey put her hands flat on the table and took deep breaths, willing her racing heart to slow down. But she thought maybe that horse had already left the gate, and there would be no stopping now until they'd crossed the finish line.

"Isn't a horse an investment?" Alison asked. "I mean, could you sell him for more money down the road?"

"She could," Monique told her. "But she won't. My cousin never will and she *always* says they're investments. Her husband always believes her, too. Brandon, believe Casey when she tells you that, okay? She deserves that level of trust."

"Right," Brandon said, his eyes narrowing.

"I just wasn't planning on buying a horse," Casey said desperately, more to herself than anyone at the table. "I mean, I love him. He's great to ride. That doesn't mean I want to buy him."

"But you *should* buy him," Monique said eagerly. "It's true love! I can see it in your face!"

Heather was a little more cautious. "Can you afford a horse?"

"Horses are very expensive, aren't they?" Saul asked. "I heard horses are *mad* expensive."

"Love is more important than *money,*" Alison interjected sternly.

"Not really," Brandon said.

Everyone looked at Brandon, aghast. Even Saul looked uncertain.

Brandon quickly realized his error. "I mean... you can't feed a horse love. Or use love to cover his vet bills. It has to be budgeted out first. That's all I'm saying."

Casey hardly knew what was happening around her. Things had gone from zero to sixty with alarming rapidity—but it was starting to stop feeling insane and instead feel so, so right.

She could make the math work and buy James. It was so obvious! Why had she thought she could make do with riding lessons? Of *course* she was going to buy a horse sooner or later. Why not now? Why not James?

The new ideas began to cheer in her brain; they'd bullied their way in and they'd won the day.

Suddenly everything made so much sense!

She leaned over and planted a kiss on Brandon's cheek. "Let's make a budget," she said. "Let's work it out. I know we can."

Another waiter arrived, tray of champagne flutes in his hand. "More mimosas?"

"A toast!" Kim cried, snatching a glass from the tray. "To Casey and Brandon's first child!"

The waiter's smile slipped ever so slightly.

"He's a horse," Mike corrected. "Alcohol is allowed to new horse owners."

"It's *encouraged,*" Casey said, laughing.

"Hear, hear!" everyone called, laughing and clinking glasses. Brandon gave her a pained smile as she tipped her flute against his. Casey just grinned at him in return. *This is happening,* she thought.

Then, before their lobster-studded entrees had even arrived, she sent a text to Sky. *Don't do anything with James before I've talked to you first.*

You got it, Sky replied.

The response came back so quickly, there was no way Sky had needed to pause for a moment to register her own surprise.

Sky had totally seen this coming.

Maybe she had even planned it.

Chapter Eighteen

The drive home from the beach was a quiet one. Brandon concentrated on the road, which was filled with out-of-state drivers looking for restaurants and hotels they'd never seen before. Casey's mind was working overtime, darting around everything from financials to whether or not she could fit in a ride that afternoon.

She gazed out of her window, trying to gauge the potential for an afternoon thunderstorm by the fluff status of the cumulus clouds floating over the flat Florida landscape.

Right now, they were at large cotton-ball status, but those harmless-looking cumulus could upgrade themselves to massive thunderstorms in an impressively quick progression. Far off in the northwest sky, she could just glimpse distant clouds towering heavenward, their icy tops blown into flat tabletops.

Those clouds meant business, so she'd have to hustle. She hoped Sky had some time for her. It was so difficult trying to ride in the afternoons!

They crested the causeway bridge and the car's hood tipped downward. The river lifted towards them, lined with sabal palms and fishermen.

"You're quiet," Brandon remarked.

"Wondering if I can fit a lesson in this afternoon," she replied truthfully.

"I see."

There was no judging his tone. She resumed cloud-watching. He'd say something when he was ready to. She just hoped he wasn't going to launch straight into a fight. It would be nice if they could be civil about this. Yes, she'd decided to buy a horse without his input, but she had her own money. She had that right.

She wasn't in the wrong here.

Definitely not.

They were gliding back to sea level before Brandon opened his mouth again.

"I was hoping," Brandon said, spacing out his words carefully in a way which indicated he was trying to avoid saying anything too sharply, "I was *hoping* we could go on a cruise in the fall. We talked about it, remember? Before I picked up this contract? We said when things slowed down, we could take a vacation."

Casey nodded. Of course, she remembered. That had been the day she'd first met Sky. She remembered everything about that day: the feelings, the sights, the conversations. "I'm sorry, Brandon, but I don't think this changes that. We can still take a cruise."

She had been working on a horse-keeping budget in her mind ever since the snap decision at the brunch table, carrying the ones and moving the decimal points around in her mind. There would be the purchase price, there would be the equipment cost, there would be the monthly costs of board and hoof care and routine healthcare, and then she needed to have a slush fund for veterinary emergencies. She had a general idea of what she thought she'd offer for James, so hopefully the first number wouldn't be a surprise. She would need her own tack and equipment, but Sky could help point her in the right direction for an inexpensive and well-fitting saddle, and she could buy a lot of other things second-hand, online.

As for monthly costs, Sky's board wasn't cheap, but she'd done a quick search of local barn rates while they'd been waiting for a second round of mini-lobster rolls, and found Sky was actually her best bet if she wanted a riding ring instead of a muddy field, and a barn that wasn't a glorified shed. Sky's restored center-aisle barn and shadeless arena were a bargain compared to some of the new barns with their fancy covered arenas. Hell, it was so cheap she'd practically lose money by *not* buying a horse and keeping him there.

Okay, slow down, she told herself. That was bad math and worse logic. She was getting carried away.

But who wouldn't be carried away with excitement right now? She, Casey, *she* was going to *buy* James! She was going to own a horse! A gorgeous, five-year-old horse. For the next fifteen years of her life, if she was careful, she'd have a lovely Thoroughbred horse of her own to enjoy, train, maybe even compete!

And for the next twenty-five, if she was careful, she'd have a Thoroughbred horse to feed and keep healthy.

Well, retirement was its own beast, she told herself reassuringly. She would worry about finding a horse to ride while paying for James's twilight years once that problem had arrived. For now, she was young, James was young, there were no cares in the world that couldn't be handled with optimism and a credit card with a good interest rate—the latter being something she had now, and something she hadn't even understood back when she was a kid and selling Wilson and giving everything up.

Everything was different now. Different, and better. Being thirty-something was infinitely better than being twenty-*anything.* Why did people say adulting sucked? Adulting was cool as hell, when you could do things like buy yourself a horse because you wanted to.

"Casey? What do you think?"

"What? Oh, I'm sorry. I didn't hear you." She glanced at Brandon, shrugged her shoulders. "Distracted. You know how I get. What's up? I promise I am paying attention now."

"I *said* I don't see how buying a horse fits into our cruise plans. And then I asked what you thought."

"We can still take a cruise. I don't have to tuck him into bed every night."

"I meant financially."

"Well, fine, it might be a little squeeze. Maybe we just scale down the stateroom a little bit, go for four nights instead of seven. But it still works."

Brandon sighed in a way which suggested he had not wanted to scale back his stateroom or go for four nights instead of seven. "Are you really going to just jump into this?"

"I'm doing the numbers first," Casey explained. "So I know what I'll need each month. I'll write them down when we get home, and I'll show you then."

"But your mind is made up."

Casey shrugged and looked back out the window. They were still surrounded by the wide, tranquil waters of the Banana River; driving on the long, narrow causeway between the barrier island and the mainland. It was just wide enough for the four-lane road, the scrubby grass on the shoulders, and the long-legged egrets fishing in the tangles of mangrove which lined either shore.

Everything in their part of the world was like this: a tiny piece of land with just enough room for humans and their interests to balance, with water lapping all around them. Swamps and springs, rivers and beaches, canals and ditches: Casey and Brandon had made their home in a precarious place. People here looked out at all that water and they thought of recreation: fishing, jet-skis, kayaking, sailing. Casey looked at it and thought about the problems it posed: flooded pastures, softened hooves, a general shortage of land to ride on and graze horses on. She'd always seen it this way; she'd never bought in to the water-first lifestyle of most of her friends here, even while she was accepting their grown-up play-dates to skip around on Sea-Doos.

She'd always been thinking of horses, she realized. Even when she hadn't thought she was, they were lurking there, permanent residents in the back of her mind.

This passion wasn't going anywhere. Why deny it?

"My mind is made up," she told him with finality in her tone, "but to be fair, it was made up a long time ago. This is just all of the pieces falling into place."

Brandon's silence was like a third person in the car, somehow filling up all the extra space around them. Casey felt it pressing against her. She turned her face back to the window to escape it. The low buildings of the barrier island swept by, vacuum cleaner repairs and ammo dealers and tropical fish outlets.

"Casey," Brandon finally said, braking for a sudden red light, "suppose this is a phase. A moment in your life. This is a lot of money and a whole living creature that you're taking on with almost no thought."

She bit her lower lip to avoid shouting in reply. She told herself there was no point in replying, because he wouldn't have listened to anything she'd said anyway. He wanted to believe it was a phase? Fine. Let him think that. Let him think that for the next year as she enjoyed riding *her* horse. Maybe that would be enough time for him to accept that being an equestrian was simply who she was, the girl she'd always been, deep inside.

The seconds ticked by. The light stayed obstinately red. Casey watched a man on a bicycle wobble along the cracked shoulder of the road, one hand on the handlebars and one hand cradling an enormous paper bag from Burger King. Really enormous, like, there must be enough food in that bag to feed ten people. She wanted to point the man's load out to Brandon, but figured he was in no mood for it.

"I wouldn't just buy a boat without your approval," he said

finally.

The light turned green. The bicyclist wobbled onward, never having paused for the red, completely confident in his timing.

Casey turned to stare at Brandon, incredulous. He kept his gaze on the road. Avoiding her, she thought. Because he knew he'd said something idiotic. "A boat is not a *horse*. That's just not… these things are not comparable." She tried to focus all of her ire on the first half of his sentence. She didn't know *what* to say about the second half.

"It's a big expensive investment with ongoing bills," Brandon persisted. "In that way, they are comparable. It's a financial decision which affects us both. In *that* way, they're comparable. They're a hassle to get rid of when you decide you don't want them any more. Again, a fair comparison!"

His voice was so technical, so monotone, like he was schooling her, giving her a lesson he was already bored with teaching. Casey felt a sudden and dangerous desire to wrench open the car door and fling herself out of the car, to run away from him, to scare him half to death. She'd do it at a red light—she wasn't an idiot—but she'd take off so fast he wouldn't know what to do, and she'd be halfway down the next street before he got the car going, and he'd be panicking and he'd be sorry and this entire conversation would disappear, he'd never bring it up again.

The car stopped at a red light.

Casey sat quietly, her face turned away from Brandon.

She didn't jump out of the car.

Except in her mind, she did. Over, and over, and over.

When Casey came downstairs that afternoon wearing breeches and a long-sleeved sun-shirt, Brandon was watching golf in the living room. She paused in the doorway, giving him an opportunity to speak to her, but he didn't look up from the game.

Silently fuming, she went into the kitchen and started rifling through the junk drawer for her checkbook. She'd last used it to cover a plumbing disaster which had left two inches of gray water on the kitchen floor. There hadn't been enough in their shared account to cover that particular repair, coming so quickly on the heels of a roof repair after a hurricane last summer. Casey had *cheerfully* covered the plumber's bill with money from her own savings account. No questions asked! No request for repayment! No further conversation necessary!

She found the checkbook and slipped it into her purse with a prim smile. She had the money. She was getting the horse. What better way to spend it? What on earth had she been hoarding savings away for, if not this? She and Brandon had no plans. They lived entirely in the present. There was no house fund, like some couples might have shared—houses here were ridiculously expensive and the insurance, because of hurricane season, was ruinous. There was no wedding fund, either, because neither of them saw much reason to get married. The future was still an abstract thought to Casey, but at least now, she thought, she'd have a horse in hers.

She stalked back down the hall, past the quiet living room, and stopped in the entry to pull on her boots. There was a small but earnest patter of applause from the golf game.

Casey figured she'd better say something before she left. She lifted her voice to carry above the polite clapping. "Text me what you want for dinner and I'll pick it up. I'm feeling fried chicken, if you need a hint."

There was a long moment of silence. She heard Brandon rearranging himself on the couch, probably so that he could look through the door, see her standing in the entry, bent over her the zippers of her boots.

He said: "Are you going to own that horse when you come

home?"

"I hope so," she replied, looking up and meeting his gaze steadily.

He looked disappointed. "I think this is a mistake."

"You could try being happy for me, instead."

"I'll be happy for you when you do this in six months, or a year. Not now. Not after two months."

She'd been lifting her purse strap over her shoulder, ready to turn on her heel and stomp out, but his words made her pause. Was six months really all it would take to make Brandon okay with all of this? He just wanted a longer waiting period before she bought a horse?

But James wasn't going to be around in six months. Casey's heart twisted at the thought. He'd be gone, in someone else's barn, his soft nose wobbling as he begged someone else for cookies.

And maybe that was the worst of it: James didn't need *her*. James would thrive with anyone. He was a lovely, willing, easy-going horse. James would make whoever took him home incredibly happy, and as long as they were good to him and kept the treats coming, he'd be happy with them.

Casey just needed that person to be *her*. She couldn't bear the thought of him going off with someone else, being their best friend, being their sweet, special boy when he was *her* sweet, special boy. The way Wilson had been, before she'd sold him.

She couldn't stand the thought of falling in love with another horse and then watching him load up in a trailer and leave her forever. Not again.

"It's this horse, Brandon," Casey said softly, wishing he'd understand, wishing he'd just *try*. "And this horse is right now. There's no James six months from now. I didn't mean for this to happen. It just did. Can you please understand that?"

"I could," Brandon agreed, "if I was sure it was a good idea."

"Sometimes things aren't good or bad," Casey snapped, finally done with the conversation. "They just *are.*"

Chapter Nineteen

The drive to the barn had never felt longer.

"Come on," Casey muttered at stoplights. "Come on, come on, come on."

It was a mantra, a request to the universe. Just *come on*. Just something, please, work out.

She drove up the barn lane faster than she should have, the car bouncing and complaining on the ruts, but remembered to slow down when the trees cleared, so no one would remark upon how unsafely she was driving around horses and kids. She didn't need any criticism now. She just needed a straight line from this moment to the moment in the future where she had secured James, the horse was hers, and there was no turning back.

Why would she want to turn back?

She got out of the car and waved to Sky, who was perched on the roll-top in the middle of the arena, shouting directions to a beginner class.

"I'll be inside in fifteen minutes!" Sky yelled from across the distance. "We'll talk!"

Casey went into the barn feeling like she would explode before fifteen minutes had passed. She stalked down the aisle and into the tack room, looking for a place to sit and calm herself down. Her heart was racing and her hands were shaking. Her body's reaction seemed like too much, but she felt like she was about to click on *buy now* for a concert a million other people were waiting for. What if she didn't get tickets? What if she was shut out?

There was a little cluster of girls in the tack room. Gwen broke free of them the moment Casey burst inside. She grabbed Casey's arm and steered her back into the barn aisle, walking them down a few stalls until they were out of easy eavesdropping range. Casey was grateful for the distance; some girls had followed them out and she could feel their stares on her back. Somehow, everyone must know she wanted James. Nothing escaped the eagle eyes and sharp ears of teenage girls.

"Well?" Casey hissed urgently. "What happened with the buyer?"

"Talented junior rider," Gwen said gravely. "Looking for a jumper prospect. Wants to take him up through the levels, take him to college with her. She really liked him."

Casey felt a frown creasing her forehead, deeply irritated by the existence of girls in this unfair world who could buy a horse *to take* to college, instead of having to sell their horse to pay for tuition. It made her doubly determined to buy James right now, tonight. No spoiled rich teenager was getting her hands on that horse. "Well, that's too bad for her," she hissed. "She'll just have to keep looking, won't she?"

Gwen's eyebrows went up. "So you're really serious? You're going to buy him?"

"You don't think I should?" Casey was taken aback by the younger girl's reaction. She had counted on Gwen's support in all of this. If no one else believed James was the right horse for her, at least Gwen would back her up. Gwen thought she could do train him. Gwen was...

Gwen was *fourteen.*

She'd counted on a fourteen-year-old's support, but not her boyfriend's.

The realization came over her all at once, shocking and cold, as if she'd turned her back on a calm ocean and then been slammed from behind with a rogue wave.

Casey wondered if she had somehow regressed and gone back to her teenage self after spending so much time hanging out with all of these young and vengeful girls. Was she buying James because she loved him, or because she was trying to keep other people off of him?

What if those were the same things?

"I think you should, absolutely," Gwen said. "If you can."

"I can buy him." She had the checkbook in her purse. She had the money in the bank. She had the will to sign her name.

"Well, then." Gwen shrugged. "Make Sky your offer, and tell her that even if it's not what she was asking, you'll keep him here and keep riding him here, and she'll take it. I've seen her do it before. A boarder is worth more to her than selling a horse to someone who is going to take it away, even if they pay more."

"What did she ask for him? Were you there?"

Gwen told her the figure.

Casey swallowed. "I don't have that much." If she spent that much, she wouldn't have a slush fund for emergencies. She wouldn't have enough for board and tack. She sensed her plan starting to collapse. Her hands were jammed in the slim pockets of her breeches, and she could feel them shaking wildly. Her body was spinning completely out of control.

"That's my point," Gwen said urgently. "Offer what you *can*. You're her client. This other girl would be paying someone else board and training."

"Got it," Casey said, calming down a little, although she was still pretty horrified at the price the other buyers were willing to pay. On paper, James was nothing but a green-broke ex-racehorse, for heaven's sake! Sure, he knew the basics and could get around an arena without giving anyone a heart attack, but back when she was a kid, a horse like James would have been practically free.

Either things had changed, or Sky was extremely good at horse dealing.

Or maybe, she thought hopefully, maybe James was simply *that nice* of a show prospect.

There was a sudden parade of horses clattering into the barn; Sky's lesson had ended. The first kids inside claimed the cross-ties with hoses in triumph, the stragglers had to tie up in the aisle to wait on the hoses to come free. Last of all came Sky, laughing loudly and encouraging a tween with a balky paint horse to keep on tugging at those reins. She saw Casey with Gwen, and her smile became knowing.

"Casey! Just the girl I want to see."

Casey expected to be closeted in Sky's office, but when Sky waved her over to stand in front of James's stall, she realized the trainer was more seasoned than that. Why sequester her in the confines of the office when the horse pulling at her heartstrings was right there, ready to step in with fluttering nostrils and big hopeful eyes should the negotiating get ugly? Casey wondered if Sky was going to strong-arm her, and if she was going to end up promising more than she could afford.

Her fears of being less a friend and more a business prospect lurched back upwards from wherever they'd been hiding, happy to be of service again.

Sky slid open the stall door, and they stepped inside.

Within the heavy wooden stall walls, the noise of the kids untacking and hosing off their horses was just muffled enough for a quiet conversation to take place. James was delighted to see them, especially without a halter in sight. He nosed at Casey's pockets, hoping for cookies, but she had left his treats in the car, too rattled to remember them.

"You wanted to see me before I sold him," Sky said.

"That's right." Casey hesitated, running her fingers up James's nose. He wiggled his upper lip along her palm, his whiskers tickling her skin, and she was instantly lost. Any misgivings she'd had went right out the window at the familiar touch of his affectionate nuzzling.

"I've *got* to buy him, Sky. I'll keep him here and train with you and everything, but I've got to buy him."

Sky smiled happily, and Casey knew for certain that every minute of this, since the moment she'd stepped onto the property, had been one long play, scripted and directed by Sky herself. The thing was, Casey thought, she didn't even mind.

"I know you do," Sky said, her voice warm. "Let's make it happen."

Chapter Twenty

For that entire first, heady week of horse ownership, Casey rode James without instruction, and without incident. In order to fund the massive upfront of buying James, like paying two months' board—because Sky, like any other landlord, required a hefty safety deposit— she had to cancel both of her riding lessons for that week.

"And I'll have to drop down to one lesson per week," she told Sky nervously. Casey felt like she was letting Sky down by cancelling one of her weekly lessons, as if she was the only one keeping Sky's business running. "I hope that's okay."

"You'll be just fine," Sky told her absently, flipping through her lesson book and drawing a quick line through each of Casey's Wednesday lessons. "I wouldn't have let you buy James if I didn't think you could handle him. If he gives you any trouble, we can address that in your Saturday lesson. Just remember not to get into a fight with him." She smiled sweetly at Casey. "No one is going to win that fight."

Casey had only been thinking of finances and had not considered that dropping down to one lesson per week might threaten her ability to continue James's training. Now, she felt a sudden flutter in her stomach. What if she wasn't really capable of training an ex-racehorse to be a nice, quiet amateur horse?

The questions started flying around her brain. Did she actually remember the things she had done as a teenager? And why on earth had she not asked herself this *before* she'd bought herself an off-track Thoroughbred who was proficient in walking, trotting, cantering, jumping off-balance, and not much else? Was she as good at training horses as she was at her own crippling self-doubt? *Not likely!*

Casey walked out into the barn aisle feeling sweaty and a little sick to her stomach.

Everything had been done in such a rush, she thought, falling headfirst into a full-on panic attack. She'd fallen for James, she'd found out James was a hot item on the local market, she'd gotten that breakneck encouragement from her (non-equestrian) friends to buy him right away, she'd defied Brandon and bought him, and she was in the process of buying an incomprehensible amount of money on *stuff* for him because horses needed things, they needed entire wardrobes for every season, from boots to bonnets and everything in between, and it was *all* her responsibility.

This whole situation had cascaded out of control so quickly! The only person who had urged her to slow down and consider her options more carefully had been Brandon, and now they were barely on speaking terms.

Oh, and now she had a horse who needed a substantial amount of work, *years* worth of work, and she hadn't done this sort of training in more than a decade.

Oh, *god.*

James was leaning over his stall guard, still thrilled with the novelty of the open door and his ability to look up and down the aisle instead of being shut up behind bars. Casey had been so delighted with the stall guard when it arrived. She'd hustled to attach the snaps to the screw eyes that were already in the door-frame, then rolled back his door so that James could enjoy his new perspective. Several of the horses in the barn had stall guards, and she'd considered the purchase a must.

Sky had wandered down the aisle and given it an appraising look. She patted James on the neck and asked him how he liked his view. Then, she'd explained to Casey that she didn't mind private horses having stall guards, but, she'd stressed, they could only be used when the owner was in the barn, and Casey had to be careful the horse didn't start getting territorial and nipping at other horses as they were led past. She'd given this directive to Casey with a hint of sternness, giving Casey the impression she should have asked permission before putting up the stall guard.

Casey had felt very small at that moment.

Now she pushed James back into his stall and slid the door closed. She looked at the door, her hands trembling against the steel bars, while James lurked at the back of his stall, feelings clearly hurt.

She definitely shouldn't have bought the stall guard, Casey thought. She probably shouldn't have bought the horse. All of her instincts were bad and should be ignored for the safety of herself and others.

James came back over, not able to resist a human for long. He lifted his upper lip to her fingers, still gripping the stalls bars, and started wiggling his lip against them, tickling and shoving. His signature move was still endearing enough to clutch at her heart.

Casey couldn't help but draw a long, shuddering breath, swallow a sob, and then start laughing… or was she crying? It was hard to tell the difference.

"You're so silly," she sobbed. "I love you."

James allowed the sharp edge of his front teeth brush against her skin and she flicked out her fingers against his nose, making him jump away before he came right back for more, lips pushing against her skin, gaze fixed on her. It was a game to him, she realized, her heart overflowing with adoration. He was *playing* with her.

Casey understood then that they would make things work.

"Let's tack up, buddy," she told him. He was her horse, and she could ride him whenever she wanted to.

James followed her happily down to the cross-ties. He stood still as she clipped the ties to either side of his halter; he stood quietly while she brushed him and lifted his hooves nicely when she asked him to. Despite his good manners, Casey felt overly aware of every move the two of them made, as if someone passing by would see her and think: *that girl is going to ruin that horse.*

"That's ridiculous," Casey told herself. "You're doing fine. You know what you're doing."

When she lifted the saddle from the rack and approached him with it, though, James sidestepped away and craned his neck in the cross-ties to glare at her, ears half-pinned.

Casey took a step back and wondered what she'd done wrong. There had to be a reason he was angry about the saddle. What if he had an awful pain internally? What if he had ulcers? What if he had, oh, what was that awful vertebrae problem, *kissing spine?* Oh dear god, James was broken. She had a broken horse. Casey's nerves came back, her heart pounding so hard she thought it must be moving her riding shirt upwards with every beat. What was she going to do now?

"Oh, what a silly racehorse," Gwen sang out, walking by with a halter over her shoulder. "Be nice to your mother, James."

James shook his head, the halter buckles rattling, and his ears swung forward again to watch Gwen as she went off down the aisle. Casey took a deep breath. He was just being a little bit of a racehorse, messing around to pass the time. She *knew* that. She had brushed these gestures off before. Why was she panicking over his every little move now? Nothing had changed.

Nothing had changed except ownership.

At the mounting block, James took several minutes to get his act together and stand still. Casey stood on the top step and watched him spin around her, feeling more and more like a failed circus ringmaster, feeling closer and closer to tears. Why couldn't she make him halt and stand for her?

"Stop it, James!" she snapped, yanking on the reins, and James halted and stared at her with wide, shocked eyes before resuming his circle. A few loops later, he settled and stood still. Casey mounted, feeling like an idiot. He was *always* hard to mount without help. Maybe today he was tougher than usual, but that didn't mean she couldn't ride him. What was going *on* with her today?

The arena wasn't any better. Casey was hyper-aware of every twist of his head and ears, somehow forgetting that just yesterday she'd found his curiosity cute. Now she was tense, waiting for a spook showdown the next time he spotted a squirrel or a sparrow who looked suspicious.

Gwen came out to the arena with one of the school ponies who needed a tune-up and mounted him with a quick, easy gesture in the center of the ring. She rode up alongside James and Casey, a pint-sized power rider on a thirteen-hand bundle of trouble. "You look different today," she observed in her blunt way. "Everything okay?"

"Hmm? Oh it's fine, I'm fine," Casey replied, pretending nonchalance. She didn't look down at Gwen. It was important she that she sat precisely in the middle of the saddle with her heels down and her hands just so above James's withers, in case he spooked and bolted. Did it matter that James had never spooked and bolted with her? No, it did not. Anything might happen. He was young and green, and she was old and out of shape, and somehow they had to improve together.

"You're sitting really tense. Like, your ass is sore? Maybe that saddle isn't going to work out for you."

Casey shifted in her saddle, her mind eagerly seizing this new topic of potential trouble. What if the saddle *wasn't* going to work out? She'd bought it used, there was no way to return it. She'd be stuck with a saddle she couldn't use until she convinced someone else to buy it! And she would need that money to buy a new one! She'd be saddle-less for days, weeks, months!

But no, the saddle *was* comfortable, she realized. And if she had to sell it, she'd just go back to borrowing a school saddle until she got the money to buy another one. She let out a gust of breath she'd been holding unconsciously and felt her seat sink down in the saddle.

"Oh, that looks better," Gwen said cheerfully. "Looks like you just forgot to breathe."

Breathing, the most basic of functions, and she'd forgotten to do it. *Finally,* Casey thought. *Something else to berate myself over.*

"Well, I have to hustle and get this little monster warmed up. I need to jump him over a course before his afternoon lessons—he's been stopping at fences again." Gwen waggled her crop as she thumped the pony's sides with her heels, and trotted away.

James watched them with interest, his head high as they moved across the arena. Casey just concentrated on breathing. Maybe if she remembered how to breathe, she'd remember how to ride.

Because right now, everything was feeling pretty confusing.

"Hey, how are things going?"

Casey turned in the saddle. Sky was riding towards her, mounted on a school horse named Moose. "Hey, Sky," she said, trying to sound chipper. "Just got on."

Sky reined up a few feet away. James looked at Moose, who chewed at his bit and sighed. The big bay horse was past the point of being interested in work. Casey had heard Sky trying to pep him up in lessons with some enthusiastic chirrups, but not much got him past a slow jog these days.

"Trying to give Moose a little change," Sky said, patting the horse's neck. "Hoping some jumps will perk him up. He's had beginners on his back for too long, I think. He needs some excitement, don't you, Moose?"

"You think he's so lazy because he's bored?"

"Yeah. He knows his way around a hunter course. I should sell him. I just haven't found the right person for him yet, the right combo for his experience and his size, because he's so damn big... and it's hard to give up a really quiet horse once he's in the lesson program."

Casey had a feeling Moose was the kind of horse she should have bought. If she should have bought a horse at all, which was debatable.

"You look nice on James," Sky said, interrupting her dark thoughts. "You guys are the right match. I'm really glad it worked out."

"Thanks." Casey looked moodily at James's ears, flicking this way and that as he took in his surroundings.

"Everything okay?"

What could she possibly say?

"Boyfriend not too upset with you?"

Casey's eyes met Sky's, astonished.

Sky laughed. "Oh, Casey, I'm sorry! It never fails. Boyfriends do not want horses around. He'll come around. Do something nice for him."

"Like what?" Casey asked woefully.

Sky waggled her eyebrows.

"Oh. Well, I mean..." She was surprisingly embarrassed, but things *had* been pretty quiet in that arena.

"I'm serious! Show him that riding gives you serious muscles. Give him a reason to root for you to ride more." Sky picked up her reins and gave Moose a poke in the ribs with her short spurs. "Let's get to work, old man. Casey, trot that horse around the arena and wear him out. You've been too easy on him this week. I still have to muck his stall, you know. I can tell when he's spinning in circles and when he's tired enough to just stand still and eat!" She laughed and trotted off.

"You hear that?" Casey asked James. "You've been making a mess of your room."

He flicked his ears to her for a moment, then switched his focus back to the other horses in the arena. He tugged at the reins, eager to follow them.

There was nothing else she could do. With her trainer's eyes on her, every barn kid gossiping about her, and Brandon at home angry with her, Casey just had to pick up her reins, deepen her seat, and trot on.

She'd spent so much more than she'd expected.

Casey thought she'd be happy to borrow everything she needed for James until she had saved some extra money for her own supplies, or at least that she'd pick up some essentials on the second-hand market, but she hadn't been prepared for how owning her very own horse things would make her *feel*.

There was no shame in using the school horse supplies to groom her own horse, as she reminded herself over and over during that first week of ownership, but there was no pride or fun in it, either. She *owned* a horse, so she should have her own lovely things, in her own lovely grooming box. Accordingly, aided and abetted by the barn girls and Sky, Casey set about filling up her empty tack locker with shining new supplies.

"That's half the fun of having a horse," said Rachel, a sunny blonde who never stopped smiling. They were sitting on their horses not doing anything in particular; Rachel had done ten minutes of rising trot without stirrups and considered her weekly homework assignment from Sky completed, and Casey had just tacked up, originally planning on taking James for a long, quiet walk around the arena before doing some schooling of her own. But she'd met up with Rachel at the in-gate and they'd been sitting in the watery evening sunlight, swinging their legs free of the stirrups, ever since. James was the sort of Thoroughbred who appreciated a good long pause in his day, and he had already stopped asking Rachel's horse to play with him and instead settled down for a nap. His ears twitched gently, flicking away flies.

"I'm afraid you're right," Casey confessed. "I told my boyfriend I wouldn't go crazy, though. He wanted to go on a cruise at the end of summer, so I have to save for that."

"Boyfriends," Rachel scoffed. "My boyfriend knows if he wants to do anything that isn't hanging out at the barn, he has to pay it for himself."

Casey gazed at the girl next to her and wondered how a sixteen-year-old could have such confident control over her life. "We share a lot of things," she felt compelled to explain. "We live together, we have a townhouse. So we have to be able to split bills and things."

"I'm living alone forever," Rachel declared happily. She ran her hand down her horse's mane, flattening the raven-black flyaways. "As soon as I can, I'm buying a piece of land, putting a trailer on it and just training my horses. No students, no boarders. I don't like having a lot of people around. Maybe a working student to help with stalls."

Casey remembered having a similar dream. Then she'd given it up, gone straight, accepted the American Dream of college and desk job. Maybe Rachel would do that, too. Casey had to believe that; otherwise, she was going to feel jealous of the teenager, and that seemed abnormal. "That sounds really nice. I kind of wish I'd done that. But I'd still want Brandon around. He's really great."

"Guys are fine," Rachel agreed, "if they know their place. Any whining about the horses, though, and he's outta there."

Casey considered whether Brandon was going to start whining about James. Maybe if he was willing to say anything to her at all that wasn't strictly necessary, he would... but they weren't exactly speaking at the moment.

She'd known Brandon could be a passive-aggressive beast when he wanted to be, but even with the knowledge of several years' worth of relationship and co-habitation to guide her, she hadn't been prepared for the cool civility of his silent treatment. The past week had been like living with an excessively polite ghost. Casey almost wished he'd start shouting so they could have the argument she knew was just below the surface, waiting to explode.

If Brandon had been a horse, he would have been terrifying, she thought now, stroking the quiet neck of her snoozing Thoroughbred. She would never have bought him.

She wouldn't have known how to control him.

"Tell me you still have these rust breeches," Arden exclaimed, pouncing on an old photo which Casey's mother, in a state of surprising enthusiasm over her new grand-horse, had posted to Facebook with a helpful tag to Casey's account, so that all of her friends could see it.

In the photo, a pre-teen Casey was sitting on a large pony, sometime in the wilds of the early 1990s, wearing rust-colored breeches she had protested from the moment her mother had brought them home from the second-hand tack shop. Her helmet was equally cringe-inducing: a big bulbous dome which had been nicknamed a "mushroom hat" back in the day, with inch-thick styrofoam lining for the very latest in noggin-saving technology at the time.

"No, thank goodness," Casey sighed, wincing a little at the

memory. "Those were old when I got them. It's good of you to think I might still fit the breeches I wore when I was twelve, but I'd want to spring for a new pair anyway."

"I was thinking more for me."

Casey looked at Arden's slim hips. "Oh, right. You would have fit them."

"I gotta find some," Arden said, shaking her head regretfully. "Rust is so retro. But they're like, impossible to find."

"They made everything out of cheap polyester then," Gwen said, without looking up from her own phone. "None of it survived to the next century."

"If you'd kept these, they'd be worth like, so much, as vintage wear," Arden informed Casey, ignoring Gwen. "I bet all of your old riding stuff was like a treasure trove."

"You guys are acting like I'm a dinosaur," Casey protested. "I'm telling you, these were old when I got them. And *ugly.*"

"I heard Kristin Fontaine has a pair," Gwen remarked. "You know, the rich-ass girl from Royal Palm with that jumper who was on the World Cup team a couple of years ago."

"She would," Arden said darkly. "She has like, twenty thousand Instagram followers. She gets to make her own trends now."

"If rust-colored breeches come back, I'm getting out of horses," Casey said, taking her phone back from Arden. "They're ugly, plain and simple."

Arden and Gwen shared a *look,* which clearly stated Casey was definitely out of touch. Casey shrugged and removed herself from the tack room, wandering out into the quiet barn aisle. The background noise of the stable was all peaceful repetition: a whirring of box fans, the occasional snorts of dozing horses, a shuffle of hooves in sawdust as James walked over and put his head over the stall guard, which she was forcing herself to use despite the guilty feeling Sky's speech had given her.

Casey put her hand out, let him lip gently at her cupped palm. "There's nothing there," she said, but he didn't really mind. He licked at her skin anyway, motivated by salt or boredom or maybe, she thought, maybe even affection. Lord knew she loved him, and he had the things to prove it.

There was a new halter hanging on his hook, dark leather, a brass nameplate shining gently in the sunlight spilling in from the barn doorway. There was a new fly sheet hanging on the blanket bar on his stall door. His bridle path had been freshly clipped with the new trimmers she'd thrown into her order at the last minute, though not his whiskers; those were long and luxuriant—Casey had read enough about the controversy of cutting off a horse's sensitive whiskers to make her vow that James's chin beard would remain forever fuzzy.

There was one reassurance in Casey's life now that made all of the money and all of those looming credit card bills worthwhile: James would never judge her. The girls here would always be younger and cooler than her. Brandon would always be confused and worried by her return to equestrian life. Her girlfriends, though they had championed this choice, would never quite understand how she could give up carefree weekends and oceanside brunch to get hot and sweaty with a horse. But James—he would always regard her with the same dark eyes, the same affectionate touch, the same simplicity of thought: *hi, hello, do you have cookies, where do you want to go next?*

Could horses replace everything else, she wondered?

Should they?

Chapter Twenty-one

"So," Heather said around a mouthful of bacon, "how goes horse ownership?"

"It's amazing." Casey made her declaration without hesitation. She tipped back the dregs of her second mimosa. "It's the best."

Everyone around the table smiled and made little cheering noises.

Casey accepted their appreciation with a broad smile as she accepted a third champagne flute from the circulating waiters. *Why not?*

They didn't need to know the truth: that she'd spent the past week spiraling downwards from a competent, confident rider relearning all of her old skills to a nervous rein-clutching mess who didn't have the first idea of how to ride a novice horse. That she'd been revisiting that old horsemen's wag, *green plus green equals black and blue,* over and over in her thoughts. That she'd been grabbing a handful of mane every time James flicked an ear at a passing butterfly.

She *wasn't* a green rider, she'd been telling herself over and over, but the speech was hitting her psyche with waning success as the days went by. She *felt* like a green rider. Let James make one silly move, and she didn't know how to react.

Last night, while she was riding in the arena with Gwen, had been the worst of it. She'd gotten up the nerve to trot and was posting ungracefully around on the rail, her balance shifting as James first sped up and then slowed down, reading but misinterpreting all of her body's unconscious cues. Sometimes she caught up to Gwen, who was trotting little Shadow around the arena as well, and sometimes she fell way behind them—that was how uncoordinated her riding was, and how inconsistent.

Although, she'd had to admit to herself as she'd hosed James off after the ride, her good little horse hadn't let her ineptitude bother him. He just stuck his nose out and trotted on, and didn't get freaked out by the changes in tempo she inadvertently forced upon him.

There was something to be said for that, anyway. James was a Good Boy. He wasn't going to punish her for being a terrible rider.

The only truly rough moment had come when he'd wanted to canter after Shadow, and she just hadn't felt ready for that shift in speed. He'd tugged at the reins as Gwen's pony went past, lifting his head and gaping his mouth when she tried to hold him back, and for a horrible moment she'd felt her legs sliding behind her and her upper body tipping forward as he wrenched her out of the saddle. Then the end of the arena came rushing up to meet them, the fence naturally slowing him as he turned to avoid a crash, and Casey had managed to get herself back in the middle of the saddle where she belonged.

"Well, you stuck it out," Gwen had said later, listening to Casey's tale of woe in her no-nonsense manner. "So I'm not sure what the problem is."

The *problem*, she'd wanted to shriek, was that she'd forgotten *everything*. And now she was in completely over her head.

"He's just a really good horse," Casey now told her smiling friends, the bubbles of mimosa still fizzing at the back of her throat. "I'm so lucky to have him."

There were smiles and murmurs all around. Alison and

Heather and Tyler and Monique and Saul: they all agreed, Casey was so very lucky.

The only one who didn't say anything was Brandon.

"So I know you want me to admit it," Casey said, pitching her voice higher than usual to overcome the noises all around them: the roar of the ocean surf, the screaming of gulls, the shrieking of children splashing in the waves around them. "And tell you that buying James was a mistake."

Brandon looked at the sky and then at the sand and then back at the sky. Anything, Casey thought, to avoid looking at her. "That's not what I want."

Casey scooped up a broken shell and threw it over the breaking waves. The afternoon sun slanted over them, casting a golden glitter on the water which made everything hard to look at. "You haven't said anything to me besides goodnight, good morning, and 'did you make coffee' in two weeks. You're mad at me. So what *do* you want?"

"I want you to be happy," Brandon responded stiffly. "I want to support you. And since I haven't been able to, I have been quiet about it."

Casey was suddenly glad they'd gone for this walk after brunch.

As their party had broken up early, she'd thought about heading home, changing into riding clothes, and leaving the heavy quiet of their townhouse for the fun of the barn. Even if she was having trouble riding right now, at least the atmosphere there was lighter than the oppressive one at home.

She'd chosen the beach, though, and now they were having a conversation which was long overdue. *Good choice, Casey!*

Now, if only she knew what to say to keep it going. She looked out at the hazy horizon and thought hard, but nothing sage came to mind. Finally she said the only thing she could think of, the only thing she could feel, with the only words she knew held every last drop of honesty within her: "I just don't want you to be angry with me, and I don't know what to do about it."

The waves crashed on the beach; the surf's roar was echoing in her ears. Brandon's pause was long, an agony to wait out. How far was too far, she wondered fleetingly. Had she already told him something about herself which he could not accept?

I shouldn't have to choose, she thought rebelliously. *It's just a horse.*

But there was no such thing as "just" a horse, and she knew it, and now, so did Brandon.

He took a deep breath beside her; she curled up her toes in nervous anticipation. But he didn't have a big speech for her. "I'm just trying to let you do what you think is best, and stay out of your way."

Casey let her muscles relax, watched her toes sink into the wet sand. A bubbling wash of foamy water swept past and then withdrew, dragging shell and silt across the tops of her feet. She spotted a tiny crab, just an instant and then it was gone, pulled out to sea. "I don't know what's best."

"It's too late to second guess now."

She looked up at him sharply, but Brandon wasn't looking at her; he was studying a shell, holding it up to the light, squinting as if he'd plucked a raw diamond from the surf. "What is that?" she asked, desperate for anything else to talk about, now that she knew this conversation was a non-starter, too confusing to even properly begin. If they were having problems, they weren't through with them yet. "Is that a nice shell?"

"It's nothing." He threw the shell into the waves. "Why now, why today? You know I'll get over it eventually. You can't wait me out?" Brandon gave her a half-hearted grin.

She didn't know anything of the sort. How could she know for sure? How could either of them be sure of anything about each other? They were young and they were flexible, they weren't made of granite, their personalities weren't fixed forever. People changed. People got mad and people drifted apart. People decided they could only take so much.

Casey thought all of this but none of it could make its way to her tongue.

"It's not anything," Casey said finally. She watched clear water tumble over her bare feet. "It's nothing."

"*Something's* going on." Brandon stepped in front of her and put his hands on her shoulders. "You have to tell me. Or I'll start guessing."

"It's *nothing.*"

"So it's finally happened," Brandon sighed. "You decided to take up deep-sea fishing and you don't know how to tell me."

"Ugh, Brandon. That's ridiculous."

"So it's finally happened," he tried again. "You're devoting your life to building cat towers."

"I still don't like cats," she reminded him, biting back a grin despite herself.

"So it's finally happened," Brandon intoned solemnly. "You and James are moving to a remote mountaintop to study Zen together."

"A horse monastery sounds like a real thing," Casey mused. "But seriously? James and I could use a little Zen. I thought he'd be teaching me how to be chill, but suddenly he seems being quiet is no longer cool."

"So you guys aren't getting along." Brandon didn't sound triumphant. He just sounded curious. And concerned. "What's going on? Tell me."

"We are, but we aren't. He's a good boy, I swear, but when he does something silly, I just don't know what to do with him. And he's being silly *all* the time, all of a sudden. So I'm realizing… this impulse, I… I bought a green horse when I've only been riding a couple of months. Only an idiot would do that. It was a *big* mistake, Brandon." She stopped short of saying he was right. There were only so many weights a girl could bear at once. "I should have waited."

Brandon absorbed her confession in silence. He nodded slowly, his eyes on hers. Then he took her hands in his. "But, you love him, don't you?"

"I do! I really love him." That part was easy, at least. "And that's why I had to buy him but—did I have to?"

"Look, if you love him, it wasn't a mistake, not for *that* reason, anyway." He grinned and winked at her to take the sting away. "And it's kind of crazy to say you've only been riding a couple of months. You've been riding for years."

"Not *recently,* I haven't. That was all so long ago."

"There's no way you forget how to ride a horse. I refuse to believe that. You'll figure out how to fix this."

"But I don't know how," she said desperately. "I'm not sixteen anymore. I wasn't scared of anything, then. Now I'm… god, I hate to say this, but I *am* afraid. I'm afraid of getting dumped, getting hurt. I'm afraid I just don't know how to train him. I *know* I don't."

"But you did know this stuff, right? You said you trained horses like him before. Racehorses. Well, ex-racehorses."

"When I was a *teenager,*" she insisted, still feeling this was a critical difference which was being overlooked. Teenage girls on horseback were capable of anything. Adulthood changed that. And why were they talking about her training skills now? When had this stopped being about the silence between her and Brandon? When had the silence… stopped?

"But you don't just forget how to do things," Brandon insisted. "It's like riding a bike, right? You pick it all up again, as you go. You're just rusty."

Casey considered this possibility, remembering the way she'd felt when she'd first gotten back into the saddle: that sensation of *rightness,* as if she'd been walking on her hands for years and had suddenly been tipped back onto her feet.

"It *should* be like that," she sighed, looking up at Brandon. "I wish I could explain it better."

"For something which has you turned so completely upside-down, I kind of wish you could, too." Brandon's smile was tender.

They gazed at one another for a long moment, Casey feeling as though the world was slowly righting on its axis, the realization flowing through her that she had waited it out, and now she didn't have to choose—she had *both!* And as for Brandon, he was looking more soft in the lips with every passing second, his face seeming to cross the little gulf between them...

They were both surprised by a big wave, which slapped against their calves with a resounding *clap.* Casey's dress was splashed wet to the waist, and Brandon's shorts didn't fare much better.

Casey shrieked and they both burst into hysterical laughter, doubling over as the water churned around their calves. "Oh my god," Casey panted, hugging herself. "That scared me to *death."*

"A timely distraction," Brandon chortled. "We were both getting too serious for this nice public beach. There are children here, Casey."

They started walking again, splashing their feet in the shallow water. Brandon was pointing out birds, as if their earlier conversation had been decisively ended by the rogue wave. Casey let her mind stay on James, and the fears she had confessed to Brandon. She'd better work through this, she thought, or things weren't going to get better.

She thought about the horses she'd ridden in the past, and all of the silly, foolish, even dangerous equine quirks which she'd overcome. She hadn't paused back then, she'd just ridden through their foolishness and pushed for the result *she* wanted. Why couldn't she get that back?

Casey shook her head at herself. The answer, of course, was that back then, it had all just felt like instinct. The horse moved one way, she moved another way in answer. Amazing to think things ever been so simple.

She turned to Brandon, who was taking a picture of some sandpipers playing in the surf. "Hey, did you ever drop something and then come back to it later?"

"Guitar," Brandon said after a moment's pause, with the air of admitting a weakness.

"Guitar? When?"

"While you've been riding James. I thought... I had some time alone... better do something productive with it that wasn't *working...*"

"Brandon, that's amazing!" Casey turned to him, planted a kiss on his lips. "And is it just coming back to you right away, or is it taking time?"

"It's taking time," he assured her. "I couldn't even remember how to move my fingers at first, I was like a toddler with no hand-eye coordination. Now and then, something good happens and I make nice sound come out of it."

"Oh yes," Casey agreed happily. "That's exactly what I feel like when I'm riding. Most of the time, anyway. And then every now and then, I get it all right."

"Well then," Brandon smiled, "I guess that's just what it's like, when you're an adult."

They kept walking, passing a golden retriever wagging his tail over a sodden tennis ball, three small children being dragged on a surfboard, a waif in a two-piece posing while her friends took photos for her Instagram career. A hippie in beads and fringe rode past on a bicycle. The flotsam of Cocoa Beach floated all around them.

Awash in this sea of good vibes only, Casey ruminated on how much better she was feeling about James, and about Brandon, and about life in general. She thought about Rachel at the barn, daydreaming about a boyfriend-free life with no one to come between her and her horses. She thought about Arden, brazenly declaring there was no point in working a job unless she was utterly passionate about it. She thought about Gwen, who would never let a single human soul get between her and horses. Would they grow up to be horsewomen, or would they grow up like her, lapsed and struggling to get it all back, balanced with the needs of a partner in her life?

Best not to get too hung up on the wisdom of teenagers, she told herself. They were all ideals, and no experience. Better to get her advice from Brandon, a fellow actual Adult, and hey, how great was it that he was relearning how to play the guitar?

Of course, she thought later, looking out the car window as they soared over the causeway bridge towards home, forgetting how to play a guitar probably wouldn't get you killed, except for in very specific thriller-movie situations.

Horses, on the other hand, held a little more danger.

Chapter Twenty-two

Casey overslept on Monday morning, exhausted from a full weekend of brunch and Brandon and horse. She came running downstairs half-dressed, and found Brandon lounging at the kitchen table, munching toast and flicking through the Internet on his laptop.

"I poured you coffee," he announced as she dashed into the kitchen, wild-eyed. "It should be cool enough to drink."

"God bless you," Casey gasped. "I can't believe I slept so late. Why didn't you wake me up?"

"I thought you were up. I got up, you said, 'oh god this sucks,' and then you just didn't come downstairs right away. I thought you were taking a long time upstairs."

"I choose the worst times to talk in my sleep." Casey took a pull of coffee. "Mmm. That's good. I guess I have five minutes for coffee and chit-chat. What are you looking at?"

Brandon smiled to himself. "Cruises."

Casey rolled her eyes. "Do you ever think about anything but vacations?"

"Can you think of anything better?"

Casey could not. But the question was almost comically unfair. Ask her this on any Monday morning, with the prospect of another week to be spent in that godforsaken office, and there was only one possible answer: *get me out of here.*

The walk-in bathtub campaign was this week, she remembered grimly. That's right, folks, a four-part email campaign about walk-in bathtubs. She needed a drink in her hand and an ocean view just to contemplate such a horror. Unfortunately, she had to confront it head-on, sober and landlocked, in about thirty-five minutes.

She needed toast.

"When are you thinking for a cruise?" Casey asked, popping bread into the toaster. "Late September?"

"Most likely," Brandon replied absently, eyes on his screen. "I'm waiting for some late deals, though. They're still pricey."

"That's peak hurricane season. There will be last-minute sales. They're just holding out as long as they can, but we've lived here long enough to know they're relying on us locals to fill their staterooms." Casey wrapped up her toast in a paper towel, and pulled down a tumbler for the rest of her coffee. "I'll be home after riding tonight, unless it rains late and washes me out."

Brandon turned up his face for a kiss like a fifties housewife sending her husband off to work. "Have a nice day, dear."

The early morning humidity was oppressive, but Casey still felt a wrench of unhappiness when she walked into the blue-tinted light of her office building's lobby and the ice-cold air hit her cheeks.

Now that she spend so much time at the barn, Casey had grown even more keenly aware of how much she had loved growing up outside, running around barns, specifically barns in Florida—hot, humid, buggy, stormy Florida. Sure, the place had its shortcomings, most of them fairly substantial: a daily threat of being fried by lightning, felled by sunstroke, or contracting dengue fever all came to mind.

But Florida was so richly *alive,* so violently *awake,* so committed to its own moody, dangerous, beautiful patterns, that Casey didn't see how a person could grow up here and fail to absorb the place into their blood. Spending so much time indoors, with her hair blown back by air conditioning, had numbed her to Florida's summer spell-casting, but now she felt that singing exhilaration in her veins again every time she stepped outside into the bright tropical light, or felt the cold gust of wind from a storm racing her way.

So on her Saturday mornings and weekday evenings out at the stables, Casey felt her spirit move in synch with the world around her, and rejoiced in the outdoors even as she alternately melted into a puddle, ran away from lightning, swatted away mosquitos, and generally fought back against the elements.

During her weekdays, she felt like racing through her work so that she could get back to the farm. All she wanted to do was chase that summertime feeling, to be daring and young again, on horseback beneath the dynamic Florida sky as it shifted from clear blue, to cotton-ball clouds, to dark-bellied, ominous thunderstorms.

She missed so much while she was stuck indoors, she thought gloomily, climbing the stairs to her office.

She missed being outside underneath that changing canopy; she missed the taste of salt on the sea breeze as it rushed inland; she missed the rattling of palm fronds and the first rumble of thunder— sometimes a faraway growl, sometimes a huge crack from somewhere terribly nearby, a storm arriving with the impact of a giant knocking down one's door.

Meanwhile, she was tired of air conditioning (most of the time) and insulated walls which silenced the rumble of thunder, and tinted windows which kept her from seeing the true brightness of the day.

Casey put her things down at her desk and trudged to the kitchen to put away her lunch bag. She poured herself a cup of office coffee and stirred it glumly while she gazed out the stupid blue windows.

She was still standing there, completely checked out, when Mary came up behind her.

"Casey," her manager said lightly. "What's out there?"

Casey nearly dropped her mug. She recovered herself before answering. "Oh, there's nothing. I was just looking out for a minute before I got started, and I guess my mind wandered."

Mary studied her for a moment, while Casey squirmed inwardly. "Your head isn't here today," Mary pronounced eventually. "Is anything going on?"

"Nothing's going on. I'm just looking at the clouds."

Mary glanced out the window. "Summer's so boring. The same thing every day for months. Listen, I'm taking you off the appliance outlet account."

The change in topic made Casey's head spin, and she replied before she could think about her tone. "I'm sorry—*what?*"

"The conversion rates have been abysmal," Mary said, shrugging. "I'm taking you off the account and giving it to Alan. The company is ready to walk as it is."

Casey thought of her portfolio, such as it was. The patio furniture liquidation store, the flooring warehouse outlet, the walk-in bathtubs, and the appliance outlet store. She hated every single one of them. The more she considered the idea of losing her daily deep dive into washing machine close-outs, the less she cared, even if this was technically a punishment. Why not insist she deserved something better? She steeled herself, took a fortifying gulp of coffee, and looked Mary in the eye.

"Mary, I have to tell you, I think I could give you better numbers with a different industry. Before I moved to email, I was doing really great work on social ads—"

"Make the numbers work on the email accounts you have, and you can get bigger accounts." Mary sniffed and turned away, the conversation over as far as she was concerned.

"No one is going to succeed with these accounts!" Casey insisted, addressing Mary's back as the woman walked down the hallway. "They won't spend the money on good leads, so I'm basically sending spam to thousands of people every day, hoping someone is dumb enough to open it and buy some deck chairs or a bathtub from a company they've never heard of."

Mary stopped. She turned slowly, her mouth compressed into a single grim line.

Casey had the distinct impression she'd gone too far.

"Your job," Mary said tightly, "is to send out emails that *aren't* spam. That's what separates a marketing agency handling email campaigns from the owner's sister who is 'good at computers' doing them. If you think you're sending out spam, maybe you're not in the right job."

Casey bit back the urge to reply that this was exactly what she'd just said, that she'd been better in the advertising department, building social media campaigns. But she'd also had decent clients there: a local health and beauty company, a small chain of family-friendly beach bars, a decent-sized city zoo. Fun, interesting companies whose offers people *wanted* to see in their social media and their inboxes. She'd been adding value to people's lives.

This was always going to be spam, no matter how nicely she wrote her copy.

Her life's work was sending out spam. Perfectly written, perfectly designed spam.

Casey watched Mary walk away, her knee-length black skirt and sensible heels propelling her away from Casey's problems, Casey's crises, Casey's collapsing career.

It's not that bad, she told herself.

When she turned back around, rain was pelting the blue glass of the window.

"It's too early for rain," she said blankly. "Why is it raining in the morning?"

"Florida," a coworker sighed as she walked into the kitchen. "Who can explain it?"

I can, Casey thought. *When I'm not cooped up inside.*

Chapter Twenty-three

Having gotten the rain out of the way early, the Space Coast seemed content to bake for the rest of that Monday, and Casey drove to the barn under a blazing-hot sun in a yellowish, hazy sky. Everything was looking a little worn, from the median flowerbeds in town to the thin grass along the roadside out in the country. All it took was one hot, dry afternoon in July, and Florida wilted.

Sky was in the office, air conditioning blowing into the barn aisle, when Casey arrived. She poked her head inside. "Hey, Sky."

"Hey, Casey! I hope you're not planning on riding anytime soon. It's like, ninety-eight degrees or something."

"I guess not. I didn't really have a plan." She should have gone home, but after just a few weeks of horse ownership, she'd gotten so used to coming straight to the barn after work that she didn't know what she'd do with those extra hours at home. Brandon was probably practicing his guitar or working out or something; he'd have learned to fill his time by now without her. "Maybe I'll just give him a bath or something."

"You want to come in and talk to me? I could use your advice."

Casey's eyebrows went up. Sky wanted *her* advice? "Sure," she said. "What's up?"

Sky pushed her tablet over to Casey, showing her a spreadsheet on the screen. "This is where I'm at," she said, pointing. "And this is where I *need* to be."

Casey looked at the discrepancy. "Those are very different numbers," she said eventually.

"They are." Sky leaned back in her chair and looked at the ceiling. She looked a little older than her quarter-century. "They are very different."

"What do you think is missing?"

"Oh, students. Sales horses. Commissions and training fees. Everything, really. You know, what we talked about a couple weeks ago with the whole lesson and show program. I have a nice little crew here, but I need more. About three times more. I don't have any lessons this evening. None! And I own six lesson horses. I haven't had a lesson for Sage in three weeks. I've been riding him myself in the morning, just to keep him tuned-up."

Casey looked at the spreadsheet. This was what Sky had seen coming back in May—this was why she'd reached out to Bluewater for a marketing proposal. Isolated in a quiet corner of the county, she didn't have the option of putting up a sign inviting the public in for riding lessons. She had to find other ways to advertise, and the money to do it.

Just so happened, Casey was very good at alternative advertising.

"Sky, we need to get you a marketing plan and we need to do it now."

"Well, that's what I wanted to ask you about…"

Casey cocked her head.

"I know I can't pay you what you're worth, or even anything, really…" Sky laughed and shook her head. "So this is really presumptuous. But Casey, have you ever considered a trade?"

Casey sat up in her chair, her heart fluttering. This was *just* what she needed: something *fun* to work on, something that she actually cared about! "I'm considering it now," she said eagerly. "What are you thinking?"

"Riding lessons to start," Sky said. "I know you're feeling a little nervous on James right now, so we could bump you back to two lessons per week, and then if we think he needs it, I could get on James and help you out a little."

Casey couldn't hold back her grin. "That would be absolutely amazing, Sky! I would feel so much better if I was getting some extra help. I've been really nervous lately."

"I know." Sky winked at her. "But you're doing great. So if takes a little bit extra of me yelling at you every week to help you realize that, I can happily take your marketing wisdom as payment."

"Thank you," Casey said. "I can't tell you how much I appreciate this."

"That's what I'm supposed to say to you!"

"I mean, I'm just dying to do something *fun*. Something I care about! Work has been… let's just say it's been boring and leave it at that."

"Boring, or soul-sucking misery?" Sky grinned.

"Oh, you know it's soul-sucking. I wish I could work more with horses." Casey said the words without thinking, but she immediately realized they were true. "I'm excited to work on an equine marketing job, for sure. But I think I'd take mucking stalls over writing more of the emails I've been working on the past couple of years."

"Mucking stalls is a sure cure for desk burnout," Sky laughed. "Although it gives new meaning to the phrase 'same shit, different day,' right?"

They were laughing together, with possibly unmerited mirth, until Gwen poked her pixie's face into the office. "Are we missing something good?"

"No," Sky hiccuped. "All business. Very boring."

"Well, *you're* missing out," Gwen said with a smirk. "Because the horse show committee is meeting again, and things are getting serious."

Casey looked from Gwen to Sky. "The what?"

"Crap," Sky said.

Despite her protests, Casey was designated as the official St. Johns Equestrian Center spy. Her job: to figure out exactly what the girls were up to in that tack room, and help Sky put a stop to it.

"The girls have been plotting to make me put on a horse show on Labor Day weekend," Sky explained, "and needless to say, I do not want to do it. But I need to know what they're talking about in there or I can't defend myself properly."

"Why does it need to be Labor Day?" Casey asked, confused. "Don't people go to the beach or out boating on Labor Day?"

Gwen and Sky exchanged looks.

"What?"

"You've been out of the horse business for a while if you forgot that horse-people do not go to the beach or go boating on holidays," Sky chuckled. "Very civilian thing to say. The *beach*. Gwen, remember the beach?"

She and Gwen guffawed.

"I'm not sure I've ever been to the beach," Gwen laughed. "What is this beach place you speak of?"

"Whatever. Just tell me why this is a big secret and why I have to be a spy."

Gwen took over for Sky. "There used to be a Labor Day Horse Show at a farm called Blackjack Acres. We went every year."

"Hey," Casey interrupted, a memory from her teen years rising up like a ghost. "I used to go to that show, too! I completely forgot. I guess there *was* a time when I didn't go to the beach on Labor Day."

"Sure you went," Gwen scoffed.

"No, really! Everyone went. We used to wear our barn colors, act like it was a big A-circuit show. I can't believe I forgot about that. So what happened, why aren't you going this year?"

"Because they closed," Gwen sighed. "It's going to be a development. I drove past it with my mom last week. There's a billboard advertising resort lifestyle homes, whatever that means."

"Very large pools, lots of grand columns," Sky murmured. "Like in Wellington."

"But without horses," Gwen said, as she might have said 'but on fire.' "So anyway, everyone wants to go to a horse show as soon as possible, and Labor Day was the earliest Sky would take us anywhere. Now there won't be any shows around here until late October, and we need at least a jumper show to prep if we're going to go to any events up in Ocala this winter. Because Sky won't take us to the sunset jumper shows at Lone Palm, even though there is one every single weekend all summer and we would all do really well at them."

"It's too hot for those," Sky groaned.

"They're the sunset shows. It's in the name. They don't even start until eight o'clock."

"It has been in the nineties until past sunset every night for the past month," Sky pointed out.

"But there's no *sun* after sunset," Gwen persisted. "Hot without sun isn't that big a deal."

Sky flicked her gaze back to Casey. "Oh, to be young."

Casey did not bother pointing out that Sky wasn't even close to thirty yet. She knew from personal experience that teenagers were a special breed when it came to horse shows. If asked, Casey would agree with Sky about summer horse shows being the sweaty devil, but back when she'd been a teenager, she'd been determined to spend her weekends at shows.

Now the idea of getting up at four o'clock on a weekend morning to schlep a horse across town to a new place, full of new things to spook at, all in order to enter a ring and be judged by a stranger in front of a crowd of strangers sounded absolutely dreadful, not even considering the weather.

Masochistic, even. *Riders, you are being judged.* Just consider the implications of that phrase! To be judged on purpose! To pay for the privilege!

Casey wasn't sure what sort of high she'd been seeking as a sixteen-year-old, but horse showing certainly wasn't going to produce the same level of euphoria on *this* side of thirty. Riding lessons were stressful enough.

But teenagers simply lived for them. Plus, they were very good ways to showcase a farm... both the facility, and the lesson program. Casey began to think like a marketer instead of a nervous adult rider. "Sky, it's think about this. So the kids are building up a coalition to force you into a horse show. Sounds crazy, but a horse show would be the perfect goal for a marketing campaign. Bring a bunch of people here, show off the property, have your students ready to win a bunch of ribbons... it's hard to think of better publicity."

"So now you're on their side?" Sky rolled her eyes. "Great, just super! Just do me a favor. Before you force me into this, go listen in and see what they're up to. Then... I guess we'll talk about it."

Casey got up and joined Gwen in the doorway. "Lead the way," she said. "Take me to your people."

Casey walked into the tack room and immediately found ten pairs of suspicious eyes locked upon her.

"Hello?" she asked the group, while walking over to her tack locker as nonchalantly as possible. She had been instructed to Act Normally, which she assumed was the first rule of spying anyway. But the teens were making that impossible. She decided to make her accusation without showing her hand. "I'm sorry, have I stumbled onto some sort of secret meeting?"

She let her gaze flick around the room, seeing who the conspirators were. Arden, Rachel, Roxy, and Callie were all prominently seated in the center, with a few other girls sitting on tack trunks facing them. The entire group was mostly comprised of the older barn girls, who were now regarding her carefully, waiting for her next move. Casey began to doubt they'd say anything while she was there.

"Well, I'm just going to get my tack, then," she said, heading for her tack locker. "No one murder me, please."

"Hi, Casey," Arden said as she passed.

Otherwise, there was silence as she went over to her locker and started shuffling around saddle pads. Casey knew there were still some questions amongst the juniors about where she fit in the barn mix. Some of the younger girls, following Gwen's lead in most things, fully accepted her as one of their own. A few others—the older and more suspicious girls like Roxy, Anita, and Callie—were not so sure. They were generally nice enough to her, but she'd found that if they were whispering anything they didn't want to get back to Sky, they clammed up the moment she entered their airspace.

Casey knew that with this mission from Sky, she was risking the tightrope balance she walked between being a responsible adult and being one of the gang. She tucked James's bridle over her shoulder and knelt for her brush box, moving slowly, stalling for time.

Anita, who at seventeen was generally considered at the top of the farm totem pole, shifted uncomfortably on the folding chair she had placed front and center of the group—she was clearly chairing this meeting. "Casey," she began regally, with a meaningful glance at Roxy and Callie, her cohorts in the front row, "how do you feel about horse shows?"

Casey recognized that at this moment, she had an important choice to make.

She could tell the truth, or she could tell them what they wanted to hear.

The mere idea of going to a horse show seized Casey with a lung-squeezing anxiety. But she looked at the closed faces of the girls she wanted to accept her, and she smiled—the kind of big, fake, corporate smile only a grown woman who has sold out on her personal ideals to get a job with a semi-decent paycheck and almost-affordable health insurance could make with such ease. These girls simply had no idea how much vapidity and how much deception were really out there in the doldrums of adulthood. At least she had that on them.

"I'm for them!" she lied happily, her grin practically splitting her face in two. "Did you know I used to show all over Florida? Fox Lea Farm? Florida Horse Park? Have you guys been to those places?"

There were fewer proud nods than reluctant head shakes. Casey had them. She was the most experienced rider in the room right now.

"They're great," she went on. "Huge show-rings, lots of shopping. Makes for an awesome weekend." She turned back to her locker and pulled out her saddle, propped it against her hip. She knew they were still watching her, intrigued by this hidden side of her, this hint of coolness behind her boring grown-up life.

Anita's voice shifted to a more welcoming tone. "Then you definitely want to help us convince Sky that she should put on a barn horse show!"

Casey flitted a glance around the room and saw gazes of interest and approval from everyone—except for Gwen, who was watching her steadily, a thoughtful expression on that solemn pixie's face of hers.

"Absolutely! I think that's an amazing idea!"

Only Gwen's face remained unchanged, cool and appraising, as everyone else broke into excited chattering. Apparently they thought if they had the support of Casey, the one adult with a locker in the boarder's tack room, they were sure to win their case with Sky.

"You know what I think?"

"What do you think, Gwen?" They were in the cross-ties, or rather, Casey was. Gwen was standing nearby, watching as Casey groomed James.

"I think you want to have a horse show just so you can compete in it, too."

"You think wrong."

"Do I?" Gwen shrugged. "It sure seemed like you were excited about it."

"Maybe I'm just a really good spy, Gwen. Did that ever occur to you?" Casey tossed a body brush in the tote and picked up the hoof-pick. James shifted to watch her, his shoes grinding on the concrete. "Ugh, be still, buddy. That sound puts my teeth on edge."

"I don't know if I'd call you a good spy," Gwen went on. "You were supposed to find out their plans, not tell them what an amazing idea having a show was."

"That was how I got them to tell me their plans! And you have to admit, it was very well thought-out. Sky wouldn't have to do anything but call the vendors and get a judge." The teens had done all the work, even putting together a list of classes to offer and a number of services they'd need to organize, from port-a-potties to a lunch truck. Casey suspected that if Sky gave them a budget and the farm credit card, they could probably handle the entire event themselves. She'd told Sky as much, reporting out quickly before she fetched James from his stall. The evening shadows were growing longer by the minute, and now it was almost cool enough for a ride to be a marginally good idea.

Casey was just settling her saddle onto James's back when Sky herself appeared, looking a little frazzled. "Casey, can I talk to you quick?"

Casey cast a furtive glance at her watch. Nearly seven o'clock already. She wasn't getting home until nine tonight, she could tell already. Brandon was going to be a little shirty about dinner. But now she was already late, might as well commit. "Of course, Sky, what's up?"

"Look, this is a crazy idea. Feel free to tell me no. But... this horse show. You're right. I could do it, especially if it's the focus of your campaign and we try to build up buzz around it. I mean, we're only in July. We have two months."

"Sure," Casey agreed. She slid the girth under the saddle flap and started buckling it into place. "The great Labor Day horse show. We can do that."

"Well, I don't know about Labor Day, and here's why. The kids go back to school in mid-August. They're my help, and without them this place kind of goes to hell during the day. It takes me all day to get through stalls and all the other chores." Sky laughed, shaking her head. "I rely on my free labor."

"We're happy to do it for you," Gwen told her solemnly.

"You're the greatest," Sky replied. "And I mean that. But here's the thing: I can't function all by myself for three weeks and also put on a horse show."

"So where does that leave us? No show?" Casey concentrated on tightening the girth, not wanting Sky to see her disappointment.

"I might be able to do it closer to the end of September," Sky said. "If, and this is the crazy part... *if* you think you could help me out around here."

Casey looked around James's shoulder and peered at Sky under his neck. "Excuse me?"

"I know it's impossible. But I thought... if you really wanted a break from your job... maybe you could take some time off and just work for me. Just for September. Just to see how it goes, and see how much business we can build up, and survive the horse show. I mean, you were saying you wished you could work more with horses and... I can't pay you much but I can cover your board and lessons, and obviously your show fees are on me... Casey? Is that presumptuous?"

Casey, still leaning down to look under James's neck at Sky, had dug both her hands into his black mane, and was hanging on for dear life. He tossed his head and shifted his forelegs, but she just moved with him, her forehead tipped against his warm neck. She felt like James was the only thing keeping her anchored to the earth. "Are you serious, Sky? Work for you for a whole month?"

"It's crazy, I know," Sky said apologetically. "I just... it came to me and I thought it wouldn't hurt to ask..."

"No," Casey said slowly. "Never hurts to ask."

Chapter Twenty-four

Casey managed to get home before nine, but only by a few minutes. Brandon was on the sofa, watching TV. She slipped off her boots, steeling herself for a chilly reception. But she was pleasantly surprised. Brandon hopped up and came to greet her in the hallway.

"Babe!" he said, holding out his arms. "You're here! Go get cleaned up and I'll warm up your dinner."

What has him so chipper? Casey wondered, heading up the stairs for a hot shower. He should have been annoyed with her. She was crazy late.

When she came back downstairs, robed and wet-haired, she found a plate of a deceptively simple-looking pasta awaiting her, along with a glass of red wine. Brandon was sitting across the table from her place, sipping at his own glass and looking slightly smug. Casey slipped into her chair and eyed him. "What's up with you?" she asked suspiciously.

"I have some news." Brandon took another sip of wine and waggled his eyebrows at her. "Go on, eat up, don't let that get cold."

"Okay, weirdo." Casey picked up her fork and set into her meal. "Um, this is good," she said around a bite. "Is your news that you're quitting your job to start a restaurant? Because I think I'd support that whole-heartedly."

"That's not it. It's work-related, though."

Casey thought of her own bizarre work offer and wondered if today was just an auspicious day to make changes. She should look at her horoscope more often. "Okay, tell me."

He put down his wine glass and leaned forward, commanding her full attention. "I've been offered a full-time position running my department," he announced proudly. "From a six-month contract to executive-level, how do you like that? And the company's throwing all kinds of money at oceanic research. It's going to be the focus of all of their marketing campaigns for the next year. This is going to be a huge deal. I can hardly believe it's really happening…"

Brandon kept going in that vein, but Casey had such a buzzing in her ears she could hardly hear him. Running his department? The company was based in West Palm Beach! Was Brandon proposing that they *move?*

"Where would it be?" she asked urgently, interrupting what was apparently a very lengthy speech about his potential with the company. "Would you still be working remotely?"

Brandon's smile grew a little more guarded. "Well, there is that. Obviously the job is in West Palm, at the home office. But I think there's a ton of potential for us there, babe. I didn't accept the position yet—I wanted us to talk about it." He must have seen her face change. "I'm sorry, I was excited… I know this is a big deal, moving…"

Casey put down her fork with a clatter. "Brandon, it's amazing that you got this deal, but *moving,* and to *West Palm* of all places…" she shook her head, imagining it: the traffic, the sprawl, the expense. Her chest felt tight. "I just never pictured myself down there, you know? This is a big shock. I'm sorry. I just… need a minute."

"Sure," Brandon said, a slight catch in his voice. "Sure, sure, I understand. It's different. But there are some really great aspects. There'd be a better job for you, for one thing. Much better agencies, bigger clients. We could live in a nice building close to everything, there are great restaurants, beaches..." He trailed off. "You look more upset than I'd expected. I knew it was big but... Casey, don't *cry.*"

Casey bit down on her lower lip, feeling the hot prickling in her eyes. "It's just... I *like* it here."

That wasn't all of it. She liked their house, she liked their friends, she liked their rituals. She liked living half an hour from her parents, from the house where she had grown up. She liked the beaches where they walked and the restaurants where they dined and the stores where they shopped. Casey hadn't come back to her hometown because she'd lacked the courage to step off the shore and swim to the nearest big city. She'd come back because she loved her home.

But even all of that emotion had to take a backseat to the looming elephant in the room. Or rather—the Thoroughbred in the room.

She'd just been offered an incredible opportunity of her own... one that seemed to be equally implausible to accept and impossible to refuse. One she didn't even know how to put into words. She had come home swallowing her growing excitement because she hadn't yet known how she would explain it to Brandon... but he'd been too consumed with his own success to even realize what a painful difference it would make in her life.

The injustice of it stung, and she pushed back from the table.

"Casey," Brandon said, getting up as well. "Casey, wait."

"No," she managed to say, working the syllable around the growing lump in her throat. He'd never considered that this could hurt her, he had only seen his own success and couldn't wait to gloat about it. He'd had to see her face fall to understand his mistake. She couldn't stay in the room with him. Casey pushed into the hallway and headed for the stairs, desperate to be alone.

"Casey, please don't be upset. We can work this out. Casey—is this about James? There are stables down there. We'll find a place for him. I'll help. Come on, Casey."

Was this about James? Part of her wanted to scream: *yes, of course it was about James!* Because how would she ever afford to keep her horse in the rarefied air of ritzy Palm Beach County, where everything cost three times what it cost up here?

Another part of her wanted to snap: *there's more to my life than James.*

"It's not just about James," she hissed, not turning her head as she pounded up the stairs.

"What is it, then?"

"It's *everything!*" Casey screamed down at him as she reached the landing. She'd never raised her voice to Brandon; his startled expression nearly made her burst into hysterical laughter. The shock of emotion helped her snap out of her sudden rage. She pulled herself together with a physical shrug. "It's too much right now," she continued in a more level tone. "I need a minute. Just leave me be for a minute."

"Okay," he said, contrite, but he stayed at the foot of the stairs, blinking up at her like a lost puppy, until she turned away and went into her room, shutting the door with a soft and final *click.*

Casey sat alone in bed, the pillows bunched behind her back, for a solid hour. She heard no noise from downstairs; from next door, she heard water run in the shared walls as her elderly neighbors prepared for bed. They had been married thirty-seven years, Casey remembered—a few years longer than she'd been alive. Where would she be in thirty-seven years? She'd expected to be with Brandon. Neither of them had been fussed enough about the future to talk about marriage, but it hadn't ever really mattered.

Neither of them had ever asked the other one for a sacrifice like this before.

How horrible, how hilarious, that both of them needed to ask a huge favor of the other at the exact same time!

Casey had gone over it all on the drive home. She had been going to ask for his help with an unpaid leave of absence. Just a month's forgiveness for her share of the household bills, while she took some time away from the agency to help Sky. At the end of the month, she'd know better if she was cut out for a couple of different things: for freelance marketing instead of working for an agency, or for running a barn instead of working full-time in marketing. Or she might even realize that she should go back to the agency and keep working while she figured out a better next move. Three possible outcomes, and one desperate purpose: she *needed* to know so that she could move her life forward.

She needed something more from her days than sitting in that office, listening to the coughs and murmurs of a dozen other people, writing words that would all be thrown away. Maybe the answer was in another office, maybe that answer was in a barn full of horses, or maybe it was inside of her, all of the work she could do if she was released from what had become nothing more than daily chores. But she wouldn't know unless she made the leap.

Sky had offered her the leap, and Casey knew she wouldn't get another chance as good as this. She was thirty-two years old. How many chances at a do-over would she get?

Just as Brandon wouldn't get another chance like this. He was being offered a place at the top, working on a cause which meant the world to him. Casey tugged a blanket up to her chin and sniffled into it, because she knew the choices they were going to make were game changers, and they were going to hurt like hell.

* * *

"I'm not going without you," Brandon declared.

Well, that's to his credit, Casey thought, burying her face in her hands for a single, painful moment of release. Then she lifted her eyes back to his. They were red, but they were dry. She had cried it out in bed, alone. She'd taken that advantage from Brandon, and she didn't feel bad about it—this was his punishment for forgetting her feelings earlier. It wasn't a terrible punishment. He'd be fine.

"Listen to me," she told him now. "I'm not talking about forever. I'm saying that right now, you and I have to follow these chances. Neither of us can turn these down without wondering forever what would have happened. Can we live a couple of hours apart for a few months? Yes, *of course* we can."

Brandon sat down at the other end of the couch and looked over at her, his expression searching, as if she was already miles away. "Casey, if you want to quit your job and try out other things, you can do that with me. You don't owe me anything. If this is about money—"

"It's not about money," Casey interrupted. "Thank you very much, though. I'm the same as you right now, babe. I got a job offer I can't turn down. So did you. Mine just happens to start the month after yours does. And it's *temporary.*"

"Meaning you'll come to West Palm after it's done?" Brandon winced. "I shouldn't be asking you like it's a done deal. I shouldn't be demanding you move away because of me."

"No, it's fine." Casey closed her eyes again. "I'm past that. I'm not mad. I understand. I'm just saying the timing is… bad."

"Casey? Did you know you were going to take this job when you came home tonight?"

She hadn't, not entirely. She'd come home with an idea she wanted to talk out with him, and instead she'd been rattled to the core and needed an hour to herself to breathe deep and think hard. But she'd come downstairs knowing exactly what she needed to. "I didn't expect any of this," Casey said truthfully. "But I'm guessing you didn't, either."

"No," Brandon replied. He reached out for her, and she gave him her hand. Then he grinned at her, an unexpected flash of a smile which made her heart lift in her chest. Oh, she loved Brandon! Why did it sometimes hit her like a bolt of lightning? That must be what happened when people grew comfortable together. You forgot how much someone truly moved you, it became a part of you somehow, until that person moved just so and your heart simply couldn't take it. "That damn horse. I've been wanting to say that for a while. Now it really feels right."

Casey laughed shakily. "Brandon, I could not agree more. That damn horse."

That damn horse, and her horse-addled brain, she added silently. She couldn't blame James for all of this. James was a result, not a cause.

But if it made things easier for Brandon, she'd let him blame James. Her horse wouldn't mind.

Chapter Twenty-five

"So, the horse show's a go if you are," Sky was saying, her voice sounding high-pitched through Casey's earbuds. "Have you had enough time to think about it?"

Casey glanced at the clock on her computer screen. "Yes, Sky, fourteen hours was the perfect amount of time for a major life decision, but I spent some of it sleeping so maybe I should get an extension."

Sky laughed. "I'm sorry, I'm sorry! I just... I think it would be good for both of us. If I'm really honest..." Sky's voice trailed off for a moment, while she decided just how honest she could be. Casey certainly understood *that*. "I'm sinking here. I'm exhausted, and I'm barely holding it together, and yet despite all this work, I'm not pulling in enough to pay the bills. I need business to pick up, but I also need to have the energy to keep up with it when it does. So your help, even for a month, would change everything for me. If I can have you for a month, I can afford to pay someone else the next month... or you, if you decide to stay on."

Casey bit her lip. She wasn't ready to face the idea of moving just yet, so she'd decided to compartment that little issue neatly in the back of her head and leave it parked there until she could handle taking it out and examining it properly. That wouldn't be right now. Nor anytime soon, not as July ticked slowly down to August, and what was going to be a long, strange month alone with

Brandon heading to West Palm.

Which he'd be doing kicking and screaming, if this morning's mournful breakfast had been anything to judge the future on. But Casey wasn't taking no for answer. She wasn't going to be the reason for Brandon to give up his dream job, and *he* wasn't going to be the reason she didn't explore her new possibilities, either. Asking someone to move when they didn't really want to was one issue, something which could be dealt with. Letting someone back away from a dream was another issue altogether, and one she was fully prepared to face head-on, with a stiff upper lip and enough work to keep the sorrow away.

"I'm going to give you September," Casey told Sky, looking around as she spoke, but no one was loitering near her cubicle. Even if they had been, they couldn't have known what she meant. "That's a promise."

"Casey! That's so exciting!" Sky's voice nearly overpowered her earbuds, and Casey hurriedly pressed down the volume button. "You're going to have so much fun. *We're* going to have so much fun! I can't wait to have you all to myself!"

Casey smiled and shook her head. Sky had no idea just how 'all to herself' Casey would be. "I'm really excited, too. But we have to get started on planning for the show and how we're going to market it right away. We don't have a long time to build things up."

"I'll do whatever you say," Sky promised. "I'm going to be the best client you've ever had."

That wouldn't be tough, Casey thought ruefully. She had an inbox full of annoying clients to prove it. "Well, let me get back to the current clients," she said. "Tuesdays are always busy for me with client requests."

"Not for me," Sky declared. "Not *yet.*"

Grinning, Casey ended the call and took out her earbuds. She didn't take many personal calls while she was at work, but she'd been nervous when she saw Sky's number pop up so early on a weekday. She should have guessed Sky was just too impatient to wait another moment for her answer.

So this was her future! She was going to spend all of her spare time for the next few weeks getting Sky's phone ringing with prospective students, and then filling up the horse show with entries. And come September, she'd give her desk a little vacation and spend some time regaining her horsekeeping chops. Despite the impending emptiness of her house, Casey was excited. These were good choices. They *had* to be, for the sacrifices they were making.

She'd have to email HR about a leave of absence. Casey glanced at her inbox, filled with demands on her time, and decided the clients could wait a few more minutes. Her personal life was much more interesting. She opened a new email draft and thought about how to begin her request.

"Casey, what happened with the Senior Assist campaign?"

She looked up, startled. Mary was standing in her cubicle doorway, clutching a paper cup of office coffee and looking disgruntled. Casey struggled to bring her thoughts back to office work. "Mary! Hi! Um… Senior Assist… I was just reading that." She clicked on the email hastily, hoping Mary couldn't see that it was unread. "Well, they are saying the copy didn't get clicks, but, listen, they also used an email list they bought from some shady website. There's a decent chance most of the emails aren't even active, let alone for seniors or caregivers. I don't see how they can blame—"

"The click rate they reported is *well* below average, even for you."

Casey squeezed her fingernails into her palms. What was that *even for you* line about? She was far from a poor performer. Mary was just going to stand there and pretend Casey was subpar? This, on top of everything else in her life, on top of losing the stupid appliance account—had that really only been yesterday?—was simply too much.

"My click-through rates are the second-highest in the agency," she whispered.

Whispered? She'd meant to roar it. A dangerous heat pricked at the corners of Casey's eyes. Great, she was going to cry in front of her boss. The perfect response.

"Send them a rewrite for a new send before lunch. And the same goes for that furniture outlet. Get it right this time." Mary's sharp voice flicked hard on Casey's raw nerves.

And Casey, tired of Mary's constant injustice, tired of being blamed for everything that went wrong with these cheap clients, and tired of all the drama of simply being alive, stood up from her chair, letting it roll out from beneath her. She carefully ran her thumb and forefinger over each eye, as if she was rubbing them wearily, rather than brushing away a few rogue tears, wrought of exhaustion and frustration, that she just couldn't help.

"These are unreasonable requests," Casey announced, her voice remarkably steady considering her mental state, "and I'm not going to send them rewrites for free. They're trying to take advantage of the agency."

As if I gave a damn about the agency, she thought savagely.

"That's for me to decide," Mary said smugly. "And I think they're right. I think you could have done better."

"You approved them," Casey pointed out. "You read every line before I send it out."

Mary almost, but not quite, rolled her eyes as she lifted her paper cup to her maroon-painted lips. The message was unmistakable. Casey needed to shut up and get to work on those rewrites.

Casey considered her next move.

Mary drank her coffee, waiting.

An uncomfortable moment (for Casey, at least) passed in silence.

Then, Casey's phone buzzed. Once, twice, three times. She was generally good at holding off on answering texts when Mary was around (Mary did not appreciate being interrupted), but something about the urgency of its vibration in her purse was too significant to ignore. *Three* texts in a row? Something had to be up. Casey looked over at her purse uncomfortably.

Mary's eyes had shifted to her bag as well. "Something going on?"

Casey pulled out her phone and her eyes grew wide. The messages were all from Sky.

Casey sorry to bother you at work again but James is colicky.

Calling vet really sorry

He was trying to roll but we stopped him. Walking him now. Hopefully nothing. Just wanted you to know. Will update when vet comes.

There was no question what she had to do next. This decision, at least, did not come with a thousand subtexts.

"I have to go," Casey said, dropping her phone back into her bag like a hot coal. "Right now."

Mary stepped aside, confused. "Really, those rewrites *have* to be done by—"

"I won't be back today," Casey said. "I'll take a sick day, thanks." She was pushing past Mary, she was halfway down the aisle between the cubicles.

"Sick days are for when you're *sick!*" Mary called, in a last-ditch effort to be a bitch.

"It's a family medical emergency," Casey shot back. "And it's *personal.*"

"Fine," Mary said, looking alarmed at last. "Fine. Let me know —"

Casey was out the door and in the corridor, pulling out her phone again as she headed for the stairs, thumbing a reply to Sky.

She ran headlong into a mass of paisley and peanut butter.

"Casey, is everything okay?"

"Leslie! I have to run, Sky texted—James is colicking, she called the vet already—"

Leslie dropped the Tupperware of peanut-butter granola she'd been munching on as she walked the hallway, getting her steps and eating breakfast at the same time in a rather astonishing act of multi-tasking. As she knelt down to clean up her mess, she looked up at Casey, her motherly face schooled into soothing lines. "It's going to be fine. Sky knows what she's doing. You just drive carefully out there, now, and don't take any risks."

Casey was gone, flying down the stairs, before she could even finish.

Two blown red lights and a few very dicey slides through stop signs later, Casey was running into the barn, barely managing to calm her pace down to a fast walk as she entered the aisle. The vet's truck was already parked out front, and at the far end of the barn she saw a cluster of women grouped around a horse in the cross-ties: James.

He was looking very sorry for himself, despite all of the feminine company, and barely looked up when Casey entered his space. That's how she knew he was definitely ill. James would never ignore her presence, and the potential for cookies, if he was feeling like himself.

"Oh, buddy," she sighed. "What did you do?"

"It's not too bad," the vet said, filling up a few syringes and lining them up on the seat of a folding chair. "Sky caught him before he did anything silly. All he was doing was digging a hole in his stall and looking fussy. No rolling, nothing to worry about in his gut. Just your average everyday gas colic. Turns out he's a baby about tummy aches. Most Thoroughbreds are, in my experience."

"Sky," Casey breathed. "Thank you so much for handling this."

Sky held out her arms and Casey fell into them, grateful for the sticky hug. "That's what I'm here for, girl."

By the time the vet had finished using James for a pincushion, the horse was flicking his tail around and looking irritable. Casey wished she could give him some cookies to cheer him up, but Dr. Winslow was pretty firm on his diet for the next two days. *The bland diet,* she thought, remembering days home from school with a stomach bug, living on dry toast and cherry Jell-O. *Poor buddy.* Casey wrapped her arms around his neck, and he shifted his hooves but didn't step away from her.

"Best thing for him is grass," the vet added, packing up her duffel and slinging it over her shoulder for the walk back to the truck. "Just graze him for as long as you've got."

"I have all the time in the world," Casey vowed, her hands wrapped in James's short black mane.

Dr. Winslow gave her a wry grin. "That's unusual."

Casey watched the vet heading for her truck, and a new worry seized her. She shot a panicked glance at Sky. She had never paid a vet bill—that's what her parents had been for! What was the etiquette here? *"Sky!* Does she send me a bill or what?" she hissed.

"A bill? No, you can pay her right now. She takes credit cards. Just follow her and she'll get you taken care of once her supplies are put away." Sky put her hand on James's neck. "I'll hang out with this boy for you."

Wondering how much this visit was going to hurt her savings account, Casey anxiously followed Dr. Winslow down the barn aisle and out to her truck. The vet was middle-aged, grays taking over her brown curls, which were tucked severely up into a mass of elastic bands and bobby pins. She had a lined, tanned face and a no-nonsense demeanor which Casey could only envy. Dr. Winslow would not be intimidated by demanding clients or domineering managers. Dr. Winslow would work for no one but herself. Casey wished she'd teach seminars.

The vet hunched over a tablet and tapped out a review of the visit, then printed it on a small bluetooth printer sitting on the passenger side seat. Casey's eyes widened at the sight of all this mobile office tech. She remembered vets carrying metal clipboards and triplicate bills, with handwritten cases and recommended treatments scrawled out in an untidy, rushed hand. Clearly, times had changed.

Dr. Winslow handed her the print-out with her observations, diagnosis, treatments, and instructions all laid out in tidy 12-point Arial. "Will that be cash or charge?" the vet asked, pulling out a mobile credit card device.

Casey looked at the numbers at the top of the page and swallowed. "Charge," she said.

Of all the shocks of the past twenty-four hours, Casey felt most unsettled by the cost of an "it's not too bad" vet visit. Casey couldn't even begin to imagine what a bill for a *bad* visit would be, but she supposed something had to pay for all those mobile office gadgets.

Casey sent a text to Leslie, back at the office: James would be fine but needed to be grazed as long as possible today, and could Leslie please let Mary know that Casey would be back in the office tomorrow? She shuddered at what Mary would be like to deal with the next morning even as she tapped out the words, but she figured she'd deal with that when she had to. Right now, she had James to worry about.

It was starting to feel like she spent *all* of her time worrying about James.

But no, she wasn't going to think about that.

"I'm going on a Publix run," Sky announced, walking out to the lawn where James was moodily nosing at the grass. "You want a sandwich?"

Casey patted her thigh to check for money, but there was no pocket there. With a surprised start, she realized she wasn't wearing her usual riding breeches. She looked down at her clothes in exasperation. She was still wearing beige slacks of that precise shade and fabric which attracted stains from anything that came into its vicinity, and a floral polyester blouse which was wet through with sweat just from walking around in the humid air. She didn't even want to think about what was happening inside her under-wire bra.

"Gosh, Sky, I'm an idiot. Can you wait five minutes and let me change into my barn clothes?"

Sky laughed, shaking her head. "I'm sorry, Casey! Somehow I didn't even notice. Please, go change. I'll deal with this booger."

Casey handed over the lead rope but lingered, watching James as he pawed at a thick-rooted weed. "He's going to be okay, isn't he?"

"Don't worry! He's going to be fine."

Don't worry. The words hammered at Casey for the next two hours, as she stood in the blazing summer sun and watched her horse grow gradually more interested in the poisonously green grass.

Don't worry! You've just put a large vet bill on your credit card.

Don't worry! You ran out of the office after being disrespectful to your manager and leaving deadline work undone.

Don't worry! You're about to take a leave of absence from your job to clean stalls while your boyfriend moves to a new city for his dream job.

Don't worry! You just bought a horse and he's literally all you can ever think about and you think it might be destroying your life.

Don't worry!

It's fine!

Chapter Twenty-six

Despite the chaos they seemed to cause with every breath, horses somehow also offered a perfect respite from the outside world. Casey couldn't quite explain their effect, and would have readily admitted to any outsider that a significant leap in thinking was required to accept such a gap in logic. But it was true. It was true in mundane tasks like cleaning stalls, and in close contact like grooming, and nowhere was it more true then while riding.

In the saddle, nothing mattered but that very moment. Everything fell away: relationship troubles and job miseries and financial woes. Nothing was left but the act of riding, of getting it right with a partner who didn't speak but definitely had opinions.

The act of riding required focus, laser-sharp, and a consciousness of one's body that extended from the toes to the forehead. Casey could recall having a certain level of focus in her teen years, but her hazy memories felt nothing like what was required of her now.

James was young, and he was green, and because of these things, he needed constant change to maintain his steadiness. This was one of those fantastic contradictions of plain English which riding required a person to learn.

If Casey let herself think about anything else but James, and where James was headed and how James was moving and what to expect from James in two, three, five, ten strides—*anything* but

James, to be perfectly clear—things went wrong.

She couldn't be trotting along with her heels down and her elbows in and her chin up, looking masterfully in control of her own equitation, and start thinking about Brandon's new job, or her back-and-forths with HR about the leave of absence (Mary was dragging her heels on signing off on it, unsurprisingly), because if she did, James would wobble and change pace or change course or spook at a leaf and everything would go to hell.

Casey had to remember her basics, and think about them all the time.

Basic number one: riding a horse down a straight line was a series of corrections from left to right and back again.

Basic number two: getting a horse around the arena at a steady trot was actually a game of *go* and *whoa*.

Basic number three: the smoothest gaits were built from a combination of half-halts (a subtle gesture which could only be described as asking for a halt but then pushing the horse forward instead, causing the horse to rebalance) and pushing with more leg —*all* of the leg, from the hip to the heel, but not necessarily all of the leg all of the time.

It was complicated, and Casey struggled, but she pushed on.

She pushed on because when she was riding, she forgot everything else. Once she finally centered, she stayed that way. When it took her awhile to find her balance, it was obvious to anyone watching: poor green James came apart at the seams when he wasn't held together by his rider, with his legs going one way and his head going another, shoulders pointing in and hindquarters pointing out.

"Remember to breathe," Gwen loved to call to her laughingly, trotting past with preternatural elegance atop any number of horses and ponies: her own Juniper, but also the school horses and project ponies Sky handed off to her tween protégé.

But sometimes Casey thought remembering to breathe was simply asking her mind to do *too* much all at once. She generally had enough to manage, with her hands and her feet and her toes and her nose and her pelvis and her hips. Anything situated more internally than those, like her lungs, became an afterthought.

Breathe in through the nose, breathe down through the seat bones, and on through the heels, Casey thought when she was able to spare a moment to consider her lungs. But mostly, she had too many other things to think about. Things like oxygen supply would have to manage themselves.

On this particular summer Saturday, the sun was filtering down through midday clouds, fleecy puffballs preceding an afternoon's rain, and a steady sea breeze was sailing inland across the farm, ruffling James's short black mane. Casey wiped sweat from her forehead with the cotton back of her gloves; she'd found she got so drenched during these sweltering summer rides that she had to buy special gloves designed specifically to mop up sweat. Sky had gone one step further and suggested she stick a pantyliner into the front lining of her riding helmet, avowing they were incredible for absorbing sweat, but Casey wasn't ready to go that far yet. There were certain aspects of the romantic dream of horse-riding she would like to keep intact. Pressing her forehead into a pantyliner during every ride would definitely burst at least one bubble.

Now, Casey took a deep breath, considered her entire body, and rocked back onto her seat bones, opening her pelvis up to give James the cue to stretch his spine. He took the suggestion happily, shoving out his neck and pulling the reins through her fingers until his nose was dangling just inches above the ground as he walked along the rail.

"You're a good boy," Casey crooned. "Such a good, *stretchy* boy."

Across the arena, Gwen was trotting Juniper in spiraling circles, turning big loops into small, and then big again. Casey watched the pair hungrily. There was something breathtaking about Gwen in the saddle, so tiny and so naturally talented on her big, spring-loaded warmblood. Something unattainable, too: Gwen would always have some special polish Casey would not, no matter how hard she worked in the saddle. Gwen would never have to hesitate about becoming a professional, would never have to hem and haw about whether she could make it as a trainer or if she'd have to get a "real" job. Gwen would probably be scooped up by some Olympian as an apprentice before she was out of high school. Her whole life was laid out in front of her, a glittering golden road of one good horse after another.

"It would be nice if things were that simple," Casey told James, who was still being a good stretchy boy. He snorted, shaking his head hard to free himself of some flies which had taken advantage of his slow pace, and as he lifted his head again, Casey shifted her weight and shortened her reins, asking him to shorten his back and come back into a working frame. James, still feeling fresh despite the heat, cheerfully obliged with a pluckier, up-tempo walk.

"He looks so good!" Gwen called, sitting down to give Juniper a break. "You two are having a really great day!"

"You're too sweet," Casey replied, but she gave James an extra pat on the neck before shoving herself back into her work zone. She had learned to remind herself to mentally and physically rebalance. It wasn't enough to just pick up the reins and nudge for a trot. She had to place herself in the center of her horse, check her seat, check her legs, check her hands, check her breath, check her *horse,* and then, when everything was lined up for a split-second of balance, push into the trot.

Casey didn't remember riding being this much work when she was Gwen's age, but at least she was getting similar results now.

James didn't exactly spring into a working trot, but he did step eagerly into a gradually strengthening trot, and that was something. Casey did her body checks over and over as they went down the long side of the arena:

tighten stomach muscles,

drop heels,

straighten wrists,

inside leg to outside rein,

slow his rhythm by slowing her body,

prepare for the turn,

look *around* the turn,

inside seat bone and inside leg,

outside rein again,

leg, more leg, good!

All of that, she thought with exhaustion a few minutes later, to get a horse to trot around a large rectangular arena. She brushed the sweat from her forehead again. Her gloves were wringing wet.

"Really nice," Gwen said from her slow, smooth circle in the center of the ring. Her attention didn't seem to waver from Juniper, who in turn didn't waver from his perfectly curving track.

Casey waved her thanks, too out of breath to reply. It *had* been really nice. Maybe it was just a trot around an arena, but it had felt like magic.

And it hadn't left her a single spare second to think about her insane life outside of the saddle.

That's the real magic of horses, she thought, slackening her reins so that James could stretch again. *Horses take everything, but they offer the perfect escape in return.*

"Hey, let's go on a trail ride," Gwen suggested, walking Juniper over.

Casey's gentle meditations were stopped short. "A what-now? We don't have any trails." *And I don't exactly trust James outside this ring, anyway.*

"We'll just ride down the driveway and along the road a little. It's fine, Juniper knows the way and Sky doesn't mind us going as long as we don't go alone."

"Trust me, my company will basically make it the same as going alone. *Double* alone. I'm not ready to take James out of the arena."

"Casey." Gwen's voice was long-suffering. "It is *past* time you take this horse out of the arena. Come on. Do this for yourself."

Casey was, as usual, bullied into obeying the teenager. She really wished she would grow a spine one of these days. Gwen just seemed to overpower her so easily!

They rode through the grass alongside the barn, horses inside looking out through their stall windows with interest. Sky was at the front end, talking to a riding student's mother. Casey hoped she would beckon them back and tell them not to go wandering down the road, but she just waved and went back to her conversation.

James now had his head up high, surveying the scenery around him with pricked ears and wide eyes. Quick breaths fluttered through his nostrils, rippling the fine skin and turning into little snorts. Casey held the reins short, but managed to keep her hands forward, so that she wasn't yanking back on him. She wasn't stopping him from doing anything; she was just... ready. Prepared for the worst.

Almost next to her, walking a scant half-stride ahead, Gwen rode absently along on a half-asleep Juniper. She was watching Casey and James with amusement. "Look at those ears! You know he's having fun, right? He needed this."

Well, he *felt* like he was going to jump out from under her. If Casey had been looking for a way to build up James's energy into an extended walk, she had certainly found it. Unfortunately that wasn't going to be on her training agenda for years... if ever. She concentrated on her heels, sinking her weight deeply into them, and shifting her lower leg forward ever so slightly. It was her old safety seat, a remembered position from riding the silly, snorting ex-racehorses of yesteryear. If nothing else, her body still knew how to prepare for an emergency situation.

"Casey!" Gwen's voice was bubbly with laughter. "Relax! For god's sake! You're going to set him off."

"I don't know how to relax," Casey said tightly.

"Laugh."

"What?" They were nearing the end of the farm clearing; the white shell driveway which led through the palmettos and Australian pines was waiting just ahead, a dark tunnel of branches interlacing overhead. She wondered what animals were lurking in those stiff palmetto fronds, waiting to take off and rattle through the underbrush. One raccoon on the move and James would be off like a shot. Would she stay on? Casey imagined herself at the hospital, Brandon leaning over her. *I can't move to West Palm now,* he said softly into his phone. *Not when my girlfriend's in traction.*

"Laugh! It will loosen you up. And if he spooks—you just laugh at him. If you react, he's going to freak out. If you laugh and loosen your body, he'll realize he's being a dork and pull himself together."

Casey tore her gaze away from the narrowing driveway and looked skeptically at Gwen. "If he spooks, he's going to take off. He's a *Thoroughbred.*"

"He's not scared until you are, Casey."

The words rang with authority: they smacked of a simple truth of horsemanship. Casey looked through James's pricked ears and bit her lower lip as he jigged sideways, realizing Gwen was absolutely right.

Either she was in control of this situation, or James was. There was no in-between.

As soon as they made it between the trees, a lizard set off into the palmettos, making a racket far larger than any tiny reptile should be able to, and James blew out his breath with a *huff*, looking hard into the woods for the source of the sound.

"Hahahaha!" Casey chortled. "James, you're so silly. Hahaha!" She pressed her legs gently to his side and he jogged forward, tossing his head when she reined him back. "We're walking, we're walking, we're walking," she sang, sounding like an absolute idiot.

"We're walking, we're walking!" Gwen warbled.

"We're walking, we're walking, we're walking!" the two of them chorused, their horses' ears flicking back to listen to them, their attention utterly captivated by the crazies on their backs.

All the way down the driveway, they sang ridiculous nonsense songs, laughing like gulls when James hopped over a puddle and stopped to gaze distrustfully at the leaning mailbox. Casey managed to be brave enough to walk him a little ways down the gleaming white road, keeping well to the center and away from the dark, glittering water in those deep drainage ditches.

By the time the horses had turned back up the barn lane, she was utterly relaxed. She could feel her weight sinking into her seat and legs as if she were a weighted float, her hips bobbing below the waterline. When James moved quickly, scooting past a suspicious squirrel, she just swayed with him and laughed.

When he'd settled back into a smooth gait, Casey reached forward and rubbed the hot neck of her horse with one gloved hand. They'd ridden down the road! They'd gone out of the arena! Anything was possible now!

She felt unstoppable. She felt like a goddess. She felt like a horsewoman.

Brandon was packing when she came home that afternoon, sweaty and half-dizzy from too much sun and not enough water. He shook his head at her when she came shambling up the stairs.

"You shouldn't have ridden in the middle of the day, Casey. You're going to get heat stroke."

A loud boom punctuated his words, and the light which had been streaming in the bedroom windows suddenly winked out.

Casey pulled off her sweaty shirt. "That's why I did it, dear."

The storm lasted the better part of the afternoon, as August storms were liable to do, and Casey settled down at Brandon's desk in the guest room, trying to get through some of her marketing work for Sky. He came in and out of the room quietly, looking for files and books he'd need to take to West Palm with him. He was planning a lightweight move, as if he was just going out of town on a business trip. Casey was deeply grateful for this. It made the whole thing less real. If Brandon had been packing up all of his clothes and the bits of furniture which had been his before they'd moved in together, she wasn't sure either of them would be handling this change with any grace at all.

As it was, they were kind to each other, even though Brandon couldn't quite believe the future she'd convinced him to accept.

"Casey," he asked at one point, "will you need the printer?"

"I don't think so," she said, turning away from her laptop. He was surveying the printer without pleasure. "Are you going to set it up in your hotel room?"

"Not in the hotel, but in the sublet, when that opens up. I just wouldn't like to be without it if I should need it... but if you think you might..."

"No," she replied, "I never print anything," and then she thought of the empty space on the shelf which would be left behind, and of the printer sitting on a bland kitchen counter in some bland corporate rental, and suddenly she felt tears prickling at her eyes. She sniffed and turned back to her work, determined to be the tough one. She was, after all, the one who was staying behind *and* the one insisting he go. If she wasn't the tough one, who was?

"I cried over a printer," Casey confessed later, on the phone with her mother. She had gone down to the kitchen to escape Brandon's suitcases, slowly filling with his favorite button-down shirts, and in the watery evening light had a sudden urge to call her mother for advice. "Is that normal?"

"Perfectly," Casey's mother insisted. "Blank spaces are going to be the weirdest part of all of this for you."

"Am I doing the right thing?" She whispered this, half-afraid of the answer.

"In terms of Brandon? Yes. Sometimes we have to push people into doing things." Her mother's tone was knowing; Casey suspected her mother had pushed her own father out onto plenty of limbs during their marriage, and maybe beforehand. "In terms of the horse thing? I don't know about that one."

"I wasn't asking about that one," Casey said, struggling to keep irritation out of her voice.

"Luckily, I'm your mother, so I don't have to wait to be asked," she replied comfortably. "But since we're on the topic, Casey, I know why you have to do it. Horses have always been your thing. I couldn't expect you to react any other way to this kind of offer. And I think you'll find your answer pretty quickly."

"Meaning I'll either love it or hate it?"

"Exactly." Her mother chuckled. "I think by October, you'll know exactly what you want to do next."

Casey looked at the rain streaming down the kitchen window, the smeared green and brown of her little backyard and the high wooden fence surrounding it. It seemed like an amazing feat, to know exactly what she wanted to do next. It seemed impossible.

If such a thing could happen, though, that would make all of this heartache and upheaval worthwhile.

For *both* of them.

Chapter Twenty-seven

"Oh man, it's so weird being here without Brandon." Casey slipped into a chair across from Heather and Alison. The other two women were already sipping mimosas and giggling over something on Alison's phone, but they were nice enough to look up and be attentive once Casey had arrived.

"You said he's coming later, right?" Heather waved down a passing waiter, pointing toward Casey and tipping her hand back in the classic "girl needs drink" gesture.

"Yeah, when he's done with packing. He had to pick up some last-minute stuff since he's leaving tomorrow and it was kind of stressing him out. I told him I'd bring him home some lunch if he can't make it here."

Alison raised an eyebrow. "So, you ready for him to be gone already?"

"Why would you think that?"

"Because you're sending him to West Palm alone?" Alison turned from Casey's shocked face to the waiter, who was just arriving with a tray of fresh drinks and a hopeful expression. "We need the breakfast potatoes. ASAP. For the table, please and thank you."

"Anything else?" He glanced around the table. The breeze off the water ruffled the pages of his notepad.

Casey held up her hands helplessly. "I just got here. And we're going to be here a little while. Maybe just the potatoes to start?"

The waiter scowled at her and stomped away.

"I don't know why that's such a weird request," Alison complained, watching him storm back to the kitchen. "It's like the brunch version of a big plate of fries."

"It's exactly like that," Heather agreed. "We should make that a thing. Start calling them brunch fries."

"So, Casey," Alison said, flipping the subject back around with ease. "Brandon's hitting the road in the morning. When should we be prepared for you to leave us, too, or is this the last you'll see of Brandon?"

Casey tipped back her mimosa in three big gulps, ready for that bubbly feeling to start spreading from her tongue to her toes. She needed it today. "Guys, I am not going to talk about this."

"The hell you aren't," Heather insisted, pushing her dark hair back from her face. "Here's something we need to discuss.: you're going to move to West Palm. Maybe not tomorrow and maybe not in two weeks, but eventually."

"I don't think it's totally decided. I don't have a job down there, for one thing. It's too expensive a place to move without a paycheck."

"So, what, we're supposed to believe you're just going to let Brandon walk?" Heather shook her head. "You two are good together."

Alison looked knowing. "Maybe they're not that great."

"He's not walking," Casey said stoutly, ignoring Alison, whom she knew had a "hangry" issue. Once the potatoes arrived, she'd be nicer. "He's just going down ahead…" She stopped, caught. The other women knew it.

"Ahead of you, go on, you can say it." Alison drained her glass. "You're just dragging this out, Case. Go down there and stay with him instead of working at that barn for a month, and you can use your unpaid leave for something useful, like finding a good job that pays you a ton of money. You can get a place at a *way* better agency down there. Waiting won't help you."

"I already made a commitment to work at the barn," Casey pointed out. "You want me to break that?"

Alison rolled her eyes. "It's that horse," she pronounced. "You're going to give up Brandon over that horse. We should have known this was going to get out of control."

Heather nodded hesitantly. "I hate to say it, but Alison might be on to something here. I know you love James, but are you really going to pick a horse over Brandon?"

"That's not what is happening here!"

Alison tipped back her chair with the air of a wise bettor. "Yup, saw this one coming a mile away. Casey, that horse is behind this decision, and it's going to cost you."

Casey was so angry, she thought the top of her head must be lifting off. She felt *dizzy*. She shook her head to try and clear her brain. "You encouraged me to buy him! Both of you! So don't act like that, alright? It's not fair. Did either of you consider how I am actually feeling right now? I thought we were friends!"

The women looked moodily at their empty glasses.

"I'm sorry," Heather said eventually. "That was unkind of me."

"I'm sorry, too." Alison's pale cheeks flushed red. "I just... Casey, listen to me for a sec. I knew you in high school. Four years. And until senior year, it was like you didn't exist. You went to classes, you disappeared. The only thing you thought about was your horse. I guess I'm just afraid that's happening again."

"And if it is, should I give him up?" Casey asked, her voice sharp. "I should just stop riding because, I don't know, I like it *too much?*"

Alison blushed even an even rosier red, although previously Casey would have laid money on that being an impossible feat.

"You're right. When you put it like that, you're right. I'm really sorry."

Casey sighed and shrugged. "Thank you," she said. She noticed a passing waiter and lifted her glass, waving it in the air. He held up a finger, nodding. "Let's talk about something else," she suggested. "Anything else."

Just then, a runner deposited the breakfast potatoes in the center of their table: a gargantuan platter of sausage-flecked fried potatoes sprinkled liberally with spices and flecks of green parsley. It was very hard to think of being angry with a plate of goodness like that between them. Casey felt her mood lift immediately. She looked around at her friends and felt a stirring of sympathy. They were just worried about her. They cared what happened to her, and she might resent their opinions, but that didn't mean she couldn't appreciate their concerns.

"I really don't think Brandon and I are going to split up, if that's what you're worried about," Casey told them. And she didn't. That was the one thing she had. If she really thought they were on the outs, she'd probably have a proper breakdown. But Casey saw them making it through this, and so her spirits ultimately remained high even when she felt depressed about the move. "It's nice of you guys to worry about me, though."

"So we *can* talk about this, then?" Alison quipped, and popped a bite of potato in her mouth.

Casey grinned and nodded. "Yes. I can listen to you."

Heather cracked her knuckles. "Okay, where to begin? Let's be clear: I'm not actually worried about Brandon doing the leaving. I'm worried about *you*. Because I'm pretty sure you're hellbent on crashing your entire life right now, and if the whole problem isn't the horse but is actually your job, I think we should fix that before you go off the rails completely."

"That's kind of mean," Alison scolded, who was transforming

back into her kind self now that she'd had a bite to eat.

"Eat your potatoes." Heather tugged the platter closer to Alison's plate. "Yum yum eat-em-up."

"There's no need to be rude," Alison said, rolling her eyes at Heather, but she picked up her fork and started digging in anyway.

"Listen up, Casey." Heather leaned forward, her eyes piercing. "At my job, we don't beat around the bush."

"Too bad we don't know what your job is," Casey said lightly, wishing things would ease up. Whatever happened to fun brunch?

"Not important. At my job, we see a problem, we call it out. That's not industry-specific, it's a culture, and it's a good one. So, I'm calling you out. What do you want to do?"

"Maybe what she really wants is actually what *you* do," Alison cut in. "You should tell her what that is, so she can decide."

"Maybe it is." Heather popped a potato in her mouth, as if to illustrate just how casual she could be about her secret job. "You never know."

Casey shook her head at both of them. "So you want to know what I want to do? At this moment? Right now, I really just want to ride my horse for like, a solid month." Casey stuck her fork into the potatoes, ignoring the serving spoon and dishes set out for more genteel company. "Maybe spending this month working with Sky will help me figure it out. Maybe I won't even stay in marketing. Maybe I'll end up wanting to work with horses full-time."

She could have bitten off her tongue as soon as she'd said it. She'd made this mistake before, musing about being a professional equestrian in front of civilians. They did *not* like this sort of thing. Made them very nervous.

"Oh, Casey, that's not a good idea." Alison's voice was now deeply sympathetic, as if she was just now realizing how serious Casey's crisis was. "That's not what you want, I promise you."

Heather was less gentle. "Are you crazy? Give up your

marketing career to ride *horses?* Casey, this is a classic quarter-life crisis. Do not do anything rash. Whatever you do, do *not* quit your job for that horse. This too shall pass. Or we'll find you a job you like. But cleaning up after horses is not it."

The mimosas arrived, a tray of glasses clearly meant to serve more than one table. "Hey, my mom has horses," the runner said cheerfully as she set new glasses out for each of them. "You have horses?"

"I have *a* horse," Casey admitted, much as she might have admitted to a pack-a-day habit. Her friends shook their heads and looked slightly scornful.

The runner brightened. "That's cool. My mom has five. Ages five to thirty-five. The oldest one, she's had him since she was like, in high school. She said she could never give him up."

"That's really nice," Casey said weakly.

The runner recognized that she'd said something wrong and quickly departed, leaving behind the entire tray of glasses as a peace offering. The women went in for fresh drinks with one fluid, simultaneous motion.

"Maybe you just need some adult time," Alison said a few sips later. "You've been hanging out with those kids."

"I *like* those kids. They're so single-minded. They know exactly what they want. You know what sucks? They look at me and see their worst fears. I'm the girl who gave up horses for school and a good job. The thing their parents all keep telling them to do. And they think it's a fate worse than death. Literally. Every one of those girls will tell you they'd rather die in a riding accident, doing what they love, rather than live to be ninety but work in an office." Casey shook her head. "Think about that."

Alison rolled her eyes. "That's so stupid. Imagine wanting to die riding a horse. Why would you listen to them? They're *teenagers.*"

"What do they know about anything?" Heather agreed,

stabbing at a chunk of sausage. "When I was a teenager I wanted to be a secret agent."

There was a pause as Alison and Casey regarded Heather.

"Fair," Heather said finally. "But I don't carry a gun or race around the Alps on Her Majesty's secret service or whatever. Which was teenager-Heather's goal. I don't do anything like that."

"Not *yet,*" Alison snorted.

"Would you even tell us if you did?" Casey asked pointedly.

"Whatever. Listen, the point is, you can't be judging yourself at thirty-something against what you wanted when you were fifteen. That's just crazy. You didn't even have a fully developed brain yet."

Casey didn't have a response to that. But, she thought, moodily poking around the potatoes with a fork, she had never felt such clarity of mind as she had when she was fifteen. She'd known exactly what she'd wanted from life. It was a few years later, when —*presumably*—her brain was fully developed, that the confusion had started to set in. What sort of sense did that make?

"Brandon!" Alison's voice after four mimosas was a shrill chirp, piercing enough to make Casey nearly jump out out of her seat. "You made it!"

"Was there any doubt?" Brandon slid into the chair next to her; Casey offered her lips and received a cool kiss. "Just had to write a few thousand lines of code and then brave Target for some kitchen supplies, all in a morning's work. Now I'm ready for girl's brunch. What are we talking about? I hope it's *The Bachelor.*"

"You caught us in a lull," Casey said. "We're not talking about anything. You get to choose the next conversation!"

"That's a lot of pressure," Brandon sighed. "I'm not sure I'm up to the task. Alison, you want to take over?"

Alison ran her finger along the lip of her champagne flute. Her eyes fluttered up to meet Casey's, and for a moment Casey's breath held tight in the back of her throat. Then, she smiled: slowly, reassuringly. *I've got this,* her smile said.

"I was just telling Casey," Alison announced brightly, "about how busy the wedding business is. Seems like *everyone* wants to get married on the beach this year. I have to hire an assistant! Someone to do my social media and emails and things."

"Oh really?" Brandon leaned forward, helped himself to some potatoes. "Mmm, these are really amazing. Casey, you probably know some junior in your office who could be Alison's assistant. Maybe convince them to leave as your parting gift to the agency. Oh, there's the waiter, let me wave him down and we can put in our orders. Unless you guys are just living off potatoes. Heather, can you pass me that menu?"

Casey let Brandon's chatter take over the table. He tended to get talkative after a long morning spent working alone. It was nice, though. It took the pressure off her... as Alison had surely known it would. She'd wound Casey's boyfriend up and set him down like a children's toy, leaving him to wobble and weave all over the place while the women sat back and relaxed.

Alison caught Casey's eye a few minutes later and she gestured; Casey hopped up and they went to the restrooms together. Under the watchful eye of a plaster pelican mounted above the mirrors, they washed their hands, checked their teeth, fiddled with their hair, and flitted around the subject at hand.

"Thanks for not saying anything to Brandon about... the whole working-with-horses-forever thing," Casey said finally. "I don't think he knows about that part. I wouldn't even know how to explain it, so I'm not bringing it up unless I have to."

"Well, it's really none of my business," Alison replied briskly, as if she and Heather hadn't just spent the last fifteen minutes grilling Casey on her personal life. "You guys will have to deal with that when you're ready to."

"I'm not going to *do* anything. Everything with us will work out. I'm just—venting, I guess. Putting my thoughts out there so they're not stuck inside anymore. It doesn't mean anything." If she said it enough times, it would be true. She would stop daydreaming about roads not taken and just concentrate on filling the potholes on the one she'd chosen.

Alison flicked her eyebrows into place. "You know, Casey, here's the thing. You might do something."

Casey looked at her in the mirror, waiting.

"I mean, six months ago I never would have believed you were going to take up horseback riding again. And then I never would have believed you would buy a horse. But here we are. You've been following some serious inner signals lately."

"You think?" Casey forced a laugh.

"Um, *yeah*. So just... watch yourself, okay? You've been a little impulsive. I say this as a friend."

"Yeah, thanks."

"A friend who doesn't want to see you unemployed and homeless."

"I get it—"

"A friend who doesn't have a spare bedroom or even a nice enough couch for you to crash on."

Casey looked over at Alison. There was no trace of humor on her thin face. "It's going to be fine, really."

Alison shrugged and shook her head. "If you say so, horse girl."

Chapter Twenty-eight

On that first Monday, that first dark morning without Brandon, she went to work late.

Brandon had left the house early, before traffic could clog Interstate 95, his route south to West Palm Beach. He hadn't wanted to drive down Sunday night and leave her alone an extra night… and he hadn't wanted to drive down to an empty hotel room when he could be at home in his own house.

"Sure, I'll get down there in the thick of morning traffic, but at least there are more lanes to soak it all up," he'd reasoned. "And the office is right off the interstate. So I'll check into the hotel after work. There's no rush, it's not like I'm moving into the place." He was staying in an extended-stay hotel for the first week or two, then he had found a short-term rental in a condo tower that he was actually quite excited about. He hadn't seen it in person, but the photos promised a sleek and modern atmosphere which would be very different from their aging townhouse, with its brown carpets and unfortunate yellow kitchen counters.

Casey found the idea of moving to a building she'd never seen deeply unnerving—what if the pictures were all computer-illustrated fakes? What if the building had been hastily built during the housing bubble and there were a million code violations?—but she managed to keep her anxiety to a minimum around Brandon.

"I can't wait to see what the view is like," she'd told him

instead, having promised to come down for the weekend any time she could get away from work. But she didn't expect that to happen too often once September arrived. Then the horse show would be just weeks away, and between working and riding, Casey would be swamped with preparation.

So this morning, Brandon had driven away into the dark, after a farewell full of kisses and promises, and Casey had gone back into the house and sat herself down at the kitchen table and cried, forehead against a placemat, for a solid twenty minutes. Then she went upstairs and took a shower for another twenty minutes to try and steam out the headache she'd given herself, and then she went downstairs in her bathrobe and drank half a pot of coffee and ate three brown-sugar-and-cinnamon Pop-Tarts, cold, straight out of the foil packaging, before she managed to get herself together.

"Casey, my friend, this will never do," she whispered to herself, because speaking at full volume in this suddenly empty house was not going to work.

She folded the foil back over the last Pop-Tart, dropped it into her lunch bag along with a Lean Cuisine, and forced herself to go to work.

Mary was on her case before she'd turned on her computer. "Casey, where were you this morning? You just decided to skip the Monday meeting?"

Casey found she wasn't in the mood for Mary. Not after the morning she'd had. There was just no space in her life for this woman's antiquated managerial skills. "I had some personal things going on this morning," she said simply, not bothering to look up. She pulled out her planner and pen, ready to make a list for the day as soon as her inbox revealed the state of her week to come.

Casey could feel Mary standing over her, waiting for her to go into more detail. She reached for the keyboard and entered her password into her computer instead. She had nothing else to say to

Mary; the sooner Mary figured that out, the better.

Mary hovered a moment longer. Casey decided she wanted coffee, Mary notwithstanding. She shoved back her desk chair so quickly that Mary jumped to one side, and Casey had to bite back a laugh. She suddenly heard Gwen's voice in her head: *If he spooks, laugh at him.*

The joy of Saturday's ride came flooding back over her, and all she wanted to do was throw her purse back into her car and drive out to the barn to see her horse.

Instead, she nodded at Mary and went down the aisle between the cubicles to the kitchen, ignoring the eyes she could feel on her back all of the way, like two icy daggers.

She called Brandon at lunch.

"Hey, babe," he answered, sounding startled. "Is everything okay?"

"It's fine." She looked at her reflection in the rear-view mirror. She was sitting in her car with the air conditioning running, parked outside of a sandwich shop near the office. A white paper bag on the passenger seat held her lunch; she hadn't been able to deal with the Lean Cuisine and the office break room after all. Today was not a day for cheerless spaces and microwaved pasta. "I miss you."

"You're not usually with me at lunchtime," Brandon pointed out.

"So you're going to choose this time to be the sensible one?" Casey asked, stung.

"I think it might be wise."

She closed her eyes. "Brandon, I just wanted to talk to you for a minute. Let's not be wise."

"I'm sorry."

There was a moment of quiet. She tried to think of something to say. Talking on the phone was new to their relationship—or, rather, it was something so buried in their past, she had never considered the possibility it might make a return. She tried to remember what they had talked about years ago, when they had been dating, when things had been fresh and new and exciting.

Nothing came to mind.

Brandon spoke first. "Are you going to ride James tonight?"

Casey laughed despite herself, surprised at the question. "Of course I am, the minute I can get out of the office."

"Good. I want you to work hard and do well at that horse show, Casey. You need to win a blue ribbon and make me proud."

"Oh, well I think a blue ribbon might be a little bit strong." Casey was secretly dying for a blue ribbon. "I will just be happy to survive it in one piece."

"A blue," Brandon said firmly. "If you're going to leave me to languish in West Palm alone, I expect you to bring home top honors. It's the least you can do."

"Well, when you put it that way…"

"I do. I have to be able to tell everyone you're so accomplished you wouldn't even consider moving with me until you'd put on a huge horse show *and* won it. Hey, listen babe, I'm getting called into a meeting. This whole day has been nothing but meetings so far. On-boarding stuff, totally boring. I forgot about this part of being someone's employee. You're good, though, right?"

Casey met her own eyes in the mirror again. She smiled at herself, winked her silly half-wink. *You've got this, girl.* "I'm good, Brandon. I was feeling sad, so I went and got a sandwich from Ziggy's."

"You got a Ziggy's—okay, now I'm jealous. I have to go into this HR meeting and all I can think about is Ziggy's. You're wrecking me, babe."

"That was my evil plan all along."

When he was off the phone, Casey turned up the radio and

considered her sandwich. "One lonely car lunch," she decided. "And then I'm going to behave myself."

Going forward, she would eat the lunch she had packed, keep her spirits up, and concentrate all of her energy on James.

Actually, that sounded pretty awesome.

"Casey! Just the girl I wanted to see." Sky burst from her office doorway just as Casey was hustling down the aisle, moving in a hurry to beat the weather. An impending afternoon storm was rustling the fronds of the palm trees and rumbling in the distance. Casey felt like she had been racing the dark clouds all the way from the office to the barn, and she was *this* close to beating the lightning. She could probably wedge in a twenty-minute ride if she got James tacked in the next five minutes…

"What's up, Sky? Is this about the marketing plan? Because I need to ride and I think I'm short on time." She gestured down the aisle at the dark clouds gathering in the west.

"Actually I think you may have to wait this one out," Sky said with a shrug. "It'll probably pass quickly. And no, this is something else."

Casey didn't know what else Sky could possibly need from her. Her board and lessons were on the house this month and next. She shrugged. "Humor me, will you? We can walk and talk."

So Sky followed Casey closely as she gathered up her tack, took it down to the cross-ties, and turned again to retrieve James from his stall, talking all the while. "Here's the thing. My mom's birthday is this weekend. And usually it's not a big deal, but my dad has suddenly decided he wants to put on this whole surprise party and he wants my help. Actually—" Sky lowered her voice confidingly, "I think he wants me to do all the hard work so he won't have to. But either way, it's such crazy late notice."

"I'll say." Casey slipped James's leather halter over his nose and reached up to push the strap behind his ears, a bit of a chore since the treat-happy horse was trying to nuzzle her fingers with his wobbly lips. "Your father knows how horse-people live. What was he thinking?"

"Well," Sky sighed. "He doesn't quite know how I live. He thinks I have a barn manager. They both do."

Casey laughed as she buckled the halter and tugged James out of his stall. "Well Sky, why would they think that? You work your ass off here." She finished and looked over at Sky, saw her expression. "Oh. Is this one of those conditions of keeping the farm things?"

"Along with having a dog and eventually breaking even? Yeah. I'm not supposed to be cutting corners. But we're working on the money thing, you and me. It'll come together. I'll be able to hire someone."

"In October, for sure. And you'll have me in just a few more weeks." James walked alongside her, his hooves beating a pleasant rhythm on the concrete. Casey stroked his neck with her free hand.

"I know. I'm so grateful! But that's a whole other thing. Just for right now, Casey, I was wondering, maybe, please…"

Casey glanced at her sidelong, wondering what could be so serious that Sky could barely get the words out. The wind gusted suddenly, blowing her bangs from behind her ears. Hair flew into her mouth. "Ugh," she muttered, tugging at loose strands. She was so occupied with her mouthful of hair, she barely heard Sky's request.

"Can you stay here and watch the farm this weekend, so I can go down to the party?"

Casey stopped walking, pulling James to an abrupt halt beside her. She stared at Sky. And just as she opened her mouth to say she couldn't possibly be responsible for all of these horses and people for an entire weekend, the light went out of the barn aisle like a blanket had been pulled over the farm. Rain began pouring down, huge tropical drops drumming so loudly on the metal roof that even if she had told Sky *no* in that first shocked moment, the younger woman wouldn't have heard her anyway.

"I'm not the right person for that," Casey said to her a few moments later, as the first heavy downpour subsided.

"You are," Sky said. "You really are."

"It's too soon. I haven't even started working here yet. I don't remember anything about keeping a barn running. I'll panic at the first thing that goes wrong."

Sky smiled and shook her head. "Casey, you know what the difference is between a boarder and a barn manager? A boarder panics. A barn manager takes charge. I know you think you'll panic, but something tells me that you're the take-charge type."

"Why would you ever think that?" Casey was pretty certain she was the panic type.

A peal of thunder echoed through the barn. Sky waited until it was finished, its long slow bass seeming to vibrate the ground beneath their feet, before she answered. "You're the adult in this barn," Sky told her at last. "I hear you with the kids, but that's nothing. You should hear yourself with *me*. You give me strict instructions. You tell me the things I have to fix about myself, and my business. Casey, I'm telling you, if you ever want to run a barn, you'll be a success, because when the going gets tough with other people, you have no problem telling them what to do."

Casey laughed nervously. "I don't know how to take that."

"Like the compliment it is. And also… you can barn-sit for me this weekend. Right?"

"Barn-sitting," Brandon repeated, sounding amused. "Well, that was fast."

"I'm terrified." Casey shifted on the sofa, trying to find a more flattering angle for her face. The laptop was balanced on the armrest, so at least she wasn't looking down at the camera lens, a classic webcam mistake. "Anything could happen. A horse could get sick, a kid could fall off, we could run out of feed, there could be a rabid raccoon in the tack room—"

"The sky could fall," Brandon supplied, grinning at her. "We could have a surprise hurricane."

"We could! It's August and we haven't had a hurricane in a couple of years. We're due. One could pop up at any moment."

"There's no such thing as a surprise hurricane. The Weather Channel would tell us about it so that we could panic-buy all the bottled water in the state at least a week in advance."

He had a point. Casey granted him that. "I just don't know that I'm ready for this."

"But you said yes."

"She's very persuasive."

He barked a short laugh. "Now *that* I knew."

"It's not too much work, anyway. Some of the kids will help. Arden and Gwen and a few other girls are deputized on weekends as barn help, and Sky will have them helping me all weekend."

"It's amazing how a teenage workforce of privileged white girls is a thing in horses," Brandon observed. "You really would not see that coming."

"I think we need to be careful with the word privilege," Casey sighed. "Parents give up a lot to keep their girls in horses, because it keeps them away from bad elements at school. Do you want me to give this talk again?"

"I don't, I don't! I'm so sorry." Brandon laughed and shook his head. "I will never bring up the complex socioeconomics of equestrian centers again. God help me."

"It's kind of scary, to think of being alone out there, too." Casey mused, changing the subject. Just being alone in her own home was a slightly upsetting. She had already closed all of the blinds tightly, but the empty townhouse still felt a little creaky, a little dangerous, without Brandon in it. The thought of being alone in that mobile home, out there against the empty grasslands and the winding river, was deeply alarming—even with Sky's noisy dogs to protect her.

"That part is scary," Brandon said thoughtfully. "I can see that being an issue. I don't think I love you being out there alone all night. You can't come home?"

"I could, but then there would be no one with the dogs. And something could happen to the barn overnight... I don't think I could deal with the stress of driving up the lane not knowing if the whole place burned down overnight."

Brandon raised his eyebrows at her. "You really *do* have an active imagination, Casey."

"I can't help it!"

"Well, tell you what. I've got nothing to do down here this weekend. I'll just come back up and stay with you."

Casey's jaw dropped. "You *will?*"

"Of course I will. It's only a couple of hours to drive. I'll come up Saturday and drive back down here on Sunday."

"I'll be so busy. You'll be bored."

"You don't want me to come."

"No," Casey said. "I mean—that's not what I meant. No, you're wrong. Yes, I want you to come."

"Then I'll come." He smiled at her, his face lit slightly blue by the monitor, and Casey smiled back, her whole heart in her eyes.

Chapter Twenty-nine

The first barn-sitting problem presented itself about twenty minutes after Sky left for Wellington, driving down the barn lane in a cloud of white dust. And it was caused, predictably, by a pony.

"Snowshoe turned over his hay bucket," Arden reported, poking her head into the office. "He flooded his stall."

Casey, sitting behind the desk in Sky's usual spot, looked up from the list of instructions Sky had left her. She'd been reading it over and over for the past half hour, pausing only to bid Sky a safe journey and agree that yes, she was overthinking this and yes, everything would be just fine. "Oh, no. Is it completely flooded?"

"Pretty much," Arden confirmed, with the pleasure of bearing bad news written all over her smug face. "We'd just refilled the muck tub his hay goes in. There was at least two buckets' worth of water in there."

So, that's ten gallons, Casey thought. *Super.* She followed Arden down the barn aisle, which was already bustling with Saturday boarder activity. Even with riding lessons cancelled for the weekend, there were kids everywhere, either just hanging out in the aisle or hauling horses out of stalls and leading them down to cross-ties, ready to get down to the serious business of grooming and tacking and bathing. The barn echoed with the sounds of horseshoes on concrete, sliding stall doors, and girlish shouts and giggles.

Casey peered through the bars of Snowshoe's stall. A small chestnut pony with four white socks and a big white blaze blinked back at her. He was standing in a puddle of water, with soggy hay spread all around him. The overturned muck tub was next to him, more wet hay spilling from inside.

"Why, Snowshoe. Why."

The pony did not answer her, but he did look suspiciously pleased with himself.

"The tub wasn't fastened to the wall right," Arden informed her. "He always tests it and if the bungee cord isn't tight, he'll tip it over. *Someone* didn't check it." Her tone begged Casey to find and punish the guilty party.

"Why is his hay even soaked?" Casey asked, stalling for time while she figured out what to do with the pony's stall. She had never paid much attention to Sky's handful of lesson ponies; they required little attention as they ate almost nothing and generally never got sick or injured, as ponies were made entirely of iron and bad intentions.

"His owner thinks he's allergic to dust." Gwen had strolled up to join them. Her voice was bland—almost, but not quite, masking her opinion of Snowshoe's owner. "She insists it gets soaked even though there's zero evidence he needs it that way. And since she leases him to Sky for almost nothing, Sky goes along with it."

"Oh, that's annoying," Casey said absently, mentally processing the potentially problematic fact that Sky didn't actually own Snowshoe. She'd had no idea any of the lesson horses didn't belong to the farm. *Dammit, Sky!* This might have been useful information if a vet call was needed at any point.

"So, you want us to strip this stall?" Gwen asked, gazing dispassionately at the mess.

There was really no choice. The pony couldn't be left on wet bedding. It was bad enough that the paddocks were so muddy from the ongoing rainy season. Time spent indoors was the only chance that soft hooves got to dry out during the entire summer.

"I guess so," Casey sighed. "Do you need help?"

"Well, next question." Gwen held up a finger. "We might not have enough in the shavings pile to get through the weekend. The delivery is Monday, but we're already low. Sky topped off the stalls yesterday so you wouldn't have to worry about it unless there was a problem... like this."

Casey didn't ask Gwen how she knew when the bedding delivery would be. She just allowed herself to be marched over to the shavings pile where she found that inventory was, in fact, very low. Gwen held up the blue tarp and Casey ducked under it, breathing in the wet, shop-class smell of wood shavings. There were blades of grass poking through the thin remnants of last month's truckload. It would take serious work to scrape up enough bedding to fill Snowshoe's stall.

"But his stall is soaked," Casey said helplessly. "It has to be stripped."

"Well, we can do a really low bedding for him," Gwen assured her, appraising the shavings situation with her hands on her hips. She looked like a small and serious contractor. "I'll sweep it back from the door and the edges so he just has some in the middle. I've seen some barns do it that way, seems fine."

"That works."

"Of course, if Wendy stops by, she'll be a little upset. You'll be able to tell her why it's like that, though. Should be fine."

"Wendy?" Casey had never heard of anyone named Wendy. "That's his owner?"

"Yup. She comes every couple Saturday afternoons to visit. Like around one or two, when it's really hot. You're not usually here that time of day, so you've probably never seen her."

"She needs to not come," Casey decided. "That would be really important to my mental health."

"Well, we'll just explain the situation to her. Horses do these things."

Casey went back into the office and sat down in Sky's creaking chair. The dusty little alarm clock on the desk told her the morning was young—only quarter past ten—and there was plenty of time for the horses to make more trouble.

Brandon arrived in the steamy midday, with an armful of lunch from Ziggy's and a devilish smile. Having never been to the farm at all, he parked at the house rather than the barn, and carried the food up to the front porch, which set off the usually sleeping dogs. They bayed bloody murder against the front door as Casey hustled across the lawn to intercept him.

"Is that dogs I hear?" Brandon asked, looking concerned. "Or wailing spirits from the depths of hell?"

"Just dogs," Casey panted. "I told you about them, remember?" But maybe she hadn't gone into detail. The Catahoula hounds were so rarely in sight during barn hours, she didn't think about them much. They slept like tops all day in the air conditioning, and came out in the late evening to sniff and inspect the detritus of the day. "They're fine with everyone, really. Just loud."

She slipped inside the trailer and slammed the storm door closed behind her before the dogs could escape. They pressed their noses to the glass and slavered ferociously at Brandon, who took several steps back in response. "Are we sure?" he called through the glass door. "Absolutely fine with everyone?"

Casey was *not* sure. Come to think of it, Sky had never actually said the dogs were good with people. She'd just said they were so crazy she kept them inside when there were people in the barn. That, and the fact that they stole everything that wasn't nailed down. The dogs had never had a problem with her, but they definitely seemed to have an issue with Brandon.

"Maybe they're some of those dogs that don't like men," she said helplessly, trying and failing to pull them away from the door. "Sky did say once she *had* to have crazy dogs because she lived alone out here."

"Maybe we eat in the barn, then."

There wasn't much choice, although Casey wasn't thrilled about trotting out Brandon in front of the teens. She hadn't wanted their one-week reunion, not to mention his first visit to the farm, to include the brat pack.

As they walked across the grass towards the barn, the dogs quieted. Brandon shifted the deli bag to one arm and held out his free hand to Casey. She took it, smiling at him.

"I missed you," he said softly. "I have too much time on my hands down there. I have to sit and think about how I left my girlfriend and my home to sit in a hotel room near I-95. It has not been a good trade."

Casey looked down at the grass, letting her hair swing over her face. "I miss you, too," she replied. "I've been spending all of my time here so I don't have to think about it."

Brandon shook his head. "Why am I not surprised?"

The lounge was crisply cold (someone had turned the air conditioning down too far again, teenager-style) and they had just settled down at the card table in the corner to dig into their sandwiches when the door opened and half a dozen girls filed in, not bothering to hide their interest in Casey and Brandon.

Brandon froze, his sandwich halfway to his mouth, and watched the giggling procession pass him by. They settled into the chairs facing the picture window overlooking the arena and commenced whispering, their shiny pony-tails pressed close together.

Brandon looked back at Casey, eyebrows in a questioning arch.

She shrugged, trying to keep things casual, and called over her shoulder: "Hey girls, who is riding?"

"Gwen and Rocket," Arden replied, her voice full of suppressed laughter. "The new pony."

Casey vaguely remembered hearing something about Rocket's reputation. "Doesn't he have a nasty stop or something?"

"Drops his shoulder before fences, spins, and bucks," Callie recited with relish. "He's a total dick."

"Should Gwen be riding him while Sky isn't here?"

There was a series of shrugs.

Casey and Brandon exchanged glances.

"Uh, guys, I don't know…"

"It's fine," Callie said, flipping her pony-tail over her shoulder. "Gwen won't jump him. She's just doing flatwork."

Casey had her suspicions about that—why would the entire group settle in for a show if Gwen was just going to do flatwork? But, she had to admit, Sky hadn't given her any restrictions on what the girls could do with their usual rides. This was supposed to be an ordinary weekend, minus riding lessons.

"Fine," she said finally. "Let me know if he gives her trouble." She didn't know what she'd do about it besides ask Gwen to bring the pony in, but she had to say *something*.

Brandon gave her an encouraging smile. "You're the boss-lady now!"

Casey shrugged. She didn't *feel* like the boss-lady. She felt like a baby-sitter, with a group of kids who thought they'd outgrown having a sitter watching over them. "I'd rather pretend they're not around and just enjoy having you here with me."

"Nope, you're in charge." Brandon winked at her. "You have to make the rules. Don't let me get in the way."

Casey laughed and covered his hand with hers. His skin felt so warm and alive; had he really been gone just a week? She felt like she hadn't touched him in forever. "You couldn't get in the way!"

"Brandon! Get out of the way!"

There was a general shrieking as the pony went racing through the barn again at previously undiscovered pony speeds.

Brandon flattened himself against the wall and inched back towards the open door of the lounge. All of the girls had raced out to the arena the moment Rocket had shown his demonic side and bucked off Gwen. Brandon and Casey came following hot on their heels. Rocket had opted to gallop straight back to the barn, ears pinned and short legs spinning wildly, racing right past Brandon with a velocity which matched his name. He'd stared after the departing pony in obvious shock, and if only Casey had been able to pause and enjoy the moment, it would have been fun to photograph his expression when he realized Rocket was coming back at him.

Unfortunately, there was no time for fun. She left Brandon to save himself, abandoned the runaway pony to the girls who had stayed in the barn, and went running back out to the arena, where Gwen was just sitting up, shaking her head.

"Jesus, Gwen, are you okay?"

Gwen took off her helmet and shook dirt out of it. Her face was, as usual, devoid of expression. "Fine, I think."

Casey dropped to her knees beside the girl. "You were down for a long time."

"Knocked the wind out of me." Gwen ignored Casey's outstretched hand and stood up slowly. "Oof. My whole side is sore. It's *nothing,"* she added quickly, seeing Casey's face shaping itself into a lot of questions about broken bones and internal injuries. "I'm fine. That pony isn't very high off the ground."

A few dozen feet away, the barn seemed to lift itself off the ground on the strength of ten girls' screaming. There was a rattle of hooves on concrete and then Rocket was flying out of the barn aisle again, his reins broken and the loose ends snapping around his forelegs.

"Brat," Gwen said grimly. "I need to get back on him or he's going to do this every day."

Casey's safety-first brain wanted to disagree, but her horse-trainer brain knew Gwen was right. "Well, we'll have to catch him first. What's going on in there? Didn't any of those girls think to grab a feed bucket?"

When the dust settled, Casey found Brandon in the lounge, picking morosely at his potato chips. He'd been alone for a while, and she felt bad about it, but there was no denying the afternoon's events had redistributed her priorities for an hour or so.

Things had gone smoothly once a feed bucket was acquired and shaken loudly for Rocket to hear. The pony had been caught, Gwen had been remounted, and they'd all trooped out to the arena to offer advice and keep tabs on her while the girl got the pony around the ring with her heels, her elbows, and her sharp voice.

By the time they came in, Rocket dripping with sweat but chastened, Gwen looking appropriately queenly in the saddle, and everyone chattering about what a brat he was and how tough Gwen was, the blue midday sky was beginning to transition to afternoon clouds. There was a low rumble in the distance as thunder began to wake up amongst the cumulus.

"Hey," Casey said, closing the door behind her. The lounge was tremendously, miraculously cold on her skin after standing in the blazing sunshine for the past half-hour. "Sorry about all that."

"I put your sandwich in the fridge." Brandon gestured to the little fridge humming in the corner. "I had to move some weird meds around to make room."

Casey laughed as she pulled her sandwich free from between two bottles of Gentocin. "Just antibiotics," she assured him. "Injectable, since they don't make bubblegum flavor for horses."

"Too bad, I loved that stuff when I was a kid."

"So did I!" She slid back into the folding chair across from him. "So, that was an adventure."

"I saw. That kid really had a tough ride."

"Gwen's tougher than the worst pony," Casey confided. "She's going places, that kid."

"What places? Like, the Olympics?"

Casey bit into her sandwich and chewed slowly, considering. "Everyone thinks so. She has the talent. But you know, I think even if she just has a barn like this and trains good horses, she'll be fulfilled. The Olympic team… that's a teenage dream. I think you grow out of it. Most of the time."

"Did you grow out of it?"

"I did," Casey said honestly. "I have no interest in riding in the Olympics. Those huge jumps! No, thank you."

"What about a barn like this? And the good horses? Is that something you'd want?"

She dropped her eyes, wishing he wouldn't bring this up immediately. She didn't want to think about their future right now. She didn't want to make any plans. She wanted to eat her damn sandwich. *"Brandon,"* she muttered. "Why do you want to do this?"

"I'm just trying to understand what you want, Casey." His voice was gentle, but she could hear the strain underneath. He was stressing over all of this.

She wished he'd just stop. She wished he'd hit pause.

It was hard enough for her to get through these days alone without stressing constantly. The last thing she wanted right now was for this worry to spill into her relationship when they were *together.*

More than anything right now, what Casey wanted was to be left in peace to panic over her future alone. She wanted Brandon to stay unchanged, a steady rock. Then, once she had sorted everything out to her satisfaction, he would be right there waiting for her, a hand extended to pull her up to join him.

Now he was staring at her, waiting for an answer, unwilling to let sleeping dogs lie long enough for them to finish their dreams.

Casey picked up her sandwich, sighed, put it down again. She flattened her hands on the table and met Brandon's gaze. "Can't we just let this play out? I don't *know* what's coming next. I want to get through this weekend. I want to get through this marketing campaign. I want to survive the next two months. And then? I'm sure things will become more clear."

Brandon leaned back in his chair, his gaze not leaving hers. "I don't want us to decide we want different things."

She drew in a quick breath. When she spoke, her throat felt tight, thick with all that emotion she'd been trying to tamp down. "I don't want that either," she managed to say. "I don't think that's what's happening."

"I'm not saying we are. I'm just… there's just been a lot. You're right about that. And all week I've been asking myself: is it me, or is it the move, or is it the job, or is it the horse? I am not trying to start a fight, please don't misunderstand me, but things didn't get strange until the horse came along."

Casey put down her sandwich, her appetite gone. "He's not The Horse, Brandon. Have you even met James? You haven't, have you? How did we leave that out?"

Brandon shook his head, his gaze suddenly furtive.

"Come on. It's time."

Chapter Thirty

"He's not going to hurt you," Casey sighed, shaking her head.

Brandon was hanging back from James's open stall door, looking a little leery of the sounds and smells emerging from within. He'd never been a natural around animals, Casey was remembering. He hadn't been allowed to have pets as a child.

"Come on, you can give James a cookie," she urged him. *That* would win him over. What was more innocent, more delightful, than a sweet horse eating a yummy cookie? When James ran his lips over Brandon's palms, he wouldn't be able to resist the horse's charms another moment.

They had a large audience, as the entire stables' worth of horses were currently inside and waiting for their afternoon hay. Each horse was watching them with great interest, leaning over nylon stall guards or running their nose up their stall bars. James knew he was the chosen one, and he strained to get to Casey as she neared his stall, one foreleg slowly tracing the concrete in front of his stall so that he was almost, but not quite, performing a forbidden paw.

"You better put that foot back!" Casey warned, and he dragged it back into the shavings, the shoe scraping gratingly on the pavement beneath. She glanced at Brandon; he was looking at her, not the horse. "What?"

"Does he know commands like that?"

"He knows when he's being bad. Tone of voice, mainly." She pulled the package of peanut butter cremes from her barn bag. "But it's all in the name of cookies. Here, take one."

"Um." Brandon took the cookie from her fingers, still looking uncertain. By now they were standing right in front of James, who was leaning over the stall guard and straining to reach Brandon with everything he had, eyes popping with the effort to get his neck to reach just a little longer. "How do I—"

"Just hand it to him. When his lips touch your fingers, let go." It wasn't the petting zoo-approved way for a beginner to feed a horse, but Casey had no patience for that whole lay-your-fingers-flat song-and-dance. Try that with James and he'd just knock the cookie on the floor and then get mad at you while he was searching for it.

Brandon offered up the cookie, but he yanked his fingers back as if he'd touched something hot the moment James's searching lips encircled the treat. James crunched the cookie and regarded Brandon with a bland expression before turning to Casey, reminding her that she still owed him one.

She happily handed over a treat, then turned to Brandon, who had taken a cautious step backwards. "Okay, you've gotten off on the right foot. And it sounds like that storm is moving on past. Let's clean him up and go for a ride."

With a cool breeze and gray clouds overhead taking the edge off the afternoon, all of the barn kids had solemnly gathered alongside the arena. They perched on the neighboring picnic table with their legs folded and their expressions grave, ready to judge Brandon for every move he made.

Casey could have strangled them... but at the same time, she couldn't fault them, either. She would have done the same thing if placed in their position. It was a privilege of being a barn kid: the entire stable community was your personal reality show, put on for your amusement. If anyone had asked them to stop watching Brandon as he walked hesitantly behind Casey in the arena, they would have responded with wide, injured eyes and a hurt tone: "But we're just *sitting here!* We can't *sit here?*"

It was a sign of their enhanced investment in Brandon's fate that they'd all trooped out to the arena instead of settling back into the air-conditioned comfort of the lounge where, after all, they'd been watching Gwen's adventures with Rocket quite contentedly.

She supposed that was a compliment.

Brandon was watching her with his own bewildered expression, as if he wasn't sure how she had morphed from normal girlfriend to Amazon on horseback. For her part, Casey was starting to wonder if he'd ever listened to any of her barn stories at all, or indeed if he had actually unfollowed her on social media at some point. She posted plenty of photos of James to her accounts! There was no way this was the first time he had seen her mounted! The way he was looking at her, though, it was as if he'd had no idea she was capable of riding a horse.

She pulled up after giving James a few turns around the arena at the walk. James had settled into a routine with their rides, and was generally dead quiet until he'd started trotting. Then he started to anticipate canter work and got tougher. But if she just walked him, whether it was for ten minutes or sixty, he'd stay as quiet as an old trail horse. That was exactly what she wanted right now.

"Okay, now you get on," she called to Brandon, hopping down from the saddle. "You should feel what it's like up there."

"Me? I don't think so."

"Oh, come on. He's half-asleep."

"I've never been on a horse!"

"That's my point!"

There was some verbal tussling, but Casey was determined and

Brandon gave in at last. She situated him at the mounting block, and got James to stand quietly, then waited for Brandon to put a foot in the stirrup.

There was an air of great anticipation from the picnic table.

Brandon stood on the top step and looked at her.

"What do I do?"

"You put your foot in the stirrup and swing on." Casey pointed at the stirrup. "You're strong enough to get up there. Just don't slam onto his back."

Brandon looked helplessly at the saddle.

"Dude, you've seen enough *Game of Thrones* to know how stirrups and saddles work."

This was an indisputable point. Brandon was devoted to *Game of Thrones*. He put his foot in the stirrup, bent his knee, and launched himself upwards from the mounting block. James flinched from the effort, his ears flicking backwards, but he didn't move a hoof. Brandon's seat made contact with the saddle and for a moment he was sitting successfully. Then he slowly began to topple forward.

"Sit up! Don't end up on his neck!" James was sidestepping now, nervous about the sack of potatoes someone had hoisted onto his back. Casey wriggled the reins to settle her horse, and shook her head at Brandon. Really, he was being this obtuse? Surely he knew he had to sit upright, that he wasn't settling into an armchair? The fact that she had basically forced him into this position had already faded from her mind. She was just annoyed that her boyfriend couldn't sort out how to sit on a horse without looking ridiculous.

The picnic table was shaking with laughter.

Brandon managed to pull himself together and sit upright at last. James settled down and stood still, mouthing at the bit. Casey smiled up at Brandon and reached forward to set his right foot in the stirrup. They looked at each other for a moment. Casey tried to think of something to say. Brandon didn't look particularly happy about sitting on a horse. She wasn't sure, now that she considered it, what reaction she had expected. If he'd wanted to ride a horse, he probably would have said so at some point in the past few months.

"See," she declared finally, "nothing to it."

"If there was nothing to do it, you wouldn't be spending a fortune on lessons and practicing at all hours," Brandon pointed out.

This was such a true statement that Casey decided they were best off leaving it alone. "Let's walk," she suggested. "Let your body move with his motion."

They started to talk and Brandon was almost immediately off-balance. "Whoa!" he cried.

Casey stopped James and stared up at him.

"What did you say?"

The picnic table was in paroxysms.

"I said *wo-uh*," Brandon repeated, emphasizing the syllables.

Casey grinned. "It's *ho.*"

"Excuse me?"

"Whoa isn't pronounced *whoa*. It's pronounced *ho.* Sometimes *ho-a.* It depends on the person and how serious they are."

Brandon had forgotten about how uncomfortable he was sitting on a horse and was staring at Casey with undisguised disbelief. "That's not true."

"I've never, in my life, been around anyone who said *whoa* to a horse. Un-ironically, I mean," she added.

Brandon shrugged, and apparently decided to leave it. Casey led him around the arena a few times, and then he expressed a wish to dismount and she said *ho* to James, who halted cheerfully, and she helped him down from the saddle without looking too triumphant.

They went into the barn in single-file, Brandon trailing behind, and as she led James along in what felt like a mutinous silence, Casey was forced to consider that maybe today had not been a success, that maybe Brandon was simply never going to like or understand horses and there was nothing she could do about it. Suddenly, all of his concerns from the lounge were echoing in her ears, and she wasn't able to dissuade them.

She was not going to get over this phase. She was not going to want to ride *less;* instead, she was almost certainly going to continue down this equine rabbit-hole, riding more and possibly even acquiring the accessories that came along with a complete and total devotion to horses, in their proper order: a truck with poor gas mileage, a horse trailer, another horse, a piece of unaffordable land in an economically depressed area with a very long commute to her job, a small barn which was a constant money-pit of repairs, an inability to string together two sentences without talking about horses.

She wasn't exaggerating any of it. This was what *happened.*

Or could she just be normal and be a person with a life who also had a horse?

Gosh, that would be nice, wouldn't it? Casey nearly laughed out loud. Her goals were really shifting from day to day. *And this is why I can't have a conversation about the future right now.*

She led James into the cross-ties and started unbuckling his bridle. James, delighted with the undemanding scope of the day's ride, helpfully leaned into her, rubbing against her shoulder and chest until she swatted him away.

"Get off me!" she chided him.

James immediately stood straight and tall, as if he could never even imagine behaving so rudely.

Brandon, standing awkwardly nearby, suddenly began to laugh.

Casey stared at him, her fingers still on the buckles. "What?"

"You... it's just... this great big racehorse and you just knock him around and yell at him like he's a bad dog." Brandon gasped for breath and went back to laughing. "And he *listens!* He's totally worried that he's offended you. It's just crazy. I didn't realize it was like that... I thought horses were different, somehow."

"Different how?"

"Oh, I don't know... not mean, exactly, but imposing. Like a statue of a Civil War general. Their horses always look like they'd trample anyone in their way and they'd *like* it. But James... would he ever trample someone? I thought he'd be a war horse, but he's more like a golden retriever."

"He'd trample someone for a cookie, maybe."

James swung an ear around at the sound of that magic word.

"Should I get him one?"

"After I get his halter on," Casey said, sliding the bridle down over his ears.

"Just say when." Brandon had picked up her barn duffle, slung over her brush box to keep it off the ground, and was rummaging around for the cookies.

The action had James nearly running her over with his excitement, but Casey let it slide. Brandon had made a connection with horses. The lectures could wait.

As she watched Brandon feed James one cookie after another, laughing at the horse's waggling lips, there was a clatter of shod hooves on concrete from somewhere down the barn aisle, and an exasperated voice, shouting *"Ho! Now listen to me! You ho!"*

Brandon and Casey's eyes met and then they both dissolved into a puddle of laughter. Some things about the horse world really were hilariously wrong... it just took an outsider to point them out.

Casey had barely finished scraping the water from James's back when there was a wail from down the aisle. She looked around the corner of the cross-ties and saw Arden holding Phineas in the center of the barn. "What's going on?" she shouted, really making an effort to get her voice to carry over the sounds of box fans blowing into the stalls.

"Phineas is *lame*," Arden cried. "Three-legged lame!"

"Oh, shit," Casey said to James, who was still watching Brandon for signs of hidden cookies, and didn't pay any attention to Casey's distress.

"What's up?" Brandon asked. He was leaning against the wall watching her work, finally looking somewhat comfortable in the presence of horses.

"Something's going on with Arden's horse. He's lame."

"Lame? That's kinda mean."

"Sore in a leg. Can you watch James for a minute? I have to go see."

"I guess?"

Casey had already headed down the aisle.

Arden had only taken Phineas a few steps from his stall before stopping him, and now she was leaning against his neck and making a sound suspiciously like choked sobs.

Casey found herself thinking this level of drama was unwarranted. Why couldn't Arden just be calm and try to figure out the problem? What good was panicking going to do?

Wow, she thought a half-second later, *you really are turning into a barn manager.*

Maybe Sky was right about her.

"Which leg?"

Arden mumbled something incoherent. She was quickly proving herself useless; Casey sighed and took the lead from her. She walked Phineas a few strides down the aisle, watching his head and neck first to see which leg was the problem. But this was more than a head-bobbing lameness, when the horse gave away a sore spot by picking up his head abruptly when it touched the ground. Phineas lurched to avoid putting weight on his right foreleg for more than a second or two. When she stopped him again, he actually let the hoof hover above the ground, the toe just touching the pavement.

Damn, Casey thought, running her hand down his leg. *This looks very bad.*

But she found no heat or swelling in the horse's leg, no cuts or abrasions. She looked at Phineas for a long moment, the seconds ticking by while Arden heaved her sobs against his shoulder and the other girls watched with dark fascination.

Then, something stirred in Casey's mind: a slowly emerging memory. She picked up his right hoof and called for a hoof-pick. Someone pressed a metal pick into her hand and she dug out the bedding and debris caught in his hoof. Then she tapped the sole of his hoof with the metal tip.

Phineas yanked his hoof away from her.

"Ah-hah," she announced triumphantly. "We have an abscess!"

The dogs had finally stopped barking, and had come onto the front porch to get to know Brandon. Casey brought out iced tea, and they looked out over the farm. There was lightning flicking through towering clouds to the north. The thunderheads' western fringes were touched by gold as the sun sank below the horizon. The horses were all outside, the girls had all gone home, and the barn lights were out. Saturday—exhausting, frustrating, frightening, exhilarating Saturday—was over.

"You were pretty impressive today. Especially when you put that big bandage on that horse's foot."

"Oh, the diaper wrap?" Casey smiled. "Yeah, that was an old trick my trainer taught me when I was a kid. The sugar and iodine draw out the abscess, and the diaper and duct tape keep it all watertight so no dirt gets in. Plus it's padded, gives the horse some comfort."

"Pretty good that you remembered that."

"I didn't, at first. Then it just… came to me. I was panicking for a minute there. I forgot a horse with a bad abscess acts like he just broke his leg."

"You were pretty smooth with that pony lady, too."

Casey had nearly forgotten the visit from Snowshoe's owner, it had been so brief and so simple compared with the rest of the day. The woman had questioned her pony's rather austere bedding situation, and Casey had simply explained the situation: water bucket, flood, bedding delivery on Monday. She'd said it in a straightforward, professional manner that gave Wendy Pony-Owner no room to complain.

"I have to agree, that was a high point in my day."

"You're a pro," Brandon sighed, putting his hands behind his head and stretching out his legs. One of the Catahoulas wriggled closer to him, whining for attention. Even the dogs now loved Brandon, Casey thought with some amusement. The day really had gone remarkably well, all things considered.

A flock of ibis flew overhead, their curving red beaks a tarnished gold in the sunset. "Man, it's beautiful out here," Brandon remarked. "You can see why a person moves out to the country."

Casey couldn't help but watch him closely as he sat on the deck chair, gazing out over the countryside. Brandon was a self-avowed city boy; their townhouse was, he often said, as much suburban life as he could take, and he had a disconcerting habit of looking at real estate listings for beachside condos in the thick, relatively speaking, of Cocoa Beach's tiny downtown district. He liked walking to restaurants and biking his way through his errands; he liked looking out of his windows and seeing bright lights on busy streets. Like any horse owner, Casey liked to indulge in innocent little flights of fancy about having her own farm, a horse in the backyard, but she'd figured Brandon would never go for it.

Could a few visits to the farm change his mind?

Would that matter someday?

"So what happens after this weekend?" Brandon asked.

Casey blinked at him, still lost in her cobwebby thoughts of the future.

"When Sky comes back," he clarified.

"Oh, nothing special. Not for a while yet. She'll be home in the early afternoon tomorrow. Everything goes back to normal for a couple weeks. Then I'll start working here so we can prep for the horse show."

"Right, the horse show. And then..."

"And then we see what's next," Casey finished for him.

Brandon was still gazing out over the farm. The sun was gone at last, and the thunderheads were turning a lush pink at the edges, binding the dark gray clouds with cotton-candy swirls. "And then we see," he repeated.

Casey reached out and took his hand. He squeezed her fingers in his. Together, they watched the afterglow fade from the sky.

Chapter Thirty-one

"So, I guess this is happening now," Casey laughed nervously. "Wish me luck?"

"Good luck, you!" Brandon's voice was tinny coming from the phone's speaker, but his face was coming through clearly on the screen. She smiled at him, thankful for video calling. Maybe the future hadn't given them flying cars, but at least they had video calls. "Just… try not to have *too* much fun. It's still work, you know."

Casey picked up her phone; she'd left it propped up on the bathroom counter while she braided her hair, prepping for her first afternoon as a groom. Or as the barn manager; Sky seemed to alternate and call her both interchangeably. It didn't really matter what her title was since she wasn't being paid. Whichever word they went with, her duties would be the same: help tack up school horses, clean stalls, oversee evening feeding, and sweep up the barn at the end of the night while Sky went over her books in the office. There was quite a lot of work waiting for her, and she wasn't sure how she was going to be feeling in about six hours' time, but she still thought even the worst day in the barn had to be better than sitting at her office desk all day.

"I'll try to," she replied solemnly. "I will think of you slaving away over code down in West Palm, then going out with your work buddies for tiki drinks."

"Hey! We did it that *one* time!"

Casey savored his grin, the way his face lit up when he laughed. They'd spent the past weekend together; she'd driven down to West Palm and helped him unpack his things in the high-rise rental. With its bland white walls and dusty blinds, the place had needed some serious decoration help—Casey brought down some pictures and posters just to make the place feel less sterile. She'd been partially right about the rental's online charm; the apartment had looked a lot fancier in the website photos, though it didn't seem to be riddled with contractor shortcuts, as she'd feared. (Brandon told her she watched too many "special reports" on the local news.)

Not that the apartment's disappointing interior really mattered to Brandon. He was barely home at all, working constantly on the infrastructure of his employer's ambitious research projects. She'd barely been able to keep his attention for the entire weekend; a few times, he'd had to put his phone on night mode just to stop himself from answering constant texts from his team.

This weekend, she was making him come home to *her*. For one thing, she was out of free weekends; she had to work on Saturdays now. All day Saturday, every week, and a couple of Sundays, too—that was the barn schedule. Brandon had been surprised by how all-consuming her new schedule was, but Casey waved away working weekends, saying it was just part of the horse game, nothing to worry about.

The truth was, she was a little pained about the whole working Saturdays thing, too... but still determined to give this job the test run she thought it deserved.

"Well, no matter what, next Sunday we can go to brunch together and see everybody, so be ready for some serious boozing. They'll be thrilled that you're back for the weekend."

"Agreed. Well, my lunch is about over... and you must be heading out now, right?"

She glanced at the clock on her bedside table. "Yup. It's that time."

"Well listen… good luck! I love you!"

"I love you," Casey replied, and then ended the call quickly, before she could get too emotional about their goodbye. After four weeks of living apart, she was starting to figure out how to keep sane.

Keeping music playing downstairs constantly was the main thing, so that when she went down to the living room or kitchen or out the front door, the house never felt empty. The worst thing about being alone was definitely the silence.

The easiest way to avoid that, of course, was to head to the barn.

Today had been her first day out of the office, day one of thirty—*at least* thirty, she thought to herself with a little grin—and she'd spent the morning working on marketing for St. Johns, with a little marketing for herself as well. If she could find a couple of paying clients during this downtime from the agency, maybe she could make this lifestyle work and simply never go back to the office. Maybe. It was worth a daydream, anyway. And a robust online portfolio never hurt anyone.

Now she stretched her arms over her head, checked her barn bag to make sure her breeches and boot socks were inside (she sure wasn't going to do hours of barn labor in tight pants while the September afternoons were still sizzling-hot), and grabbed her cold cup, topped off with ice and water, from the fridge.

"Time to go to work," she sang to herself, tapping her toes to the jazz music playing quietly from the living room while she plucked her keys from their hook in the hallway, and then she was out, the front door closing behind her, chasing a dream.

When Casey walked into the barn, Sky was in the aisle,

standing next to a cross-tied school horse and looking rather wild-eyed.

"What's up?" Casey asked, assessing the situation and seeing nothing alarming. The horse leaned on the cross-ties and let his eyelids drop, unconcerned with life.

"Ugh," Sky replied unhelpfully, kneeling down by the horse's left foreleg. She tapped at his hoof and Casey noticed he was missing something important. "Before you do anything else, can you call the farrier, please? This idiot pulled a shoe while he was in his stall. How does that happen? He took off a chunk of hoof wall with it. And I needed him for two lessons tonight. Both new riders! *Casey!* What am I going to do? How does a horse pull off a shoe inside his own stall?" Her voice was approaching a wail.

"I'll call right now," Casey promised. "And if the farrier can't make it, then we'll just duct-tape it up and see what we've got."

She went into the office with the satisfying feeling that she was already a steady head in a crisis, a sensible voice in a sea of insanity. *Casey the Reliable! What did we ever do without her?*

Five minutes later she returned to the cross-ties bearing a roll of sheet cotton and some duct tape. Sky looked up at her bleakly. "He's not coming?"

"He'll be here tomorrow morning." Casey did not reveal that just getting the farrier to promise to come tomorrow morning had required several minutes of pleading. "First thing tomorrow morning."

"Tomorrow morning! I have to pick up feed tomorrow morning. In *Melbourne*. It takes half the morning to drive down there and back."

"Then I will be here to meet him and hold this goofball," Casey declared without hesitation. *Casey the Dependable! How did we ever manage without you?* "Now, let's wrap this foot up and see if he's sound enough for walk-trot lessons."

The barn kids began trickling in an hour later. A few girls settled down at the patio tables set up on the barn's front deck and began hustling through their homework. Several others wandered down to play with the school horses waiting in the cross-ties for afternoon lessons to begin. No one was in a hurry to ride; there was still a blazing sun in the blue sky, with just a few white clouds trying lazily to puff up into storm clouds. The afternoon routine was always the same: everyone who didn't have a scheduled lesson would wait to see if any clouds thickened over the sun, then hustle to groom and ride their horses before the day turned stormy. Rain meant clouds, and clouds meant shade.

Casey led the one-shoe school horse back out of his stall and into the cross-ties; she'd given him a little hay break after she'd wrapped up his hoof. She waved to the teens doing their homework, and they waved back.

"Look at you," Arden hooted. "A groom!"

"That's right," Casey said happily, even though she didn't think Arden had been complimenting her. For some people, the grunt work was always going to feel like a comedown. She was thankful she wasn't one of those people.

Gwen came over to inspect Casey's work. "What's wrong with him?"

"Nothing now," Casey announced triumphantly. "He's sound as a dollar with his hoof wrapped. There's nothing really wrong, anyway, he just pulled a shoe and the farrier won't be out until tomorrow."

"Oh, is the farrier coming?" Arden called across the aisle. "Because Phin could really use a reset. He's not due for two weeks but his hooves are growing like crazy. Let me show you."

Before Casey could tell her a show-and-tell session was not necessary, Arden was dragging Phineas out of his stall and leading him down to her. "See," she said, pointing out the offset nails and overhanging toes. "He needs done badly. Can you see if the farrier will do him tomorrow, too? And he has to be held. You *can't* cross-tie him with the farrier."

"I'll see what I can do," Casey promised, still feeling a little bit of warm glow for being Casey the Dependable, but also starting to feel a rising anxiety about how far behind she was going to be on the long list of projects she had planned to work on the next morning. She had advertising copy to revise, an interest list to contact, some spec work to get up on her portfolio… and falling behind on her second day of freelance/barn work was not an ideal scenario.

By the time she had the school horses tacked, the farrier phoned and convinced to take on a second emergency job, and the stalls cleaned up, the sky had begun its afternoon rumbling and everyone was racing to get into the arena ahead of the rain. Normally Casey would have been tacking up too, but by the time she finished the last stall, she didn't see how she could beat the lightning and rain. Still, she pulled James out of his stall and put him in the cross-ties, determined to try and get in a quick ride. Sky wouldn't need her to do anything again until later—

"Hey, Casey, can you grab Citizen and put the old Collegiate saddle on him real quick?" Sky was advancing down the aisle with her phone to her ear. "I've got Laney's mom on the phone and she wants to ride in the five o'clock lesson. They're on their way right now. The six o'clock is definitely going to get canceled with all this rain on the way."

Was there *that* much rain on the way? Casey left James in the cross-ties and ran to fetch Citizen, checking the radar on her phone as she went. *Yikes.* After the front line of the storm moved over the river, there was a veil of heavy rain trailing behind it that reached back past Orlando, almost to Tampa. It looked like at least two hours of rain—starting in a few minutes and lasting until past sunset.

Dammit, Casey thought fiercely. She'd been here since two and she wasn't going to get to ride? That would be a colossal fail. She hustled Citizen into his tack so quickly the poor horse was barely awake before she had saddled and bridled him, looped the reins under his throat-latch, and put his halter back on so that he could be cross-tied.

"You stand there nicely and wait for Laney," she told him firmly. "No shenanigans." Then she turned back to James.

Fresh raindrops were already plunking into yesterday's puddles by the time she led James out to the mounting block, and he was shaking his head as sprinkles of water flicked against his sensitive ears. He'd never been much of an outdoorsman, Casey reflected, mounting up and walking him over to the busy ring. More of an indoor kind of horse.

By now the five o'clock lesson was in full swing and the riders were using the entire arena. They were intermediate kids who didn't have their own horses yet. Casey knew Sky liked this group, but didn't feel she could afford to spend too much time on them. They were clients with just enough money for weekly lessons, but not enough to lease or buy a horse and pay board.

They weren't really competitive either, Casey reflected, watching them canter unsteadily around the ring. They needed to ride more than once a week, poor kids. Riding built an entirely new human; a new schematic was required in order to feel and mimic every movement of another animal. After a certain point, only constant practice could make perfect. She wished there was a way they could get more riding time. She wished there was a way *she* could get more riding time… starting with right now.

She sat on James by the arena gate for a moment, listening to the low rumble of thunder, and finally considered it distant enough to risk the ride. She nodded gratefully as a watching lesson mom pushed open the arena gate for her.

They actually made it as far as a few trots around the arena before lightning struck nearby, causing a colossal crash of thunder which had students and moms alike shrieking and stampeding for the barn, and *then* the rain began in earnest. By the time everyone human and equine had managed to crowd into the barn aisle, comically large raindrops were crashing down on the metal roof, sounding like a waterfall pouring over their heads. Horses and riders alike were thoroughly drenched, and kids were losing their grip on slippery reins as their mounts turned restlessly in the aisle.

It was pandemonium.

"Casey, can you help students untack?" Sky shouted over the din of rain and shrieking riders and horseshoes grinding on concrete.

"Just a sec—I have to untack James!" In the crowd, she had nowhere to do it. Finally she dragged James through the mass of horses, got him into his stall, closed the door, and untacked him there. She had to follow him around the stall as he paced anxiously, confused by the change from normal procedures.

"Could you just *please* stand still?" she hissed ferociously, but evidently he could not.

Once James was finally untacked, she tipped her saddle against the stall wall outside and draped her bridle over it, hoping no one would let their horse step on her tack, then darted over to snatch the dangling reins from the closest student, a tween girl gaping wide-eyed at the scene, who apparently had no plans to deal with her steaming-wet horse. Casey took the horse into his stall and started to strip his tack. This served as a wake-up call for the lesson group, and after a few moments of confused circling around one another, the other students found their way into their horses' stalls and got to work. The rain went on hammering down, too noisy for anyone to talk, but at least the aisle was emptied of horses at last.

"There goes my six o'clock lesson," Sky chirped over the din, holding up her phone so Casey could see all the text notifications.

And there goes any chance of riding this evening, Casey thought glumly.

"It sucked a little bit," Casey admitted.

Brandon gave her an encouraging smile. "Well, it was just the first day."

Casey pushed wet hair back from her shoulders and took a plate out of the microwave. "Well, at least I have an excuse to eat this lovely Stouffer's lasagna."

"Casey!" From his spot on her phone, tilted against the coffeemaker so she could make dinner while they fit in a quick chat, Brandon's face looked pained. "You're eating garbage without me there to stop you!"

Casey stuck a fork into her dinner. "I didn't get home until after seven, I took a shower, now it's eight, and you want me to cook, too? I don't think so. I'll eat how I want while you're gone."

"There's so much salt in that," Brandon chided. "You spend all afternoon outside and then you overload on salt. Casey, come on."

She took a bite of lasagna. It was too hot and it burned her tongue but she managed to choke it down. "Mmm, this is good. *This* does not suck, anyway."

"So, today was that rough? You only want lasagna when you've had a tough day."

"It was a lot," Casey admitted. "I didn't even get to ride more than ten minutes. Sky was constantly asking me for help. I'd think I was done and she'd start asking for something else. Then it stormed and everything went to hell. And I have to go in early tomorrow to hold horses for the farrier while she goes to Melbourne for the feed run."

"But you've got your own stuff to work on."

"Don't I know it." Casey toyed with her lasagna. "Maybe I can take my laptop in."

"Does the barn have wi-fi?"

"I'm not sure. Sky does some stuff on her computer but it might just be spreadsheets."

"Well, you'd need that."

They both knew it was impossible to pull together anything without the Internet these days.

"Or you could come home for a couple of hours, then go back for the afternoon."

"I doubt there'll be time for that." She took another bite. It *was* too salty. Dammit, Brandon! Always putting ideas in her head.

"You know, when you're freelancing, you can't overextend yourself."

"I know."

"You have to be able to keep your schedule workable."

"I know."

"Knowing how much to take on is part of—"

"I *know.*"

"Sorry! I'm sorry. I'm just… I just don't know how to help from down here."

She ate in silence for a few minutes, Brandon waiting her out on the phone.

"It's just for a month," Casey said eventually. "I'll figure it out. That's what this month is all about. Helping Sky and figuring out what I want to do. And how to do it, I guess."

Chapter Thirty-two

By the end of her first week as barn groom/manager/general dogsbody, Casey felt ready to pack in horse-work and go back to an office. Possibly even the office she'd been working at before. She was exhausted, she was frustrated, she was disappointed... everything she *hadn't* wanted out of this experience. It was incredibly daunting.

The problem with the job didn't stem from the way Sky treated her. The young woman wasn't a bad boss. The problem was, Sky had learned to lean on Casey for, well, *everything,* and with startling swiftness.

Not only that, but business really was picking up, just as Casey had promised. The phone was ringing and the inbox was pinging and new cars were showing up, excited children in jeans and old sneakers arriving for their very first riding lessons in a steady, enthusiastic stream. A few horse owners had also come to tour the property, nodding their heads appreciatively at the air-conditioned lounge and the full course of jumps in the arena. Casey was bringing in the prospective clients. But every single hour that Sky had to devote to welcoming and selling new clients on the farm was an hour of work which Casey had to step in and cover.

"I feel really conflicted about the whole thing," she confessed to Brandon, home for the weekend. She was snug in bed, pillows scrunched up behind her back, relishing the feel of him next to her in bed. Her hair was still wet from her shower, and the fiercely blowing air conditioning was making her head cold. "I'm doing the marketing that's bringing all of these people in, and I'm thrilled that it's working. But then I have to work my ass off because all of these people are coming in. So I've taken all the fun out of my second job, by being good at my first job. It's a real problem."

"Well, it's only for a month," Brandon replied reassuringly. This was his go-to response. He had already said it just about every day on their phone calls. "And you're already a week into it. Three weeks to go."

And then what? Go back to the office? Casey wondered if she could fit job-hunting a few hours a day into her insane schedule. No prospects had responded to her inquiries about freelance work; maybe that was a dead end.

"Have you told Sky yet?" Brandon asked.

"No, I haven't been able to bring it up," Casey admitted. She didn't want to disappoint her friend. Sky absolutely loved having Casey around. She talked about how much she loved Casey's presence all the time. Then she asked Casey to do something else for her.

When Casey wasn't so tired she wanted to cry, she wanted to be at the farm working with Sky, just as much as Sky wanted her there. But working for Sky made her so tired she wanted to cry.

It was complicated.

Everything was so complicated.

"Are you worried about the horse show?" Brandon asked, putting a comforting hand on her knee. "That's coming up, too. Or is that too much for you to even think about?"

"Basically." Casey chewed at her lip, thinking about the past week, which she'd spent mostly *out* of the saddle. "I haven't had time to ride in a few days. I'm trying to keep this really strict schedule with computer work in the morning, and barn work in the afternoon. And it's just wall-to-wall lessons and stall cleaning and requests while I'm there. And then it's dark out and I come home. The clocks changing in a few weeks will make things ten times worse, by the way." Casey thought of the impending doom of six p.m. sunsets. Nothing good could come of them. "I guess this is just a slow month for James."

"Bad timing, I guess."

"Yeah."

They were both silent for a moment. Casey chewed at the inside of her cheek, considering the horse show and the potential implications of not riding James every single day beforehand. It felt like a bad idea.

Brandon broke the silence at last. "Hey listen, have you thought about going to bed? It's all the rage these days."

Casey glanced at her bedside clock. It was past eleven. How had that happened? "Oh man, I better." She leaned over and kissed him. "You home today, brunch tomorrow before I go to work for a few hours, it's like life is normal again!"

"Almost normal," he murmured, turning off the bedside light. "Maybe as normal as it's going to get."

Brunch was a welcome change after the week of lonesome meals taken at her kitchen table. Alison and Heather were agog for details on her first full week as freelancer/groom, and Brandon's friends Monique and Tyler had come along as well. They were equally eager to hear about the triumphant first week of Casey's sabbatical.

"It's been a bit of a nightmare," Casey confessed.

"You miss the buzz of the office," Monique guessed, her voice sympathetic. "I hear that's the toughest part of freelancing."

"Not really," Casey laughed, following it up with a shrug and small, regretful smile. "I mean, definitely *not* my office. I can't see ever missing that place. It's actually such a pleasure to wake up every morning and realize I don't have to go in there."

Brandon looked over at her with a startled expression. Maybe he hadn't realized she felt so strongly about the agency. If he wanted her to quit and move south with him, he shouldn't look so upset, Casey thought impatiently.

"What about the horses, though?" Alison asked. "Are you loving being a—whaddya call it, a horse helper? I mean, that's what you wanted to do, right?"

"I'm not loving it," Casey sighed. "It's kind of taking the joy out of my barn time."

Brandon's face slipped into more relaxed lines. Casey had to bite back a laugh.

"But the marketing piece I'm doing for the barn? I like that."

"Do you think you might see a business in it?" Heather asked. "Marketing for stables seems really, really niche. Maybe you can build something around that."

"Maybe. I think I'd like to try. But I don't know how it will fit into my life when I have to go back to work. And I don't think there's enough there to run a full-time business… at least, not right away. It would take a while to build up enough paying clients. Most stables are pretty low-budget. I mean, I'm not working for cash right now."

The waiter slipped a plate of eggs Benedict in front of her, and Casey smiled up at him. "This looks amazing."

"Here's hoping," he said, and dashed back to the kitchen.

"Huh," Alison said. "That was kind of weird."

Casey took a bite. "Well, they're amazing, anyway."

"He's just not a marketing wizard like you," Monique chuckled. "Not everyone has your way with words. Mmm… these *are* amazing."

For a few moments the table was quiet while everyone devoted themselves to their food.

It was after the third round of mimosas that Alison made her proposal. "Casey," she said, her voice a little hesitant, "So… I'm definitely hiring an assistant for the wedding business. And it's mostly social media, I swear. Just a *little* bit of picking up linens from the dry-cleaners and maybe some light floral arranging every now and then. But honestly, what I really need is marketing help. Are you sure you won't do it?"

Casey was too surprised to answer. It was one thing to joke about working together. An outright job offer from across the table was totally unexpected. And… not really feasible. "I just don't see how being an assistant could pay me enough, Alison, and it wouldn't really solve my problem if I want to branch out into freelance work. I'm sorry, really. It sounds like fun. But with James…" she glanced apologetically at Brandon, "if I want to live anything like the life my boyfriend is accustomed to, I have to pick and choose my opportunities carefully. I feel like I'm going to have to go back to the agency for a while." The idea was depressing, but she knew it was true.

"I need you part-time," Alison persisted. "Flexible. From home. I'd just need your help in person at some of the bigger weddings. But it could mostly be remote. And we could be… I don't know, maybe your second client, if you want to go off on your own. But it wouldn't be a tiny account. I *do* have a decent marketing budget, even if I don't get much payroll to throw around."

Everyone was looking at Alison with approval, and then the gazes shifted to Casey, who was still astonished by the offer. She realized she hadn't put enough thought into her business idea. How much would she charge, how would she fit it into her crazy days, how would she even begin to take on a client?

Everyone was looking at her expectantly.

"I don't know what to say, Alison. Thank you."

"Well," Alison shrugged. "It's the least I can do to help you get started. You deserve a shot."

"I'd have to get some numbers together for you," Casey said helplessly, feeling that the brunch gossip had fallen hopelessly and rather gauchely into a business luncheon.

But everyone clearly loved it, because they were watching her breathlessly, waiting to see what she'd say next.

"I'll email you," Alison said. "I think we could really do some awesome things together."

"This is *great!*" Monique was clapping her hands. "It's all going to work out, Casey! The power of friendship. I'll look around and see if I have any connections I can send your way, too."

"I might know some people," Tyler added. "Brandon, you remember the Peterson boat people? They were talking about bumping up their marketing in the fall. Well, it's fall already and I haven't seen a single move on their Facebook page since July."

Suddenly everyone at the table was talking about marketing prospects for Casey's new business. The one that didn't exist yet. And there she sat in the middle of it, a foolish grin on her face, watching as her friends swapped names and companies, wrote down notes and looked up contacts.

The waiter came back and stood behind her, surveying the activity. "I hope they're not all writing bad Yelp reviews right now," he said finally.

"Nope," Casey said. "I wanted to tell you. The eggs were amazing."

"Well, that's a relief," he replied, mysteriously. "Let me get you some more drinks."

As it turned out, the waiter knew something was up with the eggs. Two tables over, a gray-haired man stood up and demanded to see a manager, trembling with the sort of rage not seen since Moses threw down the tablets. There was a hush, and then a mad roar of noise, as the occupants of the restaurant paused to consider the situation and then rushed straight into crazy theorizing.

"These *eggs Benedict!*" The man was shouting. "Are you *joking?*"

The waiter had been hovering behind Casey's shoulder. She heard him suck in air, a suspicious sound which made her whip around. He was doubled over, clutching her chair's back and choking on his own laughter.

"What did you *do?*" she hissed.

"It wasn't me," he whispered, wiping away tears. "The chef is quitting at the end of his shift. As he runs out of ingredients he's just throwing the empties out and not getting anything new."

"That seems like lot of rage for missing... what? Salt? There's salt on the table."

The waiter rolled his eyes at her. "Lady, this is a brunch restaurant in Florida. Most of these people can't have salt. No, there's literally nothing on that guy's plate but one coddled egg, half a biscuit and some slices of melon. And the chef just left."

Casey didn't know what to say.

"That's terrible," Heather put in. "Where are we going to eat next week? A new chef might suck."

"My breakfast potatoes!" Alison wailed. "Please tell me you won't lose the breakfast potatoes!"

The waiter shrugged at Alison and went off in search of the manager.

"Well, I want to talk to the manager after that guy is through," Alison said, watching him go. "I cannot allow anything to happen to those potatoes."

Casey turned to Brandon, who was watching the goings-on without any especial interest. "You okay, babe?" she asked, squeezing his thigh.

"Yeah. I'm ready to go."

"You look tired."

"I could use a nap, actually." He leered at her.

"Oh!" Casey burst out laughing. "Well, I have a little bit of time before I have to head to the barn."

They walked out to the car side-by-side. Casey was glad to leave the tumult of the restaurant behind.

"That was strange back there," Brandon remarked.

"It took the heat off me, anyway."

"What does that mean? They were being nice."

"None of that will come to anything, you know that. People can't just assign marketing tasks. Companies have procedures for these kinds of things."

Brandon shrugged and leaned over to open the car door for her. "Or maybe you are afraid to take it on right now?"

She didn't answer him, but his look, as she swung into the passenger seat, was knowing.

Casey managed to leave the barn early that evening, after convincing Arden, Heather, and Roxy that they wanted to help Sky with the last couple lessons of the day. It wasn't hard to do. She just dropped some heavy hints that she might be convinced to clean their tack for them later in the week if they gave her this time to spend with Brandon now.

They drove back over to the beach, despite Brandon's potential kvetching about sand, because there was an unseasonably cool breeze blowing off the water, and Casey wanted to pretend for a few minutes that she had a normal life.

Just to sort of feel it out, remember what it was to not be working at her kitchen table or mucking out stalls, with nothing in between. It was amazing how one week at St. Johns could make her feel as if months had gone by since she'd done anything that wasn't horsey in nature. And all of the talk of marketing work today had completely confused her. She felt like she could only focus on one huge life change at a time. Right now, it was the horses, and every time she tried to grasp something else, things got stressful.

So, the beach. The golden strand was shadowed already by Cocoa Beach's low-slung old condos, and the tourists were packing up for the night.

"The water is getting cool already," she said, dipping her toes in the water and drawing them back quickly. "September is still horribly hot, but the ocean turns chilly just like that."

"And the sun goes down an hour earlier soon, like you were saying last night." Brandon pointed at the pink clouds behind them. "Are there lights at the barn arena? I'd hate for you to miss out on more riding because the days are shorter."

"There are! But they're very expensive to use, so we have to be sure there are at least four riders in the ring to turn them on and then we're only allowed thirty minutes unless it's a lesson. It's going to get crowded. But, thank you for thinking of me like that."

"Like what?"

"Like a rider," Casey said, feeling herself blush a little bit. "It feels like a whole other identity from the person I've been all these years. It's nice to know you can see it too, that it's not just a person I am in my head. If that makes sense."

Brandon chuckled. "Kind of? Look, all of this is a big change, but I admit, I like seeing you devoted to something. You deserve that kind of happiness. It took some getting used to, but... this is who you are. And it's beautiful to see someone so passionate about something."

His voice sounded oddly moved, and Casey felt a sudden suspicion. But when she turned up her face to his, she saw he was just smiling in his usual way. There was nothing hidden behind his back—or in his eyes. That was good, she thought. Now was really not the time for any more life-changing decisions.

Not that it would be a stretch, emotionally. If Brandon dropped to one knee, she'd say yes. They'd been together for years, and she had no opposition to marriage. But she couldn't even begin to think about a wedding right now. She would have been slightly disappointed in Brandon for popping the question now, solely on the basis of bad timing and worse judgment.

"Someday, you'll get settled down with exactly what you want," Brandon went on, almost echoing her thoughts, "and I know horses are going to be involved somehow. But… I have to admit, I'm glad this week has convinced you that you aren't going to run off and turn into a professional trainer after all."

"It seemed like a good idea for a few minutes," Casey admitted. "It's what I wanted when I was a kid. But it's not right for me now. I like to sit and think, you know? I like my computer time, I like coming up with interesting copy and finding the right places to run ads and all of that. I *do* like marketing, really. So maybe the guys are on to something with all of their ideas. Maybe Alison is right. I can't say I really see myself doing beach weddings but… it's better than what I've got, I guess."

"You should hold out for something you want," Brandon suggested.

"That's kind, *really* it is! But where does that leave me in the meantime? Do I quit my job at the end of all this? Do I take on Alison's work, and hope that's enough?"

Brandon looked at her. The sun was setting behind the dunes and the golden light was shifting on his face. He looked utterly calm when he said: "I don't know what you should do. But I'll support you no matter what you choose."

Casey felt unreasonably close to crying. She settled for squeezing his hand.

Chapter Thirty-three

The next two weeks were a whirlwind of work… and emotions, if Casey was being honest with herself.

She found herself working fourteen days straight, for starters, which had not been in her original plans. But putting a horse show on the calendar meant prepping the horses as well as the property, and every single school horse needed multiple spa sessions to get them ready for their time in the spotlight. Casey was given a pulling comb and a list, and she used gaps in her daily chores to pull manes into tidy four-inch bobs, ripping away with the comb until her fingers bled. She had to tug gloves over her ragged nails to ride James, who was entirely too enthusiastic about the farm's sudden change in atmosphere.

"He's bouncing like a kangaroo," Casey complained to Sky. They'd fit in a lesson on Thursday morning, when Casey should have been home working on a proposal for Alison's hotel management team. "I haven't gotten enough time into him with everything else going on."

"Well, we can make up for lost time, or you can drop down to walk-trot classes." Sky did not seem to think this was particularly devastating to consider. "It's his first outing."

Casey knew she was very lucky to have a horse, and to know how to ride, and to be able to enter a horse show in ten days' time. She knew all of this, but it did not make the prospect of taking him in walk-trot classes like a total beginner feel any more palatable. With the full awareness that she was bowing to her ego instead of her intellect, she insisted: "No, I'm sure we can canter if I just put in enough work over the next week."

Sky nodded, her blonde pony-tail bouncing over her shoulder, and clapped her hands together, making James shy. "Alright, then, let's see you trotting on the rail, and pick up a right-lead canter at the corner!"

James burst into a happy trot and Casey had her hands full collecting him into a decent, balanced gait before they reached the corner. He knew exactly what was coming. Maybe they'd done too many transitions here, Casey thought, closing her fingers on the reins and unconsciously setting her jaw as she tried to stop him from anticipating the cue to canter.

Casey saw the bird before James did. *Gosh, that's a big sandhill crane,* she thought, tensing in the saddle. *Almost the size of a person.*

The crane, gray and slim with a red-crowned head, slowly emerged from the shadow of the oak tree near the top of the arena. Tall even for his own lanky species, the bird was at least five feet tall.

James spotted the crane as Casey was counting their strides down to the corner. His head came up and his ears pricked. She heard his breath come a little harder. But he wasn't so fussed that he stopped to stare. Relieved, Casey thought that if she could just get his attention back to her by asking for the canter transition, they'd be fine.

Casey shifted her leg, tightened her outside rein, and signaled James to canter.

The crane spread his wings to their full extent and beat them once—twice—three times.

Casey wasn't even sure what direction James went in. Forward, backward, up, down? It didn't matter. She was spitting out dirt and shoving herself up on her elbows, her right hip aching where it had made her body's first contact with the ground. Off to her left, James was galloping around the arena, snorting and wringing his tail as if he'd been hit with a cattle prod.

Sky ran over and knelt alongside Casey. "You okay?"

Casey ran her tongue over her teeth. "I could use some mouthwash. Your arena isn't very tasty."

"I've heard that. Haven't tasted it lately myself." Sky winked. "That's what my crash-test-dummy teenagers are for."

"Guess I should have hired one for James." Casey took Sky's hand and staggered to her feet. She rubbed her hip regretfully. "Where is he?"

James was at the other end of the arena, looking in their direction with his head held high.

"Doing his best Black Stallion impression," Casey observed dryly.

"Very majestic," Sky agreed, grinning. "You ready to get back on?"

Casey had absolutely no desire to get back on that fire-breathing monster. She would like back her nice, zen James, please. But there was no way to avoid it. "Of course. As soon as we catch him."

Fortunately for Casey's sore hip, James was not particularly hard to catch, although he *was* pretty upset about that damn bird. The crane decided to hang out between the barn and the arena for the rest of their lesson, pecking at the ground and occasionally stretching out those massive wings for a beat or two. James saw no reason to get over it, and snorted and shied every time he got to the top of the arena.

Casey was exhausted from pushing him forward and trying to catch him before every leap. By the end of the lesson, they'd

managed a few decent canter transitions at the end of the arena...
but nothing back at the top.

"That was discouraging," she admitted to Sky, although
discouraging wasn't the half of it. Her perfectionist brain didn't
need this kind of backwards slide a week and a half before a horse
show. Add in her general stress levels about working and having
Brandon living out of town, and Casey felt like she might be on the
verge of teeny, tiny little breakdown. The sort where you start
picturing yourself crying in the bathtub with a bottle of wine close
at hand before you've even had lunch, and the vision is appealing.

"You'll have bad days," Sky said lightly, evidently not very
bothered by their poor lesson. "You know that, though. This isn't
your first rodeo."

It wasn't, Casey thought, shaking her head slightly as she
untacked James in the cross-ties. He was drenched with sweat, his
veins standing up on his neck and his nostrils still spread so wide
she could see the pink skin inside them as he huffed away. All of
those canter transitions and the stress of the sandhill crane had
really taken it out of him, and yet he hadn't slowed down at all.
Casey remembered something she'd heard once about
Thoroughbreds, from an old riding instructor: *they just don't know
how to be tired.* Or, to put more more accurately, she thought:
Thoroughbreds were like toddlers. They had an on-switch and an
off-switch, and nothing in between.

"You were quieter before," Casey told her horse, a slightly
accusing edge to her voice. She slipped the saddle from his back,
and the sopping wet saddle pad fell to the ground. James flicked an
ear at it nervously and stepped away. "You weren't a spooky
monster two months ago. So what happened to you? You've seen
birds before, James!"

He eyeballed her, neck bowed against the cross-ties.

She picked up the saddle pad. "I just want one thing to be calm and normal. I just want one thing about my life to not be insane. Couldn't that one thing be you? You were supposed to be *fun*."

Casey leaned her forehead against the barn wall, the wooden plank cool and damp against her skin. Behind her, she heard the ring of metal on concrete as James shifted again, trying to keep an eye on her. *Mom's being weird again,* he was probably thinking.

"Casey? Are you all right?"

It was Gwen. Casey pushed back from the wall and turned around. The girl was standing at James's head, letting him wiggle his upper lip against her outstretched palm. "Don't let him bite you," Casey warned automatically. "He just about caught me with his teeth the other day."

"He's getting more of a personality," Gwen observed, flattening her hand and watching James snap his teeth together right above her palm. "He's getting really funny. He was so quiet when he got here. Just his lip thing, and even that's getting more animated."

"He's getting to be a pain," Casey sighed. She unraveled the hose from its dock. "And it seems like the farther along we should be, the dorkier he is getting. I can't explain it."

Gwen yanked her hand away before James managed to bite a finger off. Then she put it straight back out again for him to nuzzle. "In my experience, that's how ex-racehorses are when they start getting fit and happy. They come in kind of loopy from racetrack life, they fall out of shape really quickly because they're not galloping miles a day anymore, and then it takes some time for them to rev back up to their old selves."

Casey watched Gwen fiddle with James's nose until he started licking the girl's hand with his long pink tongue. She tried to remember how Wilson had behaved when she'd first started riding him, or any of the other off-track Thoroughbreds she'd ridden as a teenager, but her memory just didn't extend to that level of detail.

"He *has* gotten sillier," she admitted, "and not in a necessarily bad way. He's been pretty cute, actually. Although the constant licking is getting excessive."

Gwen nodded, her hand still being swabbed by James's tongue. "Yeah, he seems to have a problem stopping." She took her palm away and James stepped after her, raising his head when he hit the tug of the cross-ties on his halter. He lifted a leg to paw with impatience and Gwen shook her head at him, hard. He put it down again obediently. "That's pretty good," she said, and then wandered off.

Casey concentrated her efforts on getting James hosed down, but she was thinking about what Gwen had said. He *did* have more personality these days. When she'd first met him, he'd been quiet and still, watching her from within his stall and only perking up for cookies. She'd called him "zen" for that, but maybe she'd been mistaken. Maybe he'd just been out of his element, feeling a bit lonesome, and disoriented by the sudden changes in his life. After all, he had no frame of reference for the abrupt switch from Gulfstream to St. Johns. To go from a bustling racing barn to a suburban boarding stable had to be a bit of a shock when there was no way to explain the change. One day your life was A, the next day your life was Z, with nothing in the middle. You'd be a little subdued or a little crazy, most likely. James had chosen to be subdued.

Casey laughed as she realized something that should have been obvious from the start: she and James were in the same boat, just at different times.

"James, you realize that's the same way I feel right now? Like, where did my old life go? And what on earth is my new life? And since everything I'm doing is temporary, I'm reacting the same way you did. I'm putting my head down and hoping things start making sense." He leaned into the cool water as she let it play down his sweaty neck.

"It's nice to be understood, I get that," Casey went on. "But do you think we could somehow make this horse show thing work out it becoming too much of a disaster?"

James didn't answer, but he *did* swing his head to look at her, and she would have sworn the look in his eye was mischievous.

"Great," She told him. "Super."

Chapter Thirty-four

The September horse show was everything a Florida horse show should be: hot, sweaty, supremely regrettable.

James was jumping up and down like a pogo stick.

"Ugh, maybe this was a bad idea," Casey said for the twelfth time, watching her idiot horse bounce around at the end of the reins. They'd had a pretty decent week of training despite the bird incident. Casey felt like Gwen's little speech about James's personality finally shining through after months of uncertainty had been really helpful. She could look at James and see a fun-loving, high-spirited horse instead of a misbehaving troublemaker who had suddenly decided he didn't want to be a good boy anymore. She could work with fun-loving and high-spirited; it was a completely different proposition from a horse who was simply up to trouble to get her mad.

Armed with a better insight into James's intentions, and feeling like she'd found a sympathetic ally as she dealt with her own general confusion about life, she'd been able to finesse him through some of his sillier moments during their rides.

Plus, and this part was important: the sandhill crane had not come back.

The horse show set-up had changed things, though. For the past two days he'd been bouncing off the walls. Casey's hands had been full as all of the little bits of rental equipment Sky had been reserving for the show began arriving. Small tents sprouted alongside the arena, a flat trailer for the hired horse show judge and her scribe had been parked right up against the fence, and portable toilets were leaning together companionably near the far end of the barn.

Everything looked completely different, and Casey understood why James was so keyed up about the additions. All of the horses were spooky to some degree. But deep down, she still wanted to throttle him.

"It *was* a bad idea," Sky said, from behind her.

Casey jumped. "What?"

"Sorry, I meant, having this horse show was a bad idea. Jesus. I'm losing my mind here and we haven't even started holding classes." Sky looked around, taking in the scene. Riders from other barns were already in the paddocks she'd designated as warm-up arenas, their trainers bawling out orders and lashing lunge whips. "Let's never do this again."

"That's fine," Casey agreed. The whole thing hadn't been fun for her, either. Between working at home, all of the lesson horse and farm prep, and getting James into showing order, she felt like the past week had aged her several years. She had *definitely* spotted some new grays in her hair this morning, just before she braided the dark waves into a coil at the nape of her neck which wouldn't be released before sunset tonight.

As Sky hustled off to deal with a new crisis by the arena, Casey led James in a wide circle to try and release some of his trembling excess energy. The dark horse skipped after her cheerfully, as anxious for a leader as he was to be in motion. His hindquarters swung out in a wide arc, cupping the soft ground and sending mud flying.

"Hey! Watch out!" Arden was walking a pony out of the barn, looking mutinous. She had donned beautiful white breeches and a gleaming white ratcatcher shirt for the day, and looked as if she was prepping for her hunter rounds in the Dixon Oval at Devon Horse Show, instead of spending the morning helping Sky's lesson kids get on and off ponies in the walk-trot classes.

Her job was Casey's fault; it had been Casey's suggestion that Sky give all of the barn girls assignments to keep them busy until they had to prep for the afternoon jumping classes. Gwen was occupied in the barn, tacking up the next pony in the long queue of school horses who needed to be prepped for students. Anita and Roxy were manning the registration table in the barn aisle, handing out show numbers and taking checks from participants as they arrived. Callie was runner, charged with taking care of the judge's needs, handing over entry sheets and returning with score sheets so that the right people got their ribbons. Hannah, Alli and Martina were all variously stationed as ground crew and ring stewards.

They were an army of whippet-slim teenage workers, all clad in breeches, with their long hair elegantly braided. Casey touched her own uneven bun, low on the nape of her neck to fit beneath the harness of her helmet, and tried not to think about how comparatively wide her thighs looked in her show breeches.

Arden's role of pony-runner, getting the right kid on the right horse before each class, was important, but she evidently thought this work was beneath her. Maybe because she needed two hands to lead around ponies, and that didn't leave any appendages free for her phone and the Instagram feed she needed to maintain with constant updates on her glamorous equestrian life. Now she glowered at Casey, flicking at non-existent mud stains on her breeches.

Casey smiled apologetically. "Sorry, Arden. James is just a little worked up."

"Well, that's what you get with a *Thoroughbred*," Arden snapped nastily, and stalked off, dragging the pony along in her angry wake. Near the cluster of nervous children and parents by the arena in-gate, a small riding student waited, hard hat on head and jumping bat in hand, for Arden to deliver her mount.

The walk-trot classes were about to begin.

Casey had struggled with her class choices all week, but had ultimately decided she couldn't bear to compete against a bunch of eight-year-olds in the walk-trots, even though she realized her competency level was roughly equivalent to theirs when the horses they were all mounted on were figured into the equation. The ponies and horses in these early-morning classes were extremely well-behaved animals; they were the lesson drones and expensive packers belonging to small beginners and well-heeled intermediates from not just St. Johns Equestrian Center, but from all of the local barns—because *everyone* had turned out for Sky's first horse show.

From old ranches and backyard lean-tos and private barns and shiny new show stables, the locals had come. Anywhere there was a rider, a horse, and an English saddle within an hour of St. Johns, they'd loaded up in their trailers and arrived ready to perform for the hired judge. Everyone, it seemed, was sick of the hot summer and ready to compete; everyone was feeling the absence of the old Labor Day weekend show. The grass lawn on either side of the driveway and behind Sky's house was packed with horse trailers of all sizes and all styles: rusty old stock trailers with canvas tarps for roofs, two-horse bumper pulls towed by the family SUV, white goose-necks with tack rooms, even a gleamingly new six-horse rig from the posh newcomers to town, Wellstone Equestrian—and it couldn't be denied that the ponies and horses Wellstone had brought along were turned out nicely enough for the A-circuit shows their riders would frequent in the coming winter.

The entire property was packed. No wonder Sky looked like she was the general in charge of the losing side. She was in way over her head today. Casey felt for her, but she couldn't help her—not yet. *She* was in way over her head today, too. Once her classes were done and she had put James up in his stall, she'd be at Sky's side, but first she had to fight through her own battles.

James was hustling in a nervous circle around her again. "Come on, man, can you please chill?" she pleaded, desperation cracking her voice. She was going to have to *ride* this thing in a few minutes? She couldn't even hold him still long enough to tighten his girth.

"Casey! We're here! Now let's see that horse of yours."

"Mom?" Casey turned, astonished, dragging her snorting horse beside her. Her parents were emerging from the chaotic bustle of the barn aisle. There was a familiar bag hanging over her mother's shoulder. It was a fat canvas tote with Casey's initials stitched over the front pocket: her mom's old horse show bag! Casey felt like she'd gone back in time. "You still have that bag?"

"Of course I do." Casey's mother eyeballed James with an expert Horse Show Mom gaze: it was the assessment of a woman who did not know how to ride a horse, but who certainly knew how to handle one when necessary. She made a quick decision about James's sanity level and held out one hand, stopping Casey's father while he was mid-step. "He's bigger in person," she observed lightly, changing the subject before anyone could note her precautionary move. "For some reason, I thought he was maybe fifteen-three."

"He's just sixteen hands," Casey said, "but right now he seems to be seventeen or eighteen. He grows when he's upset." James began to dance and she dragged him in another circle. Her parents stepped back to avoid the flying mud.

"You're going to ruin the grass right here," her father said. He had always been very interested in the health of grass. *Overly interested,* her mother would say with a shake of her head, watching him stand in the front yard investigating the growth of his sod.

"It's going to get ruined by the end of today anyway," Casey replied. "A lot of horses coming out of that barn."

"It's really something to see you with a horse again," her mother remarked. "Looks very fitting. I guess we were right, weren't we? And you told us you absolutely weren't going to buy a horse. When was that, Memorial Day? *That* stand didn't last very long."

"Oh, don't hassle her about that, now," her father rebuked gently.

Casey's mother shrugged. "We knew you were going to buy a horse. I'm just saying, it's interesting. And I'm happy for you. I'm not here to start a fight." This last assurance she made while pulling Casey's father back two steps, as James's anxious spinning took him ever closer to their tidy clothes.

"Thank you. Um, why *are* you here?" Casey had not invited them or requested their presence in any way. This was supposed to be a quiet first horse show, not a big event with a cheering section. Those, she had supposed, might come later, when they were more experienced at this kind of thing. Assuming they survived today.

"I got a new camera," her father said, patting the horse show bag. "And your mother wanted to meet your horse—I mean, *we* wanted to meet your horse," he amended.

"Well," Casey replied, shrugging, "if you got a new camera, I suppose I'll allow it."

No self-respecting horse girl was going to turn down a private photographer at a horse show, even if it did look like a disaster in the making. There'd still be some cute photos amongst the train wrecks. And if she was being quite honest with herself, it was nice to have her parents there. She needed *some* support, and Sky was too busy with all of her young students to hold Casey's hand. She had wanted Brandon here, but she'd managed to push through her initial unhappiness when he'd said he couldn't come.

More and more, his absence was starting to feel normal—and Casey hated that. Having her parents there would make this feel just like a normal horse show from the old days... before Brandon had been around, when it was just Casey and her horse. She'd use that energy and channel it into an amazing first horse show for James, Casey decided.

Because it was that simple, of course. You just... decided.

Then again, maybe not. Twenty minutes later, sweating and swearing under her breath, Casey had to admit that the warm-up was not going well. She could just imagine what the entire reel of photos would look like when her father triumphantly uploaded them: Casey white-faced and terrified aboard a towering giraffe of a horse who couldn't keep his head in the stratosphere, let alone in the game.

The loudspeakers, temporary and crackly, spat out the winners of the final walk-trot class. There was just the walk-trot cross-rails to go, and then the hunter pleasure and hunter equitation classes—Casey's classes—would be called to the arena. There was only a handful of kids signed up to trot through the cross-rails class. She had maybe fifteen minutes left to prep.

Unfortunately, she hadn't had the guts to canter yet. Every time she thought about asking James for a canter transition, he seemed to grow another inch and lengthen his trot stride by another foot.

"You look great, Casey!" her mother called as she trotted by them yet again. Casey would have said thanks, if she could have gotten her voice-box unfrozen.

She was slowly, but surely, being overtaken by fear. She could feel terror prickling in the balls of her feet, and tingling in the tips of her fingers, and slipping tightly around her neck, cutting off her breathing.

She couldn't do this.

James was quaking beneath her, feeding off her nerves as she fed off of his. His head was swinging to watch all of the other horses, his mouth was pulling at the reins. They were cutting into her hands, but her palms and the insides of her fingers weren't sensitive anymore, they had toughened up from all those blisters, calloused over—she'd been riding for five months now, she was experienced again, she should be able to handle this!—but he was tugging away at her, tugging so hard he was going to rip the reins free and run away with her. Casey's eyes roved across the paddock, looking for an escape route. This was over.

"Canter him," her mother called out, her voice carrying across the paddock as if she were one of those strident, confident riding instructors bellowing at her students.

Casey didn't look back at her mother. She kept rising to the trot. She tried to count strides to herself, to find a rhythm and slow James down to match it, but he was too powerful, hauling too hard on her with his big strong neck, too much for her to overcome with the motion of her body alone.

She couldn't *do* this. She needed to pull up, get out of this paddock, dismount and drag him back to his stall. This had been a bad idea. She wasn't sixteen anymore! If something went wrong she wasn't going to bounce off that hard ground, and everyone would see her, and James would take off and get some little kid dumped off *her* horse, and it would be a chain reaction of awfulness.

"Casey, *canter* him," her mother shouted now, her voice sharp with irritation. "He needs to get it out of his system. Take him for a canter right around the arena three or four times until he flicks his ears back to you and is listening again."

There were other moms out there yelling to their daughters, and riding instructors yelling to their students, and Casey suddenly remembered being a little girl on this very farm, being yelled at just like this. What had she done next?

Exactly what she'd been told, that was what.

Casey felt like she was eight years old, and every bone in her body rebelled against listening to her mother like a child, but she didn't see what choice she had. James was being a nut. He was not going to get any better either way. She might as well do what she was told. It wasn't as if *she* had any better ideas.

"Go on! Canter him!"

Casey sat down in the saddle, nudged slightly with her seat, and let James pop into the canter he'd been dying for.

He went too fast at first, his breath snorting from his nostrils with every stride, and Casey knew they were frightening small children as her ridiculous ex-racehorse went plunging around the slippery paddock. But she stayed well inside of the other riders, and since all children rode against arena railings as if the fencing was a magnet and its mate was wedged inside their boots, she had a fairly open path around the middle of the paddock for James to canter through.

She sat down in the saddle to make it harder, not giving him the satisfaction of a half-seat. If James wanted to canter, he was going to have to work for it, using his body properly and carrying her weight with his hindquarters. They didn't do a lot of sitting canter work yet, so she knew he'd find it tiring and distracting.

By the third time around his little oval, James was starting to lower his head and look for an opportunity to break his stride. His ears flicked back to her, begging for her guidance. *I messed up! What do I do?*

Casey lifted her hands and tightened her core, sitting deep and still in the saddle—or as deep and still as she could, she wasn't exactly a world champion at the sitting canter just yet—and James broke into a trot, his breath coming hard. He arched his neck and let his weight fall on his forehand, asking her to let him walk.

Asking her for a walk! What a coup! What a triumph! What a surprise!

Casey turned to look at her mother, who gave her a thumbs up.

Suddenly, she thought, feeling eight years old again was not bad at all. Not when you had a practiced, reliable horse show mom looking out for you.

Chapter Thirty-five

Then her class was being called, and suddenly she was riding James into the show-ring, and everything felt much scarier.

Casey wondered how the show-ring version of their arena could feel so different, when it was the same arena in which they rode every single day. But this fishbowl, surrounded by people and horses and tents and the trailer where the judge was sitting, was nothing like the arena they knew.

In fact, Casey thought, the entire farm had become an alien place. No wonder James didn't feel up to task. His quiet home had transformed. There wasn't even the rustle of prairie grass in the breeze or the trilling of mockingbirds in the trees; instead there was the faint hissing of the rented P.A. system, threatening to crackle to life at any minute, and the buzzing of chattering observers, the shouts of riding instructors, and the wails of disappointed children who hadn't gotten the right color ribbon.

Casey looked around her, taking in the other riders in her class as they all searched for positions along the rail. They were nearly all strangers to her, people from other farms. She looked forward again between James's pricked ears, feeling very alone. She had no allies here to help her out if she got into a tight spot and needed room for James to canter comfortably. Her mother wasn't allowed to yell suggestions, either, if she got flustered again. Now, Casey was on her own.

James had quieted since they'd cantered through the muddy paddock, as if he'd needed to blow off that steam in order to move at a normal pace. But he was quivering a little now as they walked around the arena, waiting for all of the horses to enter so that the announcer could say those five alarming words: *Riders, you are being judged.*

Poor ex-racehorse James was still struggling with the concept of a horse show, and Casey was trying to steady him with a soothing wiggle on the reins. She could tell that he just couldn't understand what was going on. In his experience, all of this hustle and bustle said *race,* but there was nowhere to race. They were walking around the arena in single-file, which must have felt a little like going to the post, but there was not an outrider or a starting gate in sight. So what the hell were they doing out here?

James waggled his ears at the onlookers along the rail, and he looked from side to side at the jumps and the other horses, and Casey's heart went out to him as she saw how hard he was trying to just figure it all out.

She reached down and stroked his hot neck, careful not to loosen her grip on the reins lest he get any ideas about speed and forward motion without her hands ready to stop him. The last thing she needed from this day was a bolt in the show-ring while crowds of people from the local horse community were in attendance. The gossips in this group had long memories. No one remembered gaffes as well as horse-people.

James seemed to arch his neck backwards into her touch, his ears flicking back to her. Encouraged, she started murmuring to him. "You're going to be just fine," she told him softly, taking care that her voice didn't travel—speaking in the horse show ring was a big no-no in hunter divisions. "This is like a big group riding lesson. We're all going to tr—to *move* together at the same time," she amended, realizing she'd almost said *trot* out loud. James had picked up voice commands pretty early in training. She didn't want to accidentally give him the wrong cue.

The loudspeaker did its crunching static thing and he staggered sideways a little, as if the sound had physically shoved him. Casey put her lower legs on and squeezed gently to keep him moving forward. Behind them, there was a quiet clink of metal as the ring steward, Alli, closed the gate behind the last rider.

"Riders, you are being judged at the walk," the announcer said.

This was it, then. Casey checked her position, sucked in her stomach, pushed back her shoulders. James felt the roll in her pelvis and put up his nose, anticipating a cue to trot; she wiggled the inside rein and pushed her inside leg against his girth, asking him to bend and soften his mouth. He gave in, happy to have a request he understood, and arched his neck with pleasure.

There, she thought. *He looks good. Let's just keep this up for a minute*
—

"Riders trot! Trot your horses, please."

Well, a short minute, anyway. Casey tried to gather James up for a tidy trot transition, but he'd already noticed the other horses stepping it up and decided he would go with them without being told. He jounced into a fast trot with his head high, and for an awful moment Casey thought they were about to break into a gallop and run down the horse a few strides in front of them. She took a quick look around, judged the space around her clear, and bent James into a circle, taking him off the rail and away from his perceived competition.

James had clearly thought he'd figured out the game and now he wrung his tail with frustration, tossing his head—they were supposed to *catch* that horse and *pass* him, not let him get away, and who ever heard of circling off the rail anyway? What kind of race was this?

Not a race, Casey thought, hoping he'd hear her thoughts. She was trying to keep her motion rhythmic, counting in her head *one-two, one-two,* moving her body as slowly as she could post without falling behind James's rapid footfalls. After a half-dozen strides, he began to relax and comply with her body's request, slowing to match her posting.

Yes, she breathed. *"Good boy,"* she whispered. His ears flicked back to catch her voice.

They came out of the ring two flat classes and a million heartbeats later, Casey ready to drop dead from expended energy and jangling nerves; James hot and sweaty and yet somehow still fresh as a daisy. He wouldn't feel how tired he was until later, she figured. His racehorse adrenaline was up and he'd go for hours if he was allowed his own way. He'd already proven that on far quieter days than this one.

Her parents were waiting for her a few strides from the in-gate, her father clicking away with his new camera and her mother looking proud. Casey was again besieged with the overwhelming strangeness of feeling eight years old. Maybe horseback riding was more stress than her psyche could handle, she thought fleetingly.

Oh well.

"That was good!" Casey's mother announced. "I have water here... hop down and we'll loosen his girth and then you can have some."

"I can't," Casey said. "I'm doing the cross-rails next. But I'll take the water." She leaned down and snatched the sweating bottle from her mother's hand.

"Cross-rails!" her father exclaimed.

"That's right," Casey said, feeling oddly calm about the coming ordeal. "I signed up for cross-rails as well. I figured if we survived the flat classes, we could do some little jumps without dying."

"I'll pick up your ribbons, so you can have a picture with

them," Casey's mother said, and Casey's heart swelled with pleasure. *Ribbons!*

She and James had won third in pleasure, and fifth in equitation. She had no idea how they'd gotten higher marks in Hunter Pleasure, the class which was judged on the horse's behavior, than in Hunter Equitation, the class which was judged on her riding skills. Surely she'd looked more put-together out there than James had! But that was a question she would have to wrestle with later.

"We'll wait until after cross-rails, then," her father said. "You'll have one in that, too."

"If I ribbon in cross-rails, margaritas are on me," Casey said, laughing. She felt euphoric, as if she was rising high above all of her troubles. Two classes down, and she'd survived! And the next class was over fences, so she wouldn't have to deal with any other horses in the arena! Sure, sure, there were *jumps* in the next class, but Casey didn't think James would be too outrageous while cantering around a course of eighteen-inch cross-rails. Either way, the fences were small enough to allow for errors, so if they went in and demolished the tiny course, so be it.

She handed her mother the empty water bottle and nudged James into a walk. "I'm going to let him get a drink from one of the paddock troughs and then I'll see you by the in-gate," she called.

"Margaritas," her mother said appreciatively to her father, who still had the camera to his eye. "Sounds good to me."

Casey grinned to herself. She had this. She *had* this!

Chapter Thirty-six

Casey slipped into a chair opposite her parents at the Surfside Grille. She appreciated their choice. The old restaurant had some sentimental value to her; they'd eaten here a lot when she was a kid. The views were good, with a terrace overlooking the placid waters of Port Canaveral. There was only one cruise ship left at its dock, but the carnival atmosphere of the port's eateries remained even after the terminals had cleared of partying guests on their way to their ships. Everyone here was in a very good mood.

Casey remembered sitting with Brandon alongside the water just a few restaurants down from this one, talking about their next cruise—the one they hadn't booked, the one which had been forgotten when he'd taken the job in West Palm—and her horse show euphoria began to ebb just a little. She'd sent him some photos and he'd replied with texts that showed gratifying levels of both interest and regret at his absence from her first horse show. She'd wished he'd come, but she hadn't been upset when he'd said he couldn't make it. A person with a demanding work schedule couldn't be expected to commute between West Palm and Cocoa every weekend. She knew that. If she wanted to celebrate every event in her life with Brandon, they were going to have to live in the same town.

"So," her mother said, "have you decided what you're going to do?"

Her mother's thoughts were evidently on the same page as Casey's.

"I haven't," Casey admitted. "But I do feel like a lot of things have begun to come together. I put in a proposal for my friend Alison's company last week, and they should be getting back to me soon."

"What would that mean?" her father asked.

"Some remote marketing work. Not a ton, but something."

"Casey," her mother said, "what about Brandon? What are you doing about that whole situation?"

They loved Brandon, and Casey expected her mother to sound a little impatient, but she still felt rather stung that they were more interested in her plans with her boyfriend than with her career.

Although, to be fair, she'd been with him such a long time, he was really part of the family. Any decisions she made affected their feelings, as well.

"I'm not sure what's going to happen," Casey said. "We're not breaking up, if that's what you mean."

The silence stretched out between them. Should she not have said those words out loud? Did it confirm some sort of fears they had? Casey didn't know what else to say. They *weren't* breaking up. Whatever else happened, that had never been on the table.

Her mother finally sighed and changed the subject. "Well, we're very proud of you."

"For taking up riding again," her father clarified, happy to be on to something with less potential for arguments.

"I always knew it would be a nice hobby for you when you were settled into a career. Although you used to hate my saying that."

"You wanted to be a professional rider," her father remembered with a smile. "A horse trainer."

"We told you that you'd change your mind when you found out

what a paycheck was."

"And now here we are." Casey's father beamed. "Celebrating your first horse show since high school. It all worked out beautifully."

She smiled back at him, appreciative of his role as the peacemaker.

Their drinks arrived, a big sunny pitcher of ice and margarita, and a tray of gleaming glasses lined with salt and lime wedges. The waiter poured out their drinks, promised that an order of their famous conch fritters would be delivered directly, and bowed out.

"Well, I'm really glad I got to start riding again, too," Casey began. "Obviously I didn't expect to buy a horse so soon—" she managed to say this with a touch of self-deprecation which made both parents smile—"but I really love James and I think it's going to work out for the best."

"Yes, buying an off-track Thoroughbred surprised me a little. I thought you'd wait and get an older horse," her mother said. "Remember how frustrated you used to get with Wilson when you two were young? I wouldn't have thought you'd want to repeat all that."

"Wilson was a good boy," Casey protested. "He was fabulous."

"He was, but he was a pain, too. I think you forget how much trouble you had."

Casey was astonished. "Trouble? With Wilson?"

"Oh my gosh, honey. He used to run away with you. Don't you remember? It took you months to figure him out. And all the while we were wondering if we'd made a huge mistake. That one woman with the Dutch Warmbloods, Veronica? Do you remember her? She said we were going to let you get killed riding a retired racehorse. I almost believed her, especially after the first week. Non-stop trouble." Casey's mother tipped back her glass, swallowed, and gazed into the distance, remembering chaotic scenes which Casey barely recalled. "I wish we could have bought you a nicer horse, but you figured it out in the end."

Casey found herself irrationally upset that anyone would tarnish Wilson's sainted memory. "A nicer horse! Mom, I *loved* Wilson. I cried for *weeks* after he was gone. He was the best horse in the world."

"Well, like I said, you figured it out in the end," her mother agreed, shrugging her thin shoulders. "Whatever happened to him? After he went to his new owners, I mean."

Casey took something larger than a sip from her margarita, remembering the impromptu Google search and resulting email she'd sent a year or two ago. "He died a few years ago. Natural causes. They buried him on their farm." *I never got him back,* she thought bitterly. If he'd just lived a few more years—or if she had just gotten back to riding sooner—maybe she could have had her sweet old Wilson with her during his final years.

Now, would that really have been so great? Casey didn't know. Anyway, it wasn't worth thinking about now. She was just feeling sentimental from a combination of hot sun, exhaustion, margarita, absent boyfriend, and horses in general. It was an extremely potent cocktail.

"Well, he was a nice horse," her mother conceded. "Anyway, I'm just pointing out you could have waited a little bit of time, saved up and bought something a little easier than James. Not that James isn't very cute. We like him, don't we?" She nudged Casey's father, who nodded enthusiastically.

"I didn't want something easier. I wanted a challenge," Casey retorted, thoroughly annoyed by her mother's criticism. Sure, saying she wanted a challenging horse was not strictly true, but she would be damned if she was going to let her mother insinuate that she needed a solid old packer just because she wasn't a bouncy teenager anymore. "And it will be more satisfying to make a horse myself. I don't need to pay someone else to do all the work."

There was a brief moment of silence. The nearby cruise ship sounded its horn and began its slow promenade out to sea.

"So, you won three ribbons today," her mother finally said. "Is there another horse show in your future?"

Casey drained her glass.

"I don't know," she said eventually. This was the only answer she had, apparently.

Casey's mother leaned back in her chair, looking discontented. "Casey, I am concerned about you."

"Conch fritters!" The server announced. "Here we go!" When he spotted the looks on their faces, he practically dropped the wooden dish of fritters before he skedaddled off to another, less contentious table.

Casey's father looked conflicted; he wanted to worry about her thing but he also wanted to eat a conch fritter. His fingers hovered near the bowl while he looked for something to say which wouldn't get him in trouble with either of the women in his family.

"Eat one, Dad," Casey sighed. She put her elbows on the table and looked at her mother. "Mom, I don't have any plans. I just know what I want. I want to be with Brandon. I want to keep James. I want to quit my job." The words came out in a rush. "I need to find a way to do all three of those things, and I need to figure it out in the next ten days."

Her mother studied her face for a moment. Something in her expression softened. "I can understand that. So is this it, then? Are you going to move to West Palm?"

"Brandon wants me to... but the cost... I really need to have a job. That's what is slowing me down."

"The cost of James, you mean."

"Yeah." The rates for boarding stables in south Florida were astronomical. As soon as she had to pay James's bills herself again, she needed to be making real money. Plus, she couldn't expect Brandon to go on paying for half the townhouse forever. He wasn't moving back, and she had to accept that. "You know what it's like down there. Everything costs three times as much."

"So what are you going to do? I know you *think* you don't know, but Casey… you know."

Her mother was right. She did know. Because there was only one sensible answer, one thing that let her keep James *and* Brandon while she looked for work. Alison's marketing work would be helpful, but it wasn't enough to live on. She had to find a real job.

"I can't have everything," Casey said slowly. "I know that sounds ridiculous but… Mom, I can't have Brandon *and* James right now, can I?"

Suddenly, the enormity of all her decisions swept over Casey like a cold wave. Her parents watched her; her father concerned, her mother waiting.

"I'm going to go back to work at the end of the month," Casey realized. "And look for a new job. And hope Brandon understands why it has to be that way."

He would understand, wouldn't he? He'd get that she wanted to be with him, and she'd join him if and when she could, but that right now she just couldn't afford to take James down to West Palm without securing a job first?

He wouldn't make this into a fight about James, would he?

She remembered that morning at the horse show: the fear and the nausea and the nerves, and how her overactive brain had finally moved into confidence as she'd gotten James around the arena enough times to prove it wasn't some kind of fluke. And when he'd cantered around the arena all alone in the over-fences class, jumping those cross-rails like he'd been born for this? Casey's heart had been so swollen with pride and happiness, she thought she'd burst a button on her new blue show jacket.

The high of riding James had to have been absolutely stratospheric, she thought now, for this low to feel so incredibly deep.

She swiped at her eyes and shook her head once, twice, trying to banish the sorrow falling over her. This was no way to behave at her celebratory dinner. This was no problem to lay on her parents' shoulders. Not now, not at thirty-two, when every single step she'd taken to this place had been of her own choice. "I'll work it out," she rasped. "There's always an answer, right?"

She would be plucky Casey again, the girl who put her shoulders back and her chin up and her heels down and went into that arena even though she was scared to death.

Her mother nodded slowly. "I know it's tough, honey. But there's an answer. You'll come to it. Probably when you're not even trying. You'll be out driving, or taking a walk, or cleaning a stall even, and it will come to you. Something always does." She picked up the dish of conch fritters, noticeably depleted now, and held it out to Casey. "Have one of these before your father eats them all. These were your favorite when you were little, remember?"

Casey gratefully took a hot fritter from the dish, her eyes meeting her mother's with a silent *thank you*. For dropping it, for letting things go, for understanding that this situation could only be allowed to play itself out.

"I wasn't going to eat all of them," her father spoke up, deciding it was safe to rejoin the conversation. "I was taking it easy."

The waiter appeared with a fresh pitcher of margaritas. He paused before setting it down on the table. "Everything okay here?"

They all looked at him for a moment, considering the question.

"Yes," Casey said at last. "Everything is fine."

Chapter Thirty-seven

When Casey had been a kid, the Monday after a horse show was considered a dark day at the barn, extra-quiet for both the horses and the barn staff. She was relieved to learn this was still the case at St. Johns. Sky told her there wouldn't be lessons on Monday and not to show up until after three, which gave Casey ample time to work through the pile of changes she had to push through now that the farm's advertising wasn't tied to an upcoming horse show.

She settled in at her kitchen table with a cup of coffee and worked straight through the morning, realizing at one o'clock she'd better stop and eat something before she headed out to the barn to help Sky with evening barn work.

Just as Casey closed her laptop and slid it across the table, clearing some space for her upcoming sandwich, she heard her email *ding*.

Casey was not the sort of person who could leave an email unread, especially when it was coming to the mailbox with that particular *ding*. That was the new work email she'd set up, the one which was attached to her LinkedIn and her portfolio. That *ding* could very well be an opportunity.

She pulled the laptop back over and flipped it open again. *"Big money, big money,"* she murmured, clicking on the inbox.

Her eyes skimmed through the email quickly, widening, and then she had to go back to the top and read the sentences more carefully, hardly believing what she was seeing.

...The quality of your work in promoting the horse show and resulting turn-out was impressive...

...We operate horse shows on more than thirty dates per year throughout Florida, from Jacksonville to Naples...

...would like to speak with you further about an opening in our Merritt Island office...

Casey read the email three times in quick succession, then stood up from the table. She carefully backed a few steps away, and then she jumped into the air, did a sweet kick, and screamed at the top of her lungs.

"Atlantic Horse Show Productions?" Sky asked, tossing a pile of manure into her wheelbarrow. "Of course I've heard of them. They run shows all over the place. Not in Wellington, of course, but anywhere that the older companies don't have a stranglehold. Jacksonville Equestrian Center, some new place near Ocala, down near Fort Myers I think... yeah, they're supposed to be pretty nice shows. Mostly hunter/jumper stuff, though, and since my kids are so interesting in eventing, we haven't done any. Maybe that'll change with this new group, though." Sky squeezed out of the stall she'd been cleaning and picked up the handles of the wheelbarrow, ready to move on to the next one. "Why?"

"They sent me an email," Casey said, passing Sky with a broom in her hands. She went into the clean stall and swept back the shavings from the doorway and from beneath the water buckets. "They want to talk to me about marketing for them."

"Well, that's amazing! Congrats!"

Casey came out of the stall and leaned the broom on the wall. She wished she felt as confident as Sky did. It *seemed* amazing, but was it really? Why did they have to be based up here, when most of the big horse shows in Florida were in West Palm? This felt like a classic case of Murphy's Law. Of *course* the one show management company in Florida that wasn't in south Florida was the one which would offer her a job.

Naturally.

"It's weird that they're based in Merritt Island though, right? I mean, there aren't even any recognized horse shows here. The closest show they put on is in Orlando."

Sky shrugged, disappearing into the next stall. "I think a hunter trainer based in Merritt Island was one of the guys who organized it," she called through the stall bars. "So it probably just started out in his tack room, and grew from there."

"Do you think this office they're talking about is in some guy's barn?"

"Could be," Sky said cheerfully. "Did they give you an address?"

"I haven't emailed them back yet."

Sky looked at her through the bars. She looked like she had shut herself into horse jail. "Casey, go sit down at my desk, take out your phone, and compose a nice reply to those people. You need this job."

Casey didn't know how to take this sort of instruction from her current boss. She hadn't told Sky she wasn't going to stay through October. Suddenly feeling hurt, she bleated: "But I work for you!"

Sky just shook her head and went back to picking out the stall, pushing aside the horse she was working around. "Casey, you can muck stalls anytime you want. But I think we both know this isn't what you want. Go write that email."

Her phone rang about an hour later, as she was walking James out for a quick grazing session before it was time to feed dinner.

Strictly speaking, she didn't need to drag him out of his stall at five o'clock on a warm September evening. She just liked his company, and Sky had gone into the house to go through some show paperwork, leaving Casey with an unusual amount of free time. Having the barn closed up on a Monday was a weird and pleasant change. She could see why some old-school trainers did it every week of the year.

She felt her phone buzzing just as James found a juicy patch of grass to work through, and she paid out some lead-rope space for him as she pulled her phone from her pocket. The caller ID just said *Merritt Island*. So this would either be the horse show people, or a telemarketer. Casey took a breath and answered, feeling a tremor in her hands as she put the phone to her ear.

"This is Casey Halbach."

Alison and Heather were waiting when she got to the port, sitting together at a waterside table. The sun was sinking behind them in a rich swirl of purple clouds and golden backlight as Casey pulled out a chair and sat down across from them. She was still in her barn clothes, but she'd washed her face and hands before she'd left, and put on a fresh swipe of deodorant as well. She certainly looked and smelled tidy enough for the port restaurants, although next to Alison and Heather in their sleek office clothes, she felt a little ragged in a tank top and denim shorts.

"It's nice to see you guys," she sighed, feeling a sense of relief at being in this other place, this table at this restaurant that had nothing to do with horses. She felt linked up with the other half of her life, the one that still had Brandon in it, and a career that she was still invested in, despite everything she'd done to escape it. "Thanks a lot for meeting me here."

Alison tossed her long red hair over her shoulder. "Well? What was so important you needed to have drinks on a Monday night?

Some of us are trying to pretend we're respectable adults to our boyfriends."

Heather snorted. "Casey doesn't know. Casey, while you've been MIA for the past few weekends, Alison finally convinced Grayson to come to brunch and now he thinks she's a boozer."

"He thinks we're *all* boozers," Alison corrected. "And when I texted him to say I was getting drinks with Casey because she was having a life disaster, he texted back *whatever you need to tell yourself*, which, I don't have to tell you, means we are now in a big fight."

"I missed Grayson?" Casey was temporarily distracted from her own problems. "But I've only seen him once! And that was from a distance!"

"That's the way he likes it," Alison sighed. "He won't be coming back out. He found us too noisy and he didn't like the food. Too many seasonings, he said."

Heather rolled her eyes and waved to someone behind Casey; the waiter, she expected. "Face it, Alison. You're living with a hermit and someday you will marry a hermit. These are the choices you've made and you must live with him."

Just like that, Casey was back in her own head. "Okay, are you guys ready?"

Heather and Alison focused on her obediently. "Yes, Casey," they chanted together.

Casey paused to consider that they'd probably rehearsed this, then got on with it. "Today a horse show organizer offered me a job. I mean, there'd be a face-to-face interview, but it's as good as mine. I'd be the head of marketing."

Her friends' faces lit up, exactly as she'd known they would. This could have been such a satisfying, triumphant moment. If only. "Here's the rub," Casey went on. "The job is in-office. And the office is here. It's actually just a few blocks from my *current* office, although it's a lot smaller… it's just a storefront in one of those professional centers… but still…" Casey was babbling, so she decided to sum it all up with a few key points. "Dream job, wrong city, help."

Unfortunately, they didn't start lobbing fixes at her immediately. Instead, her wise and wonderful friends just looked at her with worry.

"That sucks," Heather intoned eventually.

"Yeah," Alison agreed. "Like, that *really* sucks."

Casey started looking around for the waiter. She needed a refill. Or three.

Chapter Thirty-eight

The end of September was one of warm waters and warm winds, which spun up a mild tropical storm offshore. The weather forecast sent the tourists shrieking homeward and threatened to officially end summer for the Space Coast.

Casey used the gusty winds and squall lines to echo her mood as she tried to decide how her life was about to proceed. She went to the face-to-face interview with Phillip Murphy and Sharon Conrad, who ran Atlantic Horse Show Productions out of a tiny office sandwiched between a chiropractor's office and a cupcake catering company, and fell in love with both of them. Phillip was a tall, dark-haired man in his fifties who had been riding show-ring hunters since he was five; Sharon was a keen-eyed part-time trainer in her forties who had decided to give up a life of organizing massive IT conferences in order to put on A-circuit horse shows, which she said were surprisingly similar pursuits.

"It's because everyone is picky about the same things," she explained. "Both groups are used to being catered to and have a tendency to become complete divas if they don't get what they want."

Both of them were funny, down-to-earth, and passionate about horses. The office, though minuscule, had an empty spot just waiting for her, a blank expanse of desk beneath a vintage Dublin Horse Show poster. If Casey was going to return to office life, there was no question: this little corner in a run-down strip mall was the antithesis of her modern cubicle at the blue-tinted building down the street.

The problem, of course, was that Brandon wasn't coming back here. If his dream job required him to be at an office in West Palm, and her dream job required her to be at an office in Merritt Island, where did that leave *them*?

Compounding this problem, as always, was James.

Casey changed clothes at home before she went out to the farm. The sky was full of low-hanging clouds with ragged edges, rushing through the evening sky as if they were late for something interesting. Sky was on the phone, cancelling that evening's lessons, when Casey came into the barn aisle. She was surprised to find all of the horses were outside.

"Hey," Sky sighed, setting her phone down on her desk. A gust of wind rattled the window behind her. "You brought another squall line."

"I looked at the radar before I left home. They're going to be off and on all afternoon, before it settles in to rain all night."

"That's why I cancelled everything tomorrow, too. If we really get six inches of rain tonight, the driveway and part of River Road will flood. So even if the arena is usable, I don't need anyone getting their Lexus stuck in the driveway and blocking the only way in and out. The horses can have a couple of days off for a tropical storm. They just put up with that horse show, after all."

"I don't think I'm keen to ride James in all this wind."

"Lord, no. This is not an afternoon for riding, not even for you and me. That's why everyone is out. We can bring them in for dinner and they can stay in tonight through the worst of the rain."

Suddenly, the office went dark and rain pelted at the window, fat drops that exploded on contact with the glass. The squall lasted about thirty-five seconds and then passed on, leaving behind a shifting, watery sunlight.

Typical tropical storm weather, Casey thought. It would be a nice night for curling up on the sofa and watching hours of television. Over Sky's shoulder, she saw a few of the horses in the paddocks toss their heels and buck, riled up by the changing weather. James was one of them.

Mentally, Casey could have used some quiet time with James this afternoon, a nice long grooming session in the cross-ties, followed by a gentle ride in the arena, maybe even a little bit of canter just so that she could feel removed from the ground, raised up above everything in the world that wanted her attention. She could really use the mind-clearing effect of riding today, but the weather simply wasn't going to cooperate. A nice, quiet ride on a recently retired Thoroughbred during the landfall of a tropical storm: it was like a mad lib, disastrous answers only.

"You want to help me muck stalls?" Sky asked, getting up with a few creaks and pops from her protesting joints. "We can set them all up with grain and hay. Then you can get out of here before the weather gets nasty."

"That sounds fine," Casey agreed. They went into the aisle and picked up the tools of their trade: manure forks, wheelbarrows, brooms.

They started at the end, each taking a stall on opposite sides of the aisle. It was too windy to talk much at that distance, which left Casey alone with her thoughts.

If riding let a person escape her cares, cleaning a stall was a way of isolating a person with all of her deepest thoughts. Casey figured she'd either sort out all of her problems in the next two hours, or go completely crazy and run out of the barn crying.

In the end, what she got was something in the middle. She hung up her broom and tipped up her wheelbarrow against the wall and knew exactly what she wanted.

Everything.

She wanted Brandon *and* she wanted the horse show job *and* she wanted James. Well, she'd known that already, to be fair.

Now, she also knew exactly what she could have.

Either.

She could have Brandon *or* she could have the horse show job and James. Somehow, things really had come down to choosing between the equestrian life and her old life—even though she had really tried to strike a balance.

Was there no such thing as balance when horses were concerned?

"I need a Coke," Casey sighed. She went into the lounge and dug around in the fridge, unearthing some soda cans from behind a few pre-packaged vaccine syringes. Sky settled down on the sofa facing the window, accepting the can Casey offered her with gratitude.

"This is great, isn't it?" Sky said after a few moments of quiet sipping. "It's so rare to have the place to ourselves, and now we get it twice in one week. A nice change from last weekend, right?"

Casey wasn't sure the quiet atmosphere was what she needed right now. "I don't know. I could use a distraction."

Sky shifted on the sofa. "What's going on? Brandon?"

"The horse show people. I had my interview this morning."

"Oh, my god! That was fast! And what happened?"

"They're amazing. They offered me the job. They really want me, actually."

Sky nodded, seeing the rub immediately. "And now you have even less idea what to do."

"It's honestly like the universe wants me to stay here, which is the most confusing part." Casey watched another veil of rain rush across the paddocks, spooking the horses from their grazing. James was a dark figure in the gray downpour, kicking up his heels and galloping up and down his fence-line. She hoped he didn't hurt himself. "I just want Brandon to come back, and that's not going to happen. His work is there. There's nothing I can do to change that now."

She let everything else she'd gone over spill out: the exorbitant cost of the boarding stables she'd found around West Palm, the fear that Brandon had no idea what he'd be in for if he took on James's expenses while she searched for a job, the nagging worry that even if she found a job down there, she'd find it just as pointless as the one she had been doing here.

Sky listened, and drank her Coke, and nodded, doing all of the things a sympathetic friend was supposed to do. Finally, Casey ran out of words. She just sat in silence for a few minutes. The sun came back out, and then went in again just as quickly, as the tropical clouds raced through the sky.

Sky shifted on the sofa next to her, sitting a little closer. "Casey, I know this isn't the answer you want. I don't think there's a good answer at all. But maybe I can help. If you need to leave James here for a while, I can find someone to lease him."

Casey turned her head to stare at Sky, utterly speechless.

Sky's pony-tail had come undone while they'd been working out in the wind, and now she shoved the loose strands behind her ears impatiently. "Look," she went on, "I know that's not what you want. Like I said. But horses make it really hard to make life decisions. I've seen it a hundred times. They're big. They're expensive. They take a lot out of you. So I'm just saying, if I can make this easier for you, I will." She hesitated, then wrapped her arm around Casey's shoulder in an awkward half-embrace. "You're my friend, Casey."

This made things a hundred times worse. Casey swiped at the tears starting to roll down her cheeks. "You're *my* friend," she said through a shuddering sob. "And I don't want to leave you in the lurch, all alone out here."

Sky managed a tight smile. "Casey, don't think about me for a single second. I'll manage. I have the girls. And now I can afford to hire someone part-time to do stalls and groom. Because of *you,* by the way. Your work did that for me. So, I can handle James for a little while, either way. You don't have to decide right now. But I can find someone to ride James a few days a week—maybe even Gwen—and you can come up whenever you can and ride. If it takes longer than a few weeks, we can do a half-lease until you figure it out. I *promise* we can work this out. You're not my boarder anymore, Casey. You're my friend. I mean that."

Casey was overcome. She felt her throat tighten, and swallowed against the feeling mutinously. She'd been crying entirely too much lately. *Horses,* she thought, and suddenly she started to laugh.

Sky withdrew her arm, looking alarmed. "Casey? Are you all right?"

"I am," she burbled. "I'm fine, I'm fine. It's just... *hahaha!*" She tried to get her hysterical laughter under control, but it wasn't leaving her. It came in chuckles and wheezes and shaking shoulders and snorts. After a few minutes, Sky watching her worriedly all the while, Casey managed to find her words again. "Listen... I started riding what... six months ago? And it has simultaneously made my life amazing and turned it completely upside-down. I just... is that normal? Am I doing this right?"

It was Sky's turn to laugh. She tipped her head back against the sofa cushions and just let go for a moment. "I think you're doing it right," she confessed at last. "I think horses wreck your life, and you're just supposed to enjoy the ride."

They sat quietly for a little while. The wind picked up again, and there was a new moan in the eaves which promised an escalation of hostilities from the tropical storm. Casey knew she should get home before the weather turned truly nasty, but she lingered, looking for an excuse to stay longer. "I should stick around," she told Sky. "You might need help bringing in everyone. Or if the weather gets bad tonight. Want me to spend the night?"

"It's just a tropical storm," Sky told her, with the typical dismissiveness of a lifelong Floridian. "If there's a tornado warning, I'll come to the barn, just like I would on a regular day. I don't want you stranded out here if the road floods, though. So go home. And don't worry about a thing." She paused, then grinned wryly, shaking her head. "Don't worry about *me*, anyway."

Chapter Thirty-nine

The next day was a sullen, northern-looking day of rain and wind. Sky texted and told her the driveway had indeed flooded, and not to bother trying to come to the barn that day. *I can clean all the stalls myself,* she wrote. *I have nothing better to do anyway.*

With no reason to leave the house that day, Casey knew it was time to sit down with a notepad, a coffee—or perhaps something stronger—and work out exactly what she was going to do. In seven days' time, her month's leave of absence would be over. She'd already taken working for Sky through the month of October off the table. Nope, now she had to either go back to work, accept the new job, or start packing up her things to join Brandon.

She stared at her notepad for a while, until the coffee had cooled in her mug. Then she wrote across the top of the page:

Start Own Business — Agency — Horse Show — Find New Job.

Okay, she thought. *Those are my options.*

She decided to let her heart do the work. What did her heart want? To never go back to the agency. To escape Mary's condescension, to never again think about walk-in bathtub sales—at least, not while she was still young and relatively limber. She drew a line through the word.

What else did her heart want? James, certainly.

She wrote *James* under *Horse Show.*

There, she thought. That was one for Horse Show.

What else?

She wrote *Brandon* under both *Start Own Business* and *Find New Job*.

Casey looked at the notepad for a long moment. The rain tapped on the kitchen window.

She was still looking at the list when her phone buzzed urgently, vibrating across the table. *Brandon.*

"What's up?" she asked hurriedly, without bothering to say hello. If he was calling her rather than texting her, something *was* up.

"I missed you," Brandon said. "It's pouring down rain, and the wind is blowing the palm trees sideways like a disaster movie, and I just suddenly remembered sitting in the living room watching storms blow through with you, and I missed you."

She sighed. "I thought there was an emergency."

"Don't make me say it."

Casey giggled. "Oh, so close!"

A gust of wind hit the kitchen window and made the glass rattle in its thin metal frame.

"I heard that. Are you getting a squall?"

"I guess so! I've been working and wasn't paying much attention."

"It's crazy here. I shouldn't have gone into the office... the roads are flooding and it's going to take me forever to get home."

"I stayed home today. Sky said the driveway is flooded." Casey leaned back in her chair, surrendering to the pleasure of a chat with Brandon. "So I've just been sorting out my life. The usual."

"How's that coming?"

"Not great, but I figure if I stare at these words long enough, a pattern will emerge."

"Hey Casey, did I ever tell you how I started freelancing?"

She wrinkled her brow, considering. "Not really. I know you

worked for some company as a proper employee before we met, and then you decided to go freelance and it worked out."

"Well, it feels relevant now, so I'm going to tell you. This is what happened: I took a full-time job I liked, and convinced my boss to turn it into a contract job. It wasn't an easy sell, but in the end they went for it."

"Why did you do all that, when you already liked the job as it was?"

"I'd met this girl."

There was silence. Casey took a long breath and listened to the rain splashing against the windows.

"And?" she prompted finally.

"And the job was moving to Philadelphia, but the girl was here."

"Oh," Casey said.

"So I backed up my argument with numbers and figures and I convinced my boss the job could be done here. I didn't want to miss my shot with this girl."

Casey bit her lip, her eyes swimming with tears for what felt like the hundredth time that day. But for once, they weren't tears borne of frustration and disappointment. "Brandon, you never told me that."

"Oh," he said blankly. "I'm sorry, did you think I meant *you?*"

They burst out laughing at the same time. "You're such a jerk," Casey gasped, swiping at her streaming eyes. "But did you really? How did you convince them?"

"I wrote a proposal. The same way you get any freelance job. I showed them what they were paying and what they were getting, versus what they *could* be paying and what they could be getting. I took a pay-cut, all things considered, but I had my freedom, and this cute horse girl in disguise, so it worked out."

"I can't believe you did that for me. This was... were we even *dating?"*

"Oh, definitely. I wasn't stalking you or anything. But I just... I just had a good feeling. And I want you to know that you're still worth giving up a job over."

"No," she said quickly. "Don't you dare."

"I won't, because I know you'd kill me. But... I think you've got a shot with this job you want. There's no reason you have to be at that desk in Merritt Island five days a week, right?"

"No, of course not."

"And you could drive up for meetings and a day or two of work now and then if they really needed you to?"

"Easily!"

"And you're a persuasive writer who can convince people to change their minds with your writing?"

Casey tipped her head backwards, resting it against the top of her chair. Her mind was racing with ideas. "Brandon, I love you. But you know I've got to go now, right?"

"Go... where?" His voice was slightly alarmed. "There's a tropical storm out there, my dear."

"I have to write this proposal," Casey said, flipping her notepad to a fresh, blank page. "You have any tips for me?"

"As a matter of fact... yes. Watch your email. Proposal tips incoming." His voice was filled with laughter. "You're going to knock them sideways, Case."

Two days passed with no reply from the horse show firm, and Casey was starting to believe she'd ruined her chance of working there at all. It was too bad, because she'd thought her proposal was spot-on, brief, and to the point.

She'd highlighted why her work could be better done remotely, and indicated her willingness to visit the office twice monthly for meetings and shared work sessions. She also insinuated, without a shred of evidence but with plenty of confidence, that with a home base in West Palm, she would be ideally situated to give Atlantic Horse Show Productions an inside track to the lucrative Wellington-area show market. There was no actual reason to believe this, but why not try it out?

Casey was willing to try just about anything at this point.

Anything that didn't involve calling up HR at the agency and giving them her return-to-work date, or turning James over to Sky for an undetermined period of time while she began packing up her things. If she could land this job, she could actually have it all.

Was that so much to ask?

As Casey waited with increasing desperation for a reply to her proposal, the last week of September stretched out hot and dry. Casey decided to spend her last few days of freedom at the farm. She was facing the misery of returning to work the following Monday. Nothing else had panned out quickly enough: Alison's hotel had not yet signed off on her marketing proposal, none of her spec work had brought in any clients, and she'd yet to hear back from any of the talent agencies she'd reached out to in West Palm. And it was so late in the game now that even if she decided to move without a job, she'd have to give two weeks' notice at the agency or risk a poor reference once she actually found someone interested in hiring her.

A few days of playing hooky from the work search were not going to hurt at this point. Might as well enjoy her last days of indecision with plenty of James-time.

Plus, she could get the stables squeaky clean and in perfect working order for whoever took over her role. Sky was on the hunt for a part-time groom and an assistant instructor to help with the recent explosion in riding lessons, and was spending part of each morning interviewing and observing potential hires.

At least, Casey thought, things were perking up for Sky. Casey was glad she'd had the chance to make things a little better for the farm. Before she'd started helping out, she hadn't realized just how much the young woman was doing on her own, and she felt a little bad remembering that she'd once assumed Sky's wealthy Wellington mother was fully bankrolling the farm. It had become clear that her mother's assistance was something hard-won, not an easy handout offered up every time Sky's bank account looked low. Once the marketing and horse show bumped her business up to the next level, Sky had risen to the occasion beautifully. Casey was proud of the work she had done to help Sky grow—and of the new cars arriving in the parking area every afternoon, bringing new boarders and new students each day.

There was a lot of chatter in the tack room about the new clientele, too. Adding new goldfish to the bowl was proving contentious. Casey liked to time a little afternoon tack-cleaning around the arrival of the teens, just to see what the latest controversies were. She found that Callie and Roxy were particularly up in arms about the Sky's focus on finding new students for the barn. They'd aged up to the top dogs this year, which was their last year as juniors and their last year before they went off to college. They had opinions, and they thought everyone should know them.

"None of those kids from Seagrape Farm can ride worth anything," Callie confided to Roxy on Friday afternoon—Casey's last free Friday.

"Oh my god! You're not kidding." Roxy snorted, pulling her saddle out of her locker. "That girl Rachel posts with her *hands*. Ridiculous. She shouldn't even be *jumping* with that kind of equitation. Back to basics if you ask me."

"Stick her on a lunge line," Callie giggled. "Take away her reins and stirrups."

"And she says she's jumping three-six! Such a liar." Roxy braced her saddle against her hip, ready to go all-in on gossip. "Honestly, I'm sorry for her. She's going to get hurt showing off like that."

"We should tell everyone to go down and watch her next lesson," Callie suggested. "So she knows *we* all know."

Casey decided things were beginning to get a little out of control. "I hate to think what you guys say about me when I'm not around," she remarked, her tone mild.

Roxy and Callie looked at her, standing in the corner of the tack room with her bucket of soapy water and armful of bridles, as if they hadn't realized she'd been in the tack room at all. "Oh," Roxy said eventually. "Casey."

Casey shrugged as if their comments meant nothing to her. "I heard you have to watch out for people who will talk shit with you," she observed benignly, sponging off a browband. "It means they'll talk shit *about* you, too."

She glanced their way and noticed Roxy turn her head slightly towards Callie. *Good guess,* she thought. Callie was the Gossiper in Chief around this place. When she went off to college next year, the next generation would have a hard time filling her boots.

But Casey had no doubt one of the girls would find herself up to the task. Barn gossip was part of boarding stable life. She'd miss these girls, once she eventually left. They were interesting.

"I heard Sky was thinking about going to a horse show in early November," Casey volunteered, hoping to give them something else to talk about.

As wary as they were of her, the teens couldn't be blasé about a horse show.

"Yes! And Live Oak Station has *the best* footing," Callie announced, setting herself up as the resident expert. "Are you going? If you want to introduce James to a new place, do it with grippy footing. Man, I learned that the hard way. A slippery arena and a spooky horse are just not great together. Remember that, Roxy?"

"You hit the ground like a ton of bricks," Roxy said appreciatively. "That was an epic fall. I'm definitely going, though. Casey, you have to take James."

None of them knew that Casey was almost definitely going to be gone by then. She felt sad about that, but she wasn't ready to tell them until she had a definite departure date. "James really isn't ready for a show off the farm," she told them instead. "I don't think we'll go to any shows until next year."

"You've been riding him since *summer* started," Callie pointed out. "What are you waiting for? He needs miles. He needs experience. You should be taking him to every show you can."

"I'm not sure he needs all that." Casey was highly amused by all the *needs* Callie was throwing around. Had she been like this once? If so, slowing down was half the fun of growing up. "What's going to happen to him if I never show him? What if I just ride him for fun?" She had no intention of doing this, of course, but it could be amusing to push a teenager's buttons—especially after Callie had just been so nasty about a girl who was almost certainly going to buy a horse from Sky and join the gang in the next few months.

"That's such a *waste!*" Callie was aghast. "He's a really nice horse! Don't let Sky hear you talking like that. She sold you that horse in good faith!"

Casey's poker face broke into a grin. "In *good faith* of what? That I'd turn him into a show horse? She sold him to me because I wrote her a check for an amount of money which we agreed upon, and then I continued to pay her in order to board him here. I don't remember promising that I'd make him an A-circuit hunter and spend every weekend showing."

"Well," Callie huffed. "I don't know how you'll live with

yourself if you waste that horse. There's nothing worse than seeing a really nice horse just get used for pleasure riding. Anyway, everyone will be going. You're going to miss out on a good time if you decide to skip it." She tossed her hair and sauntered out of the tack room.

Casey put away her armful of clean bridles, hanging them up one by one on their hooks. Imagine the passion of a teenager, she thought. Thinking there was nothing more important in life than horse showing. She'd show James again… someday, when things calmed down.

God, she couldn't wait for things to calm down.

"Knock knock," a voice called from the doorway.

Casey looked up and saw Leslie, draped in her signature paisley, waggling her fingers in a wave hello. "Hey, you! It's been forever!" She went over and gave the older woman a hug. "Where have you been?"

"Just doing pick-up and drop-off lately, there hasn't been time to hang out and visit. And you've always been so busy! Gwen tells me you're running the place." Leslie smiled widely at her. "Is this going to last? Is it your calling?"

Casey gave a little shrug and head-shake. Somehow it felt harder to admit to someone from the office. "No, it wasn't the right fit. I still want to have a career in marketing."

"So, I'll see you again very soon? It's been a month, hasn't it?"

"Next week." Casey sat down on a bench against the back wall, pushing aside some discarded polo wraps. They needed washed, she noticed, and added a load of horse laundry to her mental checklist. "I'm just spending the next few days making sure the barn is spotless so that whoever Sky hires to replace me can't judge me."

"They'll judge you anyway," Leslie mused. "Horse-people are awfully judgy, I've noticed. Well, it will be very nice to have you back at the office. Nothing has really changed there. You haven't missed anything."

No, Casey thought, *I doubt I have.*

What could she possibly have missed? Nothing interesting had ever happened in that office, not in all her years of working there. "I'm not coming back for long," she heard herself say.

"What's that?" Leslie's eyebrows went up.

"I'm not coming back for long," Casey repeated, more sure of herself now that the words had been uttered aloud. They made sense, having been given shape at last. She had made up her mind. "I have to move to West Palm, to be with my boyfriend. I miss him."

"What about James?"

"There are barns around Palm Beach," Sky said, coming into the tack room. She smiled at Casey. "When she's ready to move James, I'll help her find the right place."

"Thank you, Sky," Casey replied gratefully. She felt a buzzing in her pocket. "Oh, what timing. Hang on." She pulled out her phone and looked at the number. Her phone had an endearing new habit of making a guess at who was calling. She guessed it dug around in her email and made connections from signatures.

The screen read: *Maybe: Sharon Conrad.*

Casey's heart began to slam against her rib cage. She looked from her phone to Sky and Leslie, who were watching her with interest. She couldn't take this call in front of them! But if she didn't answer, she'd miss it…

Casey forced her thumb down on the screen and answered the call. "This is Casey."

"Casey!" Sharon Conrad, all right. Her phone was good at guessing. "Sorry to call you so late on a Friday."

Late? It was just past four o'clock. "That's fine, don't worry about it," Casey mumbled through numb lips.

"Look, I just want you to know I think we can work with your proposal for remote work. The truth is, there's no real reason for you to be in the office every day. We think you're the right person for the job, and that should be enough. Your proposal was so thoughtful and detailed, it's clear you're able to deliver the work without listening to us chattering in the background all day. It really is a small office, and Phillip never shuts up—it's true, you don't!" Sharon burst into laughter. "Now he's mad at me. Anyway, let's talk more on Monday, shall we? We'll get this all ironed out. Can you come in to talk it over? And we'll get lunch."

Casey was too stunned to answer right away. The worried looks on Sky and Leslie's faces didn't help.

"Maybe eleven o'clock?" Sharon prompted.

"Yes," Casey blurted. "Yes, I'll see you Monday at eleven. Um, thank you. Thanks very much. I'm looking forward to it."

She took the phone away from her ear.

"Well?" Sky asked impatiently. "You have to tell us!"

"They're going to let me work remotely. The horse show job… they're going to give it to me!" Casey put her arms up in the air and let out one triumphant shriek, and then Sky and Leslie mobbed her, wrapping her up in a tight bear hug. A few girls, passing the tack room, heard the commotion and joined in. By the time the celebratory hug was finally over, Casey was sweaty and dirty and a little claustrophobic. But oh, so triumphant!

Chapter Forty

Casey cried as Sky loaded James onto the trailer.

She cried when she hugged Gwen and Arden and the other girls goodbye.

She cried at the sight of her empty tack locker.

She cried when Sky got into the truck cab and told her it was time to go.

She cried as she got into her car and put it into gear, prepared to follow the horse trailer down the driveway, onto River Road, and towards I-95 South. She couldn't help herself. Change was good, but wow, change hurt while it was happening!

Casey knew she'd gotten to spend more time at St. Johns then she'd expected to, and she felt lucky for every extra day there. With her plans for leaving suddenly crystallizing, the trouble of moving had increased exponentially. She'd had to sit through an exit interview at the agency, during which time she assured Kate from Human Resources that she had no issues with Mary and that her experiences working there had been absolutely a joy. Then she'd had to start packing up the townhouse, as most of the possessions she owned in joint with Brandon were still there, awaiting a permanent housing decision. And, most difficult of all, she'd had to find a new place to keep James.

Luckily, Sky took over the barn search. After all, she was from the West Palm area, and had grown up in that region's equestrian world. Within a week of Casey's decision to move, Sky had a short-list of six barns, and they toured them all in one marathon day. The stable Casey finally decided on was short on some amenities—there was definitely no air-conditioned lounge, for one thing—but it had an arena with lights, absolutely necessary as the days were growing shorter, and the other boarders seemed nice, and it was only about half an hour's drive from the condo she and Brandon decided on.

That was the other change: he was leaving his rental in the urban core for something a little more accessible to the stable. Brandon had taken one look at the list of addresses she'd sent him and said: "There's no way we can live this far away from your horse. That's just too much to drive every day."

"But you wanted to live downtown!" Casey had exclaimed. "I can figure out the drive."

"I wanted to live downtown," Brandon admitted, "but I'd rather live somewhere that's good for both of us."

Everything felt like a good, comfortable compromise. He was working his dream job; she was working hers. His job had required he'd move; she'd managed to make her job move with her. Knowing that he'd once done the same for her was a balm that soothed any sting she felt at leaving her hometown. It wasn't as if she was moving to a new city utterly rudderless, anyway. She had Brandon and James; what else could she need?

Or so she'd thought.

"I was thinking we might get a dog," Brandon had said a few nights ago. "I could use a buddy for when you're at the barn."

"Yes," Casey agreed happily. "We *definitely* need a dog." It was decided: they'd add another team member as soon as the new condo was unpacked and settled.

So, everything had taken a long time, giving Casey plenty of time to process the changes, and yet it had all felt good until this moment, the actual act of leaving Sky's barn. Leaving the farm where she'd learned to ride all of those years gone by, leaving the farm where she'd reclaimed her inner horse girl just over six months ago. This part *hurt*.

Her life had shifted so dramatically, all because she'd gone down that driveway and allowed Sky and the horses to transform her life.

As they merged into traffic and began the two-hour trip to Palm Beach County, Casey's tears dried up, and she started to smile. James was in that trailer ahead of her—her very own horse, her lovely good boy!—and her friend was driving him, and her boyfriend was waiting for her. Everything was going to be okay. Better than okay.

She was going into the unknown, but she wasn't going alone.

Coming Soon

Looking for more of *Grabbing Mane?*

Watch for the continuation of James and Casey's story in 2021!

Subscribe to my email list to get updates on this book and all of my other equestrian fiction series!

Visit nataliekreinert.com or bit.ly/nkreinert to sign up.

Acknowledgments

This one goes out to the Patrons!

Grabbing Mane came directly from conversations on Patreon, my subscriber-based community where I share new work and chat with readers.

In April of 2019, I posted about finishing up *Forward* (the fifth book in The Eventing Series) and asked readers what they wanted next. I had some ideas, but it was Patron Lindsay Moore who came up with the winning question:

"Have you ever considered writing a book with an adult ammy protagonist? I would love to read something written by a horse person who gets the world of non-professional riders and our different flavor of challenges/triumphs."

To which I responded, truthfully: "I really haven't. I totally should."

The conversation which followed cemented this idea. It was time to write an amateur equestrian novel. A few days later, I posted the synopsis for *Grabbing Mane* on Patreon, and got a rousing response. We were off.

I'm so thankful for my Patrons every single day, as well as all of my other readers who take the time to send me a message, write me a review, tweet with me, comment on my posts, and just generally become one of my online gang. We would make a formidable team of barn brats, wouldn't we? If you've ever thought of sending me a little message but thought I wouldn't want to be bothered, think again! Please bother me. Let's be friends!

One last thing about the writing of *Grabbing Mane:* this book took eight months to write and nearly six months to rewrite after I decided the finished version just wasn't good enough. Halfway through those six months, the pandemic lockdown began. Everything creative became exponentially harder, and my goal of writing something light-hearted and fun while asking some tough questions about the nature of horse ownership? Well, that became really tough to accomplish!

If *Grabbing Mane* isn't as funny as I would have liked, I can only say that it was written in challenging times.

Thanks so much to everyone who supported me during the writing, including my Patrons: Zoe B., Heather V., Heather W., Emily H., Lindsay M., Princess Jenny, Rhonda L., Cindy S., Emily N., Peggy D., Tricia J., Sarah S., Cheryl B., Orpu, Diana A., Liz G., Megan D., Lori K., Kaylee A., Kathi H., Liza S., Mary, Rachael R., Dana P., Ann B., Claus G., Jennifer, Brinn D., Di H., Karen C., Silvana R., Risa R., Annika K., Cyndy S., Kathy, Leeanne C., Sarina L., Emma G., Kim K., Kathi L., Harry B., Christine K., Thoma J., Mara S., Kathlynn A., Andrea, Amelia H., Katy M., Karen M., Alyssa, Honey M., Dawn A., and Nicole K.

I genuinely couldn't have written this without you!

Thanks to my Street Team for standing at the ready to read and review: Emily, Kathleen, Kelsi, Meghan, Fiona, Karen, Michelle, and April. There's some overlap in there and I love that.

Thanks to the awesome bloggers and podcasters who give me a platform and are always happy to talk about equestrian fiction!

And thanks, of course, to the people who nurture me, support me, and put up with me during all of my writing days. I'm talking about my husband, Cory, and my son, Calvin. I'm talking about my own Sky, Jess. I'm talking about my author buds, like Mary Pagones, Mara Dabrishus, Meghan Scott Molin, and Jessica

Burkhart—and too many others to list! It's good to have someone to laugh and cry with about the writing life.

Well, I guess I better get busy on the sequel.

About the Author

I currently live in Central Florida, where I write fiction and freelance for a variety of publications. I mostly write about theme parks, travel, and horses! I've been writing professionally for more than a decade, and yes… I prefer writing fiction to anything else. In the past I've worked professionally in many aspects of the equestrian world, including grooming for top eventers, training off-track Thoroughbreds, galloping racehorses, working in mounted law enforcement, on breeding farms, and more.

In my spare time I ride Ben, a clever pony with whom I aspire to run around a beginner novice event someday, and hang out with my husband and teenage son. My family also includes a foxhound named Sally, who sleeps most of the time.

Visit my website at nataliekreinert.com to keep up with the latest news and read occasional blog posts and book reviews. For installments of upcoming fiction and exclusive stories, visit my Patreon page at Patreon.com/nataliekreinert to learn how you can become a subscriber!

Follow me around the Interwebs for general nonsense: visit nataliekreinert.com/social

You can find all of my books at Amazon, Taborton Equine Books, or order signed editions direct from me at nataliekreinert.com

Printed in Great Britain
by Amazon